LAUREN L. GARCIA

Catalyst Moon: Surrender

Book Four

Content warning: substance abuse.

Please note that this is the fourth book in a series. If this is your first foray into my world, I highly recommend starting with Book One.

Check the back of the book for more information about the world of Catalyst Moon, including a character list and glossary.

The Catalyst Moon saga:

Incursion (Catalyst Moon - Book 1)

Breach (Catalyst Moon - Book 2)

Storm (Catalyst Moon - Book 3)

Surrender (Catalyst Moon - Book 4) <—you are here

Sacrifice (Catalyst Moon - Book 5)

First edition

ISBN: 978-1-7335390-7-4

This book was professionally typeset on Reedsy.
Find out more at reedsy.com

For Fred, who said "open your eyes."

Contents

Author's Note

Content warning: substance abuse.

Please note that this is the fourth book in a series. If this is your first foray into my world, I **highly recommend** starting with Book One: Incursion.

Check the back of the book for more information about the world of *Catalyst Moon*, including a character list and glossary.

Join my mailing list for freebies, new releases, and other fun stuff! https://laloga.com/newsletter

-Above all other things, this is a story about love.-

From the desk of High Commander Argent,

Esteemed Pillars,

It is with my most sincere regret that I must pen this report. Following an escape attempt by the mages of Whitewater Bastion, my sentinels were forced to execute the remaining magic-users. Of course, we did not take these actions lightly, but you understand that even a hint of a mage rebellion cannot be allowed. A sentinel's duty, after all, is to protect innocent lives from magic's treachery.

The mage Eris Echina, who previously fled Commander Talon's custody during the Heartfire festival, orchestrated this escape. It is my understanding that Mage Echina, a known shape-changer, was able to infiltrate the bastion to further incite rebellion among the remaining mages. Her most obvious collaborator was the mage Kalinda Halcyon, as the two have a long friendship.

However, my informant stationed in the sentinel garrison there has brought to light a far more disturbing fact: Mage Halcyon formed a romantic relationship with a sentinel officer, a Sergeant Stonewall, and thus convinced him – and most of his sentinel squad – to flee the bastion with her and the other rebel mages. I am told this romantic bond began during Mage Halcyon's transfer to Whitewater Bastion, when she and the sergeant traveled together alone, after thralls destroyed his former squad.

I dearly wish the sordid tale ended here, but my informant's reports contain even more disturbing intelligence. It seems that Mage Halcyon was also possessed by a thrall, although my informant claims the mage was able to "cure herself." Furthermore, Mage Halcyon has been spreading tales that thralls are caused by the Fata—the mythical race of fairy creatures—due to some ancient anger with the human race.

Although my informant was adamant that these events transpired exactly as written here, reason dictates this is simply mage treachery in action. Halcyon is known for spinning wild tales. I include the information here in an abundance of caution, and to let you know what stories might begin to find their way through the uneducated populace. I will ensure my informant is duly educated on the difference between reality and fantasy.

Sergeant Stonewall and his squad will not survive long without hematite; they have been deemed Forsworn and officially cast out of the sentinel order. Only the One god knows where Halcyon, Echina, and the other mages have gone, but my sentinels are scouring the countryside until we locate them. Rest assured, we will find these renegades.

Yours in service,

High Commander Argent, City of Lasath, Province of Silverwood

ONE

K ali raised her hands, palms facing the twin stars that burned through the mist and glided toward her, closer, closer. Only the crunch of the thrall's feet against the hoarfrost signaled this was no spirit among the trees, but a being of flesh and fury. No demon inhabited this poor man's body and mind; he had been taken over by an outside force Kali understood all too well.

She was the only one who could save him.

Heart in her throat, Kali struggled to keep her voice calm. "You don't want to hurt us."

The thrall continued to stalk her through the dim afternoon light. By now, he was close enough to distinguish as a Canderi warrior: tall, broad, and fair-haired, like most of the folks from the country to the north.

She continued speaking, hoping to hold the thrall's attention while she eased into the clearing. Her fogging breath vanished in the late winter mist. "This isn't who you are. This desire to hurt us, to consume us... It's not real."

Was it her imagination, or did the thrall's pace slow a fraction? Her heart beat faster, but not entirely with fear. None of the other thralls she had approached before now had shown even a trace of comprehension of her words. Behind her, Marcen sucked in a breath and Sadira murmured something that sounded like a Zhee prayer. Kali didn't blame her fellow mages for their fear. She wanted to run too, but by now she trusted her other allies: sentinels, hidden and awaiting her signal.

One sentinel waited less patiently than the others. Kali heard Stonewall's

1

thoughts in her own mind. *We must strike* now.

Not yet, she replied in their shared, silent speech. *Relax.*

Anxiety colored her lover's reply. *I hate it when you say that.*

Perhaps it was foolish to smile now, at the worst possible time, but Kali did anyway. But her smile died when one of the sentinels shifted in the surrounding brushwork. A few snapping twigs were the only clues to the warriors' presence – would the thrall recognize the threat they posed?

Kali did not pull her gaze from the burning stars of the thrall's eyes. "Listen to me," she said, drawing his attention. "You don't have to live this way any longer. I was like you, once. I can help you now. Please just–"

"Kali!" Sadira grabbed Kali's arm and jerked her back the instant before the thrall lunged, landing in the spot she'd stood only a heartbeat earlier.

Both Marcen and Sadira closed in beside Kali, drawing her toward the edge of the clearing. The three mages faced the Canderi man who could have broken them even without a thrall's unnatural strength. Kali's breath shortened and her heart raced enough to make her dizzy, but she pushed away her fear and gathered her concentration. The promise of magic sang through her blood and she relaxed. *Now, Stonewall.*

The armored sentinels emerged from the mist and sprang for the thrall, while Drake whirled a set of *kuvlu* toward the Canderi man. A cord connected three rounded stones at the *kuvlu*'s ends; propelled by their own weight, the stones wrapped around the thrall's legs, sending him to the ground with a solid *thud*. The warriors fell upon him: Stonewall and Beacon held his arms while Flint and Drake scrambled for his powerful legs. A piercing, inhuman shriek cut through the air—and Kali's skull—as the thrall struggled in their grips, but they held him fast.

At least, they would for a few minutes. Hopefully, that was all the mages would need. Though Kali's bum left knee already burned from the day's exertions, she knelt in a patch of snow beside the thrall and held his bearded cheeks as best she could. That same eerie sound escaped his throat and he twisted again, harder, but the sentinels holding him did not move. Seren's light…the Canderi's face was contorted with pain and fear, and her own heart constricted in sympathy for this creature.

Not creature, she scolded herself. *He's a man. Thralls are all humans. There are no monsters here.*

"Mar, Sadira," she managed as the thrall tried to jerk away from her touch. Both mages knelt with her, awkwardly putting their hands over her own as she gathered her magical strength.

"I'm ready, Kali," Sadira said firmly.

Marcen's reply was less sure. "I'll do my best."

As Kali had instructed, all three mages concentrated on the thrall's particles: the place where magic lived. Particles were minuscule pieces of matter that made up everything in the world; invisible to the naked eye, but teeming with seemingly endless power and only accessible by a mage. In Kali's mind's-eye, she saw this man's particles as a roiling mass of gnats: confused and frightened, choked by the thrall's cloying hatred.

Kali tried to direct all three mages' power to soothe the man's agitated particles. She layered her will upon them and coaxed them to quiet. *Calm.*

Nothing happened.

"I'm not strong enough," Marcen whispered.

"You can do it, just keep trying," Kali replied through clenched teeth. The others' magic pulsed, brightening in her awareness as their focus sharpened. The mages always discussed this method prior to each attempt. It would work – one day.

But the thrall struggled beneath the mages' touch; his body mirrored his particles' agitation. His sheer size and strength made the sentinels' jobs harder, but something else was wrong. The foreign presence clung to his spirit like a choking vine wrapped around an oak tree.

The other mages were trying, but their understanding of thralls would never be as profound as Kali's, and the Fata's hold on this man was stronger than any of the others they'd tried—and failed—to free. Kali made a split-second decision. "This isn't working," she managed. "Give me your strength, and I can do it alone."

She felt their hesitation as a pause in the flow of magic before Marcen relented first. It was as if a door opened between them and power poured through. Sadira followed his lead, though Kali could sense the Zhee mage

3

was still holding back. Kali inhaled. Oh, it was sweet, that power, and there was so much of it. So much strength, especially from Sadira, who burned like the sun. Marcen's magic was only a flickering torch in the wind, but he had his own mettle for Kali to call upon. Careful, though, she must be careful not to take too much, lest she do irreparable damage to either of her friends.

Kali was so wrapped up in her concentration that she only dimly noted that one of the sentinels muttered something acerbic, but Stonewall silenced his squad-mate at once. Even so, Kali felt Stonewall's uncertainty and her attention wavered. No. She pushed his emotions away. She had to focus. Another breath; another draw of strength from her fellow mages. Not much more. She could do this. She *would* do this.

Damp, dirty skin twitched beneath her palms as the Canderi tried to jerk out of her grip, but his movements were less desperate than before. His breath came slower, steadier, and more tension drained from his body. Heartened, Kali shifted her focus. Now that he was calm, the real healing could begin. Another indrawn breath, and Kali dove her awareness back to his particles, searching for... There! Deep within, a parasite upon his spirit: a foreign presence akin to infection. A disease to be burned away. Once more, Kali gathered her strength and concentrated on the infection. A flare of magic, then the thrall wailed again. But this was no inhuman shriek that reverberated through the forest. This was the cry of a man in pain.

"It's working," Marcen gasped.

"Hush, and pay attention," Sadira told him, though she, too, sounded astonished.

Kali fought to ignore both of them and the hope blooming in her own heart, for she could not afford the distraction. No previous attempt had gone this well. She squeezed her eyes shut and pressed her magic harder. She would pay for this exertion later, but she didn't care now.

The man shrieked again, twisting and jerking in pain. Kali kept up her magical assault until every trace of the Fata's thrall was gone. The Canderi man groaned, but stopped thrashing, and his breathing was even. When

4

Kali looked at him again, only a man looked back. His eyes were bright blue, like most Canderi, though red-rimmed, shadowed, and wet.

Choked words escaped him. Kali didn't recognize his speech and silently lamented that she'd never learned the northerner's language. Perhaps sensing her frustration, the Canderi took another shuddering breath and said in heavily accented Aredian, "What am I?"

Exhaustion almost made Kali topple over, but she managed a smile. "You're safe. You're free."

"Free." He glanced at the sentinels and Drake, who still held him in place.

Everyone looked at Kali, waiting for the all-clear. She leaned back to give the Canderi some breathing room, and nodded.

Stonewall spoke a soft word to the others, who released the former thrall, though Flint's gaze remained fixed upon the Canderi, her mouth a hard line. Stonewall and Drake sat on their heels while Beacon, the sentinel mender, studied the Canderi man with his keen healer's gaze.

"Incredible," Beacon murmured. "All trace of Fata possession's gone. The magic worked."

"Did it?" Flint had risen to swipe snow off her gear. Her blue eyes, as vivid as the Canderi's, narrowed in suspicion and a hand rested on one of the twin daggers at her hips. "'Cause that would be the first time."

"There's a first for everything," Drake replied, green eyes glinting with amusement.

Kali looked at the Canderi, who had sat up. "You speak Aredian?" she asked.

"Very small. Little," he corrected himself. His blond beard was tangled and his clothing was in tatters. All Canderi were taller and broader than Aredians, but this man looked as if he'd not properly eaten in too long. His cheekbones were too prominent and his eyes were sunken, and he was thinner than any Canderi Kali had ever seen. But he was still a bear of a man. Only Drake was his equal in size and strength.

"You're safe," Kali said again, hoping to drive that point home. "You were a thrall – possessed by the Fata. Do you know of the Fata? We also call them fairies, or glimmers, here in Aredia. They are strange, ancient beings who've been turning our people into their thralls."

He frowned, but did not answer. Well, it was quite a lot to take in.

Kali tried again to reassure him. "We are all your friends here." Somewhere behind her, Flint snorted, but Kali ignored the sound. "What's your name?"

The Canderi was silent for a long moment, studying his filthy hands as he clenched and unclenched his fingers, until at last he murmured, "Atanar."

"*Ah*-taa-*naar?*" Kali repeated the name carefully, though her accent was terrible. But he only nodded, his gaze distant. She tried to keep her voice light as she gestured to each member of their party. "That's Stonewall and that's his brother, Drake. That's Flint, glowering behind me–"

"Am not!"

Kali bit back a grin and continued. "Beacon is the sentinel with the mender's bag, and the other mages with me are Sadira and Marcen. Oh, and I'm Kali."

Atanar nodded again, though she wasn't sure how much had registered, and she did not miss the way he glanced at the weapons each sentinel wore. But his gaze rested the longest on Sadira, whose red-brown skin and moonstone-pale hair made her stand out. "You are…different," he said to her.

"I am Zhee." When he did not seem to understand, she added, "My home country, Zheem, is far south of here."

"Are you from Cander?" Stonewall asked Atanar. Some Canderi chose to leave the tundra and head south, for Aredia, though generally those Canderi lived as roving bandits.

Atanar nodded. "But I cannot return there."

His tone brooked no room for questions, but Kali could not suppress her curiosity. "Why?"

Steely blue eyes met hers and he said only, "*Vorunn.* I am exiled."

"Well, do you have anyone you can return to?" Drake asked.

"No."

Stonewall met Kali's eyes. *I didn't plan this far ahead,* he admitted silently. *I guess I didn't think magic would work this time, either.*

6

Nor did I, she replied in kind. *I think that means he's my responsibility.*
Our responsibility, Stonewall corrected, adding, *Aderey won't like this.*
Leave Aderey to me.

Atanar's next words came slowly. "How did you heal me, Kali?"

"Magic," Kali said.

His brows lifted. "So what my people say about Aredians is true."

"Depends on what they say," Kali replied. "But yes, some of us have magic.
And sometimes, we put it to good use."

Sadira rubbed her arms, though the fire-mage could not possibly be cold.
"Indeed. Now I understand better what you tried with the others before
this, Kali."

Marcen stood. "Aye, me too, but I'm not sure I could manage it on my
own. Especially not after your little stunt just now."

Alarmed, Kali looked up, assessing her fellow mage. He was always pale,
but were those shadows beneath his eyes more prominent? "Did I hurt
you?"

"I'm a little more tired than I should be, but otherwise, I'm fine." He
smiled at her. "Don't worry. You didn't take too much."

Is that true? Stonewall moved to kneel beside Kali, his gaze ostensibly
on the Canderi who blinked as if he'd just emerged from a dream. But
Stonewall's attention was on her; she could feel it as surely as a hand upon
her shoulder. Though neither as tall nor muscular as his older brother
Drake, Stonewall exuded a solid strength that she'd come to trust. His
tawny skin was the color of clay, reminding Kali of sun-warmed earth.

Marcen wouldn't lie, she replied, slanting him with a brief smile.

But his stern expression told her he wasn't fooled. *You will push yourself
to the breaking point.*

His concern ebbed through the words and into her own emotions.
Though the connection had taken Kali a little while to get used to, she
savored the closeness to him now. The bond they'd forged was unlike any
other she'd known in her twenty-four summers, and as far as she knew,
was unique among anyone else, mage, sentinel, or otherwise.

I won't, she replied in kind. *Besides, right now, I'm the only one who understands exactly how to help the thralls; the least I can do is teach other mages how to free them.*

So many people blamed mages for thralls. Kali knew otherwise – so it was her duty to prove it.

He placed one gloved hand over hers, resting on her left knee. The joint didn't hurt anymore, though that would change once the exhilaration of borrowed magic died and the habitual pain returned.

I know, Stonewall said through their bond. *And I want to cure thralls as much as you do. I'm just worried you're going to wring yourself dry in the process.*

Her jaw tightened in determination. *I know my limits.*

His honey-brown eyes met hers steadily. *But will you heed them?*

Heat rose in her cheeks and she looked away. None of the others seemed to notice their silent conversation, but that would change if Kali and Stonewall kept staring at each other without speaking. This was not an issue either of them could settle now, so she gave a small shake of her head. *I'll be fine,* she repeated. *Trust me.*

He squeezed her hand once before helping her to her feet, but did not reply.

As she stood, the familiar hunger for *power* nibbled at the edges of her mind. The urge she'd felt when she'd been a thrall—could it really have been only a month ago?—surfaced, stronger than she remembered.

Gritting her teeth against the hunger, Kali gave Atanar a smile she did not feel. "Would you like to come with us? You look hungry – and I think you could use some new clothes. We don't have much to spare, but we do have a little."

"Aye, it's getting late," Stonewall said, then frowned at the sky. "And I think it's going to snow again."

Flint spoke from behind Kali's shoulder. "Is he really...cured? I don't want to wake up to a berserker tearing the camp apart."

Rather than answer, Kali looked at Atanar. "Do you hear them any longer?"

Them – the Fata, whose voices had once filled Kali's mind not so long

8

ago, though she could not have forgotten them if she'd tried.

Atanar closed his eyes and his voice took on an edge of awe. "They are... gone. I am myself again. Whatever that means."

He blinked quickly before looking away, not before she caught the gleam of moisture in his eyes. Kali's heart tightened. How long had he been living as a thrall? She held out her hand to the Canderi, who accepted it after a moment's pause. His calloused palm swallowed hers but his grip was gentle. Once he was standing, she made another quick assessment of his particles to ensure no trace of the Fata's presence remained.

Kali's smile was genuinely pleased now; whatever else happened, she'd done one good thing. "Welcome to Aredia, Atanar."

TWO

Stonewall's hands trembled. Hoping to stop them, he gripped the twin daggers at his belt. But the action could not quell the desire for hematite: a relentless, gnawing urge that pressed upon every corner of his mind. *Tor help me*, he thought as Drake and Beacon helped Atanar to his feet. *I must learn to live without that poison.*

Easier said than done.

It would be full dark in a matter of hours. Midwinter had come and gone, and spring would grace this part of Whitewater Province soon, but mist and afternoon shadows had overtaken the forest.

"Can you walk?" Beacon asked Atanar. The mender was nearly as tall as the Canderi, although he was lanky as a pine. "We're an hour or so from our camp."

Atanar frowned. "I can walk. But I feel...weak. Strange."

"The Fata possession could have affected you in some lasting way," Beacon said, nodding. "We still don't quite understand how it works. You might feel weaker than normal for a while." He hesitated. "If you're amenable, I'd like to take a closer look at you. We've not had a chance to, ah, spend time with many former thralls."

After a beat, Atanar asked, "What is 'amenable?'"

Drake cleared his throat. "Fancy way of asking permission to look you over."

"The more we learn about what happened to you," Beacon added. "The better we might be able to stop it from happening to anyone else."

The former thrall seemed to consider this before he nodded. "Very well.

No one else should have to..." He trailed off, his eyes going distant.

"Are you injured?" Kali asked. "I see some cuts and bruises, but is there anything else more serious that needs healing?"

Atanar shook his head, though Kali continued to study him. Her dark brown eyes were too bright and her pale cheeks were flushed, which made Stonewall think that she'd enjoyed the act of borrowing magic from her fellow mages a little too much.

A tilt of his chin drew his squad-mates to his side. Beacon and Flint met Stonewall a few paces away from where the mages, Atanar, and Drake discussed the journey back.

Flint wasted no time in sharing her displeasure at the situation. "How can we tell if that thrall is *really* cured?"

Beacon answered first. "His pulse was steady and his eyes looked normal. And he *spoke* – none of that horrid shrieking. I can't examine him the same way that Kali or Sadira can, but as far as I can tell... he's fine."

"Kali has the most experience with thralls," Stonewall added. "I trust her judgment about this. But keep an eye on our new friend, just in case."

"Well, I'm glad your brother's here, Stonewall," Flint replied. "It's nice to have another strong arm–" She cut herself off, her expression darkening.

"Did you see Milo before we set out this morning?" Stonewall asked her. "I couldn't find him."

"He was training." She looked at her boots. "Alone."

Stonewall grimaced. He needed to spend more time with the lad, but they'd had so few chances during these attempts at curing thralls. *I'll find him soon*, he promised himself.

"Mi was alone again?" Beacon asked Flint.

She swept aside a few loose strands of her black hair as she nodded. "He *still* won't spar with anyone, even me."

"Your brother could have died when Talon stabbed him," Beacon replied gently. "Even though the mages healed him as best they could, I don't think Milo's arm will ever be as it was."

"You keep saying that," Flint muttered.

"Because it's the truth." Beacon glanced at Stonewall. "She's right about

11

having *your* brother around, though. Drake's handy with or without a blade."

It was Stonewall's turn to frown. "As you say."

When he said nothing else, Beacon nodded in Kali's direction. "Can she use her magic and...send us all back, like she did to our skiff on the White River?"

Stonewall's heart skidded to a halt. Moving through time and place at impossible speeds: such magic was beyond the skill of any living mage. Such magic was the realm of the Fata, whose blood flowed through *his* veins. *He* had been the one to move their skiff like quicksilver down the river, setting them all well out of harm's way during their mad flight from Whitewater City a month ago. Months before that, *he* had been the one to move his and Kali's horse over leagues of land in a few moments. Both times, Kali had helped by lending her own strength, but the bulk of the magic had been *his.*

Magic. The word left a strange taste in his mouth. Well and good for Kali to have magic, but for *him?* He was nobody; a street urchin trained with a sword and daggers. But during Kali's possession by the Fata, she'd sensed their interest in him, and realized the connection. In a strange way, such a connection felt...not wrong. Not *right,* exactly, but Stonewall couldn't entirely dismiss the idea. Especially not when he had proof of his abilities.

But he was *not* about to share this with his squad until he understood exactly what he was capable of. The others needed every bit of their focus as much as they needed to trust his leadership, especially now that they were not only Forsworn—cast out from the sentinel order—but short a member after their former squad-mate, Rook, had betrayed them to the sentinel high commander not a month ago.

Stonewall refused to be a burden—or a danger—to those he loved. So he schooled his voice to its most calm, commanding tone. "Kali's used enough magic today. She's...tired."

"We're *all* tired," the mender pressed. "Surely she can manage a little bit, for the greater good."

Stonewall met the other man's gaze with granite. "No, Beak. Flint, would you run ahead and warn Aderey and the other Sufani of our new… companion?"

She nodded, but another stricken look flashed across her face. "Rook always did the scouting work."

"I know," Stonewall replied, his hands tightening over his daggers again. "But she's…not here. We have to-"

"She's a sodding traitor," Flint broke in. "Writing notes to the High Commander behind Talon's back. Behind *all* our backs. We might've avoided that shit storm in Whitewater City if not for her."

Stonewall and Beacon exchanged glances, and Stonewall saw Flint's ire reflected in the mender's face. Rook had been Beacon's friend, too. Ea's tits, she'd been a friend to *all* of them, and yet she'd lived among them as a liar.

Like me. The thought came unbidden, but he pushed it away. His own secrets were *nothing* like Rook's. "Even so," he said to Flint. "*We're* still a team."

The young woman blew out an impatient breath, sending a foggy plume into the air. "Aye. I'll warn them about the thrall."

"Should she go alone?" Beacon asked.

Flint bristled. "I can take care of myself."

"I know," Stonewall said, though he still considered. "And we didn't see any other thralls today… But I still don't like sending anyone off without backup." Nor did he relish the notion of sending Beacon with her, for the two would bicker nonstop. And, foolishly perhaps, he did not want to be the only sentinel remaining in this group. Drake didn't count.

So he glanced at Kali, who stood with Drake and the other mages, still speaking with Atanar. She caught his eye and raised an inquiring brow. As quickly as he could, he tried to convey his dilemma through their unspoken bond.

Her reply was brief. *Ask Mar.*

The male mage had become a constant fixture in the group during their efforts to cure thralls. Stonewall didn't know if Marcen's presence was due to some latent attraction to Kali—she'd said that Marcen had once expressed a romantic, if unrequited, interest in her—or if the fellow had deeper feelings about their missions. Regardless, Stonewall was glad of his aid.

Kali said something to Marcen, who then trotted over to the sentinels. "Do you need something?"

"Would you mind accompanying Flint back to the Sufani camp?" Stonewall asked. "With Kali's knee and Atanar's...condition, it could take us a while to get back."

Marcen's pale eyes crinkled with amusement. "Good idea to warn them. Aye, I can keep Serla Flint company. If she'll have me."

This last he said to Flint, who scoffed at his use of the honorific. "Fine, as long as you can keep up, Mage."

"Never had any complaints," Marcen said mildly.

Flint rolled her eyes before looking back at Stonewall and offering a warrior's salute: arms crossed before her chest, bowing at the waist. "Try not to get killed without me."

"Aye, I know you'd want to watch," Beacon replied, chuckling.

Flint stuck her tongue out at him and then bounded off, Marcen on her heels. Beacon watched them disappear into the mist, then shot Stonewall a smile that did not reach his eyes. "She seems...energetic. Lucky girl."

"How do *you* feel?" Stonewall asked.

The mender ran a gloved hand through his short coppery hair, glinting garishly against the trees. "I could really use a burn."

"We don't have much hematite, and can't risk getting more. We've got to ration our stores."

"It's not enough, Stonewall." Beacon's gaze crept to his gauntlet, where chips of hematite glinted in the pale light.

Stonewall placed his hand over the mender's gauntlet. "You know what happens if you eat that stuff raw. It must be purified first, or it'll kill us even quicker."

"Hematite will kill us, regardless. All we can do now is survive as long as possible."

Something knotted in Stonewall's guts. "But we're tapering off..."

14

"Flint and Milo will probably be all right," Beacon said after Stonewall didn't finish. "Their first and only Burn wasn't so long ago. A little more than a year, perhaps. But you and I…" He sighed. "I fear the damage is already done."

"Do you know that for certain?"

"No," Beacon said after a pause. "But my training and experience both tell me that anyone taking hematite as long as we have might never fully recover, even if we stop – and don't die from the agony of being without it."

"But you don't *know* that," Stonewall pressed. "We could still live normal lives."

"I know of no one else in our…situation," Beacon admitted. "Drake's the only other former sentinel I've met, and he says that he *still* feels the urge for a burn, although he obviously can live without eating hematite. That makes me think it's too late for you and me." His voice lowered. "I suppose it's the price we'll have to pay for…leaving the sentinel order like we did."

The word hung in the air between them, unspoken, although the meaning resonated in each man's mind: Oath-breakers. Traitors.

Forsworn.

"Stonewall," Kali called, drawing the sentinels' attentions. Drake, Atanar, and Sadira stood beside her. "We should get moving."

He glanced at Beacon, who straightened. "Ready when you are, ser," the mender replied, though there was no trace of annoyance or sarcasm in the honorific. Some habits died hard. Stonewall had been Beacon's commanding officer, after all, someone both the veteran and the young, inexperienced burnie twins had come to rely upon.

Stonewall clapped the other man on the shoulder. "Get going."

The mender fell in step with the others. But Stonewall remained at the center of the clearing, listening to the crackle of boots on leaves, inhaling the promise of more snow on a shivering wind. He searched the shadows, for what, he did not quite know or understand, but saw only his breath fogging in the fading light. Was it foolish of him to be disappointed at the emptiness? *Tor help me,* he thought.

As if summoned, a warm-blanket feeling spread over his entire body, sheltering, shielding. Tor's eyes glowed gold in his mind and he heard the resonant voice as clearly as if the god spoke in his ear. *I am here, my son.*

It can't be. This thought struck him at the same time as its mirror: *It's true.*

Something caught in his chest. He'd always believed in the gods, but hearing an actual answer to a prayer… Surely it was a miracle, something holy and vast, and far too important for a Forsworn sentinel with a hematite addiction; a man only steps away from living back in the gutters he'd grown up in.

"Elan?"

The warm-blanket feeling vanished. The sound of his birthname made him glance up to see Kali waiting for him. Once she had his attention, she added silently, *Are you all right?*

He quelled the flare of irritation at her unintentional interruption and replied through their bond. *Aye. Just…taking stock. I'll be right there.*

One last glance around, though he saw nothing but shadows. Once he had reached her, he offered her his arm. Her dark eyes watched him closely even as she smiled, and she jerked her chin ahead, in Atanar's direction. "One saved, at least."

Any irritation fled at the sight of her smile. "Two," he corrected, reaching up to squeeze her hand.

Her smile broadened. "With hopefully many more to come."

*

The mage—Marcen Selle—moved silently at Flint's side as they darted through the trees. Strange; she'd never met a civilian who could step through brush and brambles without breaking a twig. Only Rook had ever been able to manage–

Stop it, moron, she scolded herself. Her distraction cost her a snapped branch and she cursed beneath her breath, though the mage didn't comment. Well, she had never pretended to be stealthy. Both Flint and her twin brother, Milo, were incapable of stealth. For her part, she just didn't care to keep quiet most of the time, but Mi was just such a burly lout that he couldn't take a single step without shaking the ground. But despite any shared failings, they'd always been a team where one took up the slack when the other faltered.

Something moved in the trees ahead. Flint paused and held out her hand for the mage to stop as well. He paused right beside her and his warm breath feathered her cheek. He glanced her way, a question in his pale eyes. Rather than reply, she drew a dagger and crouched into a ready-stance. Slowly, she edged toward the source of the movement, until she spotted...

"Ea's balls," she swore, sheathing her dagger as the possum trundled away.

Marcen chuckled. "Who knows what other horrors lurk in these woods, huh?"

"Did I imagine the sodding thrall a few minutes ago?"

He sobered. "Aye, and I'm not sure I could defend us right now. Helping Kali cure that Atanar fellow took a lot out of me."

They began to jog again. The group had initially followed a game trail through the forest at the outskirts of Whitewater Province—when would they be free of this sodding place?—so Flint and Marcen's path was relatively clear. They'd made good time; she could already smell the Sufani's cooking fires.

"Then what's the point of Kali teaching you?" Flint asked as they jogged single file down the trail.

Marcen blew out his breath in a huff. "Sadira's magic is powerful." He didn't sound annoyed by Flint's question, just thoughtful. "And Kali's is... unlike any I've seen, but also strong. I can't compare to either. I'm no slouch," he added quickly. "But...well, let's just say I hope I never have to fight either of them with magic. I'd be burned to ashes."

"Or sucked dry," Flint said.

"No," Marcen replied, a trace of regret in the word. Before Flint could ask what he meant, he continued. "Kali was careful. She took power, but not more than we could safely give."

"How could you tell what she did at all? You laid your hands over hers...

did that show you what she was doing?"

"For a sentinel, you're awfully interested in magic."

"Magic saved my brother's life." It was the only answer she needed. Even now, the memory of that sodding bitch, Commander Talon, stabbing poor Mi near his heart made Flint want to break something. *I hope she's dead.*

Marcen was quiet as they trotted through the trees. "It's difficult to explain. All I can really tell you is that, when I touch another mage as they work magic, I can sort of 'see' what they're doing."

"Can you all do that?"

"Some of us, sometimes."

She scowled. "Don't you ever give a straight answer?"

"If the question calls for one," he said, and when she looked back, he was grinning. He had a crooked smile, like his mouth couldn't quite make up its mind on what expression to reveal. None of the mages were as physically strong as the sentinels, but he wasn't…ugly. Taller than her, though not by much, his pale skin and hair always seemed to glow, like it caught what light it could and cast it back. Like Seren, one of the two moons that crept into the sky.

Flint sped up, forcing him to run faster.

By the time they reached the Sufani camp, twilight had settled over the edge of the province and shadows bathed the world beyond the glow of several campfires. When she reached the copse of oak trees the Sufani nomads had camped beneath, she slowed to a walk and searched the wooden caravans for one painted purple and gold: the home of the nomads' leaders, Aderey, and his wife Ytel. Most Sufani were chatting merrily around their fires, their colorful hoods thrown back to reveal their faces. However, the moment they caught sight of Flint and Marcen, all talk ceased. Though none of the nomads immediately covered their faces, more than a few hands twitched as if to do so.

Flint kept her face civil, but she wanted to scoff. Why did they *still* distrust her friends after all they'd been through together? Stonewall had said the Sufani had many deeply ingrained habits that were difficult to break, but that didn't sit right with Flint. How long before the Sufani told them to leave? Probably not too much longer. *I guess we'll be nomads, too.*

Well, if she and Mi were together, nothing else mattered. Blood was blood. That in mind, she searched the Sufani for a familiar figure, but Milo was nowhere to be seen. She started when Marcen spoke softly. "There's Leal."

The scout sat apart from her fellows, a half-eaten plate of food at her feet as she fletched one of the many arrows set in a neat pile beside her. Like the other Sufani, Leal wore a hood and cowl around outsiders, though both were down now, revealing her close-cropped crimson hair. At Flint and Marcen's approach, Leal glanced up, though she did not set aside her arrow.

"Trouble?" she asked in a low voice.

"Depends on your definition of the word," Flint replied. "The others are on their way back. Stonewall sent us ahead to warn you."

Leal paused in her work, her brows knitting. "Who got hurt?"

Why jump to that conclusion? Were they all so unskilled to this dreg's eyes? Flint scowled. "A *thrall*, that's who."

"Kali's plan worked," Marcen added quickly at Leal's frown of confusion. "She managed to cure a thrall of his possession. Drake and the others are bringing him back now."

"Bringing him *here*?"

"He's a Canderi," Flint said. "He has nowhere else to go."

Leal jabbed the arrow toward the north. "He can go back where he came from."

"Why don't you tell him that, yourself?" Flint replied. "The sod's as big as an oak tree and probably still not in his right mind, but I'm sure he'd be glad to chat with you."

The Sufani rose smoothly. She was tall and lean, and firelight flickered in her green eyes as she regarded Flint. "How long before the 'cure' wears off? How long before he goes berserk and kills us all?"

"Kali was a thrall too," Marcen pointed out before Flint could. "But she hasn't reverted."

Leal toyed with the arrow's fletching. "I suppose. Well, I'll break the news to my parents." She motioned in the direction of a pair of caravans set well away from the main Sufani camp. *"You* get to tell Eris."

"Has she returned from scouting?" Marcen asked.

"Not yet. Adrie's about worried sick, but I think she's overreacting. Eris knows her own limits."

Flint could not help her shudder of revulsion at the thought of Eris' *limits.* Marcen glanced at her, but did not comment, only nodded to Leal. "I'll let her know. Thanks."

Marcen turned to leave. Leal stepped away too, but Flint said the Sufani's name again. "Have you seen my brother?"

"I'm not his nanny."

Flint nearly grabbed her dagger but held the urge in check. She didn't want another lecture from Stonewall about her temper. Instead, she took a deep breath and tried to speak calmly. "He said he wanted to be alone. I wasn't sure if you'd seen him while scouting the perimeter."

Leal considered her. "No, girl. I haven't seen your brother today."

With a sigh, Flint turned to go, but Leal called her. "What?" Flint asked.

"There are some strange ruins about ten minutes east of here," Leal said, pointing. "I found them when we arrived last week. The place is quiet. Secluded. A good spot to brood."

Flint nodded in thanks and stepped off. Marcen had stopped a few paces away, waiting for her. "What are you doing?" she asked him. "Our mission's over."

He gestured toward the two separate caravans, where a small group of people sat before their own fire. "I can talk to them, if you want to find Milo."

"Because they don't want to talk to me?"

A flush rose in Marcen's cheeks, but he nodded. "You're still a sentinel in their eyes."

"I'll always be a sentinel," she shot back, though the words felt hollow. How could she be a sentinel, a protector of peace and balance, if she was Forsworn? Did the One god truly hate those who'd left the sentinel order, even for really good reasons?

Marcen's reply was apologetic. "It's better this way. For now."

"Fine. I don't care." With that, Flint stalked off in the direction Leal had indicated. As she went, she passed the ring of tents set up just beyond the wooden wagons. *Our new garrison,* she thought bitterly. The Sufani had been generous with food and clothing for all of them, and had managed to spare two wagons for the mages, but the sentinels had not been so fortunate. Well, Flint had spent many nights of her nineteen years with no roof or bed, so she could manage a few more.

She found the ruins without too much trouble. Milo *was* there, at the center of what looked like a stone structure whose roof was long gone. Despite how moss and roots covered most of the wall panels, the bits that still stood were smoother than anything Flint had ever seen. Strange, indeed.

Milo had had the foresight to bring a lamp, at least. He stood poised for attack, a dagger in each hand as he faced an invisible foe. As Flint paused at what must have been a doorway, Milo lunged forward. His right arm moved strong and smooth, but his left arm faltered and he dropped the dagger.

As he bent to retrieve the fallen blade, he clutched at his left shoulder and doubled over. "Shit, shit, *shit,*" he hissed. The bitterness in his voice set Flint on high alert, as did the curse. Milo didn't swear.

Flint cleared her throat and he whirled around. Even in the dim lamplight she could see how his face was flushed and his blue eyes were red-rimmed and narrowed – at her. "How long have you been there?" he said sharply.

"Long enough to see you make an arse of yourself." She tried to inject teasing into her voice, to let him know she wasn't serious, but he scowled.

"Leave me alone, *relah,*" he said, using the southern slang for kin.

Flint crossed through the threshold to him, though she kept out of arm's reach. "It still hurts?"

"I said leave me alone."

"How bad?"

She thought he wouldn't answer, until he held up his left hand, revealing how it trembled. "I can't even hold a dagger anymore. Mira…what am I going to do?"

He used my birthname. He never did that – she hated it and he usually tried to respect her wishes. But sometimes, when he was scared or upset, he forgot himself. Flint's throat tightened at the pain in his voice even as a swell of fury swept through her. Talon had done this to him. She ground her teeth to keep from screaming in frustration. "You can't mope about it forever. You have to–"

"You don't know a sodding *thing*," he broke in, glaring at her again. "So shut up and leave me *alone.*"

Though they shared similar features, anger didn't suit his face at all. In that moment, her twin looked like a stranger. Tears pricked at Flint's eyes but she fought them back and leveled him with her own glare. He was a novice at being a horse's ass, after all, not a master like her.

"Fine," she said. "But you should know that Kali's magic worked this time and the others are on their way back with a former thrall. He's a Canderi."

With that, she turned to leave. Milo had harbored a strange fascination with the Canderi ever since they'd met a Canderi merchant in Whitewater City a few months ago. If this didn't bring him back to camp, she wasn't sure what would.

She kept a deliberately slow pace, but Milo didn't follow.

THREE

Eris Echina stood atop the rocky outcropping and scanned the horizon. Winter wind whipped her cloak and her shoulder-length black hair, but she remained unmoved. "Where did it go?" she murmured to herself. "I know I saw..."

There! So faint, it may have been a trick of the fading light: a line of smoke trailed up from the distant trees. There were no settlements in this part of the province and Leal had not mentioned any other Sufani groups nearby, so what—or whom—was the source of the smoke? A small band of travelers, perhaps, but Eris held another hope, one she hardly dared to name.

Several steps back, to give herself a running start. Though her pulse raced and the urge to fly hammered at her heart, she paused to gather her focus, to coax her body's particles to *change* and thus fulfill her desire. Then she bounded to the edge of the cliff and leaped into nothing. For one moment the world stretched below her: dark forest, distant mountains, a graying sky. Then Eris shape-changed. Her body shrank; glossy black feathers bloomed over her skin and her bones winnowed away. Eris-the-woman fell; Eris-the-crow shot into the air and swooped forward.

The wind whistled past her ears and caressed her feathers, carrying her bird body with ease. The transformation had come swiftly, but already she could feel her strength waning. And no wonder, for she'd spent the better part of the day in crow shape. One more look, she promised herself, then she would make her way back.

Oh, it was so good to fly. Few aspects of her life brought her as much joy

23

as this. Eris opened her mouth to laugh but a shrill *caw* emerged, which made her want to laugh harder. If Gideon could have seen her, he would have laughed too. *Gid.* Her husband had been killed months ago, and though grief at his passing still cut her to the quick, she had fought to find some joy in her life.

Joy, and a new purpose: a better world for her and Gid's unborn child.

Eris scanned the trees again. The line of smoke was closer now—if only she could travel this quickly in human form!—so she angled her wings to negotiate her way down to the treetops. While keeping an eye out for predators, Eris flew toward the smoke and searched the ground below. The trees were thick here, but her crow sight was sharp. When she reached the source of the smoke, she landed on a nearby branch and studied the area.

At first glance, she was reminded of the Sufani, for whoever lived here clearly did not stay in one place for too long. Tents and wagons, though none painted in the bright colors the Sufani favored, rested around a single, smoking fire. But she saw no people and her heart sank.

Perhaps they were hunters, or fleet rider messengers, or hired blades, or any number of other travelers who might have reason to camp in the wilderness. Or... Perhaps they were *other* mages, wild mages, but they'd sensed someone coming and had chosen to hide, to wait, to watch. Just like her.

But probably not. She was being foolish; so great was her desire to find mages not held captive in bastions, that she imagined all sorts of fanciful scenarios. *I've been spending too much time with Kali if I've started to make up such stories.*

Disappointment stung, but she tried to shake it away. She would keep looking. And in any case, her scouting trips were not for nothing. She'd learned more about the outskirts of Whitewater and Redfern Provinces than any map could show. When she and her friends eventually left the Sufani, she would find the safest route to the southern province of Indigo-By-the-Sea, where mages were less reviled.

Eris ruffled her feathers in preparation of flight. Though still in the early stages, her pregnancy was starting to take a toll on her, and she felt more tired than she should. She allowed herself one last look at the camp – nothing. But as she launched into the air, she swore she spotted a woman standing beside the fire, watching her ascent. Once Eris was skybound again, she circled back, but the camp was suddenly shrouded in a mist so thick, she couldn't even see the trees.

Magic? It must be. Heart lighter despite her rapidly flagging strength, Eris vowed to return when she was able, and angled back for the Sufani camp.

*

After returning to the camp, Drake offered to help their newest arrival so his companions could tend to their own needs. He led the Canderi to his modest tent, pitched between the mage wagons and the former sentinels' tents.

As Drake pulled out his pack, Atanar surveyed the area. "You are not Sufani, yet you travel with them."

"Right." Drake rifled through his pack, searching for clothing he could part with. "I'll tell you the whole story later. It's a long and sordid tale."

As it happened, he could only spare a pair of trousers and an old coat, both of which he offered to Atanar. "You and I are about the same size, so these should fit." He grinned. "At the very least, they'll smell better than what you've got."

The Canderi man accepted the bundle without comment and Drake tried not to wince. *Guess my joke missed the mark.*

"I'll ask if Milo has an extra shirt, as well," Drake added as Atanar turned to head into the borrowed Sufani wagon. No doubt he'd have to hunch over the entire time he was inside. Drake could sympathize. The Sufani wagons were a blessing to most of the others, and Drake would never openly complain, but if he spent any amount of time inside one, his back ached for hours. As far as Drake was concerned, the tents weren't much better than the caravans in terms of spaciousness, though no one else seemed to mind. Stonewall and Kali, especially, seemed happy enough to share one.

"We're lucky your boots are in decent shape," Drake continued, following the Canderi. "Not a cobbler among us, though I think Adrie mentioned something about being able to repair leather and cloth. Tomorrow morning, if you want, I can show you where we've been washing."

Atanar paused outside the door and seemed to consider the bundle of clothes before glancing back at Drake. Ea's balls…his eyes were the same blue of the sky over Pillau in the height of summer. The color brought to Drake's mind a memory of warm sugar-sand between his toes; a feeling of *home*.

"My thanks," Atanar said. He ran a hand over his tangled blond hair. "Being clean would be…welcome. But I must not take without giving back."

"Can you hunt? Chop firewood? Mind horses? Mend weapons?"

Atanar squared his broad shoulders. "I am *vorunn*; I am forbidden from wielding a blade any longer. But I can do the other tasks, though I would prefer to tend horses."

"Ah, the famed Canderi affinity for animals. Are the stories real? Can your people truly form a…kinship with beasts?"

Drake regretted the words the moment they left his mouth, for although Atanar murmured an assent, he lowered his gaze to the bundle again, a distant, haunted look creeping over his rugged features.

"Forgive me," Drake said quickly, face heating. "I meant no offense. I'm just curious. Anyway, don't worry about compensation." He tried to keep his voice jovial and warm. "We'll find some way to put you to work."

"Good."

"There's plenty of food tonight," Drake added. He gestured to the closest campfire, where Adrie had prepared their evening meal. "Just come on over when you're ready."

Atanar nodded, then glanced at the fire the sentinels shared, where Stonewall sat, already shoveling down his supper. "He is your brother?"

"Aye. You see the resemblance?" Drake and Stonewall shared similar facial features, though Drake's skin was several shades darker and his eyes were dark green next to Stonewall's light brown.

"You are...wider," Atanar replied.

Drake barked a laugh. "Well, that's one way of putting it."

Atanar frowned. "Forgive me. Aredian words are still strange on my tongue."

"No apologies needed," Drake said, shrugging. "Elan is my little brother in more ways than one. We have the same mother, just different fathers. But blood is blood."

Atanar studied him a moment more, those blue eyes sweeping from Drake's head to his feet. "You are a mage." It was not a question.

Somehow the answer made Drake's heart beat faster. "Yes."

"But the girl, Flint, called you a sentinel," Atanar replied. "From what I know of Aredian ways, no one can be both."

"Well, I'm a trailblazer that way." Drake kept his words light, but his stomach flipped anyway at the thought. But he had nothing to be nervous about. He was a *mage, not* a sentinel. That life was over, and good riddance. Still, he couldn't help himself. "Is that a problem?"

Atanar exhaled. "I do not yet know. I should be grateful for magic, but... " He waved his free hand in the direction of the campfire – the *mage*-made fire.

"Your caution is in good company." Drake nodded to the clothes. "I'll see if I can track down something else. Once you're done, we can burn the rags you've got now. If you don't mind, that is."

The Canderi nodded. "It is...amenable to me."

Drake's own laugh surprised him. "Glad to hear it."

Atanar slipped into the carriage and closed the door. One dilemma solved, for now. Again, Drake glanced at his brother and again, Stonewall ignored him. Drake grimaced. *This* dilemma would not be rectified with spare clothes. But he knew better than to test his brother now, so instead, he squared his "wider" shoulders and headed for the outskirts of their camp to find Milo.

*

After supper, Stonewall fought not to let his tension show while Atanar and Kali spoke about the fellow's time as a thrall. Although Atanar had not shown any signs of aggression, Stonewall refused to let his guard down. It didn't help that the Canderi's gaze upon Kali was intense and searching, while she sat unruffled, idly poking the campfire with a stick to encourage a blaze.

"I only have some memories," Atanar was saying. "But faint. Like dreams that flee upon waking."

"Odd," Kali said. "I remember everything. By any chance, do you know how long you were possessed?"

"It is late winter now?" When Kali nodded, Atanar considered. "I was made *vorunn* at winter's opening. By my highest reckoning, only one summer has passed since."

"And that...*vorunn* business is what started this?" Kali asked, stumbling over the Canderi word as Atanar nodded. "Stars and moons...that's over a year." She looked at Atanar as if seeing him anew. "You might've been the first thrall to come to Aredia."

"I cannot say." Atanar sat hunched over, folded arms resting on bent knees as if trying to make himself smaller. Even so, he was easily twice as heavy as Kali and would give Stonewall a hard time taking him down – should matters come to that.

Kali must have caught a trickle of Stonewall's thoughts, for some irritation bled through their bond. *He's not our enemy.*

Stonewall frowned at his dagger and whetstone. He sat near Kali, keeping his hands busy while he tried not to watch the former thrall too obviously.

You trust too easily, Stonewall replied in kind.

Better than not trusting at all. She sighed audibly, and added, *With luck, Atanar will be the beginning of many liberated thralls. I just wish I believed curing them would get easier.*

More reason for one of us to be on our guard.

"I remember the voices best," Atanar said suddenly, drawing both Stonewall and Kali's attentions. "So many, speaking a language I did not know. Sometimes they were so loud, I could hear nothing else." He shivered.

"Those times, there would be…no memories. I would wake as if from a dream, in a place I did not remember traveling to. I think sometimes only hours had passed; sometimes days – or more."

He hunched further in Drake's wool coat. Despite his own mistrust, Stonewall would have given more than a pair of socks, but he had nothing else that would fit the Canderi man. Milo had lent Atanar a tunic, though even that was tight across the Canderi's chest.

Out of habit, Stonewall glanced around, searching for his squad to reassure himself that they were safe. Beacon and Sadira were with a few Sufani, tending a wound one of the children had received during an ill-fated attempt at a snare. Flint was sparring with Drake and Leal. Adrie and Marcen were gathering firewood. Milo sat nearby, staring at his untouched dinner.

"Do you remember how you came to be a thrall?" Kali asked Atanar.

Atanar did not answer right away. "I will never forget that night."

"Your experience might help us understand how to stop it from happening to others," Kali said gently.

"It is…difficult," Atanar replied. "There are some words I do not know in your tongue." He clasped his hands before him, and did not look at Kali as he spoke. "But I see why you wish to know. I will try.

"I was one of a hunting party that numbered half a dozen. All of them were *Caradoc*, like me. Clan," he added quickly to Kali's confused look. "*Caradoc* is—was—the name of my clan, though we were not all blood kin. Of the party, only myself and my small-brother, Nel, were of Keraasi – my mother. It was Nel's first proper hunt."

A half-smile touched his face, smoothing out his coarse features, making him seem younger even than Milo and Flint, though he'd claimed to be a few summers older than the twins. Kali, too, smiled in encouragement, but said nothing. This story would probably not end well.

"It was a difficult hunt," Atanar continued. "It was winter, but only just, and a storm fell upon us during the night. When morning arrived, the tundra was ice and snow as if winter had struck in full force. Travel was hard. We were all tired, but Nel was only a boy of eleven summers. He tried to keep up," Atanar added quickly. "He did not complain once, not *once*, but I could see misery in his eyes. So I called for a rest at the..."

He trailed off. "I do not know the word in your language, but we call this place *Tang Yaarok*."

"*Tang Yaarok*," Kali repeated slowly. "What is it?"

"A...great cave in the side of a rocky hill. Within, there is a river so wide, you cannot see the other shore. They say the river flows from the earth itself. It is a sacred place, forbidden to us."

At the mention of a river, Kali had sat up. Her curiosity spiked, barely leashed as she said, "You went inside?"

"It was forbidden." Atanar whispered something in Canderi, then said, "But Nel would not have survived otherwise. The others spoke against the idea, but I was the *samaat*'s son. It was my decision. We went into the cave."

"What happened then?" Kali asked.

Eyes squeezed shut, he shook his head with such force that his body rocked. "It was forbidden."

"Atanar, please tell me."

He did not respond, and his posture sent a thrill of warning through Stonewall's veins. "Kali," he murmured. "Leave it."

I must know, she replied, reaching for the Canderi man's forearm. "Atanar–"

When she touched him, Atanar cried something in his native tongue and grabbed Kali's throat.

Stonewall lunged the moment Atanar's hands had moved. But the Canderi wrapped his hands around the thin scar Kali still bore from another thrall's attempt to steal her blood. Her thoughts were a jumble of fear – for Stonewall, for Atanar, for herself. Heart pounding, Stonewall threw himself atop Atanar, struggling to pry his grip loose as Kali wheezed. But the sodding Canderi was too strong; he shook Stonewall away like a horse shuddering off a fly, and sent the sentinel into the fire.

Thank Tor, Stonewall was quick. He rolled out of the embers, sending up a spray of smoke and ash and lunged again. But he wasn't strong enough to wrestle Atanar alone. As he wrapped both arms around the Canderi's neck, trying to cut off the man's air supply, he thought, desperately, *Relah, help me!*

Breaths later, Drake was at his side, calling aloud for the others. Beacon and Milo rushed over and each grabbed one of Atanar's arm's, to no effect. Only Drake had the strength to break Atanar's grip around Kali's neck. Only Drake could wrestle Atanar to the ground, trapping the Canderi with the full weight of his body.

"Easy, Atanar," Drake said, voice incongruously gentle amid the scuffling. "Take it easy. She's not your enemy."

Stonewall hardly gave Atanar a second glance as he went to Kali's side. "Are you all right?"

She sat upright, hand to her throat, red-faced and coughing in her attempt to suck in more air. Several more breaths seemed to steady her, though her whole body trembled. "I think so."

Stomach in knots, Stonewall took her hands. "Beacon..."

The mender knelt beside Kali. "Look at me. Watch my finger." He moved his index finger from left to right, studying how her eyes followed his movements. "Normal reactions," he murmured. "Do you feel lightheaded? Dizzy?"

She shook her head, blinking back tears.

Sadira had come over too, gently urging Stonewall away so she could take one of Kali's hands. Without a word, she closed her eyes and ducked her head in concentration.

Beacon took a deep breath and sat back on his heels. "Sadira's taking a closer look, but I don't think he did anything permanent."

"She looks hurt to me." Flint was there too, along with Adrie, Marcen, Leal, and several other Sufani who had been drawn by the commotion. Of the newcomers, only Marcen and Flint had gone to help Milo and Drake subdue the Canderi. The rest stood in a ring around the campfire, faces grim.

Flint had spoken from her place at Atanar's ankle. Between the four of them, they'd shoved Atanar to the ground, though Drake remained by his head, speaking softly to him. Flint glared at the Canderi and added, "I guess he's not cured."

"He's been through a trauma we can't imagine," Beacon said. "Perhaps the effects have lingered."

Kali was silent, her gaze on the Canderi man who now lay limply in the dirt. Atanar's blue eyes had closed and moisture gleamed on his cheek. Stonewall clenched his jaw, fighting the urge to kick in the sod's sorry face. *He could have killed her*, he thought, looking back at Kali to reassure himself she was well. *And if not for Drake, I'd have killed him. Or tried to.*

She met his gaze. She was crying, too. "I pushed too hard."

Stonewall wrapped an arm around her shoulders, pulling her close despite Sadira's protests. "I'll be cross with you later," he murmured in her ear. "For now, I'm just thankful you're alive."

To his relief, she pressed closer to him. "I like you when you're cross."

"Well, you're the only one."

Sadira cleared her throat, causing both Stonewall and Kali to look up. "I did not see any lasting damage to your body," the Zhee mage said to Kali. "And I have held back the worst of the…" She faltered, searching for the right word. "Marks on your neck."

"Bruising," Beacon offered. "Did you see damage to her brain?"

"No."

The mender smiled at her. "Have I told you today how glad I am you're here?"

Sadira's terra cotta-colored skin flushed darker and she stood abruptly, smoothing out her skirt. "Did the cure not last?" she asked Kali.

"All signs point to 'no,'" Adrie said.

Color rose in Kali's cheeks as she studied Atanar. "I *know* he was cured… "

"Kali." It was Aderey, coming forward with Leal and his wife, Ytel. "We must speak with you."

Kali winced. *I think we're about to be homeless again.*

Stonewall fought back a grimace of his own and got to his feet, offering her his hand to help her up. *Want me to come with you?*

"Help them, please," she said aloud, nodding toward his brother. "See if you can find out what happened."

Something about the way she said it made him think she already knew, but he nodded anyway. Kali stepped off to the edge of camp with Aderey, Leal, and Ytel. The others did not dissipate, but instead cast dark glances toward the Canderi man. By now, Atanar sat upright, shaking his head as Drake spoke to him. Milo and Flint stood within arm's reach, keeping the Canderi barricaded. Marcen and Adrie had disappeared.

Stonewall sent a silent prayer to Tor for strength as he came to his brother's side. "How is he?"

"I did not mean to harm her," Atanar said, looking up at Stonewall with wide eyes. "Please believe me."

Stonewall fought back a surge of anger and forced his voice to be calm. "Your actions speak for themselves."

"Kali just wants to help you," Milo said, startling Stonewall. "She means no harm." The lad had been so taciturn lately, this outburst was unusual.

Stonewall was not the only one who noticed. Flint shot him a look of surprise before adding, "Milo's right. Kali's a bit odd, but she's a good sort. For a mage."

"So I have seen," Atanar replied.

Anger coursed through Stonewall's veins again, enough to make him dizzy. The next thing he knew, he'd grabbed Atanar's tunic at the collar and jerked the Canderi up to look in his eyes. "What in the blazing void is *wrong* with you?"

"Elan, get back." Drake shoved Stonewall away, his own gaze hard. "Can't you see he's ill?"

Stonewall bit back a retort and glanced down to see his hands were shaking. Ea's tits, he needed a burn! Even a half-dose of hematite would bring a sense of control and give him the strength to face this new threat – this new life. He took a step back, trying to rein in his emotions. Drake was right. This man was sick. How long did it take someone to come back from being a thrall? Could they ever truly be free of the Fata's influence? He thought of Kali again, her eyes blazing like twin stars, and shuddered. Was there a thrall still within her, waiting to strike? His words to her on

33

their first journey together, what felt like a century ago, trickled back: *I cannot protect you from something you carry within yourself.*

"It's all right, Atanar," Drake was saying. "No lasting harm done. You're all right."

As Drake spoke, he placed a hand on Atanar's forearm, where Kali had touched him, but Atanar's reaction was completely different this time. He took a deep breath, his eyes lidding, as he nodded slowly. It was as if Drake's touch had a calming effect.

Unless… Was Drake using magic? Stonewall had never heard of magic that could soothe a fractured mind, but then, he'd never seen anyone take and give energy the way Kali could, or turn into a bird like Eris. Who knew what other powers lay dormant in mages?

Or within himself, for that matter. Had he called to his brother without using his voice, like he could speak to Kali? Or had Drake simply been drawn by the commotion?

Stonewall had not forgotten his anger, but its ferocity had eased, so he took his seat by the fire again and began to stoke the flames he'd nearly extinguished when Atanar had shoved him away. Flint joined him, though she kept her gaze on Atanar.

"We're going to get kicked out, aren't we?" Flint muttered.

Stonewall searched the tree line and found Kali in deep discussion with the Sufani leaders…and Eris, who must have recently returned from wherever she'd gone. Nobody looked pleased. He considered reaching out to Kali through their bond, then thought better of it. No doubt she needed all her concentration now.

"Aderey and Ytel have done much for us, already," he said. "We can't stay with them forever."

Flint exhaled in a long, slow draw. "What will become of us?"

How young she looked, and frightened. He didn't feel much different. "We're alive. We're together. We'll manage."

Not much of a comfort, but she seemed heartened. "We're a team," she said, nodding again before she bit her lip and cast him a sideways look. "A family."

It was almost a question. Stonewall smiled at her. "Aye. A strange family, if ever there was one, but a family, still."

Now she smiled fully, though the expression was short-lived as her gaze slid to Milo. He had apparently decided it was safe for him to skulk back into the woods alone.

"Will he be all right?" Flint asked.

"I hope so."

"I sodding *hate* this." Her gloved fists slammed into her knees. "I wish he would just get better, but I know it won't be that easy. I wish I could do something to help him, but..."

"He's your brother, Flint," Stonewall managed at last. "All you can do is give him time to heal and let him know you're there if he needs you. I think that's all we can ever do for the people we love."

She kicked one of the newly-burning logs. "I knew you were going to say that."

A clearing throat made them both look up to see Marcen standing to one side. "It's a bit dark, but I still want to check those snares," he said to Flint, thumbing the woods over his shoulder. "Want to come?"

"Not really," she said, though she stood. "But I don't have anything better to do. May as well stock up on food before we're vagabonds again."

"That's the spirit." Marcen beamed at her, nodded to Stonewall, and the two of them made their way into the forest.

Stonewall watched Flint's armored figure disappear from sight. He and his squad—and only now did he realize how he included Kali and Sadira in that number—had needed the last month to regroup. But now they had to think forward. For starters, the sentinels' armor was too distinctive. They'd been lucky so far and not run into anyone who would have recognized them, but Stonewall did not trust that luck to hold.

He studied one of his gauntlets with a critical eye. The boiled leather had been dyed dark gray, reminiscent of the hematite embedded beneath the surface layer of the thick leather. The stitching that held the leather pieces together was tight—he should know, for he'd done it himself—but it could be undone so the hematite could be removed. Beneath the top layer was

35

another thick layer of leather, dyed dark gray, but otherwise plain. Their weapons were another matter. The hiltless daggers' triangular shapes were only found in the sentinel order, but he was not about to give them up. It was the same with his sword. He'd relied upon it too long to cast it aside. Besides, he had no other methods to defend himself or his friends. Without his weapons, he was nothing.

Perhaps, without hematite to mark them and with cloaks or scarves to make them look less uniform, the sentinels could pass as regular folk, hired blades or some such. The mages had learned how to get rid of everyone's tier marks, so no one had the tell-tale mage or sentinel marks any longer. Perhaps they could travel as a group of mercenaries without drawing too much attention.

He sighed. Hardly a flawless plan, but the best he could do under these circumstances.

Aderey and his family had returned to the other Sufani; Kali and Eris walked toward one of the borrowed wagons, not speaking. When Stonewall sought Kali through their bond, not with the intent to speak to her, only to listen, he found her agitated. The feeling was centered on Eris. Naturally. Damn that woman to the blazing void. But Kali loved her, so Stonewall resolved to at least tolerate her. If only she'd return the favor.

He turned his attention back to Drake and Atanar. By now, Drake had encouraged Atanar to get up and dust himself off. Though they made an imposing pair, the two of them spoke quietly.

Stonewall decided to test a theory. He closed his eyes and sought his brother, not with his eyes or ears, but with his mind. As with Kali, he could picture the glowing filament of their connection: the thread that bound him to those he loved most. It was clear in his concentration, such that he could hardly believe it wasn't visible to the naked eye.

Relah, he tried to reach out. *Bahar.*

Drake stopped speaking mid-sentence, his green eyes going wide as he glanced over at Stonewall, who felt about as dumbstruck as his brother looked.

Sweet Mara's mercy...it worked.

FOUR

By the time Eris returned to Leal's family, she was at the end of her strength and patience. She all but dropped beside the caravan where she and Adrie had been sleeping. Shifting back to her human form, so close to her last change and after spending the better part of the day as a crow, was akin to slipping into the most comfortable dress she'd ever owned.

When she was herself again, she glanced around the camp that the mages and the hemies had made. A large group had convened around one of the fires, but Eris could not see the focus of their attention. Strange. The Sufani nomads had gathered at their own campfires, which was not unusual, but everyone's tense postures meant something was *off*. Wary, Eris hurried into the caravan to change into clean clothes. As she was clasping her wool cloak, someone knocked at the door. No sooner had Eris replied did the door burst open, with Adrie tumbling inside, Marcen on her heels.

"There you are," Adrie said without preamble. "You have to come out– now."

The urgency in the older woman's voice made Eris' stomach clench. "Have the sentinels finally found us?"

Adrie Talar's dark blond hair swayed beside her plump cheeks as she shook her head. "Kali and…the others finally cured a thrall."

Eris frowned. "Isn't that what they've been trying to do since we left the city?"

"Aye, but they brought this one back," Adrie said.

Eris' mouth dropped open. "A thrall? *Here?*"

37

Marcen made a noise of frustration. "It's not like that, Adrie."

"Then you tell me what else to make of the sodding Canderi who looks as if he's a few apples short of a pie."

"He's cured," Marcen said.

"Tell that to Kali," Adrie shot back, gesturing as if she was choking someone.

Mar cast a beseeching look at Eris. "Our mission was successful, and–"

"*Our* mission?" Eris broke in. "I know you've been working with them, trying to learn how to cure thralls, but since when are you *allies* with sentinels?"

"Since there's a real problem that we all need to solve. Aye, this Canderi *was* a thrall, but thanks to Kali's magic, he's a man again."

This was too much. Eris dropped onto the small bed at the rear of the caravan, trying to understand. "Marcen, are you certain Kali's magic worked?"

He stepped past the bundles of dried herbs and baskets of clothes to sit beside her. "Absolutely."

Eris could not help the twist of bitterness. Kali's magic was powerful and strange – and could be so sodding useful if she'd only pull her head out of that sentinel's arse for five minutes. With effort, Eris kept herself calm while Marcen related the story of how they'd found this thrall.

"That's...well, I don't know what that is," Eris said, making to stand. "But what about someone being choked? Is Kali in danger?"

But the moment she was upright, a wave of dizziness overtook her, nearly making her topple to the floor. Adrie and Mar steered her back to the bed where she sat, clutching her temple.

Dimly, she heard Adrie's instructions to Marcen before they both rushed out. Moments later, Adrie returned with a hunk of cheese, a thick biscuit, and a bowl of hot stew. "You must eat," Adrie chided as she offered the fare. "Shape-changing takes too much out of you – both of you."

The scent of onions wafted up from the bowl and Eris fought back a swell of nausea. "If I eat that, it'll just come back up. Besides, I have to ask Kali what in the sodding stars is wrong with her." Bringing a thrall back.

What was Kali thinking? That hemie—Stonewall—he'd twisted her kind heart into knots, making her think she was obligated to serve his whims, no matter how noble they appeared on the outside.

Eris tried to get up again, but Adrie touched her arm. "Sit. Eat. You can yell at Kali later."

"I'm *not* going to yell at her," Eris replied. "Too much."

"Eris…"

"Adrie."

The other mage threw up her hands. "Impossible girl."

"I've been called worse." Eris took Adrie's hand and gave a brief squeeze. "Thank you for fussing over me, but I'm fine. I'll eat later—I promise—but now, I must speak with Kali."

Adrie patted Eris' cheek, her expression both fond and exasperated. "You give me more gray hairs every day." She sighed. "Go on, then. I'll keep your supper warm."

∗

Kali gave Aderey a wistful smile. "I'll miss your stories most of all."

The Sufani leader chuckled. "We'll discuss this unpleasantness in a moment. But first…are you unharmed?"

She turned her focus inward, to her own body and its particles. The rush of panic had faded, leaving a throbbing ache in her neck and head. Her knee burned as well, for it had bent at an awkward angle during the… incident.

"I've been better," she admitted, glancing between Leal, Aderey, and Ytel. Concern looked back through all three Sufani's eyes. "But I'll be fine."

"Bringing that barbarian here was a bad idea," Eris said as she strode to meet them, apparently having returned from her reconnaissance.

"What else was I supposed to do?" Kali replied. "Leave him to fend for himself?"

"He's not some orphaned babe." Eris crossed her arms. "This is that lycanthra pup all over again."

"This is *nothing* like that," Kali shot back. "Besides, if I remember correctly, you weren't exactly opposed to the idea of sneaking her back into our room at Starwatch."

"*You* wouldn't stop crying over how she was going to die without her mother."

Kali gritted her teeth. "She needed help to survive."

But Eris was already shaking her head. "It was a wild animal. How long could you have kept her hidden? How—and what—were you going to feed her? You just can't leave well enough alone. You always take things too far."

"Better than turning a blind eye to those who need help."

"Your compassion will be your undoing. From what I hear, it nearly was today."

"At least I'm trying to make a difference," Kali replied. "Do you truly care about anyone else at all?"

Eris' green eyes gleamed with tears even as they narrowed to dagger points. "You have no idea what you're talking about–"

"Do you know how bad it was for us at the bastion, after you and the others left?" Kali broke in, balling her hands into fists. "You didn't think how the sentinels would treat us after *you* ran away. Collars for *everyone*."

"Shut up," Eris hissed.

"You first!"

"That's enough, both of you," Ytel snapped, startling both mages into silence. The Sufani leader's wife leveled them with a stern gaze. "Honestly, I'd say you were sisters by the way you snipe at one another."

Leal rolled her eyes. "My mother is right. Now is not the time to argue like spoiled brats."

Heat flooded Kali's cheeks and she looked at her boots. They were right. There were too many other problems right now to quarrel over old injustices. Such behavior was childish. She cast a surreptitious look at Eris, hoping to catch her friend's gaze, but Eris stared stonily ahead.

Aderey cleared his throat. "Kali, I am glad you are unharmed. But I hope you understand why we cannot allow you to remain with us. Many of my people are already on edge with everything that has happened."

"We need life to return to normal," Ytel added.

"I understand," Kali replied. "And we all truly appreciate everything you've given. More than food and shelter, you gave us sanctuary when we needed it most – after you were treated so horribly *because* of us mages."

"The *sentinels* captured you," Eris said.

"After we sheltered *your* mage friends," Ytel replied sharply. She looked at Kali and her voice gentled. "You did save my life, after all. Consider your debt repaid."

Aderey squeezed his wife's hand. "We won't send you into the void with nothing. You may keep everything we've given you so far—all of the clothes and supplies—and I can spare one of the wagons, too, though not anything to pull it." A smile quirked his mouth. "Perhaps your new friend could make himself useful in that regard."

Kali fought back a grimace. Aderey was only teasing her in his way, but he'd inadvertently reminded her of her own short-sightedness with Atanar. She had insisted on curing the Canderi and brought him back to live among her friends, so he was her responsibility, yet she had no idea how to help him beyond what she had already done. He deserved better.

She tried to keep her doubts from bleeding into her reply. "I'm grateful for any assistance. Thank you. Perhaps we can hunt a bit more before we go, and see to any last-minute ailments among your people."

Aderey chuckled openly. "Never have we all been as hale as when mages lived among us. I swear, even the earth you step upon seems more vibrant, as if spring has come early."

Kali's cheeks flushed. "I think that's just your overactive imagination."

"I would agree," Ytel added. "You can't cure him of *that*, can you?"

"Afraid not."

Aderey snorted. "As I recall, my darling wife, my imagination has kept *your* interest all these years." He added a playful smack against Ytel's rump that startled Kali into laughter even as the Sufani woman rolled her eyes.

Leal pinched the bridge of her nose, then looked at Eris. "Where will you go?"

"South," Eris replied immediately. "Mages are more tolerated in Indigo-By-the-Sea Province, and I think it's best to put as much distance between ourselves and Whitewater City as possible – for now. Sirvat and the others have already gone."

Leal nodded. "My scouts have reported seeing sentinel patrols too close to our camp." She spoke to her parents in Sufa, too fast for Kali to decipher.

Aderey nodded, though his expression was troubled. "We'll leave you two to your preparations," he said to the mages. "Though, I would like to speak again before you leave."

"Of course," Kali said.

"When do you want us gone?" Eris asked.

Aderey and Ytel exchanged glances before Ytel answered. "We were planning to move on from this place in two days' time. I think it's best we part ways then."

Two days. It felt like too soon. Kali glanced at Eris to gauge her friend's reaction, but Eris' expression was unreadable. She was like Stonewall in that way; both could turn emotionless so quickly. But now was probably not the time to share this observation. Instead, Kali bowed to the Sufani. "Two days, then."

Eris bowed as well, elegant as a first tier despite her rough wool dress. Even her words were graceful. "Thank you both for all you have done. For what it's worth, I deeply regret the trouble my friends caused."

Ytel gave her a look Kali couldn't read. "Take care, Eris."

The Sufani slipped back to their camp. Leal walked between her parents while all three of spoke in hushed, hurried tones.

When Kali was certain they were out of earshot, she looked at her friend. "Do you want to fight about this now or later?"

"Neither of us is getting any younger." Eris sighed. "But I'd rather not make another spectacle."

"Your caravan, then?"

They made their way across the camp in silence. Kali glanced over to see Stonewall in discussion with Flint. She tried to reach out to him, but couldn't concentrate with the knots in her stomach.

They clambered into the little caravan. The moment the door closed, Kali said, "I don't really want to fight."

Eris plopped down on the small bed built into the far wall, making the caravan rock. "I know."

"I feel like quarreling is all we've done since we left the bastion." Kali limped across the small space and flopped beside her friend, staring at her mud-splattered boots. "Maybe even before that."

"I feel the same." Eris took up a bowl of stew left on a nearby crate. "Did you really bring a thrall to our camp?"

"We found a thrall," Kali countered. "We brought back a man. And his name is Atanar. And, despite what happened today, I believe he'll be fine." She hugged her arms around her waist and added in a soft voice, "I was a thrall once, too. I know better than anyone."

"Well, you seem more or less normal."

"Thanks for the diagnosis," Kali muttered.

Eris took up her bowl again. "What was that?"

Kali did not answer.

Eris sipped her stew and nibbled her bread. "You don't want to come with us to Indigo-By-the-Sea, do you?"

"I think my place is wherever thralls are. I've not heard of them appearing much farther south."

"You're going to *keep* trying to cure them?"

Kali toyed with the end of her plait. The strands were coming loose again; she'd have to re-braid it soon. "If not me, then who?"

"I'm sure Queen Solasar has an interest in the matter."

"But only I have the practical knowledge," Kali replied. "That's why I'm trying to teach Sadira and Marcen how to help the thralls, too. What would the queen do? Send her soldiers to hunt and kill every thrall they can?" She shivered at the thought. "Thralls are innocent people corrupted by something they don't understand and cannot fight. Something powerful and evil. I have to help."

"Surely the queen can muster up some Silverwood mages to fight this battle. The dregs can take care of themselves. They always have." Frowning, Eris looked out of the caravan's small, round window above the bed. "In a way, this serves them right."

43

Kali dropped her braid and stared at her friend. "How?"

"You know I don't believe in the gods, but I like to think that there are still consequences for a person's actions." Eris' face turned hard. "If you treat innocent people like chattel, don't be surprised when they do nothing to help when you need them most."

"That's so cruel," Kali whispered. "Mages or otherwise...we're all in this world together."

"Despite what your hemie friends may think, this thrall business is *not* our fight. If anything, you've shown that we mages must protect ourselves against this...incursion." Something gleamed in Eris' eyes and her voice was dangerously calm. "Furthermore, we must press our advantage. We must fight for our own while our enemy fights another."

A cold sense of dread washed through Kali. "What are you planning?"

Of course, *now* Eris was silent.

Kali fought to keep her voice controlled. "The sentinels don't mean us true harm; they're only doing as they've been taught their whole lives. Haven't you seen proof of that with Milo and the others? There are some cruel ones, like Cobalt and Talon, but most are good people with... misguided thinking."

"Misguided thinking." Eris shook her head. "I'll never understand how you can feel such sympathy for the hemies."

"And I'll never understand how you can be so small-minded," Kali replied, crossing her arms. "We're all connected. You, me, the other mages and the sentinels, everyone in this world. Don't you see that?"

"I see a world where Gid's and my child will be hunted, imprisoned, and exploited if I do nothing to prevent it. We mages have power, Kali, perhaps more than we've ever realized. I intend to use it. I will shape this world into a better place for all mages. But I need your help."

Kali's stomach knotted further. The calm that had overtaken her friend was vastly more unsettling than when Eris shouted. "What are you planning?"

Eris moved so that she and Kali sat side-by-side. Gently, she took Kali's hand and said, "Your magic is strong. Not only can you take and give magical energy, you can move people over great distances in a short time."

No point in denying either claim, though the latter was purely Stonewall. But, even if he wanted Eris to know he was capable of such a thing, Eris would not believe it.

"You could make a difference," Eris continued. "A *real* difference. This... mission you've appointed yourself will fail. There are too many thralls and only one *Kali*. Let it go and come with me."

Kali stared at her friend, fighting the burning behind her eyes and the lingering hunger for Eris' magic pulsing through their twined hands. "Letting go isn't exactly my strongest trait."

Undeterred, Eris squeezed Kali's hand. "You and I have disagreements, but we can work through them. Like we did with the lycanthra pup, remember? You distracted the others while I left her outside the stables for the sentinel quartermaster to find. Then she took the pup to some village woman who raised wild creatures by hand."

Kali shook her head. "I told Captain Jonas about the pup. The quartermaster would have just as soon drowned the poor thing. Jonas is the one who arranged for her to go to Old Cinna." She gave a weak chuckle at the memory. "Stars and moons, he was *livid*, but then I started bawling... He could never be truly cross when I cried, so he promised me he'd take care of everything."

Eris had pulled her hand back at the mention of Captain Jonas. "Why would that stone-faced lout have cared if you cried?"

Shit. Well, there was no point in keeping this secret any longer. Kali took a deep breath. "Captain Jonas was my father."

A tiny, immature part of her was pleased at the way Eris gaped at these words. "This must be one of your peculiar jokes." She pulled a face. "Besides, everyone knows the hemies can't have children."

"It's rare, but not impossible." Kali hesitated. "I never really believed him, but Da told me that I was a gift from the One."

Eris snorted. "Naturally. Although I'm surprised he considered his own mage daughter a gift at all, since he kept you a prisoner your entire life."

Kali bit her cheek to keep back the first words that sprang to her lips, the sort that, once cast into the world, could never be reclaimed. The taste of copper flooded her mouth. She focused on the pain and on the growing hunger beating against the back of her mind: the yearning for the strength that flowed so freely through Eris' veins. Would that feeling ever go away?

This thought pulled Kali out of her anger and bade her be calm. She had a long, dangerous road ahead of her, and she needed to focus. "Jonas had no choice but to keep me in a bastion. If his commander had learned the truth, my father would have been sent to the mines, and I'd have truly been alone."

"Then why'd he even tell you at all?"

"He didn't, not for a long time. I always had a feeling, and I finally got the truth out of him when I was eleven or so. We both kept the secret until he died. But you'd left Starwatch by then, and I couldn't..." Kali swallowed, overwhelmed by memories of loneliness and grief in those windy mountains. "I couldn't stay any longer. So I came to Whitewater."

"Who was your mother, then? Another hemie? Are you a true miracle from their precious gods?"

"My mother worked in the garrison scullery, and died giving birth to me."

"Did your father tell you that?"

"He did, but..." Kali's knee twinged. She recalled Sadira's diagnosis, that her constant pain was due to an old injury and not a malformed part of her, as Jonas had always claimed. Was that the only lie he'd ever told her?

"I don't believe this," Eris said when she didn't continue. "You're either playing some crude joke on me, or I really don't know you at all." She seemed to fight to collect herself, then sat upright, once more a picture of grace. "But you can still make the right choice *now*."

Kali's heart sank to her stomach. "I *am* making the right choice." Eris scoffed but Kali continued. "Stonewall and the others... We're *all* renegades, Eris. We're all on the same side of the bastion walls."

"*They* are the enemy. They will *always* be the enemy. Why can't you see that?"

"They fled with us," Kali replied. "All of them... More than that, they *fought* with us. Bled with us. For Seren's sake, Milo's own commander tried to stab his heart! What will it take to make you see that these sentinels are *not* our enemies?"

"The only reason the hemie lackeys came with us was to save their own sorry skins," Eris retorted. "That, and they're all so brainless, they'll follow their leader anywhere – and their leader wants nothing more than to sniff after *you*. Sod's probably just happy to have a willing partner. I'm sure it's a nice change from his own hand."

Kali dug her nails into her palms. She stared at her friend, but saw a stranger. Or was she only now seeing Eris' true shape? *Heartless.* "You still hate Stonewall, even now," Kali said. "Even after he helped me."

"He's a sentinel."

"He's a good man. The two are not mutually exclusive."

"He's *using* you. The moment you're no longer worth the trouble, he'll abandon you – if you're lucky. No doubt he'd just as soon slit your throat than–"

"Enough," Kali broke in, getting to her feet. "You've made your point, several times over. I'm done."

Eris' jaw tightened. "Very well. Then if you'll excuse me, I must speak with the other mages. We have plans to make."

She'd gone cold again, smooth and hard as marble, though there was fire in her eyes. Despair clutched at Kali's heart and made her reckless. "Aye, we mages have great power. But we must be better than those who would harm us. We must not give them reasons to keep us locked away."

"The dregs will do that, regardless. We mages must take care of our own." Eris stood abruptly and pointed at the caravan door. "Go back to your hemie lover. I'm sure he misses his bedwarmer."

Anger and bitterness fought within Kali such that she could not stop the tears that slid down her cheeks as she limped for the door. "I know you're angry, but please don't do anything you'll regret one day."

"I'm not angry," Eris said as Kali stepped outside. "I'm right." With that, the door slammed shut.

FIVE

Talon's breath rasped in the silence. She was cold to her bones; her chest ached and her head throbbed, and she could not get enough air into her lungs. Alone in Silverwood Garrison's detention area, chains tight around her wrists, she stared into darkness, her thoughts consumed by memories of fire and death. Her father's last moments returned to her in the few fitful hours of sleep she found each day: the calm acceptance in his face as High Commander Argent lifted his sword; the soft *thud* of his head as it hit the scorched earth.

She had nothing left but grief, but she could not cry.

Footsteps sounded down the corridor and she listened only out of habit. At least half a dozen armored people marched toward her cell. By their quick, even tread, she guessed them to be Silver Squad, the High Commander's personal contingent of elite sentinels – coming for her, no doubt. It must be time for her trial.

The cell door opened. A spear of light sliced the darkness, though the point did not reach her. Two armored figures entered, coming to stand on either side of the doorway, then Argent stepped in. Talon recognized his silver boot spurs.

Two of his long strides brought him before her. His accent was as smooth and fine as a new blade. "On your feet. The One is waiting for you."

Talon was silent and still.

Argent remained calm. "Despite the trouble you have caused, it pains me to see you like this."

If she spoke, he would hear how her voice was like a rusted steel gate

48

being pried open. Besides, nothing she could say would change her fate.

The High Commander's armor creaked quietly as he knelt before her and removed one of his gloves. Alarm flashed through Talon, startling her into looking up, into his bare face. Argent's youth always took her by surprise; he was only about five years her junior, on the cusp of his thirties, with one of those aggressively handsome faces that left some people swooning. His eyes, though, his eyes were the color of slate, of stone walls, of hematite itself, and they missed nothing.

"You are a traitor and an oath-breaker," he said in that same quiet, polished voice. "You are a failure to yourself and those you loved. Yet you have one final chance to atone for your mistakes in this life. Will you not rise to meet it?"

The words stabbed Talon's heart anew, but she remained motionless.

A faint, sad smile touched his lips, and he reached his thumb to brush her jaw with the lightest touch. Her vision blurred at the edges so that for a moment, she could only see those hematite-gray eyes. "Stand, Talaséa Hammon," he murmured. "And face the fate you have wrought."

He lowered his hand and the next thing she knew, she was standing. Her long, bronze-colored hair fell in tangles down her back and the linen shift someone had dressed her in hung below her knees, tattered and stained. A cool breeze rifled her bare legs. She could not remember the last time she'd worn a dress – nor the last time she'd heard her full birthname aloud.

When she was fully upright, Argent gestured to the sentinels who had accompanied him. "Spar, Fain," Argent said. "Please help the former commander to her next appointment."

They steered Talon out of the garrison's detention area as if she were a chair out of place at the dinner table. Talon didn't bother to look up on their journey through the city of Lasath. She closed her eyes and dropped her chin, and let herself be brought to the Temple of the One.

*

The Pillar's voice resonated through the temple, but Talon only dimly heard the elder woman's words. "Here stands before us a sentinel who has broken her oath. Talaséa Hammon, these are the charges against you."

The assembled Circle clergy did not speak, but Talon felt their gazes upon her anyway.

High Commander Argent cleared his throat. "Subversion by way of colluding with Mage Foley Clementa to cause discord in Whitewater Bastion. Insubordination by way of withholding information from myself, your superior officer. Incompetence by allowing the escape of all mages in Whitewater Bastion–"

"Weren't those mages put down?" The second Pillar was also older, though he'd still retained a semblance of the muscular man he must have been in his youth.

Put down.

Talon squeezed her eyes shut. Her throat burned with an impending cough but she forced herself to be silent. She had not raised her gaze once since leaving her cell; she could not find the strength to care about her surroundings.

"Yes, serla," Argent replied. "Most of those mages were destroyed. Whitewater City is cleansed of their dissent."

"Thorough, as ever, Argent," the first Pillar replied, a trace of fondness in her words.

"A bit *too* thorough," the second Pillar muttered. "We might have made use of those creatures."

The inhuman word sent a chill down Talon's spine, causing her to glance at the holy man with renewed disgust. He was not as tall or broad as Argent, but he had the bearing of one who'd faced many foes in battle. His white hair contrasted with his dark skin, and his eyes seemed to glow in the light of the temple braziers.

The first Pillar, a small, gray-haired woman, offered the larger man a thin smile. "There are more mages to be had."

"I suppose." The second Pillar waved at Argent. "Continue."

Argent bowed. "There is also the matter of the former commander's failure to disclose the nature of her relationship with Foley Clementa, the former First Mage of the Whitewater Bastion. He was her father."

Soft exclamations and startled whispers rippled through the audience, though the three Pillars remained silent. Talon's shoulders sagged. Cold. She was so cold inside. Even if she could get hematite, she would never be warm again, despite the memories of fire that filled her waking mind.

"No doubt the reason for her actions," the third Pillar replied. He was thin and spare, like a branch in winter.

"Subversion, insubordination, incompetence," the second Pillar added. "There can only be one sentence."

The first Pillar spoke next, her resonant voice echoing off the temple walls. "Ser Hammon, do you have anything to say in your defense?"

Talon's grief pressed upon her, heavier than armor, heavier than stone, and she could not speak.

"Very well. Talaséa Hammon, formerly Commander Talon, you are hereby stripped of all privileges granted to you by the Circle – including the ingestion of hematite. You will spend the remainder of your days in the mines of Stonehaven Province. I pray you will find a better future once you have crossed the river into your next life."

SIX

Flint watched Sadira, transfixed. The mage stood beside their campfire, hands cupped, gaze unfocused in the way Flint had come to associate with a mage concentrating very, very hard. Beacon stood beside the Zhee mage, holding a small bowl. Morning sunlight bathed them both.

"At your word," the mender said quietly.

Sadira nodded. "Now."

Flint held her breath. Beacon tipped the contents of the bowl into Sadira's palms, using the bowl and his own body to shield the hematite powder from the wind. Flint and Milo, standing on either side of the mage, served the same purpose. As the silvery-gray powder filled the mage's palms, Sadira's hands began to glow: first bright gold, then deep crimson, and then finally a yellow so pale it was nearly white.

"Not hot enough," Beacon murmured.

Pale yellow brightened into true white, like the sun that climbed the blue dome of the sky. Flint held her breath against the heat as sweat beaded on her brow. Sadira's body shook like she was in the middle of an intense sparring session. The white burn of her hands turned pale blue.

"Splendid," Beacon said. "Just a little more…"

Sadira gasped and canted forward, dropping her hands and spilling the hematite powder. Without thinking, Flint grabbed the mage's arm to keep her from falling into the fire, too. Even through her glove, Flint's hand stung, but she didn't let go until she and Beacon steered Sadira safely to the ground, where the mage sat heavily, clutching her temples.

"I couldn't keep it hot enough," Sadira whispered. "I'm sorry."

The mender sat beside her, staring at the fire where the hematite died in little tongues of red flame flickering between their bright yellow sisters. "Don't be," Beacon said. "You did all you could. Purifying the hematite from our gear was a 'maybe,' at best."

"Even I cannot melt hematite," Sadira replied. "But I thought, if I could make *myself* hot enough, that would cleanse it enough for you." She straightened. "I will try again."

But Beacon was already shaking his head. "Don't you think you've done enough magic for the moment?"

"That little stunt nearly dropped you," Flint added as she pulled off her glove to check her skin. No blisters, thank the One, but her palm was pink where she'd gripped the fire-mage.

Beacon frowned at her, but Sadira gave a weak chuckle. "Magic takes great labor. But I thought I was strong enough for this." She sighed and pressed her fingertips to her bare throat.

The Zhee mage had shed her hematite torc during their escape from Whitewater Bastion. She had always worn the torc while Flint had known her, and Flint had assumed that Sadira wore it as punishment—a way to limit her powers—but Sadira had been able to perform great magic while wearing the necklace. But it was gone now, left in the ashes of the biggest blaze Flint had ever seen, and Sadira looked like she missed the damn thing.

Mages are strange folks, Flint thought, frowning. As much as she had enjoyed the energy and strength that hematite granted her, she had seen where that road would end and she refused to travel there. Since she and Milo were burnies—young sentinels who had only taken a single dose of hematite—Beacon and Stonewall seemed to think they would not suffer withdrawal while learning to live without the substance. That was nice, but Flint had no wish to watch her chosen family surrender to a slow and painful death.

She glanced over the mage's head to catch Milo's gaze, though his attention was on the Canderi fellow who sat alone just outside the reach of the fire's warmth, staring into a cup of broth Kali had made. When Mi caught his twin looking at him, he dropped his gaze to his boots, brows drawn as he rubbed his left palm. So he was still moping. Great.

"Don't worry," Beacon was saying to Sadira. "We'll manage."

"But you need hematite to survive," the mage replied.

"Aye, how can you be so casual?" Flint added, shuddering. "Lack of hematite nearly killed you and Stonewall." *And Rook,* she thought, though she refused to say her former friend's name aloud. "It *did* kill many others back in the garrison. Ea's balls, Red *died* after eating the stuff right off her gear."

Beacon ran a hand through his coppery hair. "Trust me, I've not forgotten. But anyone who tries to ingest hematite without first purifying it is desperate. Thanks to that priestess you and Mi befriended, we have some; we're not at that point."

"Yet," Flint and Sadira said in unison. The Zhee mage held her hands up to the fire again; heat rippled off the flames stronger than before. "I will rest, then try again. The power is there; I simply must focus it better."

Beacon sighed. "You don't have to–"

"It is *my* magic, Beacon." Sadira's pale blue eyes had narrowed and her mouth was a firm line. "You all use your skills for the greater good. Let me do this."

A pink flush climbed up Beacon's neck to his cheeks. "No arguments here."

"You're coming with us, then?" Flint asked the Zhee mage. Everyone had been in a flurry since the Sufani's proclamation the previous day.

Sadira nodded.

"Good. You're handy to have around in a tight spot."

"As are you."

There was no trace of mockery in the mage's voice. Perhaps she really meant it. Flint tried to seem nonchalant as she toyed with her sword-hilt. "I have my work cut out for me, keeping you moon-bloods alive."

She inwardly winced at the slur; sometimes her tongue had a mind of its own. Beacon shot her a glower but did not comment. A faint smile tugged at the corner of Sadira's mouth. "You have done an edible job so far."

Flint pursed her lips, working over the other woman's words. The Zhee mage was apparently still learning the finer points of the Aredian language. "Thanks?"

"Do you mean admirable?" Beacon asked, and Sadira exhaled in irritation, nodding.

She seemed to consider something, then said Milo's name, startling him into looking at her. "How is your arm today?"

"Fine," he replied in a flat voice.

Flint frowned to herself. *At least he answered.*

Sadira rose and held out her palm in a silent question. Milo hesitated, then offered her his left hand. "Still numb?" she asked as she pressed her fingers to his skin.

He nodded. "But it's still attached, so I know I'm *lucky*."

"You don't sound like you think that," Flint replied, watching her twin carefully. Sadira may have helped save her brother's life, but it was Flint's job to look out for him. That was what siblings were for.

Milo shot her a glare. "I am lucky."

"Sure you are," she replied. "But that doesn't make it fun to be out of commission. It'll be nice to have a mission again," she added, hoping to keep him talking. "I'm about to lose my mind sitting around."

It was the perfect set up for a joke at her expense, but Mi didn't take the bait, only nodded absently. Like the others, he had removed the hematite embedded in his gear, leaving only gray leather so dark it was nearly black. Already, dirt and grime covered his boots and gloves, and scuffs marred his cuirass. No longer clean shaven, he wore a patchy scruff of black hair on his chin and cheeks, and dark smudges ringed his eyes.

Something caught in her throat. What would it take to make him *better*?

"Well, we haven't been completely idle," Beacon said before Milo could reply. "Even though we're short a hand or two."

Flint could have punched the mender, for Milo's face fell again and he jerked his arm out of Sadira's grasp. "I'm going for a walk. I'll be back later."

With that, he stomped into the woods, rubbing his left arm. Once he was out of earshot, Flint gave Beacon her nastiest glare. "Thanks."

"For what?" He glanced at Milo, then gaped at her. "How is this *my* fault?"

Fury filled her to the brim and she couldn't see straight. He was a mender, for Tor's sake! He was supposed to *heal* and help, not torment. *You haven't treated Mi gently, either,* her better sense told her, but Flint ignored the nagging thought.

"That joke about 'short a hand or two,'" she hissed.

His coppery brows drew together. "Ea's tits, Flint, it was just a stupid joke. I was trying to snap him out of his fog."

"Bullshit," Flint shot back, her hands balling into fists. "Leave it to a frip like you to stomp all over anyone not close to your pedigree. Sentinels are supposed to be equal in the eyes of the One, but you never pass up an opportunity to rub our noses in your third-tier finery by treating me and Mi like trash, like less than trash. Like we don't matter."

Beacon flushed pinker with every word. "That's not true, and you know it. How can you still think so ill of me, after all we've been through? Why do you hate me so much?"

His words stopped her cold. *Why do you hate me so much?* Milo had said the same thing to her, months ago, after Dev's death, when she'd been more of a bitch to him than usual. She stared at Beacon, blinking back tears and hating herself.

A warm hand rested on her shoulder. "Take it easy, both of you," Stonewall said, coming to stand beside Flint. "What's the damage now?"

Flint clenched her jaw to keep from crying with frustration. "Nothing."

Stonewall squeezed again, but in a comforting way. "Doesn't sound like nothing. Beak?"

"Tempers are high, I guess." Beacon looked at Flint, his gaze sympathetic enough to make her want to either strangle him or break down sobbing. Perhaps both. "We're all a bit on edge."

"Just ready to be moving again," Flint managed.

Stonewall looked between them, then glanced at Sadira, who'd wisely kept out of the commotion. "Any luck with the hematite from our gear?"

"No."

"She almost had it," Flint added.

Their former sergeant shot Flint a warm look before releasing her shoulder and then nodding to the mage. "Thank you." He glanced over at Atanar, who now sat staring at the fire, his gaze unfocused.

"He's been like that for a while," Beacon murmured. "Ever since Drake went to talk with the mages. The other mages, I mean. Not our mages. Ah..." The mender glanced at Sadira, his ears going pink again.

Flint rolled her eyes. The mender's affection for the Zhee mage was so blindingly obvious. He should just save them both some time and reveal his heart. No doubt Sadira would welcome such a display, though Flint did *not* want to think of Beacon in any kind of romantic way. The very idea made her want to gag.

"You lot ready to move out?" Stonewall said. "The Sufani will be departing tomorrow at dawn; I'd like to set out a little bit earlier."

"Supplies are gathered, weapons are sharpened, and we've taken out all the hematite we can from our gear," Beacon replied. "I think we're as ready as we can be."

"Me too."

Flint started at the familiar voice. Turning, she watched Marcen stride over, rucksack in hand and dulcimer case slung over one shoulder. At her look, he flashed her a wide smile. "If you've room for another moon-blood in your party, that is."

"Who says we want you?" Flint asked.

He grinned at her again. "Who says you don't?"

I do, she wanted to reply, but the words wouldn't come. Sod it all...he had a *really* nice smile. She scowled at him instead.

Stonewall cleared his throat. "Aye, Marcen, we could definitely use your help, but what did Eris say?"

Marcen's smile faded and he shrugged, kicking at a loose stone. "She's... not pleased. But it's my life, you know? For once, I want to..." A hint of his grin returned. "I want to choose."

"Could be dangerous," Stonewall said. "The odds aren't in our favor."

Marcen shrugged again. "Old news."

A half-smile tugged at the former sergeant's mouth. "Fair enough."

Flint sighed loud enough to catch everyone's attention. "So where are we going first? How can we find more thralls? Are we just going to stumble around blindly and hope to run into them again?"

"Thralls have a way of finding us," Stonewall replied. "But there have been more thrall sightings to the north, so Kali thinks that's the best place to start."

"Makes sense, I guess," Beacon said. "I don't suppose Kali's magic could move us any closer to a goal we don't yet know, either."

"No," Stonewall replied quickly. "Also, we should avoid populated areas if we can, lest we run into any sentinel patrols, or anyone else who will recognize what we are. Of course," he sighed, "all of that could change depending on what—or whom—we encounter."

Unbidden, all eyes shot to Atanar, openly listening to their conversation. Stonewall regarded him, and asked, "Any suggestions on where to find more…like you?"

Atanar shook his head. "I was able to sense other thralls, once. But I sense none now. Nor do I know where they might be." He paused. "Will Drake be coming with you?"

Good question, Flint thought as the former sergeant's gaze grew distant and unfocused. He'd done that more and more lately, making her wonder if he'd taken one too many blows to the head. For all his talk about being compassionate to one's brother, Stonewall didn't cut his own brother much slack. Not that Flint could entirely blame him. If Mi left her thinking he was dead for three sodding years, she would never forgive him.

"I don't know what Drake's planning," Stonewall said at last. "You should ask him." Without waiting for a reply, he looked at Beacon. "Was there any hematite left from our gear after Sadira's attempt?"

The mender tossed him a leather pouch, the contents clinking. "I saved most of it. Doesn't seem like much, does it?"

Stonewall peered within and sighed. "Not really."

"I'll hold onto it for now," Beacon added. "In case Sadira tries again…"

But Stonewall was already shaking his head. "No, Aderey wants it."

Flint frowned. Hematite was deadly to anyone not accustomed to it, though she'd heard of some folks who took it in very small doses as a drug of some sort. "Why?"

"It fetches a good price in the shadow markets," Stonewall replied. "And we obviously can't use the raw stuff, only what that priestess gave us."

Beacon reached for the bag. "Even so, you can't just give it away. Like you said, it's too valuable. And even if we can't use it now, we might be able to one day–"

"No, Beak," Stonewall broke in, holding the pouch out of reach. "We must be rid of as much temptation as possible, don't you see?"

The mender scowled. "That's a nice idea, Stonewall, but I fear it won't work out as you hope. Hematite is strong."

"We're stronger," Stonewall said. "And we can't go back. We must go forward."

SEVEN

As Drake crossed the clearing later that afternoon, notes of music drifted over from the Sufani camp. When Drake peered between the wagons, he spotted Kali with Aderey, Ytel, and their youngest daughter, a wiry girl named Dianthe. Kali was demonstrating something on her viol while Dianthe watched with interest. Beyond them, the rest of the Sufani prepared for their own leave-taking.

Drake had gotten tied up mending his gear, but hopefully there was still some food left. When he came to the sentinels' fire, he found the Canderi seated there, staring into a bowl full of stew. No one else was around; Drake figured that the other sentinels were sparring or cleaning their kits, or something else dutiful. No doubt his little brother was off alone, praying one last time.

Atanar did not look up as Drake approached, nor when Drake said his name. Only when Drake sat beside him on the blanket did the Canderi seem to notice his presence, dropping the bowl in his surprise and cursing in his own language as the stew spilled in his lap.

"Shit," Drake muttered as Atanar began to mop up the mess with the blanket. "Sorry about that. But in my defense, I'm not easy to miss. I think you were a thousand miles away."

"I have not left this place since I was brought here."

"Never mind." Drake clasped his hands between his folded knees. "Speaking of traveling, I'm heading out in the morning. Have you thought about what you'd like to do?"

The Canderi considered him. "Where are you going?"

This was…tricky. Drake hadn't officially *asked* Eris if he could accompany her, but he had hope. "Not sure where, yet, but I'll be traveling with Eris and her friends. She's trying to find more people like us."

"Mages?"

"That's right." Drake hesitated. "You don't care for mages, do you?"

Atanar looked thoughtful. "I cannot say. I have such small experience with mages. There are none in Cander, and even though I have been in Aredia for some time, it is still strange to know there are people who can…" He made an indiscriminate gesture.

Something inside of Drake eased at the Canderi's words. "If it makes you feel any better, magic is still kind of a new idea for us Aredians, too." He offered a friendly smile that Atanar did not return. "Anyway, what would you like to do?"

Atanar looked down at the empty bowl. "I cannot stay here and your brother does not want me to come with them."

"Probably not," Drake admitted. "But he's not unreasonable. And if Kali knows you want to join her, I've no doubt she could convince him to ease up on his over-protectiveness."

Atanar shuddered and the bowl fell at his feet. "It is a great honor to travel in the company of the *samaat*'s family. My kinsfolk used to fight each other to hunt at my side. Now I am a burden."

This last was said with a pleading look at Drake, whose heart constricted even as he puzzled over the Canderi word, *samaat*. "You're no burden," he said gently. "You're healing. It may take a long time, but I think you'll get there eventually."

"I will never be that man again."

"Then you'll become a new man."

When Atanar did not reply, Drake risked a light touch at his wrist, causing those blue, blue eyes to meet his own. Drake tried not to stare back—some folks took that as a sign of aggression—but it was difficult *not* to look into those eyes.

Drake swallowed tightly. "The shape your life takes is the shape you make it."

61

The touch had not set off another violent outburst, thank Mara, but Atanar did not look happy. "Everyone who travels with me regrets it. I have caused great suffering during my time in this country."

"Perhaps the One god has given you a chance to make things right."

A strange, sad smile crossed Atanar's face. "I do not believe in your gods, but even so, perhaps some truth lives in your speech. But I still fear the harm I could cause." He hesitated. "Could I travel with you?"

Drake stared at him. "Are you sure?"

"I refuse to cause more suffering." Atanar's face went hard as a mountain. "So if I break again, you are the only one with the strength to stop me."

Only when he nodded to the dagger Drake wore at his hip did his words sink in. Drake gaped as cold shock swept over him. "You want me to...slit your throat or something?"

"Yes."

"You can't ask that of me."

"I must. I refuse to be a...plaything of some foreign creature." Atanar's voice softened. "Please, Drake."

The faint viol song was the only sound as they stared at each other in the fading warmth of the dying fire. Finally, Drake found his voice. "Very well."

"Promise me."

"You're asking a lot, considering we just met," Drake said in a vain attempt at humor. When Atanar only stared at him, he sighed, acquiescing. "Atanar, I swear to stop you from hurting anyone else."

Mollified, Atanar sat forward, bracing his elbow on his knees. "Now," he said, his tone more businesslike. "Tell me of this mission you mages are on."

You mages. Here was one person who did not know Drake as anything else. Strangely relieved, Drake smiled and mimicked Atanar's pose as he stoked the fire.

Their discussion carried them into the early evening, when Drake spotted Eris, Leal, and Adrie slip into the mages' caravan. Sensing that now was his best chance, Drake excused himself from his new Canderi friend and approached the caravan warily. From outside the door, he could hear voices raised in argument.

"Eris, Marcen has made his choice." It was Adrie, speaking in a firm tone.

The wagon rocked as if someone was pacing within. "It's a foolish choice. He'll be killed – if not by the sodding thralls, then by the metal-blooded morons he's throwing in his lot with."

"His best friends are dead. I think he wants a new purpose."

"I know something of grief," Eris shot back. "But how can he turn his back on his own people?"

Now was probably not a good time, but there wouldn't be a better one. Drake braced himself, rapped against the door, and pushed his way inside without waiting for a response. Within, he found two mages and one Sufani all glaring daggers at his intrusion.

"What are you doing here?" Eris asked.

Drake lifted his hands. "Just wanted to chat. Please don't turn me into a grub."

He hoped to draw a laugh, but Eris only rolled her eyes. They all drew back to give him room; the mages took a seat on the bed while Leal leaned against the wall, arms crossed.

Drake shut the door and crouched beneath the low ceiling, silently cursing whoever made these wagons so blazing *small*. "I want to come with you."

Perhaps a better man would have been less amused at Eris' shock, but Drake had to bite back a chuckle at how round her eyes got at his words. "With us? You?" She shook her head, short black hair brushing her shoulders. "I think not."

He'd expected this and had a ready argument. "Why?"

"Because you're a *sentinel*," Eris said, clearly disgusted.

"*Was* a sentinel," Drake replied. "But no longer. Why else?"

She frowned. "You helped me once, but–"

"Yes, and I suffered for it," he interjected, albeit gently. "Imprisoned, questioned, tortured...all at the hands of sentinels."

This caught her up short, and she hesitated. "Yes, but I rescued you. We owe each other nothing and your loyalty is...questionable at best. I don't need another reason to turn you away."

"I think you need reasons *not* to turn me away. Aye, I have sentinel *training*, but that makes me valuable to you, not a threat."

"You *lied* about that training."

He could not help but roll his eyes. "We've been over this a hundred times. I left that life *because* I'm a mage. Like you. There will be occasions where my experience will serve you well. It already has."

She shrugged.

Drake took a step forward, bonked his head against a low-hanging basket, and resigned himself to sitting on the floor. Not the best move, strategically, but vastly more comfortable. "If I know you even a little, Eris, I know that you don't give up and you don't back down from a fight. No doubt you have something planned. You'll need me."

"Maybe," she said curtly, but her expression was thoughtful.

"Despite my sordid past as a hemie, I'm a mage. I'm one of you. And I want to..." Hope caught in Drake's throat; this was his path, his purpose. She *had* to understand. "I want to help you. I want to shape a better world for mages. For *us.*"

Thank the One, this salvo landed. Eris' eyes widened and she glanced over at Adrie, who looked dumbfounded. Only Leal remained skeptical. "You've just been reunited with your brother," the Sufani said. "Don't you want to stay with him?"

This was more difficult. Drake measured his words. "Elan is...stubborn. I think he needs some time to..." *To forgive me,* he thought, though he said, "To think. And he's got that fire in his eyes that means he's got a new mission."

"With Kali." Eris' voice was flat.

Drake nodded. "She'll keep him plenty busy."

Eris did not reply.

"In any case," Drake went on, "I think it's time for me to truly commit to one side of the road." He shot a glance at Leal, who smirked. "Yes, Eris, I was once trained as a sentinel. But I was born a mage. Will you accept my help?"

She studied him before looking at Adrie again. "He could be useful," Adrie said carefully. "If nothing else, it will be good to have another blade at our backs."

"As long as that blade doesn't find its way *into* our backs," Eris muttered, but Drake thought she'd made up her mind. To his surprise, though, she glanced at Leal. "What do you think? You'll be our other 'blade.'"

Now that Leal's mission to help free the rest of the Whitewater mages was finished, Drake had assumed she would remain with her kin. What had her parents said when she told them? He did not know of another Sufani who had left their family to travel in the company of strangers for any length of time.

"I think Drake can be a fool and an ass," Leal said at last, and his heart sank. "But he is a skilled fighter and I believe he has a good heart. You could do a lot worse than to bring him along."

Thank Tor. Drake grinned at her. "Oh, stop with the flattery. You'll give me the wrong idea."

She shot him a rude hand gesture, but he only laughed, too pleased to be annoyed. Though he sobered at once, for there was one more matter to discuss...and he did not think it would go so smoothly.

"Very well," Eris said, sitting straight. "You may come with us. For now."

"Thank you, Serla Echina," he said, bowing at the waist even as he sat. "But there is one condition of my company that I failed to mention: Atanar."

"What about him?"

"We come as a set."

Eris burst out laughing. "Why in the stars and moons would I allow that barbarian to travel anywhere *near* my friends?"

"Because I'm asking you. Please, Eris. He's suffered more than either of us can understand. He's exiled from his homeland and has no safe harbor. I will handle him," he added before Eris could protest. "I can keep him calm."

"How?" Adrie asked.

"Magic," Drake replied simply. When all three women only looked at him, he clarified. "My magic has never been very strong, but lately it's

65

been…changing. Growing a little stronger, a little easier to use the more I wield it."

Now Eris looked curious. "Kali has made similar observations about her own magic, and mine has certainly grown stronger as I've practiced. But what does this have to do with the Canderi?"

"That one will be more trouble than he's worth," Adrie added.

"Not if he's half the fighter other Canderi are," Leal replied.

"I'm strong enough to take him on," Drake pointed out. "And with both of us at your back, no one will cross you."

The faintest smile flickered at Eris' mouth, but she was not easily swayed. "Why do you ask this of me?"

He hesitated. Now was probably not the best time to bring up the brutal nature of Atanar's request, so he tried a different tack. "I've spent my whole life running. When I was a boy, I ran from shopkeepers, merchants, other kids…anyone who'd stop me and my brother from stealing what we needed to survive. I ran from the sentinels who would have taken me to a bastion if they'd discovered what I was – and in doing so, would have left my brother alone. I ran from them again when I was an adult, because I wanted to start a real life with the man I loved, away from bastions or garrisons or any of that nonsense. And through it all, I ran from my own magic too, because it had always been a burden, a curse, something that would only bring grief."

He met Eris' green eyes, so much brighter than his own. "I can't change the past, but I can work for a better future for myself and all other mages." *Other mages.* A smile tugged at his lips; it felt so good to say those words. "Kali may have freed Atanar, but he's still hurting. But I can help him with my magic – I've already done so and am learning more each day. It will probably be difficult and take time, but I've got to try. I don't want to run away any longer."

Silence filled the caravan until Eris exhaled deeply. "Very well. But he must keep his distance. And the moment he steps out of line, you're both gone."

"My father made the same arrangement with Kali," Leal said. "And you see how that turned out."

"And yet your father still respects her," Drake replied. "Look, we have more knowledge than we did before. I think we should keep our minds open, but we also must move forward."

Eris pinched the bridge of her nose. "Very well, Drake. You may both travel with us, for now."

They made some more arrangements before Drake thanked Eris and the others, and rose to leave. Though the meeting had gone better than he'd hoped, his stomach was suddenly in knots, because the hard part was about to come. He had to tell Stonewall.

Drake made a quick stop at his tent before slipping into the darkness to find his brother. Having spent the last several days patrolling these woods, Drake knew the trails enough to travel without a torch. Besides, waxing Seren cast enough moonlight to see the way ahead. Away from the fire, cold crept over Drake like an overzealous lover, and he was thankful for his thick wool coat.

He found his brother kneeling in a patch of dirt swept free of snow, before a small pile of stones that someone—no doubt Stonewall himself—had stacked into a rough pyramid shape to create a cairn: a place to worship the god Tor. Drake paused several yards away, studying his brother in the moonlight. Stonewall's face was difficult to make out, but Drake imagined his brow furrowed in concentration as he knelt motionless, his breathing steady. Even as a boy, Elan could never relax completely. That wasn't unusual for orphans on Pillau's streets, but even when they were grown men and sentinels with new names, Stonewall had never allowed himself to trust that such security would last.

And I pulled the rug from under him when I left. Familiar guilt gnawed at Drake's conscience, but he tried to set it aside for now. He cleared his throat. "You all modified your kits."

Stonewall now wore armor of plain, dark gray leather, with a deep blue cloak over his shoulders. His head inclined in acknowledgment. "The hematite's too recognizable."

"I'd avoid major cities, but you'll pass as hired blades if you stick to the outskirts. Folks aren't as familiar with sentinels there." Drake took a few steps forward. "You feeling all right?"

"I'm fine."

Something in his voice told Drake otherwise, and guilt squeezed his heart again. He came closer and knelt beside his brother, who tensed and did not look at him. "Horseshit."

As expected, this made Stonewall shoot a glare Drake's way. "Did you come out here to mock me?"

Drake removed a *biri* from his coat pocket, twirling the slender roll of paper between his thumb and forefinger. "I remember the time after I stopped taking hematite. You fight and fight, but that *want* doesn't go down easy. You try to ignore it, and you do – for a time. But it always creeps back, often when you least expect it. And the next thing you know…"

"What?"

Drake studied the end of the *biri*, concentrating on the particles of the dried, ground thalo flowers wrapped within the thin paper. After a few moments, an ember flared to life as the plant matter began to burn.

Pleased, Drake took a single drag; the sweet smoke filled his lungs and an easy calm settled over him. "You go back for more," he said, offering his brother the *biri*. "You can't stand the *want* any longer. But taking it again after cutting back… It's worse than being a burnie. The burn clouds your mind. Either way, hematite will hold you prisoner."

"I can bear it," Stonewall said, facing the little cairn and ignoring the burning *biri*.

"Not forever."

"Watch me."

Drake exhaled. "You're strong, *relah*, but hematite is stronger. And you've been taking it, what… twelve years?"

"Thirteen," Stonewall said after a beat. "They started me on it when I was eleven."

"I was twelve summers." Drake shuddered at the memory. The sentinels started their young initiates on the substance at low doses, to better prepare them for their first true Burn when they were about eighteen. But even a little hematite had been enough to drive away his magical abilities. Now that Drake's last burn was years behind him, he couldn't help but wonder if his magic would have been stronger if he'd not started taking that shit so young.

"Flint and Milo will have it easier," Drake continued, offering the *biri* again. The thin line of smoke trailed up into the still air. "But you and Beacon are in for a rough time. This will help."

"I've been doing fine without you for three years."

Damn, but the truth stung. "Accepting help isn't the worst thing in the world."

Stonewall's eyes darted between Drake's face to the *biri*. "Those are for cinders," he said at last, looking away.

"Ea's balls, you're a stubborn ox, aren't you?" Drake rubbed his temple, trying to think of another approach.

"Don't worry about me, Bahar." Stonewall's voice was so quiet, Drake wasn't sure he meant to say the words aloud. But the use of Drake's birthname banished his frustration. This was his little brother. *I must help him, no matter what.*

He threw an arm around Stonewall's shoulders, pulling him close. Stonewall tried to squirm out of his grip, but Drake used his own size and strength to his advantage and did not release his brother.

Stonewall uttered a few choice swears, adding, "Cut it out! Let me go!"

"Listen to me, you stubborn, mule-headed, courageous idiot," Drake said as if Stonewall wasn't wriggling like a fish on the sand. "I know you haven't forgiven me for abandoning you. I don't blame you; I don't forgive myself either. But *listen* to me for a few seconds. I've been where you are. Let me help you – and your squad."

Stonewall stopped struggling, so Drake released him and offered the *biri* one last time. After what felt like an eternity, Stonewall accepted, studying the *biri* before taking a tentative draw. He exhaled a puff of smoke and immediately began sputtering; deep, hacking coughs that shook his whole body.

When Stonewall sucked in a breath again, he glowered at Drake. "I don't feel better."

"Try again. It takes a little getting used to."

Stonewall took another drag, but managed to contain himself this time. He blew out a stream of smoke. "The...urge for hematite. It's fading as I speak. This is incredible."

"It's a temporary feeling," Drake replied. "Some things, like *biris* and a little thalo gel mixed with water, will take the edge off, but only time will truly dampen the urge."

Stonewall exhaled another smoky stream. Already his posture was more at ease. Thank Tor. If anyone needed to relax a little, it was him. "How long before I don't want a burn anymore?"

"When I get there, I'll let you know. But *don't* take a full dose again," Drake added. "It'll make you brasher than any burnie. A little bit here and there will get you through the worst part."

Stonewall was silent as he smoked the *biri* down to nothing, which Drake noted with satisfaction. That stuff wasn't cheap or easy to find this far north, but he had a bit to spare, and he'd give it all up for his brother. When the *biri* was done, Stonewall gave Drake a sideways glance. "You're not coming with us, are you?"

"How in all things holy did you figure that out?"

"You look like you've got bad news but don't want to tell me." Stonewall flicked the spent *biri* away. "And you'd not have given me this now, unless you couldn't do so later."

Drake forced himself to meet his brother's eyes. "Nothing gets past you, eh?"

"Why?"

"You see more than people give you credit for."

"*Relah.*"

Drake sighed, sending a puff of mist into the air. Seren had already climbed almost to the zenith of the sky, and cast a silvery light upon the world. "I'm a mage, *relah*. It's time I acted like one."

"I understand that. But..." Stonewall looked at the cairn; this close, Drake could see the lapis pebble resting on the top. "I only just got you back, and

70

you're leaving again." Stonewall sighed. "At least this time, I'll know you're alive."

Drake didn't miss the sarcasm in that last bit. "I wanted to come back for you. But Tobin got killed and I got hurt, and the whole plan went to shit. I had to leave Aredia for years before I was certain the sentinels had stopped looking for me. And by then, I didn't know where you were, or if you were even still alive." He took a shaking breath, clenching and unclenching his fists as he fought back the burning in his eyes. "I thought it would be better for you if you believed I was dead. Because I know you, Elan. I know if you thought there was even a small chance I'd survived the attack, you would never have stopped looking for me, no matter what the cost to you. And that wasn't fair."

"I never thought about what it must have been like," Stonewall murmured, almost to himself. "For you to join the sentinels, knowing what would happen if they discovered what you were. Hiding that part of yourself away. It was for my sake, wasn't it?"

He sounded like a kid again. Drake tried to pitch his own voice to be reassuring. "It was my job to take care of you. But you're a man now, and you can take care of yourself. I think you and I are meant to walk different paths. For the first time in my life, I'm able to be who I truly am. I'm not willing to let that go."

Stonewall was silent, ostensibly studying the moon-drenched cairn. "I won't be an obstacle for you any longer," he said at last. "If you feel the gods are sending you on a different path, I can accept that, even if I don't like it."

"Come with us," Drake said at once. "You and Kali and all of them. Eris will have a fit, but I don't care. We're stronger together."

His little brother shook his head slowly. "Kali's made up her mind, as have I. And the others…" A faint smile touched his face. "They're with me, as it turns out."

"If they have any sense," Drake replied, grinning.

Stonewall shrugged, all serious once more. "Be careful, Bahar," he said to Drake. "Kali thinks Eris is planning something…dramatic. I don't want you to suffer for her actions."

"I'll keep my wits about me," Drake said. "Just make sure you do, too. By the way, how did you do that, yesterday?" He tapped his temple. "It was like hearing my name called in a crowded room, or like I'd caught you looking at me. Somehow, I just knew you wanted to speak to me. What—"

But Stonewall cut him off with a shake of his head. "I don't really understand what I did," he said in a low voice. "But I think…well, I think you're right. I think I've got my own path to follow, too."

Drake studied him. "What's going on?"

Stonewall pressed his hand against the cairn he'd built to pray. "When did you first realize you had magic?"

A chill swept through Drake's veins. "Before Mama passed, but not by much, so I was pretty young. Maybe four or five summers. Why?" No one was around, but he dropped his voice to a whisper. "Do you…?"

"No," Stonewall said, though he didn't sound convinced. "Well, not like yours or Kali's, or any other mage's that I've seen. But I've…" He trailed off, frowning. "It's hard to explain and I'm still trying to understand."

There were most definitely things left unsaid, but Drake didn't press. Stonewall would tell him eventually. Assuming they ever saw each other again. "When are you leaving?"

"Before dawn." Stonewall hesitated, then, to Drake's shock, leaned against his shoulder. "I want to forgive you."

He was warm and solid and smelled like leather, *biri* smoke, and *home*. Drake wrapped his arm around his not-so-little brother and held him close. "Do what you need to do, *relah*. Just take care of yourself."

Stonewall leaned closer. "You too, Bahar."

"We'll see each other again."

They parted and Stonewall's smile did not reach his eyes, nor did he acknowledge Drake's words. All he said was, "Be safe, brother."

EIGHT

It took Eris and her companions the better part of the day to reach the campsite she'd spotted from her airborne reconnaissance several days ago. To her consternation, nothing had changed. Even the same thick mist still hung in the air. In crow-shape, she alighted on an obliging branch to wait for the others to catch up while she scanned the clearing. Surely, if whomever conjured that mist thought someone had discovered their camp, they would have left. The fact that they remained probably meant one of two things: either they did not know they'd been discovered—unlikely, given the mist's sudden, persistent appearance—or they knew and did not care.

"Eris." Leal slipped silently through the brushwork and came to crouch beneath the tree, squinting through the forest. "By the One," she breathed. "This mist...it's just as you said. Have you seen anyone?"

Eris cawed twice in reply, and Leal nodded. "Nor did I when I checked the perimeter. They must be here, even if we can't see them."

One caw to indicate agreement. Leal had insisted upon working out some sort of code when Eris was in her crow-shape. The Sufani was all business as she scanned the mist once more, her eyes narrow beneath her emerald-green cowl and hood. "The others are right behind me."

Sure enough, a snapping twig signaled Adrie's approach as the other mage crept out of the brush to crouch with Leal. Drake and Atanar emerged after, both unnervingly quiet despite their bulk.

Once their party was assembled, Eris swooped through the mist to land gracefully in the center of the clearing, beside the remains of a fire. A moment's concentration allowed her to shape her body into a woman once more. However, she took her time with the transition, savoring the stretch of limbs and the tingle of disappearing feathers, to demonstrate her power to its fullest.

Of course, her plan was risky. If those who lived here were not mages, but enemies, Eris was advertising her abilities. But Leal and Drake had planned for all manner of scenarios. Besides, Eris had a hunch and she was not often wrong.

"I know you're here," she said to the mist. "Seren's light, show yourselves. Let us mages meet as equals."

Silence.

A woman's voice trickled through the cloying mist. "There are no mages here, stranger. Leave now, and we will spare your lives."

Eris' heart leaped but she forced herself to speak calmly. "This is no natural mist. There *are* mages here, and by now you know I am one of you. Show yourselves."

More silence, longer this time, such that Eris almost thought she'd imagined the exchange. Then a figure emerged from the mist, slowly taking the form of a woman in her early fifties, with tanned, weathered skin, pale blue eyes, and dark blond hair braided down her back. She wore a patchwork coat, plain trousers, and a blood-red scarf, and her movements were at once confident and wary.

The stranger came to stand before Eris, sizing her up, then she lifted her chin. "Those gifted with magic are called Seren's Children. Who are you?"

Seren's Children. Something in Eris' heart swelled at the term she had first heard from Gideon.

She bowed low, a sign of respect too deeply ingrained to forget. "My name is Eris Echina."

"And those skulking in the bushes?"

"Those are my friends. We've come from Whitewater Bastion."

As expected, the mention of the bastion made the wild mage's eyes widen. "A bastion mage? Here? How?" She glanced at Adrie, Leal, and the men who came to stand behind Eris. "Are all of you gifted?"

"Three of us are," Eris replied. "The others are our allies."

The wild mage frowned as she studied the others, her gaze lingering longest on Atanar, then she looked back at Eris. "How did you escape the sentinels?"

"I will share the story if you wish," Eris replied. "But first, I would have your name."

The wild mage closed her eyes, took a deep breath, and released it slowly. As she breathed out, the mist at the center of the clearing blew back to form a ring around the campsite, effectively shielding them from outside view. A strange, near-bird call echoed through the trees. Adrie gasped and Eris whirled around to see about half a dozen people stepping into the clearing. All wore expressions of wariness.

All but one. The first wild mage now grinned at Eris, white teeth flashing against tan skin. "My name is Jensine Damaris." She extended her hand to clasp Eris' forearm with an iron grip. "Welcome home, daughter of Seren."

*

Several minutes later, Eris gripped a mug of tea, savoring the warmth seeping through to her palms and the taste of honey lingering on her tongue. She nodded to Jensine, who sat across the fire from her. "It's very good, thank you."

"Thank my son," Jensine replied, jerking her chin toward a sandy-haired man who stood at her side, his arms crossed. "Though I don't know why Caith insists on such niceties."

Caith Damaris looked to be in his late twenties. He shared similar features with his mother, though he wore a scruffy beard and his eyes were dark brown, like Kali's. He frowned at his mother's words. "We might be mages, but we're not barbarians."

"*Mages*," Jensine scoffed. "You may as well call us 'moon-bloods.'" Caith winced and Jensine nodded. "There, you see? That's how I feel when you say 'mages.' The dregs spit that word, as if we're a curse on their precious world."

The rest of Seren's Children, seated across the fire from Eris and her

75

allies, muttered similar sentiments. They were a motley assortment of folks of varied ages. The oldest was a wiry man who watched Eris with sharp eyes as he smoked a *biri*. The youngest...

Eris' gaze slid to the little girl. The child's mother was Jensine's daughter Brenna; a lean, brown-haired woman with blue eyes like Jensine's. Brenna whispered to the toddler in her lap, and every so often the little girl would peek at Eris through her golden ringlets.

Something in Eris' heart fractured. No matter what she did, no matter how hard she fought, Gid would never hold their child.

She clenched her jaw against the tears that threatened to spill. She had to be stronger than ever now, for herself, for her friends, and for the new life growing within her womb. She nodded to Jensine. "How many of Seren's Children are there?"

"I can't say," Jensine replied, shrugging. "We don't often gather. Too many of us in one place can draw the wrong sort of attention. I almost didn't stick around to see if you'd come back. Anyway, you said you were from Whitewater Bastion. How is that possible? I thought you bastion folk were too tame to escape your pens."

A shiver of anger ran down Eris' spine but she kept her reply cool. "Not all of us are tame. We had outside help," she gestured to Leal and Drake, "but our escape was not easy. We lost..." Her throat tightened and she clasped her hands.

"We lost some good people," Drake finished.

Eris related the story as best she could, starting with her and Gideon's plot to leave at Heartfire and ending with the trip down the waterfall. She omitted the sentinels' role altogether, hoping to avoid mentioning the hemies. The wild mages' eyes widened at the story, and when Eris mentioned Sadira and Kali's ring of fire, Caith swore openly.

"No bastion mage has such power," he said, shaking his head. "You must be mistaken."

Jensine's voice was thoughtful. "Where are these women now?"

Eris sipped her tea, debating. If she spoke about Stonewall and the other sentinels, Seren's Children might turn against her. "Kali and Sadira have gone on a mission of their own, to...cure people from being thralls. I know it sounds impossible," she added quickly when Jensine snorted. "But Kali's done it before. Now she believes it's her job to rid the world of them, though I think we have better ways to use our gifts."

"That's too bad," Caith said. "We could use power like theirs."

Jensine studied her. "There's more you're not telling me."

Eris clutched her mug to steady herself. "Me and my friends escaped... but the sodding sentinels recaptured the rest of the Whitewater mages. I could not go back for them again."

"You can't save everyone," Jensine said, not unkindly. "Besides, you're not lacking in ability, are you? Never seen anyone who can completely change their physical form. I nearly choked the other day when I realized what you were. I'd hoped you'd come back."

Eris frowned at her. "How did you know I was...not a crow?"

"I always know when one of Seren's daughters is near." She said the words matter-of-factly, but Eris' heart skipped a beat nonetheless.

Caith glanced between Adrie and Drake. "What about you two? What can you do?"

"I can hold my own," Adrie replied stiffly. "How about you, lad?"

Caith frowned but his mother chuckled. "Bastion folk aren't like us, Caith," she said. "They don't take kindly to such probing questions. Right?"

This last she said to Adrie, who scowled. "We don't often discuss our magic with strangers."

"Why?" Jensine asked.

Adrie shot Eris a helpless look, but Eris was also at a loss. "It's just... not polite," she managed, shaking her head. "Close friends and family will speak of such things, but even then...it's not common."

"Because you're ashamed of who you are," Jensine said simply. "Because you have been taught that your magic is only meaningful when it serves another. So the dregs have poisoned your minds and the hemies use you as they see fit, and you let them. You poor creatures."

Though Eris had made similar statements, the words made her bristle. "Well, we're here now."

"Aye, so you are." Jensine took a swig of her tea and regarded Eris. "Why have you sought us out? Why didn't you continue south, like your other friends?"

"We intend to," Eris replied. "But I saw your camp, and I wanted…" Her cheeks heated. "I had to know if there were…wild mages."

There was a pause, then Jensine laughed aloud, a great belly laugh that frightened birds from their roosts. The other mages joined in, save Caith, who scowled, and Brenna, who watched Eris with that same sharp gaze as her mother.

Still guffawing, Jensine flashed Eris a wide grin once more. "And what will you do, now that you have confirmed the existence of us," she snorted, "'wild mages?'"

Adrie and Drake stiffened, and Eris guessed that Leal was glaring at Jensine. But she felt only calm. "You're right, Ser Damaris. I am powerful. No doubt there are other mages like me, trapped behind bastion walls."

"No doubt," Jensine replied, sobering.

"But you're wrong, as well." Eris lifted her chin. "I *can* free everyone. But I cannot do so alone."

Caith exhaled sharply. "What do you want?"

Eris met his gaze, ensuring her own was steel and stone. "Freedom, for all of Seren's Children."

He stared at her, then looked at his mother, whose gaze was distant. "Freedom," she said quietly. "For the bastion-bound. I've considered it, myself. It will not be easy."

"Nothing worth having ever is," Eris replied. "My own liberty certainly came at a high price."

"We've all lost those we love," Jensine said. The other mages around her murmured in agreement; Brenna hugged her daughter close, not looking at anyone.

Eris nodded. "I have no doubt. So I ask: will you join me?"

Caith scoffed but his mother only gave a feral smile. "Depends on if you prove yourself worthy of joining."

NINE

A week after Talon's trial, her mage carriage jolted to a halt, slamming her into the wooden seat. She ignored the discomfort. Hunger, thirst, coughing fits, pain... Constant companions, to be sure, but she no longer paid them any mind.

The carriage door swung open, revealing the Silverwood sentinels tasked with bringing her to Stonehaven Province. Sergeant Skarn, a stocky man with a drawling Redfern accent, grabbed her cuffs and pulled her out into the open morning air, where a sliver of the moon, Seren, rose above the battered, barren landscape.

As its name suggested, Stonehaven was rich in minerals and provided a thriving mining industry to the country. Though Talon had known as much, she'd never seen evidence of it laid out so starkly. Huge rock formations dotted the landscape, but between them and where she stood was nothing but bare soil and dirt, and a few scrubby bushes. Only two features stood out: the road from a nearby town that wound beside a great depression in the ground, as if a giant had pressed their thumb into the landscape; and a massive stone structure with a circular opening, radiating heat. The air smelled like fire and rust. A dry, chilly wind tugged at her threadbare dress and made her shiver. By now, the burn of hematite had faded from her blood, leaving her cold. She ignored that, too.

"Shift it, dreg," the sergeant muttered.

Sergeant Skarn and his companion, a male sentinel named Pace, each took one of her arms and led her toward the depression: the open-pit hematite mine. Graded steps ringed the sides of the mine, creating a path to a base still tucked in shadow. The ring of steel tools upon stone echoed through the chasm as the miners tore through the rock in search of the precious ore. A gust of wind swept up, bringing the scent of water, incongruous against the dry air and landscape, and Talon could not imagine where the water had come from.

"What a shithole," Pace muttered as they approached the entrance: a dirt pathway that led down into the depression.

"Be thankful for this shithole," Skarn replied. "We'd be dead without it."

Pace snorted with amusement. "This one will be dead, regardless. How long d'you think traitors last without hematite?"

"Doesn't matter," the sergeant replied sharply, tugging Talon along a little faster. "Once we drop her off, the prisoner's fate is not our concern. We have more important things to worry about."

Not until they were several meters into the depression did anyone come to greet them. There were three: a bored-looking young male clerk with a ledger and quill; a bald, bulky man with a thick beard; and a slender, short woman who walked a pace behind the men.

The sentinels brought Talon over and the clerk ran his gaze over her with indifference before studying his ledger. "The prisoner's name?"

"Talon," the second sentinel replied.

The clerk sighed. "Her *real* name."

No one answered. Talon glanced up to see all of them regarding her expectantly. She shot the sentinel officer a look, but he only shifted in place. Did he not know her real name? *Argent's not training them very well,* she thought, and said, "Talaséa Hammon."

"Hammon..." The lad squinted at his papers and made a note. "Right. You're late," he said to the sentinels. "I had you scheduled to arrive two days ago."

Sergeant Skarn lifted his chin. "Had to take precautions to avoid those sodding thralls. They're everywhere these days."

"So I hear," the clerk replied. "Well, come on, then." He made his way down the path to an open-sided wooden structure built into the rock itself. Here was a smoking fire pit, filled with hot coals and the remains of a meal upon a metal plate. A few crates lay scattered about, possibly serving as seats, given their proximity to the fire pit.

Workers shouted nearby and the creak of wagon wheels echoed down the path, but Talon could not make out the direction of either sound. Her gaze fell upon the woman who'd accompanied the clerk and the bulky fellow. She looked to be in her early fifties, with large, dark eyes and a vaguely familiar face.

The clerk cleared his throat. "Remove the prisoner's cuffs."

The sentinels exchanged glances before the sergeant spoke. "Is that wise?"

"The hemies never run," the bulky man replied, his voice low and grating.

"And even if she did," the clerk added, sweeping his free hand to indicate the landscape. "Where would she go? How long would she survive? I doubt she'd even make it to Carver's Creek." He looked at Talon. "When was your last burn?"

Talon's last full dose of hematite had actually been three doses at once, taken over a month ago, right before Argent had murdered her father. She had not yet started to feel the chills that accompanied the need for another burn, but surely it was only a matter of time. But she saw no reason to cooperate further, and kept her silence.

The clerk sighed loudly, shaking his head. He had a plump, young face with wide eyes and rounded cheeks, but his tone reminded Talon of a trainer scolding a group of burnies. "It doesn't matter. She's not going anywhere. Unbind her."

Sergeant Skarn bristled, but nodded to Pace, who removed the cuffs. Talon's wrists felt lighter but she did not enjoy the feeling for long.

"Ottis," the clerk said to the bulky fellow who stood beside him. "Take care of her mark."

Ottis grabbed Talon's right wrist and shoved the sleeve back, revealing her fifth tier cross and the sentinel daggers inked into her skin. Without preamble, he lifted an iron rod from the fire and pressed the burning end over both inked marks. There was no pain at first but Talon still gasped in surprise as her skin blistered and the scent of burning flesh filled her nostrils. As Ottis shoved the brand back in the coals, a searing fire spread from her wrist down through her arm, making her eyes water and her throat clench. She squeezed her eyes shut against the tears that threatened to fall. When she could bring herself to look, she stared at the three ugly red slashes that now obscured both her sentinel and tier marks. Three slashes, one for each oath she'd broken. *Honor. Service. Sacrifice.*

Da, she thought, shutting her eyes again. *I'm sorry. I'm so sorry.*

"Looks like you've got things well in hand, here," Sergeant Skarn said.

"Such a keen observation," the clerk muttered. "Run along and tell your master we'll take care of this one, too."

The sentinels hurried off, leaving Talon alone with Ottis, the clerk, and the unnamed woman. The clerk shoved his ledger beneath his armpit. "Ottis, escort our new guest and Kam to the barracks. Kam, get her sorted."

"Of course, Serla Loach," the woman replied.

The clerk grunted a reply and turned to leave, heading for one of the buildings on top of the mine. Talon expected Ottis to grab her arm again, but the bulky fellow only began shuffling down the pathway, down into the open-pit mine. Kam followed, not looking at Talon. For her part, Talon glanced over her shoulder, in the direction the sentinels had gone, but it was more of a habitual gesture than anything else. But the unfortunately-named Loach was right – she wasn't going anywhere. All she'd had to live for was dead. Soon she would be, too.

*

Ottis left them at the mouth of another passage in the pathway, about midway down into the mine. As the bulky man stalked away, Talon glanced at her new companion. Yes, Kam's features were familiar, though Talon could not place how. Kam was much shorter than Talon, without an ounce of fat on her small frame. Dirt stained her nails and hands, though her face looked as if it had been recently scrubbed clean.

"Bunks are that way," Kam said, gesturing as they stepped into the tunnel. "You and I will be sharing."

The tunnel was low and wide, which meant Talon had to hunch over to

82

walk through. A few lanterns lit the way, providing a flickering light the farther back the women went. Other than their footfalls, there were no other sounds. Was this a mine or a tomb?

Both, at least for her.

Talon could not help herself. "Are there other sentinels here?"

"They're working."

A reply died as Talon's throat began to burn, and the next thing she knew, she was doubled over, coughing and gasping. Finally, after what felt like a week, she could take a wheezing breath. Her throat burned and her lungs ached, and memories of fire and smoke danced behind her closed eyes. When she managed to look up, Kam was staring at her.

"I was...caught in a fire," Talon said by way of explanation.

Kam lifted a dark brow. "Must have been some fire. You're lucky to be alive."

Not really. Talon's body was weak; even the brief exertion of walking here had worn her out. "I thought only sentinels worked in the mines," she said, hoping to turn the conversation away from herself.

Kam continued down the passage. "Considering there are rarely more than half a dozen of us here at a time, it'd be slow going, indeed. Carver's Creek folks do most of the work. We assist as needed. There are four of us here now – including you."

"What is expected of us?"

"We do as we're told," Kam said quietly. "Until we can't."

Until the lack of hematite killed them. Talon shivered; she'd seen how hematite would lay waste to otherwise strong, healthy people. How long would it be before she succumbed to that insatiable hunger?

Soon, if the One had any mercy.

"Home sweet home." Kam had stopped to gesture to a pair of hammocks slung in an alcove off the main pathway. Someone had hung a thin piece of fabric over the opening to give a semblance of privacy. "The men are down the ways a bit," Kam added. "There's also a latrine, thank the One."

Talon wrinkled her nose, imagining the stench. "Down here?"

Kam slanted her with an incongruous smile. "Can't you hear it?"

"Hear what?"

"The river." When Talon only stared at her, Kam clarified. "It's underground. Runs beneath this entire pit, though there's a dam upriver from the latrine, so we won't soil our drinking water. It's a bit unnerving to take a shit over a little hole with the water rushing beneath, but it's the height of luxury. The frips in Lasath would be jealous."

Her voice was deadpan, but her eyes were wry, and Talon felt an unexpected smile come to her own lips. "No doubt."

Kam seemed pleased with something, and then looked back at the hammocks. "I like the bottom one, but it doesn't really matter. Riba always preferred the top..." She trailed off, her gaze lowering.

Something tightened in Talon's guts. "When did she pass into her next life?"

"The townies say Forsworn sentinels won't be granted another life," Kam replied as she knelt beside a wooden box tucked against the wall. "They say we're cursed. But I think the One has more mercy than they do. Riba crossed the river about three months ago. She lasted a while, too. Longer than I thought she would." She withdrew a healing poultice, some rags, and bandages. "Most sentinels who come here never last longer than a couple months. We lost Cadmus about a fortnight ago, and I'm worried about Jasper. You'll meet him soon enough. Let me see your arm."

Talon offered her wrist, bracing herself for the sting of the poultice. "How long have you been here?"

Kam daubed at the wound with a gentle touch. "I've lost track of the years. More than twenty, less than thirty."

"Twenty years?" Talon could not help her shock. "How is that possible? The withdrawal..."

Dark eyes opened to regard her. Gods above, Talon *knew* this woman, somehow, but could not place her features. "A long story, for another time." Carefully, Kam wrapped the bandage around Talon's wrist. "Come on, we'd best head to the mines before Ottis comes looking for us."

"Aye, he seems like a cruel sort."

"Ottis?" Kam chuckled as they made their way back out. "Oh, gods no.

He's a giant kitten. Loach has the teeth."

"The pudgy little clerk?"

Kam shook her head. "Don't let him hear you say that. In fact, don't say anything to him unless he asks you directly, and even then, keep your answers as brief as possible."

"Why?"

"Because he reports everything that happens here to the High Commander. He's one of Argent's pets. They're all over Aredia, you know."

A wave of nausea swept over Talon, making her stumble. A hand on her shoulder made her look up, into Kam's dark, concerned eyes as the other woman asked, "Are you...?"

Talon nodded. "Aye, just a little dizzy. I inhaled a great deal of smoke in the fire. Sometimes it...affects me."

Kam studied her with an air of disbelief, though she nodded slowly. "I can imagine." She gave Talon a conspiratorial smile. "Come on. We have a bit of time; I can sneak into the mess and get you something to eat before supper. That might help."

Without waiting for a reply, she took Talon's arm and all but pulled Talon along. As they hurried down the tunnel together, Kam inclined her head to look Talon's way once more. "Do you prefer your sentinel name, or your given name?"

Talon opened her mouth to say it didn't matter, because who cared what she called herself any longer? She wasn't a true sentinel anymore, so keeping her sentinel name felt false, but neither could she bear to hear the name her parents had given her.

"Tal's fine," she said at last.

Kam looked forward again. "Tal, it is."

TEN

The thrall struggled in Stonewall's grip, but he dug his heels in the cold, hard ground of the field and tightened his hold on the possessed woman's forearms. The *kuvlu* that Milo had thrown had wrapped the thrall's legs securely, allowing Beacon and Flint to help Stonewall wrestle her down. Now the mages could step in.

That piercing, inhuman shriek cut right through Stonewall's brain, but he tried to focus on Kali as she knelt beside the thrall, her face a study in concentration. Sadira and Marcen flanked her, each grimly determined to see this task through. Kali placed her hands on the thrall's temples and closed her eyes; the other mages followed suit. The woman, now prone, continued to struggle in the sentinels' grips, though already her movements felt weaker. This close, Stonewall could see dirt and grease in her hair, and the stink of her unwashed body and soiled clothing was enough to make him retch.

"Look out, Stonewall!"

Milo's cry of alarm made Stonewall glance up to see two more thralls emerge from the trees, their blazing eyes fixed on the sentinels and mages. Stonewall swore inwardly. Kali was still engrossed with her healing magic, so he gripped the thrall tighter and barked a command.

"Beacon, Sadira, take the one on the left. Flint, Milo, Mar – the one on the right. Now!"

Immediately, the sentinels broke apart, Beacon and Flint each guiding "their" mage toward the thralls now stalking the group.

Except Milo, who cast Stonewall a somewhat helpless look. "I'll have to untie the *kuvlu*," he began, reaching for the thrall's legs.

"No time, Mi, just go help Flint and Mar."

Milo's eyes widened but he hurried after his twin and the blond mage, who had fallen upon their target: a stocky man who, thank Tor, carried no weapon. Flint was fast; she dove for the fellow and leveled a brutal kick to his groin, sending him to the ground. A series of jabs to his windpipe followed, before she wrapped one arm around his neck to hold him still so Milo could grab his legs. Marcen knelt by the thrall's face.

Beacon swore, and Stonewall whirled to see the mender shaking his head like he'd been struck, though there was no sign of blood. Beacon and Sadira circled the third thrall, a thin woman wildly slashing a wood-handled scythe. Though she displayed little technique, her movements were strong and fluid, and kept both mage and sentinel at bay. Stonewall was about to see if Kali was done, so he could assist, when Beacon and Sadira lunged forward in unison; Beacon struck the thrall with his sword pommel while Sadira wrapped a hand around the scythe's handle. The wood smoldered and turned to ash, making the thrall scream. Then Beacon had her in a secure grip and Sadira reached for her face.

Relieved, Stonewall looked back at Kali, eyes still closed as she pressed her fingers to the first thrall's temples. Gods above, Kali looked exhausted and his heart rate kicked up all over again. *Is she cured?* he ventured through their silent speech.

"Aye," Kali breathed, sitting back heavily before she began to unravel the rope from the former thrall's legs. When she'd finished, the woman still lay in Stonewall's grip, her eyes wide and unfocused. Stonewall released one of her arms to gauge her reaction. She blinked hard a few times, then frowned up at Kali.

"Who are you?" she croaked. "Where am I?"

Kali smiled warmly. "I'm a friend. And you're safe now."

"You're not…one of them?"

Sadness ebbed from Kali, so strong it made Stonewall's throat catch. Sadness – and a sense of purpose that bolstered his own resolve. Yes, this was the right path. He glanced at the other teams to see Beacon and

Sadira helping their former thrall to her feet, while Flint and Marcen were speaking to the fellow they'd freed. Milo stood apart from them, his face downcast. Stonewall sighed inwardly; he'd tried to give Mi a boost of confidence with the weapon Aderey had provided, but it seemed to be short-lived.

One problem at a time, he told himself, looking back at the newly freed woman.

"The nightmare is over," Kali was saying to her, offering her hand. "Come on; we'll get you home."

*

Kali tried not to listen too obviously to the former thralls' hushed tones, but it was impossible *not* to be interested. As best she could tell, they were discussing whether to take the mages and sentinels back to their village. She dearly wanted to question them about their time as thralls, but held the urge in check for now. Hopefully she could convince at least one to share their experience.

"Three at once," Flint said, beaming. "Mar and Sadira deserve commendations."

Marcen's reply was equally pleased. "We are commendable, aren't we?"

"You were both incredible," Beacon added with a glance at Sadira, who replied with a gentle smile.

Stonewall cleared his throat. "Don't get complacent. We had a victory, today, but we might not the next time."

Kali rolled her eyes. *Spoilsport*, she chided him.

To his credit, he added, "In any case, all that practice finally paid off. Excellent job, everyone."

She shot him a wry look. "Very good. I almost believed you."

Flint slapped Stonewall's armored shoulder. "He's a hard-ass, our sarge, but he's *our* ass. I know what I said," she added as Beacon and Kali snickered.

Stonewall shook his head, but he beamed as feelings of confidence and pleasure rolled off him. His smile was infectious; Kali caught herself grinning, despite her exhaustion. Only Milo remained quiet, wrapping up the *kuvlu* and not looking at anyone.

"Serla Stonewall." It was one of the villagers, the slender woman Beacon and Sadira had freed. She had a ruddy complexion and hair the color of straw. "We decided to take you up on the offer of an escort back to Estia."

"No telling what's out there," the stocky fellow added, wincing. "Your swords will be welcome."

"We'll see you safely to your homes," Stonewall said at once.

The fellow nodded, though he frowned at Kali. "Do the moon-bloods have to come?"

Stonewall replied in what Kali thought of as his professional voice: emotionless but somehow still curt. "They're with us."

"They saved your sorry lives," Flint added. "The least you can do is say 'thanks.'"

None of the villagers replied, though the slender woman and the man exchanged a glance as the group began to make their way through the empty field. Twilight hung over the fallow ground, crickets chorused, and a cold wind rifled through Kali's unraveling braid. Her knee ached, but not as bad as she'd feared, so she was free to observe the newly cured thralls.

All three villagers were ragged and tired, though the third, the woman Kali and Stonewall had helped, seemed the worse off. Of the three, she was the only one who'd not spoken since those first few moments after Kali had freed her mind. She walked a pace behind the others, with her head bowed and her hands hanging limp at her sides.

Kali fell in step with her. "I never learned your name, ser."

"Delly."

"How are you feeling?"

She put a trembling hand to her temple, where Kali had touched her to break the Fata's hold. "I don't know. Strange."

"You'll be all right," Kali said. On an impulse, she squeezed Delly's hand. "It will take time, but you'll recover. I know; I was a thrall, too."

Delly's skin was warm, if grimy, and she did not pull away from the touch, only studied Kali with pale eyes. "But you're a mage."

89

"I am."

"But didn't mages...do this to us? That's what folks have been saying."

Eris' words came back to Kali. *The dregs will think ill of us, regardless.*

No, she wouldn't let that be true. Kali kept her voice calm and warm, and squeezed Delly's hand again. "Thralls *are* magic-made, but there is more than one kind of magic in the world. Human mages can't create thralls, only cure them."

Delly frowned. "If mages don't make them, who does?"

That was a more difficult question to answer. Now was probably not the right time to go into her knowledge of the Fata, so Kali kept her reply simple. "I'm not entirely certain, so I'm trying to figure it out. But the important thing is, you're safe now. Do you remember anything about what happened? How you came to be a thrall?"

Delly bit her lip and seemed to consider. Ahead of them, the two villagers exchanged looks again, but neither turned. At last, Delly said, "What day is it?" Kali gave her the date and Delly's eyes grew wide. "Two months after Heartfire?"

"Aye," the female villager said, glancing back. "But you've been gone since well before that. We all thought you were dead. Aster will be overjoyed to see you."

"My wife," Delly murmured to Kali, though her gaze was distant. "It's been so long."

"Do you remember what happened right before you became a thrall?" Kali asked.

"I was gathering mushrooms in the forest. I saw a woman – a stranger. At first, I thought she was a lost hunter, but her eyes shone and she..." Delly shuddered and pulled her hand out of Kali's grip to hug her stomach. "She cut me, here." She showed Kali a scar on her forearm. "After that, I only remember bits and pieces. It was like a waking dream – a nightmare. And the voices..." She described a similar sense of hearing a great number of people, as Atanar had also described and as Kali had experienced. "At the very beginning, I could *feel* them, in a way," she continued as they walked. "So much anger. It wasn't mine, but I still *felt* it, and the longer I felt it, the

90

more it *felt* like my own. I started to hate everyone: my family and friends, even myself. I hated us all so much, it scared me. I don't remember much past that." She shook her head. "I'm insane."

"You're not," Kali replied.

Delly looked at her. "There's more going on than what you've said."

The moon Atal shone high, a silver coin in the darkening sky. Seren, the mage moon, was long set. Kali shivered as well. "There usually is."

*

It was well after dark when they reached the village of Estia, and Kali's knee throbbed something awful. Estia wasn't much more than a handful of buildings: a trading post, a smithy, and of course, a humble temple. Most of the inhabitants seemed to live on nearby farms, but apparently the town magistrate lived in the center of the village. The villagers bade the group wait outside the magistrate's home while they went inside.

A strong wind blew, making Kali wince. Her cloak was lined, but not nearly enough, and she could not remember the last time she'd been truly warm all over.

"Kali, you were right about finding more thralls closer to a village," Sadira was saying. "Though I am uncertain how we will be...perceived."

Kali nodded. "I know it's risky, especially when we're fugitives, but I think the risk paid off. We saved three of their people's lives, after all."

"I hope they reward us with supper," Beacon said, stamping in place to warm himself. "I know I could eat a bear." He glanced over at the young man who stood beside him. "Mi, what about you?"

"I don't like bears," Milo said after a moment. "Too much fur."

Stonewall and the others laughed, maybe a little too loud, but Kali sensed Stonewall's relief that Milo was participating in the merriment, at least for now.

Marcen ran a hand through his hair, mussing the short, fair strands so that some stuck straight up. "You know what'd really be nice? Sleeping under a roof. Feels like forever since I've slept on something other than dirt and pine needles, with nothing between me and the sky."

"You could have gone with Eris and the others," Flint pointed out. "They took the Sufani wagon."

"Aye, but then I'd have missed out on all the fun *we've* been having," Marcen replied, winking at her.

To Kali's surprise, Flint's cheeks colored, though she squared her shoulders and said, "If you think what we've been doing is fun, there's something *very* wrong with you."

"No doubt," Marcen replied.

"If we're sharing our heart's desires," Kali said. "I'd love to wash the stink off."

"I don't mind how you smell," Stonewall replied, causing Flint and Beacon to roll their eyes and Marcen to snort with laughter. Even Sadira blanched.

Kali pulled a face. "That's not saying much, considering you smell worse than I do."

Stonewall's reply was prim. "I'm a man. We're supposed to smell bad."

"Speak for yourself," Beacon replied, wrinkling his nose.

"Well, you're both doing a fine job," Kali added.

"Ho, there!"

Everyone whirled to see that an older woman had emerged from the magistrate's home. There was no sign of Delly or the two other former thralls, only two large, burly men armed with pickaxes who flanked the magistrate. She looked to be well into her sixties, and her gaze held no warmth.

"Thank you for your assistance," she said without preamble. "However, your presence here," she glared at Kali, "is unwelcome. We of Estia are godly folk with no wish to be tainted by magic. It would be best for everyone if you'd leave. Now."

Kali's face was hot but before she could speak, Stonewall did. "My friends did your people a great service. They have not 'tainted' anyone, but *freed* them from an evil you can't imagine."

"They are mages," the magistrate replied. "*They* are evil, as are those who travel with them." Her gaze lingered on Stonewall's daggers. "If I were you, young ser, I would not remain where I am not welcome."

Stonewall sucked in a breath as if about to shout, but Kali put a hand on his arm, stilling him. *The last thing we need is for these morons to alert the sentinels,* she sent through their silent speech.

He tensed further. *If they haven't already.*

"Of course, serla," Kali said to the magistrate, holding up her hands in a gesture meant to pacify. "We won't trouble you further."

She turned for the road that they'd followed to get here, the one that would eventually carry them into Redfern Province. The others fell in step with her, all silent – even Flint. Kali felt the gazes of the magistrate and her guards upon her back as keenly as if they'd been drawn daggers, and her vision swam with anger. She and her friends had risked their sodding lives to help the people of Estia when they just as easily could have killed the thralls and gone about their business. Was Eris right? Would people always view mages as evil, even after seeing evidence to the contrary? If that was the case, what did it matter what she did? Why should she bother helping anyone when insults were her only reward?

Maybe the Fata are right to hate us, she thought bitterly, swiping at her eyes as she stalked through the cold night air. *If this is how humans treat each other.*

She felt Stonewall's touch upon her mind as though it were his hand upon the small of her back. *You did a good thing,* he said gently. *An honorable thing.*

Then why am I so angry?

We don't get to choose how our service is received. Sometimes, all we see is the sacrifice. At least, he added with a trace of wryness, *that's what my trainers used to say.*

The edge of her anger blunted. She reached for his gloved hand, savoring the way it enfolded hers. So this was "normal," now. Not a bad place to be, after all.

"Someone's up ahead," Flint whispered

The road was open, with farm fields on both sides. Immediately, the sentinels moved to stand between the mages and whatever approached.

Flint went for her daggers, but Stonewall made a slashing hand gesture and she stilled. Kali's heart raced as she peeked between Stonewall and Milo, trying to see who—or what—was coming for them.

"If it's a sentinel patrol," Stonewall murmured. "I want the mages to get out of here first. We'll cover your backs."

"What if it's those morons from Estia?" Flint said.

Stonewall's voice was grim. "We do our duty. We protect those we travel with."

Dread coursed through Kali's veins like ice. When she glanced over at Sadira, she saw her own fear reflected in the other woman's eyes even as Sadira's palms began to glow. Marcen slid into a ready stance, no doubt preparing to work his own magic. They were both right to brace for a fight, but the idea of using her magic as a weapon again, even in self-defense, made Kali's stomach twist.

We're all on the same side, she wanted to cry. *We shouldn't be fighting each other.*

Then Flint exhaled a stream of fog into the air. "One woman," she murmured. "No weapons that I can see. I don't think she means us harm."

The sentinels relaxed, though they did not break formation. Stonewall called, "Who's there?"

"Aster Reeve," the woman replied as she trotted up, her breath short. She was dark-skinned and willowy, with long black hair that hung loose about her face. "My farm's back the way I came. I'm Delly's wife."

"Delly?" Kali pushed past the sentinels. "Did she make it back to you?"

Moonlight shone on the tears that streaked Aster's face. "She did, thank the One and all the gods...and you mages."

"I'm so glad," Kali replied, and she meant it. Relief chased her anger away. "She'll probably be...not herself for a long time, but I think, with rest, she'll heal completely."

Aster sniffed, wiping her nose on the sleeve of her coat. "You're Kali, aren't you?" When Kali nodded, the Estian jerked her thumb down the road in the direction she'd come. "Stay the night with us. We don't have much to offer but a barn and some supper. It's a nice barn, though. Warm and dry. If I know the magistrate, she'll have turned you out into the cold, but that's not me and my Delly's way."

Kali opened her mouth to protest. Surely they couldn't stay long. Surely they had to be on the road soon, lest the magistrate send word to the nearest garrison. But another wind blew, more bitter than any so far, and her toes were numb and her knee throbbed, and she was so tired. She looked at her friends for guidance.

We shouldn't linger where we're not welcome, Stonewall sent, though even his thoughts felt forced. *We're wanted criminals.*

I know, Kali replied. *But...*

He sighed, his shoulders sinking. *I know. Me too.*

"It's stupid to linger." Flint pointed to Aster. "She could turn us in."

"I agree with Flint," Beacon replied, though he sighed heavily. "But..."

Flint sighed too. "Aye. It's cold as Nox's tits out here." She glanced at her brother. "Mi?"

"I'll go where you go," he said quietly.

A glance showed Kali that Sadira and Marcen were just as torn, so she looked at Stonewall again. *One night won't hurt,* she sent. *It'll take the magistrate at least a day or so to find a fleet rider and get a message out.*

And we'll be long gone by then, he replied in kind.

Kali looked back at Aster, who was watching the silent exchange with furrowed brows. "Thank you," Kali said, adding a slight bow. "We'd be glad of a shelter for the night."

Aster beamed. "It's the very least I can do. Come on," she said, turning to head down the road. "Home's not too far off."

ELEVEN

Flint couldn't remember the last time she'd been properly *clean*. She sighed in pleasure as she scrubbed the rag over her armpits again, savoring the hot water from the bucket the three women shared. Thanks to the Zhee mage, the air in the stall was also as warm as any bath house back in Whitewater City. She was stuffed with roasted mutton and red potatoes. If it hadn't been for the strange but stubborn cramps in her lower belly, which had started that morning and refused to leave, she might have been truly content.

"Sadira, remind me never to travel anywhere without you," Kali was saying as she wrung out her hair. "This is the height of luxury."

Sadira smiled. She'd cleaned up already and now sat a few paces away, plaiting her long, pale hair. "I have many uses."

"I'll say." Flint scrubbed her nether regions. She'd trained and lived with other women most of her life, and had long since abandoned any sense of modesty. The men were several stalls down, washing up as well. Thank Mara for that, because they *really* stunk.

"Can Marcen do this?" she asked, nodding to the still-steaming bucket.

"Not as well as Sadira can," Kali replied. "Neither can I. And I certainly can't make it so balmy in here."

Sadira nodded. "The men won't have warm air as we do, but they shall have hot water."

"Hot water, a proper meal, a night out of the elements." Kali sighed as she ran her fingers through her damp hair; with each pass, the dark strands dried a little more. "If it weren't for my sodding knee, I'd be downright content."

Flint paused her washing to study the mage. "How *is* your knee?"

"Much more cross than usual since we started this trip."

"I'm not surprised it bothers you so much," Flint said, poking the mage's stomach. "You're all pudge and no muscle. No wonder your sodding knee can't keep up."

"Pudge?" Kali said, brows furrowed. "Are you saying I'm fat?"

Flint rolled her eyes. "No, but you've no *muscle*. Just flesh. It amounts to the same thing as flab. Here." She flexed her leg, revealing the sinewy lines of muscle she'd worked so hard to gain. "See? I'm strong; my body can take the walking and running and fighting."

Kali's reply was a little too wry to be genuine. "That's well and good for you, Flint, but I've not spent my entire life training."

"Right, so you should start as soon as possible." Flint continued her scrubbing. "I can show you some basic sparring moves. You'll see; a little muscle on your bones will make a world of difference."

Kali replied, but Flint didn't hear. All her attention was on the rag she'd used to clean herself. The one soaked with blood.

Sweet Mara, she thought as horror flooded her veins. *I'm dying.*

"Flint? What's wrong?" Kali had dried herself and was dressing.

Too terrified to speak, Flint numbly held up the rag, tears springing to her eyes. The cramps...had they been a sign that she was sick? She'd thought she'd eaten something bad, but this...

"Oh, that's obnoxious," Kali replied. "Do you have anything for it? I don't have any extra cloths, I'm afraid."

"Nor I," Sadira said. "Perhaps our hosts have some they can spare."

How could the mages speak so blandly? Flint gripped the washrag and gave Kali her nastiest glare. "I'm *dying*," she managed to choke out. "Help me. Use your magic...something, *anything!*"

Kali stared at her as if she'd started speaking Canderi. "Is it that bad?"

Sadira rose and placed a warm hand on Flint's shoulder. "When was your last cycle?"

Flint blinked hard, fighting the urge to cry. "What in the blazing void are you talking about?"

The mages exchanged glances. "Flint," Kali said carefully. "How old were you when you started taking hematite? Not your first Burn, but the first time the sentinels had you ingest a little. It's a common practice," she said as an aside to Sadira, who looked confused.

Flint sniffed. "Almost eleven summers. But it wasn't much. What does hematite have to do with this?"

Kali bent to gather Flint's cloak, draping it over her bare shoulders. "You're not dying," she said gently, hugging the cloak around Flint. "Rather the opposite. I think your body is recovering from years of hematite use."

"Bleeding means something's wrong," Flint said, heart pounding. Surely the mages were mistaken. They had *no* idea of sentinels' ways. Right?

In response, Sadira offered another rag, a dry one, and the two mages coaxed Flint to sit upon it. "Bleeding about once a month is common for a woman old enough to bear children," Kali said as she sat beside Flint. "It's a sign of a healthy body. You have nothing to worry about...except, well, bearing children."

"You should take precautions when you take a man to bed," Sadira added.

"Right," Kali said. "We mages can look over our particles to make sure no...seeds have taken root, so to speak, but there are herbs non-mages can use to prevent pregnancy."

Flint shook her head. "Sentinels can't get pregnant."

Kali went still. "That's true, for the most part. But Flint," she squeezed Flint's shoulder again, "you're not a sentinel anymore."

Then what am I? Flint's head was spinning as she clutched the cloak tight around her body. It was all too much to take in. "So...I'm not dying?"

"No," Sadira said. "But there will be other...feelings, in body and mind, that come with your cycle."

"Cramps, mood swings, strange cravings, among other things," Kali added. "Your body gives you a warning, at least. Sometimes."

"Cramps," Flint repeated, nodding. Some of her dread had started to ease; the other women's nonchalance was now a comfort rather than an annoyance. Maybe they really did know what they were talking about. "I thought I needed to take a shit."

Kali chuckled. "Well, I don't know about that, but you're just fine, I promise. We'll show you how to manage everything. It's a bit of trouble, sometimes, but not unbearable. At least, not for most."

The Zhee mage was frowning in thought. "Did no other female sentinel discuss this with you? Not even Rook?"

At the mention of her former friend—*that sodding traitor*—Flint ducked her head, her eyes stinging once more. She clenched her jaw as she replied. "Rook never mentioned anything of this sort to me." Another betrayal.

"She might not have known either," Kali replied.

Sadira shook her head and murmured something in her native tongue, something Flint could not decipher. Rather than dwell on it, Flint swiped her nose and looked at Kali, who gave her a reassuring smile. Gratitude filled Flint's heart, making her voice quieter than normal. "Thank you," she murmured. "I must sound like a complete moron." She sure as shit felt like one.

"There's no cause for worry," Kali replied warmly. "I should have seen this coming. When I got my cycle the first time, I knew more or less what to expect, and I was *still* nervous. I can only imagine how frightened you were."

"Not that much," Flint said, but her voice fell flat. She sighed and looked at her clothes. "I should get dressed. Sadira probably should rest eventually. You can't keep us warm forever, can you?"

"Not forever," Sadira replied. "But close to it."

"Get dressed, Flint," Kali said, slowly getting to her feet. "We have a lot to discuss."

As Flint donned her gear, she could not help but ask, "You're sure Milo won't get this...cycle, too?"

The mages exchanged glances in a way that made Flint think they were trying very hard not to laugh. "Definitely sure," Kali said at last.

Well, that figured. Flint frowned as she fastened her gauntlets. "Lucky sod."

*

"What are they giggling about?" Marcen asked as he scrubbed his arms with a damp rag.

Stonewall glanced across the barn, toward the stall the women had occupied. He considered reaching out to Kali to find out what was so funny, but decided against it. Perhaps it was best he didn't know. Besides, it was probably none of his business.

"Who knows," he replied, running a hand over his scruffy chin. He'd not shaved in some time; Aderey had given him a small razor and a mirror, but he didn't have the energy to manage it right now. Instead, he dipped his rag in the bucket of warm water—courtesy of Marcen—and began washing his torso. He, Marcen, and Milo stood shirtless in one of the stalls. As the Estian farmer had said, the barn was dry; the scents of hay and soapwort filled the air, which held some of the warmth that Sadira radiated. All three men were happily sated from a delicious meal and the mood was convivial. The only thing missing was...

"Anyone seen Beacon?" Stonewall asked, glancing toward the barn's entrance.

Milo had turned away from the others to hide the scar on his left side as best he could. Dry now, he reached for his gear. "He said he had to go to the latrine."

"Been a while, though," Stonewall replied with a frown.

Marcen shrugged. "Maybe he fell in." He bent to wring out his rag, chuckling. "Want to send out a search party?"

"Not quite yet," Stonewall replied with his own chuckle. His amusement died when he caught sight of Milo struggling to buckle his cuirass with one hand, while his left hung limply at his side. "Here, Mi," Stonewall said, stepping over. "I can help with–"

"No." Milo turned away. "I've got it."

Marcen shot Stonewall a sympathetic look, then cleared his throat. "I meant to say something earlier, Milo. You were practically magical with that rope-thing Aderey gave us."

"*Kuvlu*," Milo replied, though he did not turn and still fumbled with his gear.

"Right, *kuvlu*," Marcen said. "Your aim was better than Drake's."

"I agree," Stonewall added as he gathered his own gear. "And Drake is no slouch with weapons of any kind."

Milo's shoulders sank. "You all had everything under control without me."

The cuirass was fastened, but Milo still refused to look at anyone as he sat upon an overturned bucket and grabbed the armored pieces for his legs. Sleeping in one's gear wasn't the most comfortable, but it took too long to suit up, and they might have to leave in a hurry.

Stonewall quelled the urge to offer Milo any more help—the younger man clearly wanted no part of it—but before he could speak again, Flint squealed loud enough to make him wince. "Ea's balls," she shrieked. "Get out of here!"

"Don't flatter yourself," Beacon grumbled as he slipped into the men's stall. "You've got nothing I haven't seen before. And I was just walking by, for Tor's sake!"

"Oh, sod off," Flint shot back. "You have *no* idea how lucky you are. All of you." That last was said as a mutter, though the women inexplicably began to titter again.

Beacon rolled his eyes as he started to remove his gear. His movements were quick, almost clumsy, and his words came in rapid succession. "What crawled up her arse? Mi, any ideas? Never mind; she's never needed a reason to antagonize me, or anyone else. Stonewall, let go!"

Stonewall had grabbed his arm, urging the mender to look at him directly. Beacon's eyes were bright and feverish, and his pale cheeks were flushed. Stonewall released him, anger and jealousy sweeping through his veins; the emotions fed each other, making each one that much stronger – and more shameful.

"You took hematite." Stonewall's voice was a low growl that did not sound like his own.

Beacon lifted his chin. "Just enough to take the edge away."

"You weren't supposed to get another quarter dose until–"

"I don't sodding care," Beacon broke in, scowling. "Ea's tits, Stonewall, the...*want*, it's too much! I can't bear it."

"Then don't," Stonewall shot back, holding out his hand.

Beacon's arms tensed as if about to throw a punch, and Stonewall braced himself. But the mender only fumbled through his belt-pouch and removed the leather bag that held their lives, then pressed the bag into Stonewall's palm. "Fine," Beacon said. "Have it your way, since apparently you can fight the urge I can't."

Stonewall trembled as he tucked the bag of hematite away with his other supplies, suddenly chilled by anger so strong it was frightening. The longing he'd tried to ignore surfaced again, howling through his body and mind like winter wind. Gods above, he wanted a burn. *Needed* one, more than he'd ever needed anything or anyone. Life without the burn wasn't worth living.

Stop this nonsense, he told himself, taking a deep breath. *You can't have any now. You shouldn't have any again.*

It was a truth that made him want to collapse, to bury his face in his hands and give up, for all that he stood as firm as his namesake.

Stonewall? Kali's soft presence in his mind roused him from his self-pity. *Are you all right?*

He took another deep, shaking breath. *I will be.*

Her reply was warm, if alarmed. *Can I help?*

No, but thank you.

Love flooded him, like waves caressing a sandy shore, and he relaxed a little bit. Gradually, he pulled himself together enough to see that all three men were watching him warily. "I'm sorry, Beak," he said at last, fighting to keep his voice steady. "We don't have a lot of hematite to play with, and we worked out a schedule to make it last as long as possible."

Beacon lowered his gaze. "I know. I'm sorry. It won't happen again."

Nodding, Stonewall glanced at Marcen, who had stepped away from the sentinels to dress, clearly hoping to give them some space. Milo watched his brothers-in-arms with wide eyes. Chagrin filled Stonewall and he had

102

an urge to ease Milo's discomfort, so he clapped the younger man on the shoulder. "You're still feeling all right without hematite?"

Milo swallowed thickly and nodded, dropping his gaze to his boots. "Aye."

"Good." Stonewall patted Mi's back again and looked between the other men. "It's late and it's been a long day. We should get some rest."

*

But try as he might, sleep did not come. Instead, Stonewall lay awake for what felt like hours, listening to Kali's rhythmic breaths and savoring the warmth of her body as they lay in one of the empty stalls, away from the others. But there was no peace within him, only that gnawing *desire* that he could not quell. The little pouch rested within arm's reach; how easy it would be to take just the smallest amount of hematite, with no one the wiser.

Desperate for a distraction, he considered waking Kali to lose himself in her pleasure, but she needed all the sleep she could get.

Besides, she deserved better than *him*.

His own weakness made him want to hit something, or cry, or scream his frustration to the void. Or all three at once. Blood hammered in his ears and he clenched his hands into fists, straining against the need for a burn. The barn, once welcoming and cozy, now seemed cloying as a grave, and he could not take a proper breath. He was weak and foolish, and deserved no better than a dagger in his loathsome heart. Better to die in disgrace than live as hematite's slave.

Kali stirred, murmuring his name, so he clamped down on his emotions lest he wake her. After a few minutes, she stilled, lulled back into slumber.

A coppery tang filled the back of his mouth; he'd bitten his tongue in his efforts. Bitterness burned his eyes, but he fought that too. Instead, he rolled over to his pack and fished out one of the *biris* from Drake. He lit it with a tinderbox and leaned back onto his and Kali's makeshift bed: his cloak thrown over a bushel of dry hay. The sweet, earthy smoke filled his mouth and nose, and he savored the sense of calm that settled over him, like sunlight kissing bare skin.

Damn my brother to the void, Stonewall thought, closing his eyes. *Drake was right.* He couldn't fight the urge for hematite on his own; nor, it seemed, could Beacon. The *biri* smoke was helping, but the yearning lingered in the back of Stonewall's mind, waiting to ambush him again. If he couldn't control this urge…

No. He could not entertain the notion of defeat. What would defeat look like, anyway? He could not—would not—go back to the sentinels, for so many reasons. The most important lay beside him, snoring softly. Not just Kali, but his squad, his chosen family, had put their trust in him, and he would not let them down. Stonewall exhaled another stream of smoke, switched the *biri* to his other hand, and curled closer to Kali so that the dark tangle of her hair tickled his nose. No, he could not go back, even if he'd not been Forsworn. That life was over.

But how could he go forward? The obvious answer was to find more hematite, but that notion made his guts queasy. Hematite was the problem, not the solution.

His thoughts spun in useless circles until he gave up hope of a rational solution, and turned instead to his faith. The *biri* was gone now, but its calm lingered, so Stonewall focused on each deep breath and sought his patron god.

Tor, help me. His hands tensed; another breath helped them relax. *Please, show me the path I should take.*

Warmth seeped through his veins, like coming out of the cold to stand before a snapping hearth fire. A pleasant tingle touched his fingers and toes as he sank further into relaxation. Then, as surely as if someone had spoken aloud, he heard Tor's voice in his mind.

Come home, Elan.

Awe slammed into him, dispelling the *biri*'s calm. His breath caught. Tor had answered his plea, again. This was no figment of his imagination, but divine intervention. But why him? Why now?

"I don't have a home to go to," he whispered, hoping not to wake Kali.

"But I still need your guidance."

The air went still, silent. Even Kali's breathing had stopped. Alarmed, Stonewall opened his eyes to look at her, but she was gone. The hay was gone, too, as was the barn and his squad and...

Stonewall now lay upon a barren stretch of ground, rocks stubbing into his feet even through his boots. A hot wind caressed his face. Towering, moon-bleached rocky outcroppings filled the horizon and the air smelled of rust and heat, though the day had long since faded into night. Stonehaven Province; he recognized it well, for he'd been stationed here not long before he'd met Kali. But how in the blazing void did he *get* here?

A woman's scream split the night, setting every nerve on edge. Kali! He reached for his daggers but only grabbed empty air. Kali cried out again and he scanned the landscape for the source of the noise. There! The open-pit hematite mine rested not twenty meters from his feet. Stonewall rushed forward, determined to help her, but when he reached the mine, he skidded to a halt. Instead of the path that wound around the rim, heading down into the mine, there was only a sheer drop to a chasm thick and black as the void. She was not here.

Heart racing, Stonewall called, "Kali! Where are you?"

"Stonewall!"

Her voice echoed off the pit. When he looked down, he spotted her clinging to a boulder with both arms, her legs already lost in the surreal blackness of the chasm. Stonewall tried to grab her, but his feet wouldn't obey his mind's commands. He tugged with all his strength, but he remained fixed in the earth, solid and unmovable as his sodding namesake.

"Kali," he called again, still trying to free himself. "Hang on, I'll be right there!"

This time her scream was wordless; a thrall's piercing shriek. Shadows crept up from the chasm to claw at her dirt- and blood-streaked face, cloaking her in darkness until only her eyes were visible: twin stars, burning in the void.

Then her bright presence vanished from his mind. He was alone.

Dread and despair filled him and he dropped to his knees, trying to pull himself forward, but he could not move. "Kali," he cried, but it was too late. She was gone.

He knelt in the dirt, rocks digging into his hands and arms, his sweat-damp skin cooling with each moment, his breathing labored. He searched the shadows for her, but found only darkness.

He'd failed her. He failed everyone he loved. "Kali," he whispered, sinking fully to the ground. "I'm so sorry."

"Stonewall."

He jerked upright at her touch against his cheek. The scent of hay and soap and *Kali* filled his nose and her warm breath kissed his mouth as she moved closer to him. The chasm was gone and the only shadows left were natural, nighttime ones. Her thoughts reached him hazily, for she was still half-asleep, but her presence was real.

But still, he did not believe she was safe until she was in his arms again. He said nothing, for words wouldn't come, just pressed his face into her hair, breathing her in.

She nuzzled his neck and kissed his earlobe. "Dreaming?"

"I wasn't asleep."

Her cheek curved against his; he could picture her wry smile as she said, "Could have fooled me."

Kali's sleepy amusement soothed his still-racing heart, but he could not bear to explain the vision, not now. "I guess I drifted off."

"A nightmare?" She kissed him again.

With effort, he pushed aside his lingering terror for her and shook his head. "It's gone. Did I wake you?"

"Yes, and I expect you to make it up to me with your usual enthusiasm." She inhaled. "Oh, you had a *biri*."

Gods above, he hated admitting to this weakness, but there was no point in hiding it from her. "Aye."

She leaned closer to him again. "Did it help?"

"A little." He sighed and sent his next words through their bond. *Beacon took hematite. It wasn't time, not yet, but he did it anyway. And I...* His jaw clenched at the memory of his own consuming desire; even now, after the

106

distraction of his vision and the lingering, calming effects of the *biri*, he wanted another burn. *I was angry.*

Was?

It's not fair, he replied, shaking his head. *How much I still want it. Sometimes, I think it has killed me already, even though I still breathe.*

He winced. He'd not meant to admit that to her, for she would only worry. And sure enough, Kali's concern touched him, but only a trickle, as if she were trying to keep the bulk of her emotions from affecting his. In this moment, she was a healer assessing a patient. *Has the urge faded at all?* she asked.

Sometimes I hardly notice. Other times...

You mustn't go back to it. Worry flickered in her words, like a lightning storm in a cloudy sky. *Please.*

I don't intend to. He inhaled her scent again, tickling her with his nose, and she gave a squeak of surprise. Both the noise and the feel of her body against his sent the disturbing vision a little farther back in his mind, along with the fading urge for hematite.

Kali must have sensed this too, for her voice was no more than an exhale against his ear, making him shiver. "Are you tired?"

"Not anymore." All his self-loathing, all his urges for hematite fled in the wake of her touch – and the ensuing swell of shared pleasure. Kali's emotions mirrored his and stoked them to a fever pitch. This was perhaps the best side-effect of their bond. Why else would they have found each other, if not for destiny?

We should rest, she said, even as her desire spiked and she kissed his jaw. *Who knows when we'll have this chance again?*

Exactly. Stonewall slid his hands beneath her tunic and sought her mouth with his mouth and her mind with his mind. Her body softened beneath him even as her heart opened to his; they were joined again, and he was enough.

TWELVE

They left Estia at dawn, following the path of the main road from within the safety of the dense forest. As Kali had hoped, Aster and Delly provided the women with a few necessities. These, coupled with a longer and more detailed conversation with Flint, set Kali somewhat at ease that the younger woman would be able to cope with her body's changes. Though Kali had admittedly found amusement in Flint's initial reaction to her cycle, ultimately the knowledge of just how hematite had affected the sentinel's body was unsettling, to say the least.

Kali hefted her pack and scanned the trees ahead, searching for Stonewall's dark blue cloak. To help avoid detection, the group had elected to travel in pairs or singly, near one another but far enough away to scatter their tracks. While not a foolproof plan by any means, the sentinels hoped this confused any would-be pursuers. She spotted Stonewall ahead: an indigo and gray shadow slipping through trees and underbrush with practiced grace.

Would he ever be free of hematite? What sort of life would he lead in the meantime? They had both accepted that they would never be "normal," whatever that meant, but his confessions in the barn and the conversation with Flint had sparked a new thought, one Kali didn't know how to handle. Female sentinels could not bear children, of course, but it was not impossible for sentinel men to sire them. Her own father was proof of that. Would Stonewall ever be able to...?

Stop this at once, she scolded herself, stepping to avoid a tangle of thorns. *You don't even know if you'll be alive in a month, let alone ever be ready to bear a child – if you'd even want to.* The truth was, she had never really considered being a mother until Eris had admitted her own pregnancy. Now, the idea struck Kali as, not strange, exactly, but not entirely unwelcome. But there was only one man she would want to father any of her children.

"Watch out!"

Kali jerked her head up in time to see a pine tree barely a handspan from her face, and froze. She shot Milo a grateful, if abashed, look. "Thanks."

He had been walking about a dozen paces to her right, but now drifted closer. "You looked as if you were a thousand miles away."

"I know, I should be more alert."

Milo gave her a half-smile; the best he really managed, these days. "Stonewall's alert enough for all of us."

Kali chuckled. "So is Flint."

They both looked for Flint, whose cloak, a patchwork of mossy greens and browns, almost camouflaged her completely. She wasn't alone. Marcen's wine-red coat swayed beside hers and his blond hair shone in the afternoon light filtering through the bare trees. When Kali glanced back at Milo, he looked straight ahead again and adjusted his pack. "We should keep moving."

Winter still clung to the woods along the border between Whitewater and Redfern Provinces. A hawk cried in the distance and squirrels darted out of Kali and Milo's path, but beyond that, the only sound was boots crunching upon dried leaves.

They walked in silence for a few minutes before Kali ventured a question. "How tired are you of being asked about your arm?"

"Pretty sick of it, actually."

"Very well. How's your big toe?"

"Right or left?"

"Left."

He seemed to consider carefully. "I had a blister a couple days ago, but it's healed now."

Kali smiled. "Glad to hear it."

Milo shot her a shy grin and her heart lifted at the sight. She knew all too well how it felt to have folks constantly worrying over you.

"You and Marcen are friends, right?" he asked after a moment.

"Yes, though we're not terribly close. I think he's kind. I *know* he's a fine dulcimer player." She grinned. "He laughs at my jokes."

"Flint seems to like him."

Kali thought she knew where this was going. "What do you think of him?"

"I dunno. He seems..." Milo glanced over at his sister again. "He seems to like her, too. They made a good team in Estia. Just like Beacon and Sadira, and you and Stonewall. Kind of makes me..." He sighed. "I don't really belong."

This took her by surprise. "What in the stars do you mean, Mi? Of course you—"

"No wagon needs a fifth wheel," he broke in, and held up his left arm. "Least of all a broken one."

"You're not a fifth wheel, Milo," Kali heard herself say, but the platitude fell flat.

"I know I'm not the best or brightest, but I've always been some good, to someone. I've never been useless before." He sighed again and shook his head. "I dunno."

She paused to put a hand on his arm, urging him to look at her. "Do you want me to be kind or do you want me to be truthful?"

The entire forest had gone silent, as if in anticipation. Vivid blue eyes met hers; they were wide and frightened, but Milo's voice was calm. "Truthful."

"I'm broken, too," Kali said, pointing to her knee. "Only I've never been any other way, so my experience will be different from yours. But I can tell you this: if you don't want to wake up every day and wish you hadn't, you must find a way to live with being broken. You must keep going, despite it, or perhaps even because of it."

He regarded her steadily. "How long will it take to find a way to keep going?"

"I don't know. Perhaps a long while. But your spirit is stronger than your body, Milo." She squeezed his left arm. "Trust in your gods, if you want, but mostly, trust in yourself."

His mouth opened, but before he could speak, a terrible shriek broke the air around them, and Kali's stomach flipped. "Thralls," she whispered.

Kali! Stonewall's alarm filled her mind but she held her own in check as he came darting back through the woods, racing to her side. The others converged on her as well. How strange, that she would be the rallying point for this unlikely group of allies.

"It came from the road," Beacon was saying as he and Sadira hurried over. "I think–"

Another piercing, inhuman cry cut off his words, and another, and another. Ice filled Kali's veins. How many were there?

Stonewall had already dropped his pack beside a nearby oak tree. "We can't rush in," he was saying as the others followed his lead. "Even with our new system, we must be careful."

Beacon fairly danced in place, daggers drawn and eyes gleaming. "Aye, but we must go. *Now.*"

"Since when do *you* want to go charging into battle?" Flint said to him, frowning.

"I'm no coward," the mender shot back. "You should know that by now, girl."

"Don't 'girl' me!"

"Both of you, shut up," Stonewall said as another thrall's cry filled the woods. "Let's head for the road. Sentinels first; mages follow. Everyone stay out of sight until we know how many we're dealing with, and don't be stupid."

This last was said with a look at Beacon, who glared back. "Shall we take a vote, too? Maybe run it by the queen and all the Pillars? Let's *go*, Stonewall!"

Stonewall's irritation bled through his and Kali's bond, and he snapped, "Move out."

Another chorus of thrall cries filled the air as Kali set her pack and viol case at the base of the oak tree. Her heart kicked up its pace again as the three mages followed in the sentinels' wake, heading for the main road.

This part of Whitewater Province held the foothills of the Argus Mountains, so the terrain was rolling. The road was all but obscured by the trees and the hill it crested, making the upward climb difficult for Kali in the best of circumstances; after the past several days of walking, her knee was on fire. But she tried, as always, to ignore the pain and press onward, turning her focus to the forthcoming battle. Ahead, the sentinels had paused at the tree line, crouched within a thicket of brambles.

Can't make out much from here, Stonewall told Kali through their silent speech. *You all stay back, for now. We'll press on.*

Kali whispered to her mage companions, "I doubt they can see much, so they're probably going to take a closer look."

She kept her gaze on the sentinels, who crept up the final stretch of the hill to the road. The only sound was her blood hammering in her ears. The thrall cries had abated and silence stole through the forest. Even the wind held its breath.

Just when she could not bear the suspense any longer, Stonewall called her name aloud. Immediately, the mages rushed toward the road. Kali's knee screamed in protest at the pace, the rough terrain, the incline, all of it, but she forced herself onward despite the tears that sprang to her eyes. Suddenly, Sadira's hand closed over hers, flooding her with delicious warmth. The sudden spike of hunger for Sadira's magic distracted Kali from the pain, though the feeling brought its own frustration. Seren's sweet light, when could she put that thrall shit behind her?

The mages crested the hill and found carnage. It must have been a trade caravan, given the half dozen wagons tipped and splintered, with fabric, spices, and other goods spilling onto the hard ground. Horses and oxen lay in crumpled heaps, still in their traces, with the scent of blood clinging to the chilled air. There were no human corpses in sight.

"Sweet fucking stars," Kali breathed, frozen in place at the sight. Marcen, too, had halted with her, though Sadira had released Kali's hand to rush forward to the sentinels, who were examining each wagon.

Stonewall and Milo came over, their faces grim. "The thralls must have ambushed them," Stonewall said. "We didn't find any survivors."

"No people at all," Milo added with a shudder. "Just those poor creatures..."

Kali stepped forward. "Maybe we could–"

A thrall's scream ambushed her words, cut them off. She did not need to see the dozen or so pairs of burning eyes approaching to know the thralls were upon them.

"Trap," she gasped.

*

Stonewall's first instinct was to get the mages to the relative cover of the wagons. Beacon and Flint had drawn their swords, though the mender's eyes were about as bright as any thrall's. Had he taken hematite *again*? He must have kept some aside. Stonewall all but carried Kali to the wagon, mentally cursing himself for trusting the copper-haired sentinel.

If we get out of this alive, he thought as the mages took shelter beneath a broken axle. *I'm going to kill him.*

Mages secure, Stonewall drew his daggers and faced the approaching thralls. Tor help him, he could not get an accurate count, there were so many!

Kali's despair spiked through their bond. *Don't kill them! They're human!*

"We're outnumbered," he shot back, too distracted to manage the silent communication. "This time, it's them or us."

The thralls stalked closer, now mere yards away. Some wore the garb of hired blades, complete with swords, axes, and crossbows, no doubt once employed by the merchants to guard their wares. A few wore simple cloaks and bore no weapons; perhaps the former merchants themselves. Their eerie chorus reverberated off the trees along the road and within Stonewall's own heart. *Gods above,* he thought. *We won't survive this.*

Kali tried to reach him again. *Stonewall–*

"Our safety comes first," he broke in with a confidence he did not feel. "We must fight."

"We fucking know that," Flint growled. She and Milo stood back to back, next to Stonewall. "What's with the sodding lecture?"

Before Stonewall could answer, Beacon called, "What are you waiting for?"

The mender lunged at the nearest pair of thralls, both dressed as merchants, and drove his sword into the first's throat before knocking the second with his shoulder. The possessed men screamed again, enraged. Three broke off to drive at Beacon but the rest kept their path toward the wagon. The world slowed, as if coated in molasses. Stonewall pushed aside his fear and anger, gripped his daggers in preparation to strike. Beacon cried out and stumbled back, sword hitting the dirt while he clutched his stomach, where a red stain spread through the leather.

"Beacon!" Flint shouted, and she lunged, hurling obscenities at the thrall who stood above the mender, sword poised to finish him off.

Nothing for it. Stonewall surged forward. Milo was at his heels, the *kuvlu* in his right hand. Stonewall would have to keep to the lad's left, to protect his weaker side. But no time to think more than that. Only the moment mattered; the inhale, the swing, the scent of copper in the unnaturally hot air. Something stung against Stonewall's shoulder but he ignored it and shoved his daggers between the ribs of a woman—no woman now, but a monster—and she screamed for his death. The world shrank to the song of steel against steel and muscle and bone, and the long years of training ingrained in his body's memory. The gods were with him. He would do his best. If he lived, it was by their will.

Kali's touch against his mind startled him into looking up at her. *Fall back*, she cried through their bond. *To the wagon!*

Kali, Sadira, and Marcen stood with hands joined. The Zhee mage's eyes were closed and her face was slack. Sweat ran in rivulets down Stonewall's face—when had it gotten so blazing hot?—and with a flash of insight he realized what the mages intended.

"Fall back," he called to the sentinels. Flint and Milo obeyed immediately. Thanks to hematite-granted strength, Beacon had managed to right himself and hold his own for those few...minutes? Seconds? How long had they been fighting? Stonewall shoved the mender toward the wagon, harder than he should have, and followed, leaving the thralls just a pace behind him.

But a pace was enough. A rippling wall of hot air bloomed around the wagon, between them and the thralls, distorting their bright, blazing eyes. One thrall bounded after Stonewall but fell back at once, screaming and clutching his face while fire leaped to life on his clothing. A glance at Kali; her face was pale and dull, while Sadira radiated *power.* Marcen's mouth was tight with concentration. A thrall shrieked in fear or outrage again as the ground ruptured, making the creature stumble back, teetering into the furrow created by magic. The rest of the creatures screamed their rage, pacing as close as they could to the wall of magic-heated air. But none came through.

Sweat made the insides of Stonewall's gloves slick and his daggers hard to hold, but never was he so grateful to be so uncomfortable. "How long will it last?" he asked Sadira.

"Long enough."

"We can make a break for it," Flint said. "Run to the woods while the thralls are...distracted."

"She...can't...break...the circle," Kali gasped. "Whole thing will collapse."

"Then what should we do?" Milo asked. He knelt by Beacon, who was clutching his side, his face ashen. "Beak needs a mender."

And the mages were occupied. Stonewall ground his teeth. There was an obvious solution, but by the gods, he wished it were not so. He tried to reach Kali, but every bit of her focus was on Sadira and Marcen; her energy, too, drained with each passing moment.

"Shit!" Flint's cry made him peer through the wall of hot air to see a group of armored men and women riding toward them at a breakneck pace. Their swords and daggers were drawn and their hematite armor gleamed in the afternoon light. Here on the border between provinces, the sentinel squad could have been from Whitewater or Redfern. Surely they could see what was going on; surely they would recognize magic when they saw it.

Nothing for it, Stonewall realized, clutching at his daggers. *I've got to do this on my own.*

He closed his eyes and concentrated. He had no true idea of what he was doing, he only knew he'd done it before. Would the Fata magic work if they weren't all touching, or weren't all together in a vessel? Could he do anything without Kali's supplementary energy?

Tor, he prayed. *Please help me save my family.*

It hurt to breathe; the hot air seared his lungs and sweat drenched his face, and he was afraid to open his eyes lest they burn in their sockets. But he had to focus. *Away.* Where? He tried to recall his mental map of the country, but the image slipped from his memory. Anywhere but here. South, perhaps. South was home. *Away.*

Someone gasped. Stonewall opened his eyes to see the air shimmering like sunlight on ocean waves, well beyond the ripple of heat. The world began to fade as the sentinels rode into the thralls, some with swords already stained crimson. The world faded further still, but not before Stonewall caught a look at the nearest sentinel, a woman with sergeant markings on her shoulder, who'd removed her helmet in shock as she stared at him through the wall of heat and magic. *Gray.*

Forget her, he told himself, forcing his mind back on his mission. *Away.* His squad, mages and sentinels alike, clustered around him, grounding him in his duty and oath. These people were what mattered; they were all that mattered. *Away.*

THIRTEEN

"Kali."

Time to wake, already? But she'd only just laid down! Kali threw her arm over her eyes to shield her face from the sunlight. "G'way."

"Kali, get up," Marcen said, gripping her shoulder. "Beacon's hurt and Sadira's out of it, and I tried, but I can't help him on my own."

Reality came crashing back. Kali snapped her eyes open to see her fellow mage kneeling over her. Streaks of blood marred his hair and forehead, though she wasn't sure whose blood it was. When their eyes met, he gave a thin parody of a smile. "Sorry to wake you."

"Forgiven, this one time." She sat up, blinking through the accompanying rush of dizziness. Stars and moons, her body was leaden with exhaustion. They were in an unfamiliar patch of woods, the chilly air unblemished by thrall screams. Sadira sat beside her, eyes glazed, huddling beneath her crimson cloak.

Kali touched the Zhee mage's arm and found her skin clammy and cool. "I will be well," Sadira murmured, squeezing her eyes shut. "Help Beacon."

Heart in her throat, Kali looked back up at Marcen. "What happened? Where are we?"

He helped her stand. "You don't know? You brought us here, after all. Though how you managed that *and* still gave Sadira and me so much strength, I'll never know."

Kali opened her mouth to say he was mistaken, for she'd not done anything other than pass on her energy to him and Sadira…and then her gaze fell upon Stonewall. He and the other sentinels had gathered around Beacon, who lay upon his cloak, groaning. Stonewall knelt by Beacon's mender satchel, rifling through the contents. His focus centered upon the task at hand, his emotions on a tight leash.

He used his magic, Kali thought, still half-dazed from her own endeavors. *All on his own.* A sense of pride washed through her, though no doubt he would have to answer for his actions to the others soon enough.

She stepped to the sentinels, but the movement sent an agonizing sear of pain through her left knee and she crumpled to the dirt. Marcen caught her before she fell on her face, but her hands still stung with the impact. Tears sprang to her eyes at the sudden pain and another wave of dizziness sent the world spinning. Mar helped her stand again and let her lean on him so she could hobble to the sentinels.

At her approach, Stonewall looked up, his eyes wide. "Gods above, Kali! Are you–"

"I'm fine," she said. "Beacon's the priority now." With Marcen's help, she sank beside the mender. The others had stripped off his cuirass and pulled back his tunic, revealing an ugly gash in his stomach. The wound was clean and covered with a film of pale blue thalo gel, but Kali's heart sank anyway. This was beyond her skill and strength, especially in her current state. But she had to try.

"We did what we could," Stonewall was saying, clutching a handful of bandages. "He's conscious, at least, and he's taken hematite recently. But…" He trailed off and met her gaze, and added silently, *But that will make it harder for you to help him.*

"You've done your best," she said aloud. "I'll do mine."

He ducked his head. "I think we're out of danger…for now."

She swallowed tightly and looked at Marcen. "I'll need help."

He held out his bare hand. "I'm here."

"Me too." Flint offered her own hand.

Milo did as well, and Stonewall. Four bare hands extended to Kali; four pairs of eyes looked upon her with nothing but trust – and hope. It was too much. She was not strong enough. She had never been. Her father's words echoed in her mind: *"It's a terrifying gift that you have been given, Kali. The One has entrusted you with great power, so you must always use it wisely."*

I'll try, Da, she thought, and nodded. "Very well."

She directed them how to position themselves to best help her: Stonewall on one side, one arm around her waist while he held Milo's hand with the other. Marcen knelt at her other side, one hand on her shoulder, the other clasping Flint's. Beacon lay before her, his face ashen and his eyes closed. When she laid her hands on either side of his wound, he stirred and squinted up at her.

"Will it hurt?" he mumbled.

Each inhale brought the too-sweet scent of thalo gel and made her want to retch. "Yes."

"Right." He took a deep breath and stared up at the trees.

Beacon's particles seethed, blood-red and angry in Kali's mind. At first she tried to soothe them on her own, with no borrowed energy, but the hematite in his blood dispelled her efforts; her magic barely touched the roiling mass of particles. Seren's light, it was like trying to beat down an iron door with a silk slipper. Already, her strength was waning, so Kali reached for those who offered themselves so willingly.

As the only mage, Marcen was the most useful to her purposes. She could take energy from anyone, but another mage's power resonated more closely with her own, so it strengthened her more than that of a non-mage. Inhale; Kali accepted what Marcen offered. Immediately, the pain in her knee faded to a faint throb and a sweet thrill of energy poured into every muscle and vein. With some effort, she forced herself to exhale and tried to coax Beacon's particles to quiet. She did this again and again and again, with little effect on Beacon. But for Kali, each pull of energy from Marcen was sheer bliss. Though Beacon's particles slowed their frantic, swarming fury, it was not by much, not nearly enough to allow him to heal.

Very well. Stonewall was here, and while his magic was foreign to her—and how clearly she could sense that difference with so little hematite in his blood to dull her perception—his strength was familiar, so she turned her attention to him, withdrawing what he offered along with what she continued to take from Marcen. Inhale; that sweet thrill increased again, stronger than before. Euphoria swelled through her, stealing her breath, forcing her eyes to roll back. No pain anywhere, not even in her contrary knee. She didn't want to relinquish the feeling this time. But she forced herself to exhale, to focus on her task, to pass on the borrowed strength in hopes of encouraging Beacon's body to heal.

Slowly, so slowly it might as well have not happened, Beacon's particles slowed again, a little more than last time. Each exhale coaxed them into calm. *"It's all right,"* Kali imagined telling them, like one would soothe a frightened child. *"You're going to be fine. Just take it easy, now."*

Beacon's particles had slowed, but not enough, so she turned her attention to Flint and Milo. As their faces were so similar, their particles were almost identical, at least to Kali. But particles weren't reflective of a soul, were they? If that was the case, Milo and Flint's particles would be as different as a star and an arrow.

Kali pushed aside the stray thoughts like so many cobwebs and pressed her borrowed strength onto Beacon. *Heal.*

A little more, a little more. He was healing, but it could go faster. Inhale; long and slow and sweet, power swept through her body like no other pleasure. Exhale; in a rush, eager to take more, eager to return to that feeling of joy, liberated from pain. Inhale...

Kali...

Stonewall's fear bled through their bond, snapping her out of her trance. Her eyes opened, revealing how Marcen had slumped back into Flint's chest, his head lolling to one side. Flint stared down at him with glazed eyes, her face a study in mild confusion even though her skin was gray and sickly. Milo looked the same, and Stonewall...

He canted heavily into Kali, his chin on her shoulder, his breath in her ear. "Please stop," he whispered. "Or you'll kill us all."

Stop? But she had; she'd stopped the moment... Oh. Their energy still flowed into her, she'd simply grown used to the thrill of it. How easily that had happened. "Beacon's still hurt," she said, her voice calm and reasonable. "I must–"

"Kali!" Cold hands shoved her aside, toppling her to the ground and breaking her contact with the others. Dazed, Kali looked up to see Sadira collapsing back to her knees beside Beacon, her face pale but her eyes dark with anger. "Do you see?" Sadira ground out, nodding to the sentinels and Marcen, all of whom sat slack-jawed, eyes unfocused, bodies still. "Do you see the cost?"

Were they dead? Had she taken too much? Tears sprang to Kali's eyes as she reached for Stonewall. "Elan...?"

He trembled with the effort of clasping her hand in his own. "I'll be... fine."

Along with the words, a soothing pulse of relief swept through their bond, swirling with undercurrents of worry. Swiping at her eyes, Kali rose easily and examined the others. Marcen was the worst off by far, sleeping in Flint's lap but *only* sleeping – thank the stars! Flint and Milo were each a little dazed, but still conscious.

In fact, Milo even gave her one of those hopeful looks that made him seem so much younger than he was. "Did it work?"

Seren's sweet light, she'd almost forgotten about Beacon. Kali looked at Sadira, kneeling at the mender's side. The Zhee mage nodded. "He will live. But he needs more than just field medicine."

Milo rubbed his left shoulder with his trembling right hand. "Thank Mara. I'm so tired..." His words broke off with a yawn. Kali's stomach knotted.

Flint relaxed her shoulders and shifted so that Marcen would be more comfortable. "Good. I'd hate to think we went through that shit for nothing."

Kali's cheeks burned as she returned to Stonewall, who by now had sat upright on his own, hunched over, elbows on his knees. "We'll have to make camp here," he said after a moment, and his breath was short. "None of us are fit to travel in this state."

Flint frowned. "You said we were out of danger from the thralls, but for how long?"

Stonewall looked around this new patch of forest as if seeing it for the first time. "I'm not sure, but I think we're in Redfern Province."

"Gods above and beyond," Milo replied, his eyes going huge and round. "Kali...you moved us here *and* saved Beacon?"

"Remind me never to travel without you," Flint added dryly, even though she looked at Kali with similar reverence.

Kali's stomach twisted again and she exchanged glances with Stonewall, who had gone tense. *Don't tell them yet,* he said through their silent speech. *Please.*

You can't hide your abilities forever, she replied.

He shook his head once, as if that was all he had strength for. *I'll tell them, soon. But not right now. I can barely think straight.*

Guilt made her acquiesce. She nodded back and looked at the twins. "*You* helped me. You *all* did. Now you must rest."

"Our packs," Flint said suddenly. "We left them back at..." She frowned and looked around. "Wherever we came from."

"I'll get them," Kali replied. She could walk; her knee didn't hurt any longer, and magic and power still sang through her blood. By the stars and moons and all the make-believe gods...she wanted *more.* Better to be on her own for a little while. Hopefully the urge would fade.

"Alone?" Flint asked. When Kali nodded, she looked down at Marcen. "Someone should go with you."

"I can go," Milo said, struggling upright.

But Kali held up her hand, trembling with raw energy. "You stay here. *All* of you." She inhaled and swore she could taste cold stars on the back of her tongue. Magic seethed within her, eager for a release. Even after all she'd given Beacon, there was still so much left for her. "I'll be fine. Stonewall, point me in the right direction, please."

He stared up at her. Kali met his gaze but did not speak through their bond. She let her own certainty wash over him. His eyes narrowed as he studied her, his gaze flickering from her face to her knee to Beacon, and back again.

"North and west." *At least, that's my best guess,* he added silently. *I don't think we're too far from where we were. Just far enough. If you need me, I'll come.* "Be safe," he said aloud.

Kali gave a warrior's salute. "Don't worry. We'll be gnawing on our rations before you know it." With that, she set off. The day was still young. If she hurried, she could make it back before dusk.

She froze at Stonewall's voice. "What about your knee?"

There was no pain, only power. She could run across the whole world if she wanted. Kali smiled back at him. "Don't fret over me."

He did not return the expression. In fact, his misgivings lingered in Kali's thoughts until she was out of sight of the others, then she broke into a jog. Cool air rushed across her body, her blood sang and her knee moved smoothly, as if it had never known pain. All worry fell away, along with all thoughts of past and future. All that mattered was this moment. Kali briefly closed her eyes, grinning, then raced through the woods.

*

By the time Kali began her return journey, dusk was falling, the rush of power had faded, and her pain had returned in full force. She now carried all their packs, along with her and Marcen's instrument cases, and each step, once fluid and effortless, was once more a painful slog. In hopes of avoiding trouble, she kept to the forest trails. Thank the stars she saw no sentinels or thralls, for she would have been powerless against them.

Stupid, she told herself as she limped between trees, catching herself against their trunks lest she fall. She had been careless and arrogant to think she had banished her pain forever, to think that magic could truly heal her. Selfish, too, for she'd been supposed to heal Beacon, not herself! Tears slid down her cheeks. She was weak for succumbing to that hunger for more power. *What's wrong with me?*

Kali.

She jerked her head up to see Stonewall and Milo trotting her way, and she began to cry harder at their grace and ease, and for the worried tenor of Stonewall's thoughts.

He reached her first, took her viol case and two of the packs, and still had a free hand to wrap around her shoulders. Love suffused their bond, warming her from within. "Welcome back," he said, adding a kiss against her forehead. "Any trouble?"

"No." She swiped her nose with her sleeve as Milo took the rest of her burdens. "It wasn't that far, either. But I stayed away from the road."

"That's for the best." Stonewall offered her his arm and she clung to him gratefully, and the three of them made their way through the woods, moving slowly to accommodate her limping pace.

As they walked, Kali studied each man. "You both look...better."

"A little rest set us to rights," Milo said. "Flint's fine, too, though Marcen was still sleeping when we left. But Beacon's awake."

Kali bit her lip at the mention of Marcen. Stars...how much of his energy had she taken, if he was still asleep? "Is Marcen...well?"

"Sadira says he just needs rest," Stonewall replied. "Same with Beacon." He shot her a sideways glance. "Whatever you did seems to have worked."

Aye, but at what cost? She kept the question to herself.

They reached the others. By now, Marcen was awake, if still bleary, and he beamed at Kali as Stonewall set his dulcimer case down. "Thank you," her fellow mage said to her.

Kali nodded again, not trusting herself to speak as Marcen began to dig through his pack. No fire burned, for they still had to be wary of sentinels and thralls, but the air around Sadira was slightly warm again. It wasn't the fire mage's normal, everlasting heat, but it was enough to dull the worst bite of chill air.

But the warmth did nothing to drive off Kali's lingering hunger for the magic that had burned so fiercely within her friend. The pain in Kali's knee was now a welcome distraction, as was the normalcy of setting up camp for the night. With the packs returned, rations were divvied out and soon everyone sat in a semicircle, nibbling on hard cheese, jerky, and dried fruit. Kali heated some tea in a flask, so they had something hot to drink, which was another welcome comfort.

As they ate, Stonewall spread out his map. "As best I can tell, we're here." He pointed to a spot just inside the border of Redfern Province.

"Those were Whitewater sentinels who found us before," Flint said between bites of jerky. "I recognized Gray."

"They must have heard the thralls," Milo added. "D'you think they were out looking for us?"

Stonewall nodded. "We should assume so. No doubt word will get back to Argent, and we'll have every squad in the two provinces on our backs."

"We cannot keep going this way," Sadira said, sitting upright. "Beacon will live, but he still needs a healer's care, and *rest*. You *all* do." She shot Kali a dark look over her mug of tea. "Our mission must be put aside, at least for a time."

Kali grimaced but forced herself to meet Sadira's gaze. "I agree. But where can we go?"

Beacon drained his mug and lay back on the blanket. "Stonewall...where exactly did you say we were?"

Stonewall had set his tea aside to withdraw two *biris* from a pouch at his belt. He lit them both with a tinderbox and offered one to Beacon as he replied, then added, "Closest major township is Dilt, though I–"

"Ea's tits and teeth," Beacon broke in, rubbing the bridge of his nose. "No. Gods above and beyond, please...anywhere but sodding *Dilt*."

"You've been there before?" Stonewall replied dryly, blowing out a stream of smoke.

"Born and raised, and hoped never to see that sodding, spitstain of a city again. The One has an interesting sense of humor."

"Or the One has worries other than *you*," Flint said.

The mender took a drag from his *biri*. "Perhaps, but I don't have to like it."

"You never mentioned you were from Dilt," Milo replied, frowning. "Or did you, and I just forgot?"

"Believe me, Mi, all I wanted was to *forget* that sodding place after I left."

"Will it be safe for us?" Kali asked him. "Do you think your family will give us sanctuary?"

"My family..." Beacon snorted. "Aye, they'll do as I ask."

"You're certain?" Stonewall pressed.

125

Beacon's pale blue eyes fixed skyward in silent supplication, but he said only, "Redfern folk are nothing if not loyal to their kin. Blood is blood, after all."

Flint frowned at him but spoke to Stonewall. "How far away is Dilt?"

"Several leagues," Stonewall replied. "At least a full day of travel, given our state."

The younger sentinel looked at Marcen. "Can you make it?"

He'd just taken a bite of cheese. At her words, he tried to swallow, gave up, nodded and added a wink for good measure.

Flint rolled her eyes and glanced at her brother. "And you?"

Milo, who had watched the exchange, offered her a wan smile. "Don't worry about me, *relah*."

"Beacon should be able to travel tomorrow," Sadira said. "As will I. But our steps will be slow."

"Right." Stonewall glanced at Kali, a question in his eyes.

She fought the urge to look at either of her fellow mages and kept her gaze upon Stonewall. "I can make it. What about you?"

He actually looked surprised at her question. "Of course, I'm–"

"Fine," Flint and Kali said in unison.

Stonewall cast his gaze to the sky, but he was smiling, too. "Tor help me."

"Help *all* of us," Kali said. Abruptly, she reached for her viol case and flipped the lid open, both to reassure herself that her instrument was unharmed and to give herself something to do other than look at anyone. The viol's polished wood was smooth to her touch, recalling the countless hours she'd played both for amusement and distraction. During her time away from Whitewater Bastion, she had managed to repair most of the damage. The Sufani had even given her a set of strings, but Kali wondered if it was only a matter of time before these broke. She could never seem to keep the strings around very long.

"I still don't understand why the glimmers have it out for us at all," Flint said after a beat, brows knitted. "What'd we ever do to them?"

"They're angry with humans," Kali said slowly. "For…invading their world long ago."

Beacon hummed in thought. "Legend has it that the One created the world and gave it to Ea to watch over. But Ea was lonely, so the One created Atal and the other gods."

"But they quarreled," Flint said, nodding. "So Ea begged the One for help. And the One created humans for the gods to rule over, and established the proper balance of power in the world. But the part that always trips me up is how the One created humans from…star stuff?" She made a noise of disbelief.

"The Fata told me humans came from the sky," Kali said.

"So the myths aren't myths, then?" Marcen asked, eyes wide.

"If you can believe the glimmers," Flint scoffed.

Kali closed her eyes in recollection of her possession, when, in a desperate attempt to learn what they had planned, she'd encouraged the Fata to speak to her. "The Fata told me once: 'we will take back what is ours. This world. It is ours. It has always been ours. Your kind are usurpers, and you will fall.'"

Silence fell across the group before Beacon cleared his throat. "Right, Flint, that's your answer: the Fata are crazy monsters."

But Stonewall was not appeased, and continued to study Kali. "You know the Fata better than any of us. Are they really…evil?"

"All I know is they're angry," Kali replied. "And they hunger for magic."

"Why?" Beacon asked. "Other than the obvious, I guess. The stories say they have their own magic, right?"

Kali opened her mouth to reply but her voice did not work. *Sweet blood. Sweet magic. Give it to us, now.* The litany that had once beat ceaselessly against her mind returned, faint, but the memory was enough to make her sick to her stomach. They'd spoken to her *through* her. She'd been imprisoned in the sentinel garrison along with Drake and the Sufani, but what if she hadn't? What if she'd been free and near other innocent people?

She *still* hungered for other mages' power. Like the pain in her knee, she could ignore the feeling – to a point. But the moment she took strength from another mage, that hunger surfaced again, fierce as ever, if not more so.

127

Was that hunger real, or did it only exist in her mind? What was the difference, if such a hunger affected her actions? *What if I'm a monster, too?* Kali's breath came in short bursts and her vision blurred with tears, and suddenly she wanted nothing more than to disappear into the black, welcoming void.

A warm hand pressed to the small of her back, and then Stonewall shifted closer to her side. So, too, did the feelings of love and reassurance settle over her mind, soothing her heart, setting her at ease. Stonewall's strength flowed through their bond until Kali could breathe again.

"I can't speak for anyone else, but ultimately, I don't care *what* the Fata are," Stonewall said to the others. "All I care about is stopping them."

You should *care what they are*, Kali sent through their silent speech. *They are a part of you, after all.*

They are the enemy, he replied firmly, though he could not hide his own doubts.

The exchange had only taken a moment – another benefit of Kali and Stonewall's silent communication. As such, no one seemed to think anything odd had happened, thank the stars.

Flint withdrew her whetstone and slid it along her blade as she spoke. "I'm with you, Stonewall. Whatever those sodding *things* really are makes little difference. What matters is how we can stop them."

"I'd agree," Beacon said. "But I feel inclined to point out, if we knew more about them, we might find a better way to fight them. Kali, could you maybe–"

"Enough," Stonewall interrupted. "It's late and we all must rest if we're to move out first thing in the morning. We can plan more on the journey through Redfern."

Beacon blew out a final stream of smoke and twisted his head to give Kali a hopeful grin. "Pillau is gorgeous this time of the year. Maybe you could magic us there, to regroup."

"Sorry, Beak," she said, forcing herself not to look at Stonewall. "My magic doesn't work like that. I don't know where we're going, and I doubt you'd want to risk winding up in the middle of a river or lake, or worse…

in a bastion."

The mender sighed ruefully. "Can't blame me for trying."

"You must explain this aspect of your magic to me again, Kali," Sadira said, her gaze speculative. "Perhaps Marcen and I can aid next time."

Her voice was too steady; not with disbelief, not quite, but Kali's stomach twisted all the same. Before now, Sadira had not asked many questions about their magical trips across the country, but something had changed.

But Kali shoved that misgiving aside too, and tried to conceal her unease with a smile. "Your help would be most welcome, Sadira. Perhaps later, we could–"

"Why not now?" Sadira asked.

"I'm…tired," Kali started to say, but the Zhee mage shook her head.

"We are all tired, but no one is near sleep yet."

Despite herself, Kali shot Stonewall a helpless look, but he had gone tense again, his wordless plea to keep his secret filling her every breath and bone. She could not tell which was stronger: his desire for secrecy or hers for strength, at the mention of Sadira's help. How easy it would be to take more of that delicious power–

No. With effort, Kali forced her attention away from the urge, though she could not help her lingering thought: *I'm not strong enough for any of this.*

"It's difficult to explain," she said at last.

"We can strive to understand," Sadira replied. "Marcen, you have thoughts on this matter?"

Marcen coughed into his hand. "I'd rather not–"

"Leave it for now," Stonewall said sharply.

But Sadira ignored him. "I know your heart, Kali. Not like others, but I have a mind of your magic. You hold a power that grows stronger and stranger each day. But even so, I do not grasp how you helped me fight thralls, moved all of us a league to the south, and *then* healed Beacon, all without killing yourself from overuse."

The sentinels sat in silence, none daring to get between the mages. Stonewall's mouth was a thin line even as guilt crawled through him. But he said nothing. Did he expect Kali to keep his secret forever? Sadira's questioning brought her own shameful hunger to mind; her own urge for *more*. What would Sadira think of how much Kali wanted her power? What would Marcen think? Would her friends fear her? Hate her?

Kali's mouth opened and closed as she floundered for an answer. "I borrowed your energy," she managed. "Yours and Mar's, and everyone's. That's all. Nothing I haven't done before – nothing you've not seen for yourself."

Sadira's pale eyes flashed with anger and hot air coiled around the group. "You are false to me."

"Sadira, that's enough," Stonewall said, but Kali was already struggling to her feet.

"I have to find a bush," she muttered, not looking at anyone. "I'll be back." Her knee screamed with the movement, but she welcomed the pain as she hobbled into the twilight. Pain was her constant companion and the only one she deserved.

FOURTEEN

Stonewall quelled the urge to follow in Kali's wake, for it was clear she wanted to be on her own. Instead, he took a deep breath and looked back at Sadira, who watched as Kali retreated through the trees.

"I am not within your command," she said before he could speak. "You cannot keep me from questions."

Perhaps it was foolish to antagonize a woman who could incinerate him with a flick of her fingers, but he could feel Kali's bitterness as if it was his. There was guilt, too, but he wondered if it was just an echo of his own.

"Be that as it may, we're all on the same side," he replied.

Sadira frowned at him. "She hides pieces of her magic. I do not wish to mistrust her, but secrets free themselves at the worst moments – and magic can do such harm."

"Kali won't hurt anyone," he said.

But the Zhee mage gestured to Marcen and the twins, all of whom still looked a bit too pale and wan. "You truly believe that, Stonewall?"

Gods above, he could still feel his energy draining away as Kali took it in. More unsettling than that, though, had been her elation at the draw. He'd been unable to stop her. If Sadira had not interrupted...

No. Kali would have stopped. She was more compassionate than anyone had a right to be. She would not have willingly done permanent harm to her friends.

Right?

Ultimately, it was loyalty to the woman he loved that made him say, "I trust her with my life."

"She saved Milo," Flint added. "I trust her, too."

Milo bit his lip, but nodded as well. "So do I."

Beacon gave a weak chuckle. "I'd be pretty ungrateful if I said otherwise now, wouldn't I?"

Sadira looked at Marcen. "What about you?"

The blond mage drummed his fingertips on his dulcimer case, not looking at anyone. "I think she got carried away. It *was* a little frightening. And it does make me wonder what harm she could do if she really wanted."

"She broke it off," Stonewall said, glaring at the other man. "She didn't go too far."

Marcen held up his hands. "I didn't say she did, but the potential is there."

"Kali is not evil, Stonewall," Sadira interjected, not unkindly. "But I feel concern for her, and for us. Such power as hers must not be a mystery. I must know her limits – if she has them."

He nearly spilled his secrets right there, but the words didn't come. His relationship with Kali seemed like such a silly thing to have tried to hide when compared to his Fata blood. He would tell the others soon, once he could safely wield his abilities and he had a better understanding of what exactly those abilities were – and why they'd come to such an unworthy vessel as himself. The worst part, though, was how the connection to the Fata felt *right*. It was as if all his life he'd worn boots a size too small, and had now finally found a pair that fit. It reminded him of that warm-blanket feeling when he communed with his patron-god.

But none of that mattered when Kali was hurting because of *his* unwillingness to be honest with his brothers and sisters in service. He knew better – which was the worst part.

"I'll talk to her," he told Sadira. Vague enough to mean anything, but perhaps she would take it as the assurance she sought.

This seemed to mollify the Zhee mage, for she eased back to Beacon's side to check on his wound. As she lifted the bandage, the mender winced, and then looked over at Stonewall. "Ah...I might need to visit a tree pretty soon, and I hate to ask you this, but I don't think I can manage on my own, so would you mind...?"

Stonewall rose. Thank Tor, he had recovered much of his former strength with some rest and food. "Sure thing, Beak. Milo, would you come with?"

They helped Beacon limp away from the others, in the opposite direction that Kali had gone. When they stopped, Stonewall glanced around, searching the area for anything amiss and not looking at his friend. No one spoke until the three men were on their way back, when Beacon sighed deeply.

"Back in Estia, I...kept a dose before I gave you the rest. We're in this mess because of me. I'm sorry."

"Apology accepted," Stonewall said as they crunched through dead leaves. "But you can't take credit for everything."

"Right, the Fata." Beacon sighed again. "Even so, if I'd not taken that dose this morning, if I'd just resisted temptation, we wouldn't be in such a state. Sadira wouldn't be so angry with Kali, and no one would have had to get hurt just to save my miserable life."

They were all quiet again until Milo said, "But that dose saved your life, Beak. If you'd not just had a burn–"

"*Two* burns," Stonewall couldn't help interjecting.

Milo ducked his head. "If not for the hematite, you might have died."

"Or the mages would have been able to completely heal me," Beacon replied grimly. "I want to be free of it, Mi, I do. It's just...harder than I expected."

Because Stonewall could not spare his hand to give his squad-mate a well-deserved clout, gently bumped Beacon's shoulder with his own instead. "I know."

"I'm glad you're managing," the mender added. "Thank the One, at least one of us is."

The little pouch at Stonewall's belt may have been filled with lead as well as promises. He gritted his teeth against the urge to peek inside. "Aye," he replied, staring ahead. "Thank the One."

*

It was true dark when Stonewall and Milo got Beacon settled again, so Stonewall decided it was time to search for Kali. After alerting the others of his intent, he slipped into the shadows and scanned the trees, but saw no trace of her. Only when he concentrated on the link between them, visualizing it as a shining, golden thread that bound their hearts, could he sense the direction she had gone. He could sense *her*, too: sorrow etched with long-held grief and constant pain. The strength of her emotions stung his eyes. Was it so bad for her? She tried to keep a pleasant face most of the time, but this...

More resolved than ever, Stonewall hurried through the night. He found her seated at the base of a willow tree, most of its branches still stripped bare by winter, with a few dangling in a trickle of water that flowed nearby. The stars cast a meager light upon the woman curled in on herself, her left leg stretched before her.

She inclined her chin in acknowledgment, but did not otherwise greet him. He asked her to scoot forward so he could plunk down between her and the tree. Once they were situated, he wrapped them both in his cloak. "Too bad it's dark. Redfern's one of the prettier provinces."

"I'm ready to leave."

He leaned against the tree and peered up at the crescent mage-moon, almost hidden in the tree line. "I'm sorry."

Now she tilted her head to regard him, her dark eyes cast in shadow. "For what?"

"For asking you to lie for me. For causing a rift between you and Sadira." He sighed. "For doubting you."

"You doubted me?"

"Would you have stopped if Sadira had not interrupted?"

She looked away, rubbing her left knee. "Sometimes when I...take energy from another, like I did with Marcen and Sadira, the pain goes away for a while. I can run and walk freely. I can't remember another time like that. But the pain always comes back." She sniffed and swiped at her eyes. "It hurts all the time. Sometimes I just...I just want a reprieve. A *moment* without pain. With all of you, there was so *much* power. More than I've ever taken. For a few minutes, I felt truly invincible. I've never felt like that ever, in my whole life." Now she wept in earnest. "I'm sorry, too."

He hugged her closer. "It's all right, Kali. You'll be all right. I promise."

She gave a weak laugh even as she wept. "Don't make promises you can't keep."

"Well, I'm stubborn like that, so I hear."

She chuckled again and some of her sorrow eased, allowing him to catch his breath. Taking care not to disturb her overmuch, he fumbled in his belt-pouch for a *biri*, and offered it to her. "Can you light this?"

The end flared to life and he took a deep draw, sighing as the familiar calm swept over him, then handed it to her. "This will help, but be careful at first, because..."

He trailed off as she blew out an impressive stream of smoke without so much as clearing her throat. At his surprise, she gave him a saucy wink that made him warm all over in ways no magic could ever replicate.

"Eris and I used to sneak these from the cinders back at Starwatch," she said as she took another drag. "It's been a while since I've had one."

"Hard to imagine Eris enjoying anything so...frivolous."

Kali shrugged. "She's not all fangs. She's just had a difficult life. Her own parents sent her to Starwatch Bastion when she was a little girl. Jonas brought her. I remember how frightened she was, so far from everything she'd ever known, but she didn't want to show it. I think she still hates them," Kali added, handing him the *biri*. "Her parents, I mean. I never got the full story, but she never forgave them for sending her away."

"She made a life for herself, though," Stonewall replied.

Kali did not answer. Her regret rippled around her as she leaned her head against his shoulder, *biri* smoke drifting up before them. As they sat in silence, the drone of crickets filled the air, though if Stonewall listened very hard, he could make out the faintest trickle of water from the small stream.

"Remember the stream, on the way from Starwatch?" he asked abruptly. "When you fell in?"

"I was *exploring*. There was no falling of any kind."

He smirked. "Could have fooled me."

"What about the stream?"

It was getting colder by the moment, so he untied her cloak and draped it over her knees. "I never taught you how to swim."

Kali chuckled. "Of all the things to be worried about right now…"

"Beacon had the right idea about Pillau. One day, I'll take you there, show you the ocean. You've never seen it, right?" She shook her head and he smiled at the memories of warm water and sugar sand. "You'll love it. But you must learn to swim. The sea is not to be trifled with."

"Very well, Serla Sentinel," she said with a light laugh.

He tugged the cloak more securely around them both, sealing them in a cocoon of warmth. "Better?"

She sighed and shifted closer to him. "You make everything better. You're like…" She giggled. "Even I can't make *that* joke."

"I assume it's at my expense, and has to do with my chosen name."

She giggled again. "Anchor, then. You're my anchor in a stormy sea. I think I read that in a book somewhere."

"Well, if it's in a book, it must be true." Stonewall tried to sound serious, but he could summon no other feeling than pleasure at her words.

Kali was quiet, though her emotions shifted like wind upon water. When she spoke again, her voice was a whisper. "I don't want to argue with Sadira any longer. Will you tell them about your abilities soon?"

His heart fractured. "I will. I can even swear it, if you like."

"No swearing needed. Your word is enough." She took a deep breath that shook her entire body. "You are right to doubt me. There was a moment when… When I would have lost control. I nearly killed you – all of you."

Fear coiled around her, wrapping them both in its grasp, but Stonewall was calmer now than before and could brace himself against it, enough to support them both. "But you didn't. You stopped."

"Because Sadira–"

"I know you, Kali. You are the kindest person I've ever met. You would have stopped on your own. I know it. I *believe* it."

She turned her face into the crook of his arm. "What if I can't stop, next time? What if I lose control?"

He shoved aside Tor's vision of Kali disappearing into the void. "You won't."

"But what if I do?"

"You won't."

She made a noise of pure frustration. "Saying something doesn't make it so."

The *biri* was long gone but its effect lingered. In this moment, he was content to just wrap his arms around her. "Ready to go back?" he asked.

"Not yet. It's easier if I'm not near Sadira right now. Not just because she's angry with me," Kali added quickly. "But because..."

"You're away from temptation," he finished. Gods above, he knew the feeling all-too-well.

"Every time I think I'm free of the hunger, it comes back. It's worse after I take energy from another mage."

"I know." When she tilted her head to look at him, he elaborated. "It's similar with hematite. Eating a little just to take the edge off your longing only makes the longing worse, later."

"But you bear it so well."

"Ah, so I've fooled you, too." The joke made the leaden weight at his belt a tiny bit lighter.

Kali chuckled again, though her humor was short-lived. "Has the desire gotten any better?"

"A little."

"Liar."

He grunted. "Well, it hasn't been very long since I stopped taking hematite. The urge for a burn *should* ease up – eventually. In the meantime, we've got *biris*."

"Beacon was *brimming* with hematite. I almost couldn't help him at all."

Stonewall frowned at the memory of Beacon's admission. *A full dose, so soon after the last, stolen as well.* "You may not believe it, but the gods don't place more upon us than we can bear."

"I hope you're right." She shifted against his chest, contentment radiating through their bond. "I could sleep out here."

"Not me. It's too cold."

"But you're so cozy," she said, nuzzling his neck before planting a soft kiss that sent a flare of heat through his whole body, adding to the warmth they shared. "Let's stay just a few more minutes."

Tor help him, she felt so *good* in his arms; a better feeling than any *biri* could conjure. So he held her close and breathed in her scent and said, "As you wish."

FIFTEEN

The cabin slumped in a forgotten corner of Silverwood Province, shoved between rocky hills. Perhaps it had once belonged to a hunter; Eris spotted several animal pelts stacked haphazardly just outside a door that dangled from its hinges like a tooth about to fall out. Spring had already started encroaching on this part of the world and the surrounding forest was thick with creepers that clawed the cabin's sides. The damp, musty scent of rotting wood loitered in the air.

She frowned to Jensine. "Is this a joke? Where is your sanctuary?"

"Here." Jensine spread her hands, merriment dancing in her eyes. "All around you. Don't look at me like that. Argent and his hemies will never find this place."

Drake, who had been examining the cabin, glanced over at the older woman. "Because of your…magic?"

"Oh, stars, no," Jensine said. "It's just well-hidden, and we take precautions."

"That you do," Drake replied with a glance at Atanar, whose eyes were covered by a strip of dark cloth. "Can he take that off yet, or are you still worried he'll run to the sentinels the first chance he gets?"

Jensine shrugged. "We're here. May as well release him."

"They can't be too careful with anyone not like us, Drake," Eris said. "You ought to know that better than anyone."

This last was meant as a warning. She had not divulged his past to these mages, but she also needed him to be cooperative. He shrugged in acquiescence, then touched Atanar's shoulder. "Hold still. You're about to be a free man – again."

While Drake removed the Canderi's blindfold, Eris glanced at Adrie, who was scanning the forest. "Any sign of Caith or Leal?" Eris asked.

Adrie shook her head. "Not since we split up three days ago."

Eris and her friends had been traveling with Seren's Children for almost a week. It was good, if a little strange, to be in the company of so many other mages again. Good, because they gave Eris hope that her cause was a just one; strange, because Seren's Children were in many ways utterly foreign to Eris and her companions, though she still could not express exactly *how*.

"Caith will catch up, soon," Jensine said. "He knows where we are."

"And Leal?" Drake asked. "Will he blindfold her, too? Something tells me that might not go smoothly for him."

Jensine gave a wolfish grin. "My son can protect himself."

"That's what worries me," Drake muttered, but did not push the subject.

Though Jensine remained outside with Eris and her friends, the others began to enter the tiny cabin in groups of two and three, some of them shooting Atanar dubious looks before they stepped through the derelict door. The Canderi, however, did not return any of their glances, but kept his gaze upon the ground. He'd offered no trouble on the journey, but somehow, Eris could not feel relief at the fact. Rather, she kept waiting for the other boot to drop.

A touch at her arm made her look over to see Brenna, Jensine's daughter, standing at her side. "We're next," Brenna said, nodding toward the cabin. "You and Adrie come with me. Mother will bring Drake and Atanar."

"Why must we go in shifts?" Eris asked her.

"Aye, and *how* exactly are we all going to fit in that little cabin?" Drake added. "Nat and I aren't exactly compact."

Nat? Eris thought as Atanar furrowed his brow.

But Brenna only shook her head. "You'll see. You'll like it."

Brenna's daughter, Iri, clutched her mother's hand and peered up at Eris with wide blue eyes. "Big," Iri said. "And pretty."

Eris smiled at the toddler. "Well, then, I suppose I'll have to take your word for it, little one."

A soft smile touched Brenna's lips. "Iri is right. I think you'll find our tabernacle rather to your liking."

"You mean a temple?" Eris said as they headed for the door. "Like the dirt farmers build in every village?"

Brenna chuckled. "This place is one of our sanctuaries scattered across Aredia. Mother has a…unique sense of humor and started calling them 'Seren's Tabernacles.' I think she mostly likes saying the word. After a few years, the name just…stuck."

Up close, the door was little more than splinters held together by tiny purple mushrooms growing within the wood. Brenna and Iri stepped right in, but Eris and Adrie carefully ducked through to avoid touching anything. The cabin's interior matched the dilapidated exterior, down to the threadbare curtains that had long since fallen to the dirt floor. Everything was singular: one room, one table, one chair, one moth-eaten rug crumpled in the room's center.

One wooden hatch, open, revealing a ladder: a passage down into the earth.

Eris froze, staring into the maw. Footsteps scuffed the dirt leading to it, no doubt from the other mages who'd already gone through. She caught Adrie's eye and realized the other mage was grimacing. "I'm not fond of enclosed spaces," Adrie murmured. "They remind me too much of mage carriages."

"It's perfectly safe," Brenna said as she knelt to clamber down the ladder, helping her daughter as well.

But Adrie still trembled, so Eris took her friend's hand. "I'll go first."

Adrie shuddered as Brenna and Iri descended. "Thank you."

Easier said than done, though, when Eris stood above the narrow shaft, peering down into shadow. How far down did it go? What would she find when she reached the bottom? An inhale brought contrasting scents of cool water and roasting meat. "Brenna?" she called.

"Pretty!" Iri's voice echoed through the passage.

Her mother added, "It's not far. But you shouldn't linger outside."

"She's right." Jensine's voice made Eris start and turn to see the older mage peering at her and Adrie through the cabin door. "The tabernacle is safe but I don't want to push our luck by standing around."

"Can't you cover the place with your...mist?" Adrie asked.

"For a brief time, perhaps." Jensine snorted. "Who in the stars would think an everlasting fog was anything but normal?"

Eris had little desire to clamber down the rickety ladder into the void, but apparently she had no other choice. For a few moments, the air pressed cool and close about her and she could only hear her own steady descent. When her boot struck stone, she stepped off the ladder, turned, and sucked in her breath at the sight of the cavern.

She'd emerged into a relatively low-ceilinged section. Several meters ahead, the space opened into a massive dome, where the other mages had already gathered. Someone had a fire going, but the smoke dissipated before it reached the ceiling. A few burning lamps rested on the floor by Eris' feet, but they were not necessary in the main body of the cavern. Shafts of light poured into the space from fissures in the rock, revealing rainbow veins of crimson, blue, violet, and saffron threading through curving stone.

All of that would have been impressive on its own, but there was also the river.

Eris could not see its source, only that it flowed through the cavern's dome and into another, smaller cave on the far side from the mages. Although she could make out the wrinkled current, the river's surface was mostly smooth; a deep indigo that mirrored the marbling in the rock above and the twinkling lanterns set near its stone shore. Reflected light rippled along the ceiling, adding a dreamlike, ethereal glow to the entire cavern.

There were no gods, of course, and certainly no guides for souls across a metaphorical river, but Eris could not suppress a frisson of awe at the sight.

"Sweet stars," Adrie breathed, coming to stand beside Eris, jaw agape.

Brenna and Iri had waited for them. At their astonished looks, Brenna smiled. "See? I told you it was pretty."

"Wrong, Mama," Iri pouted. "*I* told."

"Of course, sweetling," Brenna replied at once, chuckling.

Adrie pointed toward the river's shore, where nearly a dozen rafts rested on the stone. "What're those for?"

Brenna gave a mischievous smile that reminded Eris of Jensine. "The river isn't just for looking pretty." She tilted her chin toward the nearest group of mages. "Let's go. I'm starving."

She led them to the mages who stood in a loose line beside the cooking area. Some mages were familiar as those who traveled with Jensine. These gave Eris and Adrie perfunctory nods of acknowledgment. The others—about half a dozen—called cheerful greetings to Brenna and Iri, but regarded the newcomers with the same wariness that Jensine's companions had initially shown. When Brenna introduced them as bastion mages, eyebrows shot up to hairlines as the wild mages exchanged mutters of bemusement – and disbelief. Eris tried not to take any of it personally, but found herself fighting a scowl as she, Adrie, and Brenna joined the others in the line to the cooking fire.

Rather, there *was* a fire, but from what Eris could tell, its only use was to illuminate the cooking area. Two mages stood between several battered tables set in a vague horseshoe shape. The space was clearly meant to serve as a kitchen, though there were no ovens. Instead, one of the mages, a woman with iron-gray hair, lightly pressed her fingertips to a slab of venison. The bubbling juices that fell to the pan beneath it and the delicious scent told Eris the meat was cooking, though her eyes could not believe it. The other mage performed the same act, but with a tray of bread loaves. A light touch; the bread rose, the crust turning golden-brown, filling the area with its warm, yeasty scent. A pot big enough to bathe in rested on the floor beside one of the tables. Within, Eris could make out vegetables simmering while a young man stirred the contents with a long wooden spoon. Baskets, barrels, and boxes had been stacked neatly to one side of the cooking area, perhaps filled with food and other supplies.

"No fire," Adrie whispered as they approached the line of hungry mages. "Nor oven...this is incredible!"

Eris' mouth watered. She'd stopped eating fowl long ago, but venison was a rare treat, indeed. "You've never...?"

Adrie shook her head, bewildered. "I never thought to try *baking* with magic. I should have, given that I can ferment wine and ale. Maybe Jensine was right about us bastion mages being ashamed of our abilities. Maybe we are inferior."

"Don't say that," Eris replied. "Don't even *think* it. We've done the best we could. Besides, everything will be different—better—now that we're free. You'll see."

Adrie still watched the kitchen mages. "Maybe."

Though the first kitchen mage kept her attention on the meat, she spoke to the newcomers. "Bren! You're just in time. Supper's nearly done."

"It smells lovely, Leera," Brenna said. "You've outdone yourselves. Jalen, is that rosemary in the bread?"

The baker, Jalen, grinned, though he also did not look up. Leera replied. "Aye, we had a feeling the Damaris family would return today, and wanted to cook up something special. Where's that overbearing mother of yours?"

"Right here," Jensine called, her voice echoing off the cavern walls. "And I come *bearing* more beleaguered bastion-bound." She strode up, Drake and Atanar in her wake. Both men's eyes bulged in their sockets as they took in the cavern, the wild mages, and the "kitchen."

Brenna rolled her eyes at her mother's words. "Unique sense of humor," she whispered again to Eris.

"I heard that, child," Jensine said as she met Brenna, Eris, and Adrie. She scooped up Iri and bounced the toddler on her hip, speaking to the little girl in a sing-song voice. "Gran likes a little wordplay, now and again. Embarrassing your mama is a happy side-effect."

There was affection in her words, but Brenna didn't look amused. Iri, however, squealed with delight and wrapped her arms around Jensine's neck. "Rain! Rain, ran!"

Eris frowned in confusion, but Brenna explained. "She can't quite get her 'g' sounds yet, but she's trying to say 'rain Gran.' Mother's got all sorts of talents."

"Oh, isn't that the truth," Jensine said, still beaming at her granddaughter. "One day, you'll have to show us what you can do, Iri. Won't you?" The line moved forward and Jensine glanced at Brenna. "Are you sure she's not shown any sign of magic, yet?"

Brenna seemed to speak with care. "Not yet. But she's still so young."

Jensine continued bouncing the little girl. "If you're like your mama, your abilities won't be much to speak of, will they? Wouldn't that be a shame?"

Spots of pink rose in Brenna's cheeks. "Mother…"

But the older mage appeared not to notice her daughter's discomfort. "Brenna, you were about her age when you started showing your abilities. Caith was even younger." Jensine looked at Eris. "How about you? How old were you when you realized you were a mage?"

Heat swept through Eris' veins at the question – and the accompanying memory. Those days were *not* pleasant to recall. But, to be civil, she kept her reply from revealing her unhappy childhood. "About eleven summers."

Jensine, Brenna, and all the mages within earshot gaped. "Eleven?" Jensine said. "Stars and moons…that's the oldest I've ever heard of abilities showing themselves! Eleven summers, and so powerful now." She shook her head, clucking her tongue. "Amazing how Seren's gifts manifest."

Cheeks hot, Eris tried to shrug. "Well, it might have been sooner, but my parents…" She took a deep breath, schooling her voice not to tremble. "My parents made me wear a hematite amulet for as long as I could remember. It was secure, most of the time, and I'd worn it so long, I never thought it odd. But one day it fell off, and…" She shrugged again. "Everything changed."

Brenna was watching her, blue eyes wide and filled with sorrow. "Your *own* parents bound you with hematite?"

"Aye." Eris swallowed a surge of old bitterness. "Shortly after, they sent me to Starwatch."

"I was born in a bastion," Adrie said before anyone else could comment on Eris' past. "Both my parents were mages."

"I see," Jensine replied, though her gaze lingered on Eris a moment longer before she glanced at Drake. "And you? How old were you?"

145

Drake swallowed. "Pretty young, I guess. Four or five summers, maybe?"

The line began to move as mages helped themselves to heaping plates of food. During the time Eris and the others had been waiting, more dishes had appeared: potatoes and cheese, piles of fresh berries with honey, and a heaping stack of some sort of fleshy mushroom. Mugs of tea, ale, and wine were passed around. There were no dining tables. The mages took their food and sat in groups around the lanterns set along the river's shore.

Jensine's arrival seemed to have changed the mood, for some of the uncertain looks that had once been cast Eris' way had lessened. But Eris did not miss how no one would go near Atanar. Drake waited while the Canderi man served himself, and they made their way to the lantern around which Eris now sat with Adrie, Brenna, and Iri. Jensine held court at one of the fires, her laughter reverberating against the cavern walls.

"This is incredible," Adrie was saying as she swallowed a bite of venison. "Tender and juicy – made with *no* fire. I must speak with Leera."

Brenna was trying to coax her daughter into eating a plum slice, though the toddler was more interested in staring at Atanar. "I'm sure she'd be happy to show you how she manages," Brenna said.

"It just never occurred to me to *only* use magic to cook," Adrie replied. "To think of all the time I wasted waiting for ovens to heat. How extraordinary."

"Never occurred to me, either," Drake replied as he tore off a hunk of bread, examining it. "Useful skill, though." He popped the bread in his mouth and looked at Atanar. "What do you think?"

The Canderi man frowned at his plate. "Cooked food without fire. Healers with no bandages or herbs." He shook his head. "You Aredians grow stranger by the moment."

"Not all Aredians can do what we can," Eris replied. "Only those of us who are gifted."

"Gifted." Atanar said the word slowly, as if tasting it.

Before Eris could reply, a commotion in one of the other groups made her glance over to see that Jensine had gotten to her feet. Several other mages had joined her, all of them heading for the ladder. When Eris twisted around to see, her heart plummeted into her stomach. Caith and Leal had returned – but they were not alone.

"Seren's sweet light," Adrie gasped, her plate clattering to the ground as she jumped up. "Hazel!"

Caith strode across the cavern, a slim girl with strawberry-blond curls limp in his arms. Leal paced beside him. Her cowl hid her face, but Eris recognized the fury in her quick stride and the way her green eyes had gone nearly gray. Eris rose as well, and hurried after Adrie, who'd rushed to Caith's side, along with several other wild mages.

"Oh, gods above," Adrie whispered as she and Eris met the new arrivals. "Is she–"

"She's alive," Leal broke in. She shot Caith a narrow-eyed look. "Barely."

Caith's jaw tightened but he ignored the Sufani and addressed Eris. "Do you know this girl, then?"

"I… Yes," Eris stammered. "She's a mage from Whitewater Bastion… What happened?"

"Good question," Caith replied, though he wasn't looking at Eris any longer, but at his mother, who made her way over. The assembled mages stepped out of her path as she approached her son. She said nothing as she studied Hazel's unconscious form.

Adrie pointed to a nasty scrape on Hazel's forehead and a splotch of bruises at her neck. "She needs healing. Why didn't you help her?"

Caith scowled. "She's alive, isn't she?"

Anger swept through Eris and she glanced behind her, where Drake and Atanar had followed. Thank the stars, she had only to look at Drake for him to understand. Without a word, he scooped the teenage girl out of Caith's arms and hurried to the nearest fire, where a young couple sat on a blanket, entranced by the goings-on.

"Move it," Drake barked, and the mages scrambled out of his way. He laid the girl down gently and stood back so Adrie could kneel beside her. Brenna joined her, having given care of her daughter temporarily to another wild mage.

Taking a deep breath, Eris looked back at Caith and Leal. "What happened? Where did you find her?"

"A few leagues north," Caith replied. "She said she came from Lasath."

"Lasath?" Eris shook her head. "You must be mistaken. She escaped from Whitewater Bastion too, but the hemies caught her – caught all of them. Hazel should be in a bastion. I can't understand how she'd have gotten to Lasath, unless…"

Ice flooded her veins at the realization. *Argent.* The High Commander had come from Lasath to Whitewater Bastion. He must have done something with Hazel. But what?

Caith shrugged. "All I know is where we found her, and it wasn't anywhere near Whitewater City."

Eris gnashed her teeth at his non-answers, but Leal spoke next. "When we came upon her, she was in a bad way, likely from exhaustion and exposure."

"She asked for someone named 'Kalinda Halcyon,'" Caith said. "I recognized the name as one of your friends, so we," his jaw tightened again, "brought her here."

Leal blew out a breath strong enough to flutter her cowl and shot Caith a venomous look. "Aye, *after* I all but forced him to not only heal her enough so that she'd *survive* the sodding journey, but not to leave her alone in the wilderness in the first place!"

"She said *his* name, too," Caith shot back. "What in the blazing stars was I supposed to do?"

"Let an innocent child die, obviously," Leal snarled.

It was too much to follow. Eris reeled from the news, but Jensine seemed somewhat more composed. She held up a hand in a plea for silence, then leveled a stern gaze on her son. "*His* name?"

"The head sodding sentinel," Caith spat. "High Commander Argent."

SIXTEEN

E ris knelt at Hazel's side as Adrie and Brenna healed the girl's wounds. Both women were skilled enough, but Eris could not shake her longing for Kali's healing abilities – and Kali's gift of comforting those in need.

The rest of Seren's Children had dissipated, giving them all a wide berth, but Jensine's voice echoed through the cavern. No secrets among Seren's Children, apparently.

"How could you do this, Caith?" Jensine said as she paced. "*How* could you endanger all of us by bringing *that*," she jabbed her finger at the unconscious girl, "back here?"

Caith glared at Leal. "She–"

"No," Jensine interrupted. "The Sufani is a dreg, an outsider with *no* say in our lives. *You* made this decision. Now you will explain *why*."

Leal bristled and stepped forward. "I may be an outsider, but if you would deny help to an innocent child because you're afraid of some hematite-addled frip, you'd do well to rethink the path your life has traveled."

"Stay out of this," Caith hissed before looking back at Jensine. "I didn't want to bring back the girl, but if we know what Argent's thinking, perhaps we can–"

"No," Jensine broke in. "That man poisons everything he touches. And you have brought that poison here." She crossed her arms over her chest, her lips tight and pale with rage. "You have doomed us all."

"She's a *child*," Eris said, rising.

Jensine gave her a look Eris could only think of as pitying. "Aye, and you

149

are, too, to be so ignorant of the world. I should expect nothing better from a bastion mage."

Eris' hands shook even as she fought for calm. "You did the right thing," she said to Leal. "Thank you for saving her."

As Caith and Jensine continued bickering, Leal stepped closer to Eris, dropping her voice to a whisper. "We must speak privately."

A knot had started to form in Eris' stomach, and she nodded. Then Adrie called to her, and Eris whirled to see Hazel sitting upright, clutching at Drake's arm as she stared at Eris with round eyes. "Eris?" the girl whispered. "I must find Kalinda. Have you seen her?"

Eris all but flew to her side to put an arm around the girl's shoulders. Stars and moons, Hazel felt bird-light and fragile. "Not in some time," Eris said gently. "You must rest. We can talk later."

Tears crept down Hazel's cheeks. "No...I have to find her. *Now.* He said it's important that I find her. I thought you would know..."

Despite Eris' bid for control, tears pricked at her eyes, too. "Dear heart, you must rest. This can wait."

"No!" The girl put her face in her hands. "I *must* find Kalinda Halcyon. It's all he asked of me!"

She leaned into Eris, her body wracked with sobs, and Eris shot a helpless look at Adrie, who now sat back on her heels. "She's weak, but she'll live," Adrie said.

"Has she been...abused?" Eris asked, throat tight. "Tortured, or...?"

"Not that we can tell," Brenna said. "From what Ser Leal told us, her injuries were sustained on her travels. Physically, she'll recover from her ordeal."

Eris hugged the frail girl closer. Hazel had once been all curls and laughter, but she was still so young...

Drake knelt by the girl again. He said her name as he carefully pried one of her small hands free and held it in his own. "It's all right," he said when she looked up at him in alarm. "I'm a friend. My name is Drake."

She blinked at him through her tears, but her breathing began to even out. "You're a mage, too?"

"Aye." He dwarfed the girl, but he held her hand with a gentleness that belied his strength. "My magic isn't very strong, Hazel, but it can make you feel a little better. Are you comfortable with letting me try?"

Hazel sniffed and nodded. Drake's eyes closed and he held very still. Eris sought to sense his magic, but saw only the result: after a minute or two, Hazel took a deep, shuddering breath, and then gave a weak smile. "That feels nice in my heart."

Adrie frowned. "What are you doing to her?"

"Just calming her," Drake replied. "Is that better, Hazel?"

"Yes. A little. Thank you." Hazel swiped at her eyes and looked at Eris. "Where is Kali?"

"Not here," Eris replied. The poor child really should get some rest, but Eris could not quell her curiosity. "Hazel...what happened after you and the other bastion mages got recaptured? I assumed the sentinels would bring you all back to the bastion."

Hazel hugged herself. "We were free for a little bit. We walked right out the gates, like you said we could. And Druce knew how to get to the docks, where you said the boat was. It was dark and freezing, and we were all frightened, so we went as fast as we could. But we got lost, and then the city guards found us."

Her voice began to tremble. "They had hematite cuffs. And we were all tired and frightened, and it was so cold. The guards brought us to the docks, but the sentinels were waiting. And Argent..." Her lower lip quivered as more tears spilled down her cheeks. "He ordered us brought back to the bastion. The sentinels made us line up in a row outside the dormitories. I was at the end. I shut my eyes after they beheaded Druce, but I heard...

"When Argent came to me, I thought I was going to die too, but he just held my chin and made me look at him, and asked me my name, and I told him, because I was so scared, I couldn't think. Then he smiled and said it would be all right, and I felt better. The next thing I remember is seeing the Sufani again, the one who came with you to the bastion. And now I'm here, but Eris... he killed all of them! Wylie and Jep, and Foley, too, but he did that at the docks..."

She forced the last words out through her weeping. After, she collapsed into Eris' arms again, sobbing and clutching Eris' tunic. For a moment, Eris could only hold her close, too stunned and horrified to speak. Foley was dead? *All* the others, too? It was too much. Adrie ducked her head; Brenna put an arm around her. Drake rose to walk toward the river. Atanar followed. When Eris looked at Leal, the Sufani's eyes shone with tears and her gloved hands were clenched into fists.

"I told you," Jensine said from Eris' side. "Poison." With that, she turned on her heel and stalked off, Caith following. "Brenna," she called. "Come on. We have a great deal to discuss."

The brown-haired mage pulled away from Adrie. "Everything will be all right," she said, and slipped off after her mother.

Eris watched Seren's Children without seeing them. Faces appeared in her mind's eye: the mages of Whitewater Bastion she'd left behind to deal with the fallout from her actions. But despite how she'd abandoned them, they'd cremated Gid so his soul wouldn't wander. And when she had returned with another promise of freedom, they had listened to her. They had all *believed* her.

Now they were dead.

My fault.

She couldn't breathe.

"Eris."

Someone touched her shoulder. Eris blinked and looked at Adrie, who knelt beside her. Adrie's nose was bright pink and her eyes were still wet, but her face was hard. "What are we going to do?" she whispered.

Eris looked again at Seren's Children. Jensine, Caith, Brenna, and a few others all stood by the ladder, in deep discussion. None seemed pleased. Her vision trembled with rage. But her reply, somehow, was cool. "Take care of our own," she said. "Trade places with me, will you? I must speak with them."

Eris made her way over to the others. Leal, who had stood aside, fell in step with her. Eris glanced her way, but said nothing. If the Sufani wanted to join her, she would not argue. Besides, it was reassuring to have Leal at her side. She did not want to be alone right now.

When Eris and Leal reached the Damaris family and their allies, all conversation hushed. Jensine lifted her chin to regard Eris, her blue eyes cool. "How is the girl?"

"Resting," Eris replied.

Jensine nodded. "She can't stay here. *We* might not even be able to return."

"Mother, I told you, we *weren't* followed," Caith said with a scowl. "I made sure of it."

"No one could have followed our tracks," Leal added.

But the matriarch shook her head and muttered, "Poison."

Eris took a breath to ensure she could speak clearly and without emotion, for if she allowed her feelings to even trickle out, she would erupt. "Are you still willing to help me?"

She was not above feeling pleasure at the way Jensine's eyes all but bugged out of her head. "Help you free bastion mages, after this? Are you mad?"

Eris ignored the way Leal had tensed beside her. "I see now that there is little hope of achieving that goal, at least without dire repercussions to the rest of our people."

Jensine snorted. "*Your* people, you mean."

"*Our* people. Seren's blessing flows in all our veins; her light shines on every one of us. Too long have we suffered just because we were born with magic in our blood. Too long have we lived by *their* rules."

"Not us," Jensine replied, lifting her chin. "Not Seren's Children."

"*Especially* you. You live as fugitives, skulking in the wilderness, living off the land. And for what? We have *power*, Jensine. And I have seen what can happen when we work together. I'm tired of hiding. I'm tired of letting them hurt us. We must fight back. Why should *we* cower in fear of the hemies and the dregs, when we have magic at our command?"

"Pretty words," Caith said. "But you're forgetting the problem of hematite."

Eris squared her shoulders. "Hematite is the problem *and* the solution. Hematite is the sentinels' greatest strength...and greatest weakness."

The other wild mages cast her dubious looks, but Jensine's regard was more curious than anything else. "Is that so?"

"I have seen the evidence," Eris added. "The sentinels depend on the stuff; without it, they'll waste away to nothing. We must destroy the hematite mine in Stonehaven. It's the only way to stop the sentinels for good."

Silence fell over the group as all eyes fixed on Eris. Within them, she saw many things: doubt, fear, confusion, anger. All mirrors of what coiled within her own heart. At last, they all looked at Jensine, whose gaze had gone distant.

"Destroy the mine," Jensine murmured. "Now there's an idea…"

"It can't be done," Caith said, shaking his head. "Can it?"

Brenna shivered. "I don't know if we could do much, with hematite around. It strikes me as a paradox."

"Hematite won't be the only thing there," Eris pointed out. "There will be rock and stone of all kinds, and," she knew her smile held no warmth, "wood. For their tools, their wagons, or whatever else the hemies and their allies use to drag the hematite from the earth."

Jensine returned the smile. "Aye, and wood burns quite well, does it not?"

"It does, indeed," Eris agreed. "But not as well as flesh."

SEVENTEEN

All dead.

At first Drake could not think, could hardly breathe. His world was grief and rage and bitterness, turned inward. He stood at the shore of the underground river but only dimly saw the cool, dark water and the shimmering light reflected upon the cavern's ceiling. If he'd been more circumspect, fought harder, his people would be alive. At best, he'd thought them returned to a life of mere captivity; their safety was worth his own head on a pike. But for Argent to have killed them *all*...

Someone came to stand at his side. Without looking, Drake knew it was Atanar, but could not summon the will to greet the Canderi, so he kept his silence.

Atanar shifted in place as he studied the river. "You told me of the escape from that...bastard."

"Bastion," Drake murmured. "Though 'bastard' also fits."

"Bastion," Atanar repeated. "Is what you told me the truth?"

"Aye. Of course. Why would I have lied about any of that?"

"If you spoke truly, you could not have prevented the deaths of those other mages."

"I should have–" Drake's words died in his throat and he looked at the river again. "I set all of this into motion. I'm a monster."

"Did you wield the blade that killed them? Did you savor their deaths? Will you sleep easy tonight?" When Drake was silent, Atanar nodded. "No. Because while you are a strange man, Drake, you are no murderer." He looked at his reflection, distorted by the rippling current. "You are no

155

monster."

Drake sighed. "You're right: *I* didn't kill those people. But my actions led to their deaths."

"I would wager they were dead the moment they left the bastion," Atanar replied. "No one kills as this Argent does unless they mean to prove a point. You should not carry shame for the actions of another."

Drake's chest tightened. "It's not that simple."

"Yes, Drake. It is." Atanar paused. "The pain here," he touched two fingers to Drake's chest, "will grow and spread if left to fester. You must turn it to good use, or it will consume you."

Gods above, he was right – and Drake would be just as sodding stubborn as his little brother to keep fighting the realization. So he gave the Canderi the best smile he could manage. "I see your point."

"But you will not stop bruising."

"Bruising...?" Drake considered. "You mean *brooding*. And no, probably not for a while. But you've given me something to think about, Nat."

Atanar's pale brows drew together. "What do you keep calling me?"

"Oh." Heat crept up Drake's neck and he tried to sound casual as he searched the ground for a suitably shaped stone. "Nothing. Just a nickname, I guess. I'll stop if you don't like it."

"A nickname." Atanar considered.

"You know what nicknames are?"

The Canderi man glared at him, but somehow the expression held no malice. "I have not had a little name in some time." Drake opened his mouth to ask, but Atanar shook his head. "I would rather not speak of it yet."

"Fair enough. But do you like 'Nat?'"

"Do you mislike 'Atanar?'"

"No. It's a fine name. A strong name." The heat in Drake's neck rose to his cheeks. To avoid looking at Atanar, he found a round, smooth stone and cupped it in one hand, assessing its weight. "I like it very much. I just... I like 'little names,' too. A foolish habit of mine, I suppose."

"Nat." Atanar considered again, as if the nickname was something of great

156

importance, and then he offered a small smile that stole Drake's breath. "It would be good, I think, to call myself something else for a while."

"Fresh start?"

"Atanar was my grandfather's name. And my great-great grandfather's. It is a name older than any living person I know."

"Yes, but does it also mean something else?"

Atanar looked back at his reflection. "My name belongs to my clan. It is fitting I should find a new one now."

Drake did not reply, sensing that he'd stumbled somewhere unwelcome. Instead, he hefted the stone one more time, aimed, and with a flick of his wrist, sent it skipping over the river before it sank beneath the surface. Only when the stone left his hand did he consider doing so might be sacrilege, so he offered a quick prayer of forgiveness. Perhaps the stone could be an offering to Tor. Seren's light, the last thing he needed was to accidentally piss off the gods.

"Thanks for trying to talk some sense into me, Nat," he said lightly, trying to smile.

The corner of Atanar's mouth twitched, but his nod was solemn. "Thank you for the fresh start, Drake."

*

When Drake had calmed down, he returned to Adrie and Hazel, who sat away from the others while Adrie tried to coax the girl into eating. Atanar—Nat—followed Drake, and Drake felt a sense of...not relaxation, exactly, but its nosy neighbor. It was good to have an ally at his side again.

"I'm not hungry," Hazel was saying as Drake and Nat approached. "I must find Kalinda Halcyon."

"I've told you, she's not here," Adrie said, a trace of irritation in her voice. She looked up at the two men. "Kali. That's all she can talk about!"

The girl shook her head. "That's *all* he asked me to do, Adrie. To find one woman isn't such a difficult task, is it?"

There was an odd cadence to her words, as if she were reading from a script. Drake exchanged a look with Adrie, who also recognized that something wasn't right, but kept his voice light when he knelt by the girl. "I might be able to help you," he said. She brightened, eyes wide, face eager. "Kali is...beloved of my brother," Drake went on. "And I have plans to see my brother again. No doubt Kali will be with him."

"When will you see your brother next?" Hazel asked.

"Yes, Drake," Adrie added, brows knitted. "*When?*"

Drake shot her a quelling look but kept his reply to the girl easy. "Can't say for sure, but I know it will happen. I feel it, here." He placed a hand over his heart. "So I think 'when' is up to the gods. But if you stick around long enough, and do as Adrie asks of you, I'm sure you'll see Kali very soon."

Hazel studied him. "You're quite stupid if you think a lie will work on me."

Drake bit his tongue to keep from laughing as Adrie said, "*Stonewall* is his brother."

Hazel's eyes widened in understanding.

"You've heard of him?" Drake asked.

The girl nodded vigorously. "Kali and that sentinel... There were rumors, but I only realized they were true when Eris came back to the bastion. She doesn't like him."

Drake chuckled. "I can't say I'm surprised." He nodded to the bowl of broth that Adrie had been trying to get the girl to eat. "That looks good. Better finish it before Nat here gulps it down."

From behind him, Atanar grumbled. "I have already eaten."

"So he says," Drake said to the girl. "But I wouldn't take the chance, if I were you."

With that, he rose and nodded to Adrie, who looked relieved as Hazel picked up the bowl. With a glance back to indicate that Atanar should follow, Drake made his way to Eris, Leal, Jensine, and Caith. The mages stood around one of the small fires that never faded, nor seemed to need its fuel replenished. Leal hung back, arms crossed, staring at the fire. At Drake and Atanar's approach, Eris glanced up but Drake could not read her expression.

"But how could we even get *into* the mine?" Caith said as he paced before the fire. "No doubt they're well-guarded."

Eris did not look perturbed. "I can scout from above. Perhaps there's a way inside."

"Aye, it's called 'the main entrance,'" Drake said as he came to stand by her.

"Now is not the time for your jokes," Eris replied.

"It's no joke. I've been there."

Caith slanted a suspicious look Drake's way. "You've been to the hematite mine?"

Shit. Now was probably not the best time to share his past life as a sentinel, so Drake shrugged. "Well, not the mine, itself, but I'm familiar with Stonehaven Province. Aren't you?"

"Never had a reason to go near the sodding place," Caith replied gruffly. "The idea of being so close to hematite makes my skin crawl."

"Well, lucky for you that I'm here." Drake looked at Eris again. "But why in the blazing void would you even want to go to the mine...?"

He trailed off as realization struck him like an arrow to the chest. Eris met his gaze and said, "It's the only way to stop the sentinels forever."

"I agree," Jensine said. "Once we're in, we can burn the place to cinders. All we need is a chance. If you truly know the area, you'll be a splendid asset."

Drake swallowed his initial outrage. "You truly think you can destroy an entire mine? It's no small operation, you know. There probably aren't a lot of sentinels there, but there *are* guards, workers, and other civilians."

Eris frowned at him. "But don't the hemies send their own to the mine for punishment?"

"I'd imagine the place would be crawling with sentinels," Caith added.

Drake shook his head. "Not many sentinels defy their oaths, or do anything that would cause them to be cast out of the order."

"I find that difficult to believe," Eris said. "Given what I know of sentinels."

Drake stared at her and she met his gaze with challenge in her eyes. He was acutely aware of Caith, Jensine, and all the other "Children of Seren" nearby. He was strong, yes, but he could not fight all of them, if his past came to light. But would Eris betray him?

"If none of you have solid knowledge of your enemies," Atanar said suddenly, making them all glance his way. "I would listen to Drake."

Leal cleared her throat. "I agree with Atanar."

"What do we care about the opinions of dregs?" Jensine said, rolling her eyes.

"Tell us what you know of the mine," Eris said to Drake.

"I'll share my knowledge, on one condition," he said, and the mages tensed. "Destroy all the hematite you want. Burn every bit of wood in the sodding place. Just don't hurt anyone."

Eris' eyes widened. "You mean the sentinels?"

"Aye, and the miners and civilians alike who work there. They are innocent. They don't deserve to die for your vengeance."

Eris glared at him. "*No* sentinel is innocent."

"Yes," Caith added, venom in his words. "And those who aid them are just as guilty of wrongdoing."

"Those people ensure hematite spreads to the world," Eris added. "They are just as much at fault for our imprisonment."

"Maybe so," Drake said. "But if you want to bring about real change, Eris, you must *think* about how your actions—our actions—will be perceived by the rest of the world. What will people say if a bunch of mages take hundreds of innocent lives?"

His heart ached as he spoke. This was the argument Ben would have made.

Leal nodded. "It is akin to an act of war. You—and all mages—would be treated worse than before."

Thank Tor, someone else on his side! "Imagine how those still in bastions would fare," Drake added.

He made a subtle nod to Hazel as he spoke. As he'd hoped, this gave Eris pause. The news of the murdered Whitewater Bastion mages was still painfully fresh for all of them. Eris' gaze dropped to the fire as she considered.

Caith made a noise of disgust. "Mother, we don't need his help. We have our own ways of getting what we need. We can do this without him."

But Jensine, like Eris, did not look entirely convinced. "I don't want to risk our people."

Eris cleared her throat. "Drake, you said we could just...walk in?"

"Well, it's not *quite* that simple," he admitted. "It's more like...anyone can enter the mine with the intention of seeking employment. Mining is a trade like any other, and a fairly profitable one for Stonehaven Province. The trick won't be getting in, but getting hired. Assuming you could get a job at the mine, it would be a relatively simple matter to look around, suss out any weak points, and," he gave Eris a knowing look, "find out a way to complete your objective with minimal casualties."

The mages exchanged glances, but Leal spoke up next. "I think it's a sound plan, Eris. At the very least, it's a better plan than trying to storm in and burn the place to shit. Even with magic, that could go sideways too easily."

Drake nodded. "It's better at least to get as much inside information as you can before doing anything too...permanent."

"And how would we go about getting 'inside information?'" Caith asked. "How could any of us find work there?"

An itch crept up Drake's wrists, from where his sentinel mark had been placed so long ago. Marcen had dissipated the ink, but he could still feel the needle's bite upon his skin. "I'll go. I don't know anything about mining, but I can swing a hammer as good as anyone."

"I will go as well," Atanar added. "I am also on good terms with hammers."

Drake clapped the other man's shoulder. "Thanks, friend." He looked back at the other mages. "What do you say? Do you agree to my terms? Information for mercy?"

"I don't like it," Caith replied. "Putting all our trust in strangers..."

"Blood is blood," Jensine said firmly. "Drake is one of Seren's sons. The other..." She made an indeterminate gesture to Atanar. "If Blue Eyes wants to risk his life in our service, I say let him. Eris, do you agree?"

Everyone turned to the shapeshifter as she considered. In turn, she met Drake's gaze; his stomach twisted when he saw only cold calculation looking back. Given her past actions, she probably did see Atanar as disposable. But what about himself? Or Leal? Well, he had to take the risk. Besides, his eyes were open, at least. He knew how ruthless her heart could be.

At last, Eris shrugged. "Very well. It's worth a try, at least. Although, there will be more details to work out."

Drake gave her a wry smile he did not feel. "There always are."

*

Night and day were difficult to assess while underground, but Drake's exhaustion meant that he didn't give a shit what celestial body was in the sky. All he wanted was *sleep*. After more discussion with Eris and the Damaris family, after checking on a calmer Adrie, after assuring Hazel that yes, this was a safe place to sleep, he *finally* found his way to his own bedroll. He settled down beside a flickering mage-fire lantern, across from Atanar, who stirred at Drake's approach.

"Sorry," Drake whispered. "Did I wake you?"

"No." Blue eyes opened but Atanar only stared at the cavern ceiling. "I fear if I sleep, the voices will return and I will lose what control Kali gave me – what control *you* gave me."

Lying on his side, Drake fished out a *biri* from his pocket and offered it to the Canderi man. "This might help."

Atanar shook his head. "Perhaps later."

Drake put the *biri* away and leaned his head back, closed his eyes, and sank into sleep almost immediately, a habit ingrained from years of not knowing when a chance to rest would come again.

What felt like mere moments later, someone nudged his side, muttering his name. Drake snapped awake, sitting up and reaching for his spear in one fluid motion, only to face Leal, crouching beside him. Her cowl was down, revealing the thin line of her mouth. "Put that away before you poke someone's eye out," she hissed.

Drake released the weapon. "Maybe think about that *first* the next time you go waking up a sleeping soldier."

He expected another bracing comeback, but she only ducked her head. "I'm sorry," she said, still softly. "But I needed to speak to you."

"I'm guessing it can't wait until morning?"

"It's about Eris."

Both Drake and Leal glanced over to the fire where the mages had been in deep discussion. All was quiet now, and Eris lay curled on a bedroll near Brenna and her daughter, about ten yards away from where Drake had bedded down. Eris' back was to Drake, and her breathing seemed steady and rhythmic.

"These mages are not to be trusted," Leal murmured. "Yet she seems... overly fond of them, already."

"I've noticed," Drake said, frowning.

"I don't blame her for craving the company of her own people, but it's clear Jensine and the others don't have Eris' best interest at heart. Caith would have killed that girl had I not intervened."

Drake's jaw unhinged. "Are you sodding serious?"

"Aye," Leal said grimly. "The moment she said Argent's name, Caith grabbed her throat and squeezed. I think he did something with magic, too, because she didn't cry out, just gaped at him like a fish before she started squirming. It took all of my strength to shove him away, and we nearly came to blows arguing over the poor girl's fate."

It took Drake several moments to collect himself. By the time the *biri* was lit and in his fingers, his hands were shaking. "Gods above and beyond... I didn't realize..." He took a long drag. "How did you stop him, dreg that you are?"

Thankfully, Leal understood his sense of humor enough now so that she did not take offense, but instead gave a rueful, if sharp-edged, smile. "I asked him what his mother would think if she saw him about to kill a helpless child."

Drake released a stream of smoke above their heads and away from Leal. "Considering Jensine's reaction when she heard the tale, she probably would have been delighted."

Leal took a long, slow breath, clenching and unclenching her gloved fingers. "I don't care what Jensine or Caith think about me. But I don't trust them and I don't think Eris should, either." She gave Drake a look he could only think of as despondent. "They're going to take her from us, aren't they?"

Now *that* was an odd thing to say. Drake kept his voice casual. "What do you mean?"

"She's been hurting so deeply, for so long," Leal murmured. "And while you and I might think Jensine and Caith are trouble, Eris does not see them that way. She sees only a chance for revenge – and a place to belong among the 'Children of Seren.'"

There was more to the Sufani's words than she was letting on. Drake recognized the desperate look in her eyes and the pained expression on her face. "Oh, gods, Leal…" He grimaced. "She's just lost her husband…I don't think she's in a mind to look for anything–"

"That's not…" Leal made a noise of frustration. "I don't feel *that* way about her, you dolt."

"But there's *something* between you," he replied. "Right?"

Leal was silent. "Aye. But it's…private." Before Drake could agree to back off, the Sufani sighed again. "Eris is helping me…transform. Into a man. It's who I am inside."

"A man?" he asked.

"Yes." She met Drake's eyes with iron.

But his bewilderment was not her burden to bear, so he kept his tone light. "Well," he said, blowing out *biri* smoke. "You'll make a handsome one." A thought struck him. "You've clearly felt like this for some time. Would it help if we called you anything…different? *He* instead of *she*?"

"Not for now," Leal replied, and some of the edge had faded from her voice.

Although he would have liked more information, he quelled the urge for now. Leal was not someone who shared her heart easily; he did not want to push too hard. So he said only, "The worse has not yet come to pass.

You and I are still here; we're still on Eris' side. Right?"

"What are you getting at?"

Drake took another pull from the *biri.* "We've spoken our minds about the Stonehaven plan. She's not unreasonable; it looks like she's at least willing to consider our words. Our best hope now is to convince her that *our* plan is the most effective way to achieve her goal."

Something in Leal's eyes changed. Because he could not see her face, he could not determine her expression, but he thought some of the tension in her body eased. "I can do that."

"Yes, *we* can," Drake replied, offering a small smile. "Maybe you should join us at the mine, eh? Do some work for once."

As he'd hoped, the playful comment elicited a slightly-less playful jab at his ribs, but Leal's reply was thoughtful. "Maybe I will come along. Someone needs to keep you out of trouble. But what am I going to do about a tier-mark?"

Drake blew out the final breath of *biri* smoke. "We're resourceful. We'll figure something out. Now, can I please get some sleep?"

EIGHTEEN

Sweat trickled down Talon's back and shoulders as she overturned the wheelbarrow, sending a stream of dirt and rocks clattering into the waste-pit at the base of the mine. Dust swirled her way, so she held her breath behind her kerchief, despite how no precaution would stop her chest from aching. Even so, a week in the hematite mine had taught her the value of inhaling the least amount of debris as possible.

The other workers, mostly townies from Carver's Creek, would chip away at the rocky, stepped sides of the open mine, while the Forsworn sentinels wheeled the detritus down to the base, to dump it into the waste-pit. Exhausting work, but Talon relished the constant exertion, for each night since that first day, she'd been too tired to do anything other than sleep. In the mine, it was easy, too easy, perhaps, to focus only on the *here* and *now,* and shut out all thoughts of the past – or the future.

Once her wheelbarrow was empty, she rolled it to the side, giving Kam room to approach the waste-pit to empty her own load. Talon took the opportunity to swipe her damp forehead, squinting up at the hematite refinery. Even from her vantage point at the base of the mine, she could see the rough shape of the squared-off pyramid over the mine's rim that dominated the immediate area – and her attention. Although she could not see them from here, she knew at least two burly guards stood just outside the refinery's circular doorway, each armed with an ax almost as tall as she was. Though she'd not been anywhere near the refinery, she had felt the heat pouring out of the doorway and from an aperture at the top, and the scents of fire and metal had been strong enough to sting her eyes.

The building was innocuous enough, but it held all the newly -refined hematite in Aredia, waiting to be distributed to the sentinel garrisons across the country.

"Won't do you any good," a male voice huffed behind her.

Talon glanced over at Jasper, another Forsworn sentinel. Despite his obvious exhaustion, he gave her a bright smile, made even brighter by his rich, dark-brown skin. At her frown of confusion, he leaned his weight on his full wheelbarrow and jerked his chin up toward the building at the rim. "The refinery might as well be a second tier feast while we're a pair of dregs. We'll never get to it, so there's no point pining."

"I'm not pining," Talon replied, though the chill in her blood reminded her that was a lie.

As Kam finished depositing her burden, Jasper chuckled and shoved his wheelbarrow forward. "Sure, sure. None of us want a burn, eh? We're all *normal*, here."

"Don't listen to him," Kam replied as she came to Talon's side. "He's just trying to get under your skin."

"Wouldn't dream of it, Kam," Jasper called over his shoulder as he dumped his wheelbarrow's contents.

Kam followed Talon's gaze back to the refinery. A trio of workers from a nearby village made their way up the main path that led to the rim, guiding a wagon and team of mules. Though a canvas tarp covered the wagon's contents, the wind made the sides flap up, revealing glints of rust-red rock threaded with hematite.

"Don't even think about it," Kam murmured.

"Think about what?" Talon asked.

"The guards may *look* like dolts, but they're well trained. I've seen many Forsworn sentinels try to get to the refinery, but Jas is right. It's beyond our reach."

"What happened to the ones who tried?" Talon asked. But Kam said nothing, only turned to push her wheelbarrow back down the path that descended to the main pit. As Talon followed, a young man rushed up toward them, pushing a full wheelbarrow up the pathway so quickly that bits of rock and dirt clattered over its sides as he went.

"Sorry, I'm behind again," he gasped as Kam and Talon eased their empty barrows to the side to give him more room, though he still had to slow to a walk just to creep by without toppling into the pit.

"It's all right, Ruddy," Kam said, smiling at the red-faced lad. Her smile faded, however, the longer she looked at him. "Is something wrong?"

"Loach," he mumbled, and rushed up the rest of the way to the waste-pit, hurrying past Jasper with another call of apology over his shoulder.

Jasper joined the women and frowned after the younger man. "What'd he say?"

Kam's face hardened and her gaze slipped in the direction Ruddy had come from. Another cadre of workers headed up the path, led by Loach and Ottis. Unlike the plainly dressed workers who had entered the refinery before, these men and women wore a hodge-podge of leather and steel armor, as if they had split several sets of gear between them. Ottis carried a familiar trunk: wooden, reinforced with steel bands and inlaid with the sigil of the sentinels. Loach glanced down at the sentinels; a thin, slow smile came to his face and he spoke to the others. The workers continued while Loach and Ottis—and the trunk—came down the side-path toward the Forsworn sentinels.

Boots and wheels scraped the dirt beside Talon. Kam and Jasper had shoved their empty wheelbarrows to the sides of the path, and moved to stand with backs pressed to the rock face, hands clasped before their waists. Talon mimicked their pose, her heart suddenly racing.

"Ruddy," Kam said, her voice just loud enough to reach the lad, who knelt beside his wheelbarrow. "Come here!"

"A rock got stuck in my wheel," he replied.

Jasper rolled his eyes. "Then sodding leave it! Come *on*, kid."

"All right, all right." Ruddy's wheelbarrow clattered to the ground as he darted to stand beside Talon. He towered over her like the distant rock formations. His sandy brown hair gleamed with perspiration and her nose wrinkled at the musk of his body odor. He took a single, deep breath and then stood stock-still, in what Talon now recognized as a modified parade rest.

Loach and Ottis paused before the Forsworn sentinels. The mine's administrator briefly swept his gaze across the others to regard Talon. Upon closer inspection, she noted again how young he looked. Had he been one of her sentinels, she would have thought him younger than Ruddy, or even Milo. But there was a hardness in his rounded face; a cruel twist to his mouth and the muddy color of his eyes.

"How's the new one working out, Kam?" he said without looking at the dark-haired woman.

"Very well, serla," Kam replied.

"Good. She seems docile enough, I suppose." Loach's eyes narrowed. "But I've heard it's the quiet ones you've got to look out for."

Kam didn't reply. Loach continued to study Talon, who kept her breathing shallow in hopes of avoiding a coughing fit. Despite her efforts, her throat burned, a telltale sign. Her eyes watered and she fought for control, but she lost, doubled over, and began to hack like she'd just smoked a *biri* for the first time. Her ribs ached with the force of her coughs, and she could hardly catch her breath.

A soft touch at her back made her look over at Kam, who had reached out to steady her. Loach, too, shot Kam a look, but it was one of disdain, though he only shrugged. "Comfort her if it makes you feel better, but something tells me this one won't be around much longer."

"As you say, Serla Loach," Kam said.

"How are *you* feeling, Jasper?" Loach asked as Talon reined in her coughs and sputters.

The dark-skinned man did not look up. "I'm...here, serla."

"For now," Loach agreed before he glanced over at Ruddy, who stiffened. "What are you gaping at, burnie?"

"Nothing, serla," Ruddy replied, though his gaze shifted to the chest in Ottis' grip.

A razor thin smile crept to Loach's face. "It's empty."

Ruddy ducked his head. "I know, serla."

"Want a burn already, do you? How long's it been since your first?"

"Nearly a year, serla."

Loach reached into the pocket of his fitted vest and withdrew a little piece of red stone. "Here," he said, tossing it to Ruddy. "I hate to see anyone suffer needlessly."

Ruddy caught the stone with ease, but his expression was grim as he examined it. Talon felt Kam tense beside her as well and knew, somehow, that Jasper's gaze was also on the little piece of hematite.

"Go on, then," Loach said in the manner of someone biting back a laugh. "Tuck in."

It was clear how Ruddy had gotten his name, for his skin flushed pink as he bit his lip and said, "I can't, serla. It's…not allowed."

"I'm allowing it." Loach's voice was mild but the guards with him snickered. Ottis would not look Talon in the eye when she tried to meet his gaze.

Ruddy shot a helpless look at Kam, who said, "Serla, you know what raw hematite will do to him."

Loach waved a hand dismissively. "He'll die sooner or later here. I'm doing him a favor by letting him choose the time." He brightened and pulled another stone out of his pocket, offering it to Talon. "Surely you'll accept my kind offer?"

When she did not move, he grabbed her bandaged wrist and pressed the stone in her palm. Pain darkened the edges of her vision, but she fought the urge to cry out. When Loach released her, she could not help but stare at the little piece of raw hematite ore: dark silver caught in veins the color of old blood. The stone was barely bigger than the tip of her thumb but would be enough to give her seizures if she tried to ingest it – unless she was weak enough for the raw ore to simply stop her heart for good.

"You don't have to thank me." Loach smiled easily, freely, as any young man might. "But it would be polite."

Talon closed her fist around the hematite and dropped her hand to her side. "Thank you, serla."

He smirked and nodded to Kam. "Get back to work. I want the rest of that overburden gone before dusk."

170

With that, he continued to saunter up the path to the refinery, Ottis and the others following. Only when they were out of earshot did Kam and Jasper seem to breathe. Ruddy staggered back against the canyon wall, rubbing his forehead. Talon's throat still burned with the desire to cough, but she held it in check.

"Are you all right?" Kam asked her. When Talon nodded, Kam rolled her eyes. "Liar."

"I've been better," Talon admitted, clearing her throat. She glanced at Ruddy, whose face was still bright red as he examined the little chunk of raw ore. "Don't eat that."

He winced. "I know." After a beat, he chucked the stone down into the open pit mine.

Kam regarded Talon, her gaze darting to the stone in Talon's hand. "Shall I give your own advice back to you?"

Talon closed her fist around the stone. It was warm, as if it had trapped the sun's heat, and she could feel hematite's promise beating in her blood: strength, power, death. It would be the easy way out. Before she could decide whether to toss it away too, Jasper exhaled loudly. "If you kill yourself now, you'll be leaving us with the rest of that fresh pile of shit. And I'm sodding hungry."

"He means the overburden," Kam said when Talon frowned in confusion. "The waste material we're dumping."

"It amounts to the same thing," Jasper replied, shoving his wheelbarrow back down the path. "Now come on. We've work to do."

Talon ignored Kam's look and stashed the stone in the pocket of her linen pants, and then turned to follow Jasper back into the mine.

✳

It took the Forsworn sentinels until dusk to dump the overburden from that day's excavation. Hard labor; no reward. The piece of raw ore felt heavier in Talon's pocket with every step.

After dusk had settled over Stonehaven Province, after a hasty scrub with a damp rag, Talon all but collapsed before the low table in the common space the sentinels had set up in their "barracks." Even after a week of labor, her body was not yet used to the work, and every muscle was sore and exhausted. Wielding a shovel and steering a wheelbarrow were nothing like sparring, though she'd not touched a blade since Foley's death, and likely never would again.

A plate of bread, hard cheese, and stringy beans plunked down before her. Talon glanced up at Kam, who offered a small smile before setting the next plate at the empty space next to Talon. As she did, Ruddy and Jasper entered the little alcove, both hunched over to fit through the doorway.

"We washed, just for you ladies," Jasper said as he sank to the woven mat beside the table. "Well, not *washed*, exactly, but you know. Scrubbed the nooks and crannies."

Kam fluttered her lashes at him in an exaggerated flirt and spoke with all the refinement of a second tier. "We're ever so grateful, aren't we, Tal?"

Talon, who had been about to take a bite of bread, inhaled deeply, then pulled a face. "Could have done with a bit more scrubbing."

Ruddy chuckled. Jasper laughed aloud, a great booming laugh that devolved into a groan as he doubled over the table, clutching his stomach. Kam's plate clattered as she rushed to his side.

"It will pass," she murmured, rubbing his back.

Jasper groaned again, eyes squeezed shut, shivering. Ruddy squirmed on the mat beside him before placing a hand on Jasper's shoulder. Just when Talon considered getting up to join them, though she had no idea what she could do to help, Jasper let out a great sigh and sagged into Kam's grip, his head lolling on her shoulder even though his breathing was steady. Talon's heart froze, but Kam didn't look distressed. It was not relief that crossed her face, not quite, but something like quiet acceptance; an expression Foley had worn so often.

"Tal? Are you sick, too?" It was Ruddy.

Only when Talon swiped her eyes did she realize she'd been weeping. She rubbed her sleeve over her face to dry her tears and offered the lad her most confident smile. "I'm well as can be."

172

By now, Jasper had sat up, blinking, and shot Kam an embarrassed look. "Thanks for being here."

"Of course," she replied, adding a smile that did not reach her dark eyes. "You're...?"

He took a deep, shuddering breath, then nodded. "I'm not going anywhere today. It's catching up with me," he added, looking at Talon. "The...the lack, I mean."

"The lack of hematite?"

Jasper nodded. "I've held on a long time. Longer than I expected. But it makes sense, I suppose. I saw this coming," he gestured to the tiny underground common space the sentinels shared, "and had an opportunity to make provisions."

"Provisions?" Talon frowned as Kam took her seat and they all began to eat.

"Aye. Mine's a sordid tale," Jasper said wryly. "The gist is that I got caught doing something I shouldn't have. Not uncommon, I guess, for those of us who wind up in this paradise of Ea's realm."

Ruddy tore off a piece of cheese and chewed as he spoke. "Didn't you free some mages or something?"

Jasper stared at the metal plate beneath his meal. "Aye, something like that. Yes, Rudd, I freed some mages. A woman named Saba and her little one. I can't remember the baby's name. You'd think I would, considering how much sodding trouble they landed me in, but that's life for you, I guess." He sighed. "Saba was a recent...addition to Greenhill Bastion. She was a renegade mage that got caught while she was pregnant; the babe was born in the bastion."

"The child's father?" Talon asked.

Jasper shook his head. "Also a wild mage. My squad had been hunting a pack of them for a few days. We..." He ran a hand over his matted hair. "It was wrong, what we did. He was just trying to protect his wife and unborn child, and we hunted them down like beasts. I didn't kill him—my sarge did, after he attacked us—but I still couldn't sleep for a week after. Every time I looked at Saba, all I saw was the sodding monster I was. One day,

I found her in the bastion, alone. I thought she'd be afraid of me, but she was angry. Called me all sorts of horrible names, which I deserved, so I think she didn't know what to do when I told her I was sorry.

"We talked a bit, grew...not *friendly*, but I think she wanted not to hate me. I'm still not sure she ever pulled it off, but desperation looks like trust sometimes, doesn't it? Anyway, I had to do something to help her. But I knew...I knew if I got caught, they'd send me here, and I'd long for a quick death. So I started tapering off on my doses. Taking just a portion of what I got on the regular and saving the rest. I used my off-duty time to help track down someone who could get Saba out of the city. Then one night..." He shrugged. "Not much to tell, really. We just walked out the gates. I timed it right. No one questioned me; they must have thought..." He shuddered. "Well, I don't wonder too hard about that."

Ruddy's eyes were as round as dinner plates. "I never heard this part! What would anyone have thought you were doing with a *mage*?"

Jasper exchanged a glance with Kam, who placed a weathered hand on Ruddy's. "Just know that an imbalance of power often breeds cruelty."

"We'll leave it there," Jasper said, nodding. "So Saba and I just walked out–"

"Wait," Talon broke in. "Forgive me, but *no* one questioned you? Not even the gate guards?" At his blank look she could not help but sit up straighter. "We always had two guards on the bastion gates in Whitewater."

"Ah, you're from Whitewater?" Jasper asked. When Talon nodded, he winced. "Well, Greenhill Bastion isn't nearly as...ah...*rigid* as Whitewater Bastion. Though Commander Spur's a brutal son of a bitch."

Talon had heard much the same, though she'd never met the man. "Please forgive my interruption," she said. "I'm just used to things being done a different way."

"Well, no wonder," Jasper replied. "You Whitewater folk are all protocol and procedure."

Talon could feel the heat from Sadira and Kalinda's fire on her face, in her lungs, across every inch of her skin. She could feel the ground tremble as Foley's body collapsed, and the resistance of Milo's flesh as her blade sank in. She shook her head. "We were."

Silence fell over the group before Kam took a deep breath. "We'll have to hear your story, Tal. But Jasper, you may as well finish."

"Right." He toyed with his beans. "Everything went great until it didn't. I got Saba out of the bastion—her babe didn't even cry!—and to my contact. Wasn't until I was on my way back that Commander Spur caught up with me. They'd figured out a mage was missing and it wasn't too hard to put the pieces together." He laughed weakly. "Stupid oaf that I am...it never occurred to me to just leave too, you know? But training runs deep, I guess. A couple weeks later, I was here."

"With your hematite?" Talon asked. When Jasper nodded, she studied him. "How did you bring it in? They searched me quite thoroughly before I left Lasath."

Jasper grimaced. "Aye, me too, but not thoroughly enough, as it turned out. Don't make me elaborate. But my little supply is long gone, so it hardly matters."

"You've lasted a long time," Kam replied. "Perhaps you'll..."

But the dark-skinned man only gave her a sad smile. "Maybe. But probably not." He glanced at Ruddy. "Your turn, and don't skimp on the details, this time."

The younger man flushed again. "I was stupid."

"Join the club," Jasper muttered.

Ruddy gave an uneasy chuckle. "Well, I was *really* stupid. I was in the Undercity marketplace, in Lasath. I was off-duty, and saw this group of ragamuffins harassing a merchant. It got my blood hot, you know? It wasn't fair; the merchant was an old codger, all hunched over and frail, and the louts harassing him were easily three times his size. I chased 'em away. Was almost sad that none of them had the guts to stay and fight." He sighed. "The merchant was really grateful, as you can imagine, and he offered me coin as payment. I shouldn't have taken it, I *know*," he added quickly. "But I'd never seen anything so pretty as that piece of silver, and I thought I'd take it to Mara's temple or something, you know, give it to the Circle. But I didn't. I just liked to look at it at night, in my bunk. I tucked it in my boots during missions, like a good luck charm straight from Llyr himself.

"There was another sentinel, a burnie like me: Tem. We went through our first Burn together, trained together, but I think he was…I dunno. Eager to please, desperate for a promotion, something. He caught me looking at the coin and reported me to our sarge. Next thing I knew, High Commander Argent sent me here to 'set an example.'"

"Ea's tits," Jasper said after a beat. "I didn't realize that bit about your friend ratting on you. Bastard."

Talon frowned. "But why send you here? Taking a single coin is a minor infraction."

Ruddy tore off a piece of bread. "That's what some of the others said. I don't understand, either, but what can I do about it?"

"Still," Jasper said. "It's horseshit. You don't deserve this. A sodding silver coin…" He looked away from the younger man, his face pinched with anger.

Talon couldn't summon similar words. No, Ruddy did not deserve this fate – any more than Milo deserved to bear the brunt of his commander's misplaced fury. Her throat burned again.

Kam studied the burnie. "Were you brought before the Pillars?"

"No," Ruddy replied. "I wasn't worth the trouble, I guess. Thank the One."

"How can you accept this so easily?" Jasper asked. "How can you sit there and not be…I don't know, sodding *furious*? I mean, *I* defied the rules, I know that, so I accepted this fate. But you didn't do *anything.*"

Ruddy only looked at him. "I broke my oath, Jas. I betrayed my brothers and sisters in service by accepting coin when we're forbidden to do so. I shattered the gods' faith in me. How could they trust me?" His gaze dropped to his hands, twisting in his lap. "How could *anyone* trust me?"

"Fuck the gods, and fuck the High Commander," Jasper muttered. "You deserved better."

Silence settled over the Forsworn. Appetite gone, Talon picked at her beans, until Kam cleared her throat. "Your turn, Tal."

"Aye," Jasper said. He was calmer now, leaning on his elbows as he studied her. "What's your story? You came from Whitewater?"

Talon looked back at her plate, nudging the green beans around so they formed a little wall around the hard cheese. How much should she tell them? She did not think she could bear to tell her whole story. But what was the point in concealing anything now? And hadn't hiding the truth gotten her here? All her hopes, all her plans, all her efforts, for nothing. Her father was dead. She'd broken the trust of those who'd once followed her. All the mages back at Whitewater Bastion were dead.

So Talon set her fork down and placed her hands in her lap. "Yes, Jasper. I came from

Whitewater City. I was the commander of the sentinel garrison."

Ruddy sucked in his breath while Jasper and Kam exchanged startled looks. "The commander?" Ruddy said, leaning forward. "You? Of the *whole* garrison and bastion?"

Talon could not help her smile at his astonishment. "Yes."

"What in Nox's void did *you* do to end up here?" Jasper said, eyes wide.

Grief swelled over Talon like a wave, knocking her flat and stealing her breath, and in that moment, she wanted nothing more than to disappear. "I broke my oath," she whispered.

The next thing she heard was Kam's voice, soothing and gentle. "We have all broken our oaths, Tal. But if you don't wish to share your story, you don't have to."

Throat tight, Talon blinked down at her plate, though she saw only the high bastion walls of Whitewater. A few deep breaths helped her regain control of her emotions but strangely, it was the thought of her father that brought the most calm. What would Foley want her to do in this moment?

She swiped at her eyes again and looked up at Kam. "My father was First Mage of Whitewater Bastion. It took me the better part of a decade, but I managed to be stationed there, and get elevated to the rank of commander. Da was a…" Again, the thought of Foley brought a sense of peace, and a half-smile quirked her mouth. "Well, he was a firebrand in his youth, but time and…other things," she could not speak of his stolen hand, "changed him. He was a good First Mage to me, loyal and circumspect. He would have been a good First Mage to anyone, I think, but I..." Now her throat burned again, but she allowed the coughs to come, and then pressed on. "He would be alive now, if I had not come to Whitewater City. He would have kept his head down and kept quiet.

"But I was selfish. I had to be near him, had to know he was safe. My selfishness was his downfall. Not only *his* downfall," she added, hands balling into fists, "but all the mages there. They're all dead because of me. Because I tried so hard to protect my father, I lost sight of everything else, and Argent..." Her words died in her throat.

"Argent found out?" Kam said softly. When Talon nodded, Kam looked down at her own plate. "He killed *all* of the mages there, because of you and your father?"

"No," Talon replied. "There was an escape. Eleven mages fled on Heartfire. One of them returned later to free the others, though they were caught and returned."

"And executed." Jasper's voice was flat.

"Aye."

Ruddy shifted on his mat, an uncertain look on his face. "Your da, too?"

Talon nodded again.

No one spoke. Talon was not certain she could, not without weeping anyway, so she tried to take a bite of bread, but it tasted like ash. She shot a hesitant look at Kam, whose gaze was distant as she hugged her arms to her sides. "Your turn," Talon said quietly.

Kam gave a hollow chuckle. "I can hardly top that."

Before Talon could inquire further, Jasper rose shakily, using the low table as leverage. "I've heard the tale before. I'm calling it a night. Ruddy?"

"Good idea, I'm beat." Ruddy rose as well and bid the women good night.

Talon frowned after them and looked back at Kam. "They left their dishes."

The older woman began to collect the plates and remaining food. "It's all right. Jasper's in a great deal of pain, and Ruddy is just a lad."

"He could still help," Talon replied, reaching for Jasper's dish.

Kam only shrugged again. "I don't mind. You don't have to help, though."

Talon fingered her plate, then rose. "It will go faster, together."

"The One knows we don't have any time to waste."

Together, they cleaned and stored the dishes, then adjoined to their alcove and hammocks. As Talon toed off her boots, Kam pulled the curtain back to let a soft breeze steal through the little space. Talon folded her legs into the too-small hammock, not caring about being scrunched like a piece of discarded parchment because it was so *good* to be off her feet.

"Kam?" Ottis' voice rumbled through the makeshift barracks.

This made Talon sit up, smacking her forehead on the low stone ceiling. Kam rose as well and called, "Aye?"

"I'm real sorry, but Loach wants you to check the dam."

"What dam?" Talon asked her bunkmate. She could not keep the incredulity from her voice. "And why now?"

Kam sighed. "Loach does this, sometimes. It's at the base of the mine, underground. There's a warren of tunnels. No one else knows the way as well as I do."

Talon frowned. It was late and although the mine should be empty, she didn't put it past the guards or other workers to leave the smaller woman alone. "Do you need assistance?"

Kam's eyebrows rose, but she smiled. "Not really, but I could use the company. And it will make you more valuable to Loach if you know the dam as well." To Ottis, she called, "I'll head there as soon as I get my boots back on."

"Thanks, Kam," the big man called back, and his footsteps shuffled away.

As the women reached for their boots, Kam shot Talon a wry look. "You're not scared of the dark, by any chance?"

Talon tried to laugh, but another choking cough stole that sound, too.

*

Several minutes later, the two women slipped out of the makeshift barracks and made their way down the path that led to the mine's base. A few torches glowed at the mine's rim—the guards by the refinery, who never seemed to leave their post—but otherwise the mine was dark, laid bare to cold stars and the inky sky. Kam had a lantern but didn't light it with her tinderbox because the stars illuminated the path ahead. By now, Talon knew the way well enough not to stumble; she was too used to this place, already.

"There's underground rivers all over Aredia," Kam was saying as they went. "One of them had to be dammed up, so the powers-that-be could construct this delightful enterprise. The mine is fairly old, but the dam is older and not, shall we say, in the best shape of its life, so Loach likes to keep an eye on it to make sure it's not going to burst any time soon. Although I do think this," she gestured to the bowl of the open-pit mine, "would make a very pretty lake. Truth be told, I keep hoping that one day the wall *will* burst when I'm down there."

Talon could say nothing to that. They reached the base and Kam lit the lantern, then led her to the pitch-black tunnel entrance. However, Kam paused before stepping over the threshold. She seemed to be debating something, so Talon tried to offer an encouraging look, the sort she'd give a young recruit still finding her footing.

Kam toyed with the lantern's handle. "I broke my oath, too."

"I gathered as much."

"I had a daughter."

Talon could not keep the shock from her voice. "A daughter? How? Before you took the Burn, or...?"

"After." Kam clenched her jaw. "I was twenty summers old."

Talon shook her head. "I've never had my cycle, though I know of some female sentinels who did. But those women were few and far between."

"I don't know about them," Kam replied. "All I know is my daughter was a gift from the One, I'm sure of it. There is no other explanation for how I could have gotten pregnant. Especially since her father was a sentinel, too."

The lantern's flickering glow deepened the lines on Kam's face as Talon stared at her. "But...how?"

"I told you," Kam said in that patient, gentle way. "The One sent my little babe. When I told Jonas, he thought I was mad, too. He looked at me just as you are now. But I was right. I knew it then. I still do."

A flush crept up Talon's neck at being caught gaping like some burnie. "Forgive me, Kam. It's just...what you've told me...it's impossible."

"Evidently not."

"But the hematite–"

"Hematite is powerful," Kam broke in. "But the gods are more so." She looked at the sky again, dark eyes searching for something only she could see. "Say what you will, but truth is truth. Kali was a gift from the gods. Nothing less. Come on," she said, swinging the lantern toward the black mouth of the tunnel. "We shouldn't dally any longer."

NINETEEN

No doubt Flint looked like a moron with her eyes bulging, but for once, she didn't care. All she could do was gape.

The trees in this part of Redfern Province were, to her view, as tall as mountains and so thick around that a dozen men with linked arms couldn't circle the trunks. As Flint tugged along the stretcher that they had made to haul Beacon, she craned her neck, trying to make out the tops of the nearest giants. She didn't know anything about trees, but these looked like oaks who'd conquered and eaten their kin.

Branches, thicker around then most men were tall, curved into a dome high above, as if the city was cupped in a giant's palms. The province's distinctive red ferns covered the branches, along with great strands of gray, curling moss that hung like old men's beards.

"Think they touch the sky?" Mi's voice held only awe.

Flint's skin crawled, so she lowered her gaze to the road ahead. "I don't want to know."

Her squad-family had spent the last day and a half trudging across the thick forests of Redfern Province. The trip had taken longer than Stonewall had reckoned, partly because they'd had to rig up a way to carry Beacon and partly because everyone was still drained from Kali's healing magic. Now, after a long, exhausting day, Flint's body ached, her stomach growled, and she wanted nothing more than to collapse in bed for a week.

But although they had reached the city of Dilt, they still had to find a way inside.

Thank Tor and all the gods, not all the trees were behemoths. However, the surrounding forest was dense even now, at the edge of spring, when winter still held the northern provinces in its frosty grip. Aside from the trees, the underbrush seemed to be mostly thorny briars, or plants that would no doubt grant any unwary traveler a nasty rash.

The group paused at the base of two of the massive trees and Stonewall glanced at Beacon, who lay on the stretcher. "Where's the front gate?" the former sergeant asked.

Beacon gave a low cough. "Right in front of you."

Everyone looked, but Flint saw only trees, leaves, and lots of brambles. "What are you talking about?" she said to the mender. She tried to inject her usual bite into the words, but Beacon made it difficult to be cross with him when he looked so gray and sickly.

The copper-haired man's eyes were closed. "Ironwood," he muttered. "Blends in rather well, eh?"

"The gate is *made* of ironwood?" Kali asked.

"I thought ironwood was rare," Marcen added.

"It is now," Beacon replied.

Stonewall, who had taken point, strode to the nearest tree and—to Flint's satisfaction—withdrew his sword as if to cut through the underbrush. "I don't see anything. Perhaps–"

An unfamiliar male voice came from above. "I wouldn't do that if I were you, outsider."

A huge shadow passed overhead and Flint's guts twisted. The sound of flapping wings hit her just before the gust of displaced air as an ox-sized moth dove for the group. It was a testament to the sentinels' training—and the mages' tenacity—that no one shrieked in surprise.

Three massive, pale green moths, each with a rider, swooped into view and landed on the loamy forest floor, surrounding the squad. Nox's icy tits, the sheer size of the moths made Flint want to run screaming; their multifaceted eyes and bobbing, feathery feelers didn't help. And people *rode* the monsters like they were horses!

Out of sheer instinct, Flint went for one of her daggers, but Beacon stopped her. "Don't! They're allies."

"Who?" Flint, Stonewall, and the lead moth rider all spoke at once, and the mender sighed. The stretcher shifted as he struggled to sit up and face the moth riders, so Sadira and Milo went to assist.

Once Beacon was upright, the nearest rider leveled him with a glare. Or at least, Flint figured she was glaring, for she wore a leather helmet that obscured most of her features. It took Flint a moment to puzzle out her words, for her Aredian held a heavy drawl. "Who are you and what are you doing here?"

"My friends and I are here to see Amilcar Dilt." Beacon's reply took on a similar, if fainter drawl, one Flint had never heard from him before.

The woman frowned and glanced at her fellow riders. "Amilcar Dilt, eh? And who are *you*, to make such a request of our great and noble serla?"

"Don't you see the resemblance?" Beacon asked, tugging at his copper hair.

All three riders nudged their moths closer so they could get a better look at the mender. With the moths' wings flattened against their bodies, Flint could make out the wicked spears each rider carried in a holster beside their knees.

"Tell me your business with Serla Dilt," the first rider said. "Or I'll be cross. You won't like me when I'm cross."

"We don't much like you now," Flint muttered, causing Milo to snicker and Stonewall to shoot her a quelling look. She ignored the former sergeant and grinned at her twin, who chuckled again. It was a small laugh, but it heartened her to see Milo in good spirits.

The rider only shot the sentinels a brief glance before staring at Beacon. "Your business with Serla Dilt?"

Beacon grimaced. "I'm his son."

All three riders jerked in their saddles. The first stared at Beacon, her moth's eyes glittering in the filtered sunlight, and then she muttered something to one of her companions. The fellow nudged his mount, and another gust of air assaulted Flint and the others as the moth lifted from the ground, swooping toward the forest.

"Stay where you are," the first rider said to Beacon. "We must verify your claim."

The two groups waited in uncomfortable silence until something creaked from the direction of the trees, where Beacon had claimed there was a gate. Sure enough, the branches and brambles that Flint had mistaken for the forest itself swung open; they covered a large, ironwood gate. Two figures emerged. They shared Beacon's build, coloring, and features, but looked only a little older than the mender. Siblings, perhaps. A trio of personal guards followed them both. Flint could not help but notice the guards' swords looked fine, the scabbards embossed with twining gold leaves, while their leather gear gleamed in the dappled light. But weapons and gear all showed traces of use, which meant these were not purely decorative items.

Beacon's relations wore furs and fine velvet, all embroidered with vines, but none of it looked practical to Flint. They strode up to the stretcher and regarded Beacon. Both the man and the woman's faces were thin, almost as if someone had compressed their cheeks together. Both had pale eyes like Beacon, but theirs were cold and flat, without Beacon's warm humor.

Ea's balls, Flint thought, shuddering. *I must really feel sorry for the sod if I'm thinking like this.*

She was close enough to note how Beacon had tensed at the newcomers' approach, but his voice was chipper. He nodded first to the man, and then the woman. "Heitor. Renata. Nice to see you both. It's been a while. Where's Father?"

Renata crossed her arms before her chest. "Dead."

"A few days before Heartfire," Heitor added.

Beacon gaped between them. "How? What happened?"

Heitor and Renata exchanged glances before Renata answered. "Infection. He fell from his moth and gashed his leg. It never quite healed."

Beacon shook his head. "But...infections can be cured. Thalo gel alone could do the job, not to mention mages–"

"Thalo is hard to come by these days," Heitor interrupted. "And as for mages..." He spat on the ground. "We tried to bring some here, but Da refused to allow a moon-blood within the city walls, let alone in his own home. Can't say I disagree with him on that score. Magic couldn't save

Mother and our little brother, could it?"

Out of the corner of her eye, Flint saw Marcen shoot Kali a nervous look. Kali, though, remained expressionless as she listened.

Beacon seemed to accept this answer, though his jaw worked as if he were holding back an angry retort. "Why did you not write to me?"

"You're a sentinel," Heitor said. "We assumed you were occupied with more *important* matters. Besides, other than the odd letter, we'd not seen or spoken to you in nearly a decade."

"He's still my father," Beacon replied roughly. "*Our* father."

"You left after Mother died," Renata said, lifting her pointed chin. "You turned your back on your home, your family. You made your choice."

"Which brings us to now," Heitor added, sweeping his gaze up and down the stretcher. "What in Ea's realm happened to you? What are you doing with these mercenaries?"

Stonewall related the story they'd concocted. "We met your brother on the road and elected to travel together. He was gracious enough to lend his sentinel abilities to our little band of hired blades. Not two days ago, we encountered a group of thralls. Your brother fought bravely, but now he needs medical care. We'd hoped you could offer some assistance."

What little color was in Renata's face drained at the mention of thralls. "We've seen thralls near our borders."

"Seen, and fought," Heitor added. "I lost two good soldiers to those monsters. Did they pursue?"

"We weren't followed," Stonewall said in his most solemn tone, the kind Flint could not quite believe now that she knew him better. But the Redfern folk looked relieved, if not totally at ease.

"You're the leader of this outfit?" Heitor asked. When Stonewall nodded, the Redfern man swept his gaze over Kali, Marcen, and Sadira. "You're hired blades too? Where's your armor?"

Kali answered, shifting her viol case as she spoke. "We're not all mercenaries. My friends and I are troubadours. The thralls killed the rest of our party. These kind folks not only came to our rescue, but allowed us to travel with them, provided we pulled our weight."

"Hmm. Where's *your* instrument?" Heitor asked Sadira.

The Zhee mage spread her hands and spoke quickly in her native tongue. Flint didn't know a whit of Zhee, but Sadira got her point across. Heitor quirked an eyebrow but said no more.

"We're lucky to be alive, serla," Kali added. "And very thankful for your brother's aid."

"I suppose," Heitor replied, his eyes lingering over Kali a bit too long for courtesy.

Flint mentally rolled her eyes, but Kali gave Heitor a friendly smile. "We're a strange group, aren't we? But these are strange times we live in. Nothing is as it should be."

When she smiled at him, Heitor cleared his throat and squared his shoulders. "Oh...ah, well. Strange times. I suppose you're right, Ser... ?"

Kali's gaze darted up at the trees before she gave a short bow. "Green."

Flint snorted in an effort *not* to laugh, but, thank the gods, only Milo seemed to notice. He shot her a lifted brow but she shook her head and looked away from him, lest she laugh in earnest. Of course, in doing so, she glanced at Stonewall, who seemed to also be fighting the urge to roll his eyes.

Heitor Dilt, oblivious to anything but Kali, smiled back. "Welcome to Dilt, Ser Green." He looked at Beacon. "Well, Abernathy, you're here. I suppose you may as well remain until you're healed."

"You're just in time for the wedding," Renata added in a less-than-pleased voice.

Beacon's brows shot to his hairline. "Wedding? Yours?" When his sister nodded, Beacon grinned at her. "Svea finally making an honest woman of you, eh?"

Renata lifted a coppery brow. "Yes, and I'll have no lewd jokes out of you."

"Wouldn't dream of it," Beacon replied, chuckling. "You and Svea, married at last. Good. I always wanted another sister. Three's a lucky number, after all."

Renata gave a stiff nod and looked at Stonewall. "We'll send word to have the guest quarters prepared for you. I'm afraid you'll all have to share a couple of rooms. Every family member in the province is in town, along with as many Redfern folks as could make it."

"Redfern weddings are always cause for celebration," Beacon added wryly. "No one wants to be left out."

His siblings exchanged long-suffering glances. Stonewall bowed to Renata. "Thank you, Serla Dilt."

After discussing further details, Heitor muttered something to the guards, who stepped forward to take the stretcher from Flint and Marcen. Despite her exhaustion, Flint was unwilling to relinquish her brother-in-arms to strangers – not without a final question.

"Abernathy?" she murmured to Beacon. "Your birthname is...Abernathy Dilt?"

A flush crept up his face. "Aye."

She studied him: the aquiline nose; the copper scruff of hair on his cheeks and chin; the blue eyes still bright with hematite, but shadowed from exertion. How she'd hated him when she and Mi had first come to Whitewater City. This fine and dandy frip; a man who'd never known a moment of hardship while her own life had been nothing but.

He scowled at her. "Well? Go on. We both know it's a ridiculous name. Have at it."

She glanced at the retreating figures of his siblings, and then looked at her own brother, who stood by her side, who would always do so without question or hesitation, even when she did her best to drive him away. No, she could not mock Beacon. Not for his name, at least.

So she handed off the stretcher to one of the Redfern guards. "Take good care of him," she told the armored woman.

As the guards took Beacon's stretcher, he shot her a startled look, but she only nodded solemnly. That would confuse the hell out of him.

The squad passed through the ironwood gates and the forest closed all around, drawing them deeper into Dilt. If Flint could have overlooked the giant trees, the township wasn't that much different from any other she'd seen: there were dozens of similar communities that had sprung up around wealthy families like the Dilts. Most of the small shops, taverns, and other buildings, including what looked like a temple, were on the ground, amid dirt roads with grooves where carriages and wagons had made their way. Some structures, however, were carved into the body of fallen trees, so vast they each could have housed at least half the Whitewater garrison. A series of bridges, ramps, and walkways connected the fallen trees with each other and with the ground, creating another sort of canopy. And while the fallen trees looked to be oaks, every other structure, from ornate bridge to rough ladder, was carved of glinting ironwood.

There were flowers *everywhere.* Garlands festooned the walkways and streets, and bouquets hung from every window. Amid the natural beauty of the city were what seemed like hundreds of people, though surely that was Flint's renegade imagination. But the place was saturated; all the inns must have been full, for some folks had set up tents inside the alleys. Specific words were lost in the general din of the chatter, but anticipation hung in the air like the scent of the flowers.

When she caught the *clang* of the gates closing behind her, the hairs on the back of Flint's neck prickled. So many places for danger to lurk; so many unknowns, in general. And she and her friends walked so willingly into this city, where mages were unwelcome. She shot a glance at Kali to see if the other woman was distressed over this, but Kali, like Marcen, was too enchanted with the township to do more than gawk.

But Stonewall, who still walked a few paces ahead, was alert, his gaze darting from building to tree, his steps measured, one hand resting near a dagger; not enough to be considered an overt threat, but close enough so that he could grab the weapon quickly, should the need arise. Flint mirrored the former-sergeant's posture, determined to meet any danger head-on.

When she glanced beside her, to ensure Mi did the same, she found only an iridescent beetle— *bigger* than a sodding ox!—hitched to a wagon, waiting in front of a bakery while the wagon's driver unloaded sacks of flour. Flint's heart jumped and she nearly yelped in shock, but managed to suppress the un-sentinel-like response and instead turned around to find her errant twin. Why was everything in this place so fucking *huge*?

Naturally, Milo had found the most wretched person around and stopped to chat. Mi stood just outside the local temple, in deep conversation with a woman who looked like she'd been washed and left in the sun to dry a few too many times. Although Milo didn't look alarmed and could certainly defend himself against a single beggar, Flint could not leave him alone, so she murmured to Stonewall that she'd catch up and hurried to her brother's side.

In Flint's eyes, the beggar was ancient, perhaps in her late fifties, and her clothes were filthy and torn. She tugged Milo's cloak, her white eyes beseeching, and only when Flint came closer did she realize the woman was blind.

"...just a coin, serla," the woman was saying as Flint came near.

Milo bit his lip, a stricken look crossing his face. "I'm so sorry...I have no coin to give."

"Even for a glimpse into your past?"

A gleam of interest sparked in Milo's eyes as he exchanged glances with Flint, whose heart stuttered at the beggar woman's words. Perhaps she was a *hadashan*, a soul-seer; someone gifted with the ability to look into a person's past lives. Conversely, this woman might well be a charlatan preying on an easy mark. What unease Flint had felt before increased tenfold. She had to get her brother out of here.

"I'm sorry," Mi said again, and damn him, he really meant it.

"You're new," the *hadashan* replied, shaking her head. "The world will open at your feet. You simply have to step forward."

Flint touched Mi's arm, drawing his attention. "Come on." She jerked her chin at the rest of their squad, who still walked ahead. "We can come back later," she added when he opened his mouth to protest. "Beacon needs us now."

Nodding, Milo glanced back at the beggar. "The One keep you, ser."

She did not respond, only took a seat on the stone steps leading up into the temple, where within, Flint could make out white and black robed

190

Circle clergy milling like wasps. When Milo did not come along quickly, Flint pulled his good arm, for she suddenly felt a strange, desperate urge to get him away from the temple, the beggar, and any talk of past lives. Who knew how such nonsense would affect Milo's fragile state?

"Fine! Let go," Milo muttered. Even though he could have easily shaken her off, he merely trotted along.

Flint's heart tightened but she released him. "Come on. We don't want to get lost here."

"Lost. Right." Milo sighed, loud enough to reach her over the din of the streets.

They caught up with the others as the Dilt family guards led the squad through a series of ironwood gates toward one of the massive fallen trees, this one carved more ornately than any of the others they'd passed. This tree had fallen at an angle, resting on a stump the size of the One's temple back in Whitewater City. It was here that the guards paused, opening an ironwood door fixed into the stump, and ushered the squad inside.

Everything, from the benches at the sides, to the rounded windows, to the stairs leading up to the second level, was carved from the tree itself. After the chaos of the street the air was obscenely quiet, and smelled faintly of lavender. Flint stood with the others on the polished wood floor while the guards maneuvered Beacon toward the spiraling staircase.

"Abe?" The cry came from the second level, where a woman about Flint's age, with a tumble of copper curls, leaned over the balcony. "Abernathy! Gods above, what happened to you? Heitor's messenger said you were hurt, but he didn't say how badly."

"It's all right, Ida," Beacon called up, though his voice sounded strained. "I'm fine."

Ida all but flew down the stairs to Beacon's stretcher. "You don't *look* fine."

Beacon gave her a warm smile. "Your eyes lie, little sister."

She huffed, but was smiling too as she glanced at the others, her gaze lingering longest on Stonewall. "Oh, Renata said you had an escort, but she didn't say how many. Are any of you sentinels, too?"

191

"These are my traveling companions," Beacon said, not quite answering the question. He gave their names, and then added, "This is my younger sister, Idalina."

"Nice to meet you all," Idalina said, blushing when Stonewall bowed a greeting. "I've had rooms readied for you. Heitor said you all could sleep in the nearest midden heap," she added to Beacon, scowling. "But he's just being an ass, as usual. He and Ren were most put out that you interrupted the council meeting, and there's a wedding on top of everything else."

"Sorry to disappoint," Beacon replied. "Am I invited to the wedding?"

"Of course! Blood is blood, after all. Presuming you're fit to attend, that is." She knelt beside him and examined his bandage. "Mara's mercy, what *happened*, Abe? Have you been fighting thralls, too?"

"More or less," Beacon said. "I'll go into it all later, but..."

"Right." Idalina straightened and glanced at the guards. Despite her simple tunic and trousers, she had an air of nobility, just like Beacon. "Take him to his room—*carefully*—and then fetch Healer Vestain. He'll want to see to his older brother." She watched as they began to carry Beacon's stretcher up, then looked at the sentinels and mages. "Would you like to go to your rooms now? They're ready."

Out of habit, the sentinels glanced at Stonewall, who exchanged a look with Kali. Something passed between them, the wordless communication that Flint had observed on more than one occasion: the shared look of two people who knew each other well and trusted each other better.

"We'd like to go with Beacon," Kali said to the young woman. "If it's all the same to you, Serla Dilt."

Ida blinked at her. "Beacon...?" Spots of pink came to her round cheeks. "Oh, silly me. I always forget his sentinel name. Of course, you can come up with him. His room's large enough for you all to wait, though I'll have to ask that you stay out of the way while Vestain looks him over."

With that, she motioned them to follow and the whole group proceeded up the spiraling staircase, into the bulk of the tree stump itself.

Flint brought up the rear, in part because she wanted to watch their backs, and in part because her steps were slower than they should have

192

been. She had felt fine before, but now that they were—hopefully—out of immediate danger, every step was an effort and exhaustion threatened to sling her to the plush carpet at the top of the stairs.

What in the blazing void is wrong with me? she thought as she fought to keep pace with the others. Why was she so sodding tired? She ran through her mental checklist: she'd gotten enough sleep last night, she'd had a nice breakfast, and she and Mi had split a hunk of bread before reaching the city. She'd felt a tiny bit weak this morning, no doubt a remnant of Kali's magic, but that had faded. So what was going on?

The answer came to her in a flash. Hematite – or a lack of it. She was about due for another burn, and although she did not feel the driving, desperate need that Beacon had demonstrated, she sure felt the void it left.

Is this what it means, then, she thought with a scowl, *to be normal?*

"*Relah.*" It was Mi, touching her arm, looking at her with concern. One word, and she knew what he was asking, and what he always gave so freely.

She didn't deserve him. "I'm fine," she murmured. "Just tired."

He offered her his arm. She pulled a face but accepted. He smiled, and they continued through the Dilt family home.

TWENTY

Kali could not stop staring. Dilt was the most wondrous city she'd ever seen, and she wanted to see all of it, all at once. *Whole buildings carved from fallen trees!* She'd read about this part of Redfern Province before, but never dreamed she would visit. Everything smelled like wood, rich earth, and lavender. And though she could not shake her unease at Heitor Dilt's distrust of mages, for the moment she was too enthralled to care. Once Beacon was seen to, she resolved to explore the city to her heart's content, for there was no knowing when—or if—she would get this chance again.

The Dilt guards brought Beacon to a bedroom dominated by a massive bed frame carved from the tree itself. Under Idalina's watchful eye, they maneuvered the sentinel into the bed, and then scurried out to fetch Beacon's other brother and a list of supplies that Idalina rattled off.

"It's not that bad," Beacon said as his sister tugged up his shirt again to look at his wound. "You're fretting for nothing."

She clucked her tongue. "Healers make the worst patients. Vestain broke his ankle last midsummer and he acted more nonchalant than you. Now hush. Let me make my own judgment."

Beacon shot Stonewall a pleading look, but it was Kali who replied. "I'm something of a healer," she said, coming to stand with Idalina beside Beacon's bed. "I can help, if you'd like."

Idalina glanced at Kali, warm brown eyes filled with worry. "You're a troubadour *and* a healer, then?"

Heat crept to Kali's neck. *Damn me and my restless tongue!* If Heitor and

Renata hated mages, chances were their younger siblings felt the same way. But if anyone was to help Beacon, they had to know the extent of his injuries – and why those injuries were healed as much as they were.

So Kali gave her best casual shrug. "You pick up all sorts of skills on the road. I'm also an accomplished whistler, but I don't care to brag."

Idalina bent to examine Beacon's wound again. But while she did so, her fingertips crept quite close to the angry red edges and her expression was distant, as if her concentration was on something only she could see. However, soon her brows knitted and she glanced up at her brother. "When did you say you were injured?"

Beacon hesitated and Kali swore inwardly, but then the door burst open. Idalina jerked her hand back as another copper-haired man strode into the room, trailed by a guard and a servant, both laden with clean linens, herbs, and other medical supplies, which they began to set up. "Gods above, it's true," the newcomer said, rushing to Beacon's side, his face alight with joy. "You're back! You're really back!"

Beacon gave a weary smile. "Good to see you too, Ves."

"I'd hug you, but I fear that would be unwise." Vestain Dilt was perhaps Kali's age, in his mid-twenties, but he had the bearing of a much older man. Like his siblings, he was lanky, with a shock of bright coppery hair that fell into his eyes. Unlike his siblings, he wore the black and white cloak of the Circle clergy.

Without waiting for permission, Vestain examined the wound. "This is bad, Abe. I honestly don't understand how you're alive."

Beacon chuckled. "Aye. Hematite's a hell of a healing potion, isn't it? I'd recommend it for every injury, but it's got some dreadful side effects." He added a merry smile at his younger siblings, the sort that was no doubt meant to reassure. Kali silently pleaded with them not to question him further.

"I've read some fascinating texts on hematite's healing properties," Idalina said, a beat too quickly. "I suppose that explains how Abe's even talking to us now."

Vestain looked at his older brother again. "Well, from what I can tell, you've come back just in time."

"Will he be all right?" Flint asked.

Vestain nodded. "With rest and time, I believe so."

With that, the two younger Dilts began to fuss over their older brother, cleaning and examining his wound to further assess the damage. While they were engrossed, Beacon looked over their heads to catch Stonewall's gaze, and mouthed, *Sorry.*

Stonewall shook his head once, as if to say, *It's all right.* But he couldn't hide his agitation from Kali, who shared it.

But rather than dwell in anxiety, she tried to arm herself with knowledge. "I've never been to Dilt before. It seems the entire province has turned out for your sister's wedding."

Vestain threaded a needle while Idalina brought a candle over. As Vestain ran the needle through the flame, Idalina replied. "Something like that. Ren's a bit overwhelmed at the turnout, though I think everyone's eager for a distraction from this business with the thralls."

"Be still," Vestain scolded his older brother.

Beacon took a deep breath. Flint and Milo hurried to the bedside, each taking one of Beacon's hands in theirs. The sentinel mender shot them each a bewildered look, then the needle pierced his skin and his eyes squeezed shut, and his knuckles turned white from the force of his grip.

Kali hurried to keep the conversation going, if only to distract poor Beacon. "I'm sorry to hear about the death of your father. My father passed into his next life, about a year ago." Had it been a year already? Her breath caught. "I know how difficult it can be."

Vestain was concentrating, but Idalina stood back and gave Kali a tight smile. "Thank you. It was sudden. Sometimes I can't believe he's gone. But Heitor's the eldest, so Father left the running of the estate to him. He's done a fair job of it, though Renata has helped a great deal." She sighed. "Still, it takes the two of them together to equal Father."

"Well, *I* think they're doing all right," Vestain said as he stitched. "They're sending all those provisions to the afflicted border towns up north, after all."

"Aye, and meanwhile, our crops are sick and our own people are fleeing here from the outskirts."

"The crops aren't their fault, nor are the thralls," Vestain said as he drew back and handed the needle and remainder of the thread to his sister.

Idalina glanced back at Kali before she set the items aside. "Father was a great man, but misguided in a lot of ways. I'd hoped my older siblings could do better, but failing crops and thrall attacks are too much for them to handle. Even *you* must see that," she added to Vestain as she handed him a poultice and clean bandage.

Her brother sighed. "Aye, I suppose you're right. We're trying, but our clergy here can't handle the demand. Our focus must be on helping Whitewater Province–"

"Whitewater has its own resources," Idalina broke in. "What happened to taking care of our own?"

"Balance is the law of the One," Vestain replied calmly, slanting her a quelling look before glancing back at the sentinels. "If others need our help more, we are beholden to assist. Besides, I've requested aid from Lasath, but they're stretched thin with the thralls at the northern border."

"Ugh, this sodding war," Idalina said.

"It's not war," Vestain replied.

Idalina sighed. "Give it time."

No one spoke as Vestain applied an astringent poultice to the wound. Beacon flinched again, but Milo and Flint held firm, and Kali smiled at the twins' determination to keep their brother-in-arms as calm as possible. No doubt Beacon had done the same for both on multiple occasions.

"Regardless, it's good of your family to send aid where you can," Stonewall said to Idalina. "Compassion is always the right choice."

The young woman shrugged, blushing despite her attempt at nonchalance. "Father always insisted on taking care of one's home *and* one's neighbors. The provincial governor is of the same mind, and has insisted that all of the higher-tiered families offer as much aid as they are able."

Stonewall gave her a warm look, and Kali caught the tenor of his intention before he spoke. "Even so, I'm sure your people are grateful." His next words were careful. "But surely, a mage or two here would ease the Redfern Circle's burden."

A slight gamble, perhaps, but he had estimated right. Idalina's face fell and her gaze fixed on the floor. "Father never would have allowed mages through our gates. He has—had—a fierce hatred of them after Mother died in childbirth, even though that was well over a decade ago."

"That's a shame," Stonewall said. "I've seen mages do many good deeds."

Idalina's gaze lifted, but Vestain snorted as he reached for a clean bandage. "That may be, but mages are not to be trusted. No one should have that much power at their command. It throws the balance of the One's world off-kilter."

"But maybe Ser Stonewall is right," Idalina said, brow furrowed. "Maybe we could contact Redfern Bastion and–"

"Even if we could change Heitor and Ren's minds," Vestain broke in. "It would be too dangerous to bring mages here. Let the sentinels worry about them, I say, and let us worry about our crops and our families. Besides," he added as he secured the bandage. "Who's to say the mages wouldn't make things worse? I've heard talk that they're responsible for the thralls. What if, by bringing mages here, we bring *more* thralls? What then?"

"Mages aren't creating thralls," Kali said. Everyone looked at her so she quickly added, "So I've heard."

"It's true," Beacon managed between sucked breaths.

"Well, you'd know, wouldn't you?" Vestain said. Idalina caught Kali's gaze, but looked away at once.

The worst seemed to be over, so Beacon's voice was less pained. "What's wrong with the crops?"

"The blue glories are sick," Idalina said as she began to clean up the items her brother had used. "They're not fruiting like they should."

"We hardly got enough of any mushroom crop to break even, this last harvest," Vestain added as he sat back, admiring the crisp bandage around Beacon's midsection.

"It's that horrible tar-mold," Idalina said. "Except now it's more persistent and widespread than it's ever been. I'm starting to worry we'll have to cull whole crops. It's even spread to some of the beacon moths."

Beacon moths? Kali thought, glancing at the copper-haired sentinel.

He shot her a quick, wry look before addressing his sister. "Is Lumi one of the sick ones?" Idalina nodded and his face fell.

She ducked her head. "I'm sorry. I've done all I can."

"Thank you," Beacon replied. "It's just...I knew coming home wouldn't be all sugar and honey, but I wasn't prepared for..." He made a vague gesture. "So much bitter."

Vestain leaned forward, resting his elbows on his knees. "The One god willing, this too will pass. I believe the crops and such feel worse because everyone is spun in circles with the wedding preparations. I'm ready for this sodding thing to be over with so we can focus on important matters again."

Beacon opened his mouth to speak, but his sister shushed him. "No. You need your rest." She glanced at the squad. "We should leave him for now. I'll show you to your rooms."

"Thank you," Kali said. "But if it's all the same, I'd really like to get a look around the township. Maybe see these mushrooms?"

"You *also* have skill with growing things?" Idalina replied.

Kali thought of the jessamin vines and tried to look demure. "A little."

Idalina hesitated, then Stonewall cleared his throat. "I'd like to have a look as well, though I'm just curious. No skill to speak of, unless you want something cut to pieces."

He added the equivalent of a mental wink, for Kali's benefit, and she had to fight to keep from chuckling aloud. The other sentinels and Marcen chimed in with similar sentiments, though Sadira only stood by the window, gazing outside.

Idalina still looked uncertain, but Vestain seemed pleased. "We should take what help we can," he said to his sister. "But I really must get back to the temple. We need every hand to ready those supplies for Whitewater. Would you show our guests around?"

She nodded. "Of course. Thank you for coming so quickly when you're busy."

He stood and kissed her head. "Happy to help. And you," he added, pointing to Beacon. "Stay in that bed, or I'll drug you, myself."

A clearly amused Beacon lifted a brow. "Now, that's a most ungentlemanly threat. Valerian or bucksbalm?"

"Well, you're my elder brother and the reason I became a healer," Vestain replied. "So I'd let you choose. But mark my words: stay in bed, or else."

With that, he swept out of the room, white and black robe fluttering in his wake. Beacon watched him go before he looked at his sister. "Good to see that the Circle has kept him humble."

She giggled. "He's insufferable, sometimes, but he's pleased you're here. We both are."

"Glad someone is," Beacon muttered, though he smiled up at his younger sister. "Will you show them the canopy as well? You'll love it," he added to the twins, who still stood by his side.

"I'll show them everything," Idalina promised. "But *you*–"

"Must rest," Beacon broke in. "Yes, yes. No need to flog that dead horse any longer."

Idalina blew a raspberry at him, and then gestured to Stonewall and the others. "Come along. We've a bit of daylight left. May as well put it to good use."

"If you don't mind," Milo said to the young Dilt woman. "I'd like to visit the nearest temple."

"I'm sure Ves will be glad to have you," Idalina replied.

"Mind if I come too, Mi?" Flint asked.

He beamed at his sister. "I'd like that."

"What about me?" Marcen asked.

Milo replied without hesitation. "You're welcome to join us, Mar."

As the group filed out, Kali realized Sadira was not with her. She glanced back to see the Zhee mage watching her from beside the window, an unreadable look on her face. Kali frowned. "Aren't you coming?"

Sadira shook her head. "I will remain and keep eyes on him."

Beacon's cheeks went pink. "Ah…that's not necessary. I'm a big boy."

"I will remain," Sadira said again, and her tone put an end to the discussion.

But as Kali slipped out of the room, she looked back at her friend once more. This time, she recognized the look on Sadira's face: fear.

*

The temple swarmed with Circle clergy, their white and black robes fluttering enough to make Flint dizzy. She and Marcen stood just outside the temple, doing their best to keep away from the activity. Milo was already inside, having bounded through the door the moment they arrived and offered aid to the first person he'd seen. One of the priestesses had directed him toward a pile of grain sacks meant for a wagon waiting outside, and after he'd explained his limitations, she had offered to load up his right side.

Milo's movements were keen and rapid, the first time they'd been so since his injury. More importantly, there was a brightness in his eyes that Flint had not seen in too long. Gods above...when was the last time he'd looked so genuinely happy?

"You don't want to go in?" Marcen's voice startled her from her trance.

"I'm not feeling very pious right now. Besides, doesn't look like there's much room in there to pray."

"Well, *I'm* curious," he admitted, looking back inside. "I've never been to a temple before."

"Never? Not even before you..." Her cheeks burned. "Before you came to a bastion?"

But Mar only rocked on his heels, seemingly at ease amid the chaos not ten paces away. "I learned long ago not to push my luck unless absolutely necessary. Even before the sentinels caught me, I stayed away from the Circle and all their trappings. But I'm still curious." He shot her a knowing look. "I suppose I'm just drawn to danger."

Flint flushed again, for there was no mistaking the meaning behind his words. But she didn't have a drop of coy in her blood and refused to simper, so she lifted her chin and stared down his pale blue eyes. "In my experience, danger will find you whether you avoid it or not."

"Oh, I'm counting on it."

Milo passed by, laden with sacks, and shot Flint a reproving look. "You're just going to stand there? They need help, *relah*."

"They might not want *everyone's* help," Flint replied, nodding to Marcen.

This made Milo stop in his tracks, as if heedless of what was surely a heavy load, and Flint couldn't suppress a thrill of envy at his sheer strength. Though he could not grip with his left hand, he could use the hand to balance the sacks on his right shoulder. He made carrying the weight look easy.

"His mark's gone," Milo whispered.

"He still shouldn't risk it," Flint began.

But Marcen was shaking his head. "I'm here. May as well go inside. Besides," he added with a shrug, "I'll draw more attention by standing around while others are hard at work."

Milo beamed and nodded toward the elder priestess he'd dealt with before. "Nisha will get you sorted out. She's lovely."

And with that, he hustled down the stairs and toward the waiting wagon, chattering away to the priests already there.

"Good to see him in better spirits," Marcen said. "I didn't know him well before our escape from Whitewater Bastion, but he always seemed like a pleasant enough fellow."

"Not like me," Flint replied, only a little in jest.

The mage looked at her and she could not read the expression on his face. "No," was all he said before slipping inside the temple. Unwilling to be left behind, Flint hurried after.

Within was organized chaos as Circle clergy prepared whatever goods they'd collected to send up north. The humble temple was built into the side of one of the great, fallen oak trees. No elaborate bronze statues or crystal sculptures adorned the plain wooden altar, but there were murals painted on the walls and ceiling: trees, flowers, and animals, all mimicking the forest outside. Currents of rosewood and sage wafted on the breeze that swept in through the open door, but the overwhelming scent was too many bodies in close quarters. As Milo had said, the priestess called Nisha was pleased at the prospect of two more pairs of hands, and immediately set them to hauling sacks of dried goods with Milo.

Although the task was not as exciting as combat or as invigorating as sex, Flint lost herself in loading supplies into the waiting wagons. The Circle folk did not look upon her, Milo, or Mar as anything other than normal people offering to help, which made them all act nice enough.

Mostly, she watched her twin. Milo grew more animated with each trip outside, and by the time the wagons were loaded, he had everyone around him grinning – and not at his expense. His eyes were bright and merry, and gods above, he beamed like she'd not seen in too long.

After the wagons were loaded, Nisha waved Milo, Flint, and Marcen over. "Fine work," she said to them, her dark eyes crinkling with her smile. "Would that we had strong backs like yours all the time."

"If you need us, we can return tomorrow," Milo replied

Flint shook her head. "Mi, we might not be able to."

"Why not?"

Flint ground her teeth, trying to think of a reply that wouldn't give away their mission. "We should at least check with Stonewall, first."

"He won't mind." Milo brightened. "He might even want to join us. Our sergeant is a pious man," he added to Nisha. "Well, former–"

Flint jabbed his side before he could give them all away.

"I heard a group of hired blades escorted Serla Abernathy back home," Nisha replied. "Tell me, how bad was his injury?"

News travels on rapid wings, Flint thought, grimacing. This interaction had gone on too long; they needed to leave before someone said the wrong thing. "Pretty bad," she said. "Actually, we really should be getting back. Right, Mi?"

Milo gnawed his lip but nodded, then offered Nisha a low bow. "Thank you for letting me help."

The priestess smiled up at him. "I should be thanking you. It's not often we have enthusiastic—and strong—aid such as yours. I only wish you could stay. Or, better yet, join Caron and the others on their journey north." She sighed. "I fear it will be dangerous, with so many thralls about. But we cannot let our fellow Aredians go without aid."

"Well, you're doing good work," Flint said. "I'm sure those folks up north will appreciate everything." She tugged Mi's right arm, but he ignored her.

"I wish I could do more to help you there," he said to Nisha. "But I'm not much good to anyone these days. I got injured," he added at her curious look, rubbing his left shoulder.

Her face softened and she rested her hand upon his left forearm. "Yet you aided us without reservation. Milo, in the eyes of the One, you are perfect. Remember that, if you remember nothing else." She smiled and lifted her hand. "Know also that the One guides your steps, always. The One will bring you where you need to be."

"Thanks," Flint said, pulling Milo along. "Come on," she muttered.

But her twin stood frozen, staring at the priestess as if seeing her for the first time. "When are Caron and the others leaving?"

Flint's heart sank without quite knowing why. She tried to urge Milo again, but the sodding lout stood as firm as one of the giant fucking oak trees. Marcen gave her a concerned look, but she ignored him. All that mattered was Mi.

Heedless of Flint's turmoil, Nisha only smiled at Milo. "The day after the wedding. Would you like to join them?"

"He can't," Flint said, just as Milo answered, "Yes, please."

Her stomach plummeted and her palms pricked with sweat. She and Milo exchanged a startled look; within his eyes was that odd mixture of confusion and hope that he so often wore. But as they regarded each other, she saw something else: that shadowed, haunted expression that had plagued him since…since that first terrible battle at Parsa. And though she could not read his thoughts—nor would she ever want to—she knew what he wanted, and what he would want her to accept.

But the very thought made tears sting her eyes. Would he really leave her?

Flint read the answer in his eyes, but hated it. "You should at least talk to Stonewall, first," she managed.

Milo's expression softened and he nodded, and looked back at Nisha. "May I come back later?"

The priestess regarded him fondly. "You are always welcome here, Milo."

TWENTY-ONE

A n hour after leaving Beacon's room, Kali stood among a throng of mushrooms that grew upon a branch of one of the massive, fallen oak trees. Some mushrooms splayed like open palms, nestled together and colored in quiet, earthy tones of warm brown, ivory, and rusty red. Another sort boasted bulbous, round heads atop slender stems, in frothy pale blues and lavenders mottled with specks of white. But sticky black speckles, carrying a foul scent, had ravaged several sections of the fungi, and would probably spread to the rest if left unchecked.

The province's distinctive red ferns grew here as well, but had been relegated to the perimeters of the mushrooms' allotted space. These ferns towered over Kali and added another layer of sheltering boughs in addition to the leafy, mossy dome of the branches above. Sunlight trickled through, dappling the world. Despite the foul mold, Kali had an overwhelming desire to place her bare palms against the branch, to run her fingers through the ferns…anything to get a closer, *better* sense of this wondrous place. Disease dwelt here, but life and beauty did too.

Stonewall stood at her side, surveying the area while Idalina detailed the situation. "There haven't been any new pests. And it was a fairly mild winter – not too damp. As far as I can tell, there isn't any reason for the mold." A wistful look crossed her face. "If only we could get some *real* mages to take a look."

Carefully, Kali said, "It's a shame your siblings won't allow it."

"They have their reasons," Idalina said quickly. She crouched beside one of the larger mushrooms, smoothing her palms over the bulbous cap. Her

206

TWENTY-ONE

gaze grew distant, as if she was concentrating very hard, and then she sighed. "Poor things," she murmured, almost to the fungus itself. "I wish I could do something to help them." She looked over at Kali. "Any ideas?"

Heat rushed to Kali's face. She'd put herself in a stupid—and potentially dangerous—position. To work magic, she first needed to assess the mushrooms' particles, but the act of doing so would surely identify her as a mage.

But Stonewall was her hero – as ever. He caught the beat of her thoughts and cleared his throat. "Perhaps we could let Kali look around a bit before she makes an assessment. But, if you don't mind, I have a few questions."

"Oh...of course, I'm happy to tell you whatever you like," Idalina said, flushing beneath his gaze. "What do you want to know?"

Stonewall carefully stepped through the nearest huddle of blue and white mushrooms to Idalina. "There are so many different kinds," he began. "How can they all live together in harmony?"

"What do you know of crops?"

"Mostly the part where I eat them."

Idalina gestured to the mushrooms. "Fungi are marvelous beings. Rather than compete for resources, as would something like wheat or potatoes, they are able to form a symbiotic relationship with everything around them – including one another. What nutrients these," she gestured to the splayed-hand mushrooms, "favor is different than the sort that those prefer." She pointed to a cluster of purple and white fungus. "So they can all exist upon the tree together, in harmony."

"You make them sound like living creatures," Stonewall said, and there was no small amount of admiration in his voice.

Kali missed Idalina's reply, for she'd crouched to examine the nearest cluster of pale blue mushrooms, all of which bore the sticky, black mold. She placed her fingertips upon the cap, closed her eyes, and concentrated on the particles within. Yes, there was a sickness there, but a slow sort. Injuries usually left a being's particles fast-moving and agitated. However, this mold clung to its hosts like a bitter aftertaste and stagnated their growth. Left untreated, the mold would leech away each mushroom's energy.

But how to cure them? She sifted through her memories, searching for any useful information. A sudden fear struck her, so she delved her concentration back into the mushroom's particles, searching for a foreign presence like the one she'd found in thralls – just in case there was a connection. But, thank the stars and moons, there was no trace of the Fata here. But perhaps she could apply the same method of curing thralls to the mushrooms: an infection to be burned away.

Kali focused on the mold's particles—sluggish and syrupy, like the slime trail left by a snail—and drew upon her own energy to heat them. Just a bit. Just enough.

She was careful, perhaps too much so, for when she looked again, the moldy spot she'd been focusing on had not changed. But further examination of the mold's particles showed her that even that small effort had been enough to stop this bit from spreading. Good news, but it would take considerable energy, not to mention *time,* to burn away all the nasty stuff.

A handful of powerful mages could succeed here, but given the Dilt family's opinion of magic-users, that probably wouldn't happen. Maybe, if Kali poured all her energy into the task, she could at least clear the mushrooms in the immediate area, but that would kill her as certainly as a fall from this height.

"Well, Ser Green? What do you say?"

So absorbed was she in her musings that Kali nearly did not answer her false name. Thankfully, a mental prod from Stonewall jerked her back to reality, so she stood up, slowly, and gave Idalina a rueful smile.

"You need mages," Kali replied. "Ideally a team of them – maybe even half a dozen, if your siblings could bear to have so many nearby."

Idalina's shoulders slumped. "I was afraid you'd say that."

"Your family really won't tolerate mages' help?" Stonewall asked, coming to stand by Kali's side.

"Magic is dangerous," Idalina replied, as if by rote. "And my family is more stubborn than oxbeetles." Her voice turned speculative. "*Maybe* I could petition for one or two mages to be brought here, but even that would be a battle."

Stonewall exchanged a look with Kali, and she did not need a projection of thought or emotion to get her disappointment across. To the young woman, she said, "Then I fear you'll need to find another solution."

Idalina rubbed her right wrist, her expression troubled. "Magic. It's the problem *and* the solution."

How right she was. What would it take for people to understand that magic didn't have to be dangerous and evil? Kali spoke without thinking. "In *some* ways, perhaps. But the fact remains: if you want to save these crops, you need magical intervention."

Idalina sighed. "I know."

A shadow passed overhead and Kali, thankful for the momentary distraction, craned her neck to find the source.

"What's wrong?" Stonewall asked, reaching for a dagger.

Kali pointed up. "See that?"

He squinted. "Oh! That's one of the giant moths."

"Aye. Aren't they incredible?"

"You didn't seem that fond of them when they met us at the front gate."

"Neither did you. Besides, I was just surprised. Can you imagine what it's like to *fly*?" *Eris is so lucky,* she added silently.

He looked up again, tracking the moth's progress through the canopy, and then glanced back at her. Now his face was open as a boy's, and his emotions fairly sparkled with the same awe reflected in her own heart. "I'd like to do more than *imagine*."

Idalina grinned between them. "That can be arranged. Follow me – unless you're afraid of heights."

*

Stonewall ran his fingertips over the beacon moth's abdomen, savoring the fuzzy texture of the pale green coat. The moth regarded him with iridescent, multifaceted eyes and the feathery feelers wavered with his touch. The creature was easily the size of a horse, but he felt no twist of fear in his gut when standing so close. No fear, only an urge to be *flying*.

He, Kali, and Idalina were in the "stable." Built into the upper canopy of one of the massive living trees, the stable's thatched roof and scavenged wood sides sheltered its inhabitants from the elements. Some outside light penetrated the roomy space, but most of the illumination came from the moths themselves. Idalina had said the beacon moths were so named because they produced some sort of phosphorescence within their bodies, so each one emanated light from either its rear or its abdomen. The moth Stonewall stood near had a glowing belly, casting the immediate area in a soft, cool glow.

Kali and Idalina stood together beside one of the other beacon moths, whose wings pressed tight to its body while its feelers sagged. Its glow was faint, almost indiscernible. Stonewall could not make out the women's murmured conversation, but Kali's thoughts were focused entirely on the creature before her. She would heal Beacon's beloved mount, one way or another.

Indeed, he could sense her determination as clearly as the light emanating from the beacon moth before him. Nothing could stop Kali when she'd set her mind to a task, but he feared the cost. Not just to her, but to their entire party, if she was outed as a mage.

Kali, take care, he sent her.

I am, she sent back, an edge of petulance in the reply. *But Stone... They're so sick, just like the crops. If I can help–*

You risk endangering yourself and the rest of us, he interrupted. The moth beneath his palm shifted; he forced himself to relax. *You must be careful.*

Trust me, was her only reply. Stonewall glanced over at her and the Dilt woman, only to see Kali kneeling before the moth, eyes closed, face slack in the way it got when she worked her magic. Silently cursing, he cleared his throat to draw Idalina's attention away from the mage.

Idalina looked up at him, but her gaze immediately slid back to Kali, and Stonewall's heart seized when he caught the spark of recognition in the Dilt woman's face. *Shit!* He left the moth's side to move closer to them, mentally assessing the stall and how quickly he could usher Kali outside if

Idalina called her guards. His hand crept toward one of his daggers.

But Idalina only watched Kali in wonder. The moth that Kali was healing fluttered its massive, pale green wings and lifted its feelers. Idalina sucked in her breath and placed her own palms against the creature's side. Then Kali exhaled and stepped back, and gave the other woman a small smile.

"She'll be fine," Kali said quietly. Through the bond she and Stonewall shared, she said, *I'm sorry.*

He had to bite his tongue to keep from cursing aloud. *Save your sorries for Mar and Sadira.*

"You're a mage," Idalina whispered to Kali.

Kali lifted her chin. "So are you."

Idalina looked at her hands, stained with dirt and grime. "Only a little bit."

Stonewall gaped. *How did you know?*

I had a hunch, Kali sent back, and he moved his hand away from his dagger as she placed her palm on Idalina's shoulder. "You have an affinity for this place," Kali said. "This forest; these creatures. But your abilities are *more.*"

Idalina nodded, biting her lip. "But I never hurt anyone! And I have nothing to do with the thralls, or the illness to our crops, I swear!"

Kali gave her a sad smile. "I know. But it's not safe for you here. Your siblings–"

"They're harmless," Idalina broke in.

"Heitor hates mages," Kali said. "And if he's the head of your family now… "

But Idalina was already shaking her head. "Blood is blood. Heitor won't harm me. Besides, this is my home. I can't leave. I *won't.*"

"There's a whole world out there–"

"*My* world is here." Idalina took a deep breath and met Kali's eyes. "You said a team of mages could help the mushrooms. Would the two of us be enough?"

Kali went still and true *fear* swam through the bond she shared with Stonewall. It filled his belly with rocks and his veins with ice, and though he fought against the feeling, he could not entirely shake it. Because there was *fear*, yes, but there was also an eagerness, a *hunger* that he likened to the kind he still felt for hematite. She seemed to be able to control the feeling around other mages…until she took part in an exchange of power. He stared at her in the dim light but did not see the *Kali* he knew so well; memory painted a thrall in her place, eyes burning like stars, eager to take what was so freely offered.

No, Kali, he sent, desperately, but she ignored him.

And in the back of his mind, as if rousing from a long sleep, Tor's voice beckoned. *She will be lost, my son. Do you see? She is not for you. She never was. Come home, Elan.*

No, he thought, shaking his head as if to clear it. *You may be a god, but you're wrong.*

Heedless of this, Kali only studied the Dilt woman. "A couple of mages could help *some* of the mushrooms," she said carefully. "Not all. You really do need more than the two of us."

"Are any of your friends mages?"

Stonewall saw an opening and leaped in before Kali could answer. "Just Kali," he replied, causing both women to start, as if they'd forgotten he was there.

"But I'll do what I can," Kali added.

Idalina was already nodding. "Good. Fine. I'll do whatever it takes." Perhaps on a whim, she grabbed Kali's hand. "My magic is sparse, but please let me help you, if I can."

"Kali," Stonewall said, putting a hand on her shoulder. "Take care. You *must* take care."

They all stood stock-still a moment, Kali caught between them, before she looked into Stonewall's eyes. "Trust me," she said, and slipped out of his grip to follow Idalina out of the stable.

*

Stonewall's stomach was in knots. He stood among the blood-red ferns

212

again, keeping one eye out for any intruders and keeping the other on the woman he loved. Kali and Idalina knelt beside the largest mushroom, which Idalina said would be the easiest way to reach the others, given how they were all connected. Both mages' eyes were closed and their hands were linked. Neither woman looked distressed, nor was Kali as...eager as she'd been in the past when borrowing magical energy from a fellow mage. But she could not hide her elation at the flow of power; in response, his skin prickled and the hairs on the back of his neck stood at attention.

Gritting his teeth, Stonewall clamped down on his emotions, forcing himself to ignore the pleasure Kali emanated. Certain that no one else was nearby, he looked back at the mushroom. The black mold was already fading, a faint line of smoke trailing into the air, leaving an acrid burning scent. Idalina's skin seemed gray and she braced her free hand on the branch below her knees. By contrast, Kali's face was flushed, and exhilaration sparkled through the bond she and Stonewall shared. There was no pain within her, only joy. A part of him, one he ought to have been ashamed of, wished she could always feel that way, regardless of the price.

So it was with some reluctance that he reached through their bond and tried to rouse her. If he started now, before she had taken too much energy from the other mage, he could stop her before it was too late. She didn't respond to him, but he'd expected that, though that fact alone screamed a warning in his mind. This was normal now.

Kali, he tried again. *Stop.*

More of the black mold dissipated, burned to nothing. The largest mushroom was free of it now and the others nearby were on their way. Idalina slumped a little more, her breath coming slower, while Kali exhaled softly in delight.

Stonewall gripped his daggers hard enough to make his hands ache, but the pain only reminded him that he was helpless while she was in the throes of her magic. Again, he tried to reach her through their bond, but again she did not respond. All her attention was on the river of magic flowing from Idalina to her, sapping Idalina's will as well as her energy. True fear gnawed at his heart. Could he stop Kali before she killed this woman?

"Kali," he said aloud, gripping her shoulder and giving a small shake when she *still* did not react. "Kali, stop it. *Kali.*"

Nothing changed, so he snatched her hand free of Idalina's, hoping to break the flow of magic. Immediately, Idalina collapsed onto her palms, her eyes glassy.

Kali's eyes rolled back into her head and her chin tilted up, revealing the scar on her throat as she laughed aloud. He still could not reach her. Nothing for it now. Stonewall grabbed her by both shoulders and shook, shouting her name. Just as he was preparing to slap her, dark eyes opened and she gasped as if breaching the surface of a wave.

"Elan!"

Stonewall's fear burned itself to cold anger, leaving him frozen to his bones. He lowered his trembling hands and turned away from her, both to collect himself and to check on the other woman – the other *mage*. Idalina was alive and conscious, but only just. How in the blazing void was he going to explain her state?

A soft touch against his side made him tense. "Stonewall? Is she–"

"Alive," he snapped, glancing over at Kali, who now knelt beside him. "Barely."

Kali's flushed cheeks went a little paler at his words, but her eyes were still bright with magic. "I was going to stop."

"Were you?"

"Of course." She drew herself upright in a painless, fluid motion, and his foolish heart lifted at the ease of her movements. She went to examine the nearby mushrooms, each step graceful and smooth. "You're overreacting."

Stonewall lifted Idalina, who stirred in his arms, mumbling wordlessly. He took a deep breath before speaking again. "You can't hide from me, Kali. I *felt* you lose control."

She glared at him over the tops of the newly healed mushrooms. "You don't understand. I was *going* to stop. I just needed–"

"I understand enough," he broke in. "You're starting to sound like Beacon with that sodding hematite."

Anger pulsed through their bond and her hands clenched into fists at her sides. "That's completely different."

Rather than reply, he ensured his grip on Idalina was sound before making his way to the walkway that would take them down to the fallen oak, where Idalina's family lived. Kali remained among the mushrooms and ferns, watching his progress. Only when he reached the steps leading down to the walkway did she speak again.

"I *was* going to stop."

He paused and met her gaze. "Third time you've made that claim. Who are you trying to convince?"

Kali didn't respond.

*

Thank Mara, Idalina started to come to before Stonewall reached the Dilt family living quarters. Not only was it a tricky business to navigate the sloping, wooden walkways while carrying her, he had no wish to explain to anyone *why* he was carrying her in the first place.

At her request, he paused before they reached the house. "Are you certain you can walk?" he asked as he set her on her feet.

Idalina fell forward but caught herself on the tree. "I'm fine," she murmured, pressing her cheek to the bark.

She certainly didn't *look* fine, but he was done playing nursemaid to mages, so he only offered his arm. "Would you like some help getting to your room?"

Warm brown eyes met his and faint spots of color returned to her cheeks. "Yes, please," she managed. "Thank you."

Though Idalina was taller and sturdier than Kali, there was a grace to her steps even in her drained state. Her clothes were utilitarian and there was dirt beneath her nails, but she was, at her core, a third tier. Far removed from a guttersnipe like him.

A pair of guards stood before the entrance to the house proper: a hatch built into the side of the tree. Neither guard gave Stonewall more than a cursory glance, though both immediately snapped to attention upon seeing the youngest Dilt sibling.

"Serla! Do you need assistance?"

Stonewall swore mentally, for he'd not been able to come up with a suitable explanation for her state. But she only smiled at the guards with familiar ease. "No, thank you." She patted Stonewall's arm. "I was just showing off the grounds, but I must rest before the feast tonight."

This seemed to suffice, for neither guard did more than nod and hold open the hatch, allowing Stonewall and Idalina to duck inside. The sun had started to set, so servants had lit sconces and lamps along the walls, casting the carpeted corridor in a golden glow.

Stonewall wracked his brain for something innocuous to fill the silence. "How are the wedding preparations?"

Idalina wrinkled her nose. "We've only two days to go, and I'm ready for it to be done. I'm not looking forward to the dress Renata had made for me, but it will look nice. I suppose that's the point." She tugged her worn tunic. "I don't much care for silk dresses and slippers. Give me my sturdy leather boots any day."

"I imagine the slippers and silk have their places, though I can't say I've ever had much use for either."

She cast a shy smile his way. "I think you'd look...rather fetching without your armor."

Perhaps she'd not meant for the comment to sound so saucy, for she slapped her hand over her mouth. Stonewall's face burned and he dropped her arm. He'd not meant to give her the wrong impression, but had fumbled that, too.

"Forgive me, Stonewall," Idalina said, touching her forehead as if to hide her face. "I'm more tired than I realized. I spoke without thinking."

"It's all right," was all he could think to say. "I know what you meant."

She peeked at him through a tumble of copper curls. "Do you?"

As he regarded her, he could not help but consider the shape his life could take. The possibility unfolded before him, like a blanket shaking out onto meadow grass. He could remain here, pledge himself to the Dilt family in service, perhaps strike up a courtship with this lovely young woman who had shown an interest in him. Life would be simpler, perhaps even easy.

But life would be hollow without the woman he loved. Despite his anger with Kali, even the idle fantasies of parting permanently from her side filled him with bitter sorrow.

Stonewall inclined his head in the direction of Idalina's rooms. "You must get some rest, Serla Dilt. You're exhausted."

The use of her title revealed his true heart. Her cheeks pinked again, but she nodded and continued. Neither spoke for the final few minutes it took to navigate to her room. He did not remember bidding Idalina good evening, nor how his steps carried him from her room back outside, where he found a place out of sight of the guards and tried to reach Kali through their bond. But she did not respond to his silent call, though he sensed her ignoring him. That realization cut to the quick.

But they'd parted in anger. Perhaps they both needed some breathing room before they could make amends. That in mind, he pushed away from the great tree. His squad-mates were hopefully still at the local temple; he would join them and lose himself in service to the greater good.

TWENTY-TWO

E ris alighted upon the rock, fluffing her feathers against the chill,
pre-dawn wind. Seren's light, Stonehaven Province was such
a *nothing* part of the world: dry and cracked as a callus. The
only interesting bits were the massive, rust-red rock formations scattered
around the landscape; twisted hunks of earth reminiscent of gnarled hands.
Distant mountains loomed, wreathed in haze, and every breath parched
her throat.

Her crow-eyes peered down at the rocky outcropping she'd landed upon.
Large boulders laid in a semicircle provided a meager shelter from the
wind, but none from what would soon be a blistering sun. Only several
days in this sodding province, and Eris was already tired of the wasteland.
Seren's Children had an ingenious method of traveling *beneath* Silverwood
Province: rafts floating down the underground river. But the novelty had
quickly worn off that trip as well, and Eris had been only too glad to inhale
fresh air once she and her allies—old and new—had emerged from the
bowels of the earth.

She cast her mind back to the map of Aredia that Jensine and Caith kept
handy. If her recollection was correct, this general area was close enough
to the mines to serve as a home base for her allies. Yes, this spot would
make a solid camp.

Eris cast her body back on the wind. Her travels had lasted too long.
Already, the sun skulked up from the horizon, drenching the world in
crimson. A bitter wind buffeted her crow shape, knocking her off-course,
and it was a fight to regain control. When she was finally high enough, the

world below felt insignificant. Eris glided over the wind like she had been born to fly, and in a sense, she had. Such was the gift of her magic.

When she landed among the scrubby trees where her allies had made their camp last night, she took a final moment to savor the lightness of her crow form before shifting back to her human skin. As she grew, a sudden, sharp pain in her belly made her gasp and double over, and by the time she was fully human once more, she could not stand. She fell against a tree, unable to do more than whimper. Her mind spun. Was her child well? What was going on?

"Easy, easy, now." It was Jensine, slipping one arm beneath Eris' shoulders so that Eris could lean against her wiry frame.

"My babe," Eris gasped.

Adrie was at her side a beat later, running strong, cool hands beneath Eris' tunic to graze her abdomen. Tears streamed down Eris' face, as much from fear as from the pain. At last, Adrie drew back. "Everything is well."

Someplace between relief and shock, Eris could only stare at her friend.

"You're sure?" Jensine asked, still supporting Eris.

"Well, I'm no midwife," Adrie replied. "But I can suss out particles as well as any of Seren's daughters."

Jensine made a noise of disbelief, and began to steer Eris back toward their camp. Drake and Atanar stood by, faces tense, while Leal hurried over, pulling her cowl aside to reveal wide, worried eyes.

"Is she–"

But Jensine brushed aside the Sufani's concern with a wave of her hand. She did the same with Adrie, and instead brought Eris to the little wagon that housed the mages' supplies, shouting for her daughter. The interior was wall-to-wall clutter, but Jensine cleared a box of dried goods and bade Eris be seated. Brenna stepped inside and came to kneel by Eris' side while Jensine explained what she knew.

"Does it still hurt?" Brenna asked, putting a hand on Eris' shoulder.

"Look at her," Jensine scoffed. "Hunched over like that, clutching herself. What do you think?"

Brenna ignored her mother and urged Eris to meet her eyes. "What were you doing when it began?"

"Shifting to human form," Eris replied through clenched teeth. "Please... my babe..."

More tears sprang to her eyes, but she couldn't swipe them away. She couldn't move or think; she almost sodding prayed. *Please let my babe be well. Please.*

Another soft touch at her abdomen. Brenna's blue eyes closed and after a few seconds, the pain began to fade, until it vanished altogether. Sniffing, Eris swiped at her wet cheeks and looked at her fellow mage. "What's going on?"

Brenna folded her legs and sat before Eris while Jensine stood behind her. "You don't have any other children, do you?" Brenna asked.

Eris shook her head. "This is my first. What does that have to do with anything?"

"Sometimes pregnant mages experience..." Brenna considered. "Pains of this sort, particularly when they exert themselves overmuch. We're not sure why it happens, but soothing the agitated particles takes the pain away."

"Happened all the sodding time when I was carrying my firstborn," Jensine said. "Bren was no romp in the meadow, either."

Brenna grimaced, but met Eris' gaze with calm. "I had it quite bad with Iri as well. I actually had to stop using magic altogether during the final few months I carried her."

Eris' heart froze. "I can't stop shifting. Our plan depends upon it."

"Drake and Leal seem resourceful," Brenna began.

But Jensine placed both hands on Eris' shoulders. "There are ways to... mitigate the risks of using magic while with child."

Eris twisted to look up at the older mage. "What risks?"

"None to the babe, that we know of," Jensine replied. "Can't help how they turn out, of course, but I took care of them while they were in my womb. No, the pain is more of a distraction to the mother, which is the real danger."

"It can become quite hard to focus," Brenna added. "Which can disrupt whatever magic you're trying to do."

"But the babe will be fine?"

Brenna offered a warm smile. "Aye, he will."

He. Eris' lips parted but no sound came out.

Brenna tilted her head. "You didn't know?"

A little boy. Gid will have a son. Eris could only shake her head as more tears slid down her cheeks.

The wild mages exchanged glances before Jensine squeezed Eris' shoulders. "Aye, he'll be just fine. And if he's anything like his mother, he'll be a force to be reckoned with. But in the meantime, I may have a solution to your dilemma."

Eris swiped at her eyes again. *A boy.* "Tell me."

"Mother, that's not a good–"

But Jensine shushed her daughter and studied Eris. "Magic gives us many gifts. Did you use magic to create your son?"

Heat crept to Eris' cheeks. "We made the decision, but used magic to… help the process along."

"Well, the idea now is the same: help the process along." Jensine patted Eris' stomach. "Encourage your little one's particles to grow."

Eris stared at Jensine. "He's not a pumpkin. It's not that simple. It can't be."

"It's not," Brenna added, looking at her mother. "You shouldn't put these notions in her head."

But Jensine scoffed. "Three babes grown and healthy, and each one given the same treatment in my belly. Bren's had *one*, and apparently she's an expert."

"It flies in the face of the One's natural order," Brenna protested. "No mage knows better than the One; using magic on a growing babe is too dangerous."

"So is being with child in the first place," Jensine shot back. "A thousand things can go wrong. Why not give those things less time to happen?" She looked at Eris again. "You could be holding your son within three months' time."

By Eris' calculations, she had nearly seven left before her son—her *son!*—would be born. Seven months; summer would be nearing its end, with another winter on the way. But three months! Surely it was too soon. Surely, there was a catch. "I won't be ready," she managed at last. "I know nothing of babies or children. I was hoping to have time to learn."

"You'll learn as you go," Jensine replied. "I did. Besides," she smiled warmly, "you'll have us."

The pain was gone, but Eris still sat hunched, clutching her midsection, her mind whirling. What would Kali say to all of this? She'd probably be delighted to learn about this new application for magic. Did Kali even want children? Too bad if she did, for her hemie lover could never give them to her.

At last Eris looked back up at Jensine. "You have *three* children?"

Jensine's face turned to stone. "I gave birth to three. Two still live."

"Sentinels killed Asa," Brenna added softly. "Nearly a year ago. Not long after, we lost Da and Iri's father, Jax, during a raid on one of our hideouts."

"And there's little use weeping over them, now," Jensine said. "So let's not speak of the past any longer. If we are to survive, we must look to the future."

Her tone brooked no room for questions.

Eris considered. "My magic is strongest on myself. Using magic on another, even a minor healing, is difficult for me."

"Growing babes in the womb is easier than raising them outside it," Jensine replied, a wry twist to her mouth.

Eris glanced at Brenna, who straightened. "The One has granted us these bodies for a reason, and I saw no point in playing god on my daughter."

"The One—if the One exists—gave Seren's Children our magic," Jensine replied. "Why not use it?"

"It's…unnatural," Brenna said, scowling. "And dangerous. What if she damages something?"

"It's magic, which is *entirely* natural," Jensine shot back. "And she won't. She's powerful, and she'll have guidance."

They both looked at Eris, who still considered. She had so little knowledge of pregnancy, but she knew her own body and its limits. Her shifting adventures had seen to that. And she *was* powerful. No other mage could do what she could. Excitement began to flutter in her belly. She could hold her and Gid's son by the spring equinox. But she would still need to shift in the meantime, and the bigger she grew, the more awkward her flying might become. Or would she simply lay eggs in crow-form? Could her son shape-change, too? Did he shift with her, or simply stay a human, trapped in a tiny crow body?

The answer came quickly; confirmation in and of itself. "I've risked everything for freedom. I've lost my husband and too many friends." Resolve filled Eris' heart. "But I won't risk my son. Not even for magic."

Brenna exhaled in relief while Jensine frowned. "Your body; your choice. I hope you don't regret it."

Eris held the older mage's gaze. "I won't."

*

Hours later, Eris scooted closer to the bubble of warmth cast by the mage-fire. Well, it was a *fire* only in the barest sense. Caith had created a bed of hot coals from some meager fuel they'd found, transforming the sparse brushwork into a glowing source of heat. Across the mage-made fire, Leal, Drake, and Atanar were in deep discussion, with Drake gesticulating to a crudely drawn map of Carver's Creek, the closest township to the hematite mine.

"I've never been *to* the mine, thank the One," Drake was saying. "But I've spent time in Carver's. There were always folks looking for work, and the mines—not just the hematite one—are *always* hiring."

"There are mines other than hematite?" Atanar asked.

Drake nodded. "Gold, gems, copper, iron, sunstone, to name a few. From what I recall, most folks want to work the gem and gold mines—the pay's better—but the hematite mine is also popular with the locals. Guess there's good coin in poison."

Caith paced around the fire, occasionally slipping off to check the perimeter. The other wild mages who'd accompanied them, including Brenna, lingered nearby, engrossed in their own conversations. But at Drake's words, all talk ceased and Caith came to stand by Drake. "You know a great deal about the hematite mine."

Drake hesitated. "I...was taken in by the sentinels as a boy, and–"

Eris jumped in before he could continue. "But he escaped that life, cultivated his magic, and helped me and my friends escape our old bastion."

The other mages had gasped at this revelation. "You're a former sentinel?" Caith said, eyes bulging, body tense. "Mother, did you know?"

Jensine, seated beside Eris, shot her a raised brow, but Eris did not react. The thought of Drake's time as a sentinel still made her guts churn, but Gid had called him friend. Besides, Drake had proven his loyalty to her cause – and to her. He had remained by her side, while Kali, her oldest friend, had abandoned her. Besides, he was only just beginning to learn the extent of his abilities. If he could keep the Canderi man calm, who knew what he'd be able to do with a bit more time and practice?

So she met his eyes over the rippling heat cast by the mage-fire. "Blood is blood," she said, and his shoulders relaxed. "Drake has suffered at sentinels' hands. He is one of us."

"What will we be expected to do at these mine?" Leal asked after a too-long pause.

"Hope you're in the mood for some hard labor," Drake replied.

"I can hardly wait," Leal muttered.

Atanar cleared his throat. "Will I be granted entrance to Carver's Creek? Some Aredian cities are unfond of my people."

"From what I recall, miners aren't as...choosy about their hirelings," Drake replied. "Less so when they see someone with shoulders like yours."

The Canderi tilted his head. "My...shoulders?"

"They're...strong," Drake said, quickly adding, "I'm sure the folks at the mines will be thrilled to put *you* to work."

Leal rolled her eyes. "Mind on the mission, Drake."

Please, Eris thought, though she kept her expression neutral. The last thing she needed was for Drake to be distracted by the Canderi, though at least he wasn't pining over the mage-hater, Ben.

Drake returned his full attention back to the map. Eris listened, but a soft touch on her arm made her look at Jensine. The leader of Seren's Children tilted her head away from the fire, and then rose and slipped off.

Adrie sat on Eris' other side, concentrating on a lump of dough; a basket of rolls baked to varying degrees rested at her feet. When Eris rose as well, Adrie made to accompany her, but Eris held up her hand. "You stay here."

Adrie frowned. "I don't like it when you and that woman go off alone."

"You don't have to like it," Eris replied. "Stay. I'll be right back."

Before Adrie could reply, Eris followed Jensine away from the others. After leaving the fire's warmth, cold air snaked beneath Eris' cloak, so she drew it closer to her body. Jensine had paused beside one of the great rock formations they'd set up camp besides, peering into the night. "All's well?" Eris asked softly as she approached.

"For the moment." Jensine leaned against the rock. "Your friend was a hemie?"

"Yes."

"You didn't feel the need to mention that, eh?"

Her cheeks warmed, but she kept her voice as cool as the wind. "No."

When she said nothing else, Jensine's eyes narrowed. This far away from the camp, only waxing Seren's light illuminated her face. "You brought a sentinel into our midst."

Damn Drake for making her *defend* his sordid past! Eris shook her head. "As I said, Drake is a mage first and foremost. He can't help what the hemies did to him as a boy."

"But still, to even bring a *former* sentinel among us..." Jensine's hands fisted at her sides; her body canted toward Eris, as if about to strike. But Eris did not move, nor drop her gaze, and after a few seconds Jensine exhaled a plume of fog. "You still vouch for him, and for those other dregs?"

"Nothing's changed," Eris pointed out. "And besides, they're doing us a great service. Unless," she lifted a brow, "*you'd* like to infiltrate the hematite mines?"

"Smart girl, to send in the fodder," Jensine replied after a beat. "But even so, you're juggling fire with that lot."

Eris turned to leave. "Don't call them dregs."

She didn't wait to hear Jensine's reply, but her heart raced faster with each step. *Send in the fodder.* Was it true? She'd done so with Ben, Brice, and Rilla, back in Whitewater City, but they had only been allies of circumstance. Drake and Leal were *friends*. Atanar...well, he hadn't caused any trouble since they had parted with the Sufani, so Eris had seen fit to leave him alone. If any of those three were fodder, it was him.

Even so, the thought did not sit easily upon her.

After a stop at the latrine, Eris began to pick her way through the rocks to their camp, thinking to try and drift off. But before she reached her bedroll, Leal said her name. The Sufani stood a few paces away, in the shadow of a massive boulder. At Eris' look, Leal shifted, rubbing her gloved hands together.

"What's wrong?" Eris asked, coming over. "Nervous about the mission?"

She meant it as a joke, but Leal only exhaled, and then drew down her cowl to reveal her stern expression. "When will it be?" Eris stared at her, uncomprehending, and the Sufani frowned. "We had a bargain, shape-changer. Your friends are out of their bastion. When will you help me find *my* true shape?"

"Soon," Eris began, but the Sufani shook her head.

"No. Now." Leal pulled off a glove and held out a hand, watching Eris expectantly. But Eris only stared at the Sufani's trembling fingers, her throat tight. The muscles in Leal's arm tensed. "What are you waiting for?"

"I can't," Eris whispered.

Leal's hand fell. "What do you mean? Your powers have grown since you left Whitewater."

"Aye, but..." Eris took a deep breath to gather her calm. "Using magic too much is painful to me now that I'm with child."

"You've been shifting plenty."

"It's starting to hurt when I do. It never used to. And Jensine told me that, while using my magic isn't harming my child, such pains are common among pregnant mages who exert themselves. I must take care. And this mission of ours requires me to shift–"

Leal spat on the dirt. "Horseshit."

The venom in the Sufani's voice took Eris aback. "What–"

"This isn't *my* mission," Leal went on. "My aid does not come freely, and my payment is long since due. And you *promised* me."

Fierce green eyes met hers. They were darker than her own, with gold flecks near the irises. Every line of Leal's face was taut, braced for a fight. Shame flooded Eris, warming her as well as any mage-fire, but she kept her expression from revealing her internal workings. "I keep my promises," she said slowly, deliberately. "I will help you – but not now. When the mine is destroyed–"

"When my friends are free, when we find other mages, when the mine is ashes." Leal's voice took on a mocking tone and her gaze was sharper than her spear. "You are a liar, Eris Echina. Or—worse—you have no regard for your allies – your *friends*."

Now it was Eris' turn to glare. "What in the stars are you prattling on about?"

Leal began to shove her glove back on. "You're aligning yourself with evil."

"Evil?"

The Sufani jabbed a thumb toward the wild mages' caravan. "Seren's Children. They don't care about *you* – or your babe. They only care what you can do for them, how much use they can wring from your magic. Don't look at me so. You must realize it. You're many things, but stupid is not among them."

Leal's words landed like a blow, recalling what Eris had said to Kali what felt like a lifetime ago, back when Eris had first realized Kali was in love with a sodding sentinel. But this was *nothing* like that! "They're mages, just like me," Eris shot back. "Their ways may be strange to you, but that doesn't make them *evil*."

"Jensine Damaris speaks openly—gleefully—of taking innocent lives," Leal replied. "She seeks to raze a city when disabling it would do. And you're keen to go along with her. Since we took up with Seren's Children,"

Leal spat the words, "you've taken to belittling your supposed friends, like Adrie. And you left Hazel with those other mages, back in their *tabernacle*."

"This mission is too dangerous, and that poor child's been through enough," Eris replied through clenched teeth. "Brenna left her daughter, too. Does that make her evil?"

"I'm not talking about Brenna," Leal replied. "Though she seems like the only one of that Damaris clan not utterly set on destruction." Her green eyes narrowed again. "You've a streak of cruelty to you, don't you? I saw it before, back when we returned to Whitewater City, but I told myself you were working for the greater good. That Vellis frip probably deserved what she got, and I know you had a vendetta against the city guards. But destroying the mine outright..." Leal crossed her arms. "You know it's wicked, but you don't care."

Eris' vision went white. "The hemies *must* pay for their crimes. They can't be allowed to continue keeping us prisoner. You speak of cruelty; I have *felt* its touch. I act as I do because the hemies and the dregs alike will eat me alive otherwise. *You* should know that, Sufani." She pointed into the night. "If you're so opposed to this mission, leave. You're a free woman. You're not in chains."

Leal flinched at the word "woman," but stood firm. She nodded to the bubble of light, where Drake and Atanar still sat together, talking quietly. If the men had noticed Eris and Leal's argument, they did not react. "Unlike you, I keep my word. I told Drake I would help him with this task, and I shall. But I did so believing that you would make good on *your* word." Her face fell, briefly, before she pulled up her hood and veil. "By the One, I hate being wrong."

With that, she stalked away from Eris, toward Drake and Atanar. Eris watched her long enough to see both men look up; Atanar nodded to the Sufani, but Drake's gaze fell upon Eris. She turned away, stepping further into the chilled night air. Only when something cold brushed her cheek did Eris realize she was weeping. She angrily swiped her tears away and rested her hands on her abdomen, seeking out her son's particles. All well. A little boy. Somehow, he felt more real than ever. She could feel the particles of his heart, beating strong. The brief contact brought a sense of calm upon her, banishing any doubt Leal might have stirred up.

This was all that mattered: her son, and shaping a better world for him. Eris swiped her eyes again, and made her way to the caravan, where Seren's Children waited.

TWENTY-THREE

The clang of tools against rock reverberated in Drake's ears. His muscles, braced to absorb the impact of the blow, had already begun to ache– and this wasn't even his third day on the job. Since the hematite mine was an open pit, the sun beat upon Drake's shoulders as sure as any pickaxe.

He skimmed his hand over the rock face beside him. Even now, hematite beckoned; power and strength buried in the threads of dark silver. Pure, raw hematite, as much as any sentinel could want. Enough to snuff out a life in a few agonizing minutes.

Eris was right to destroy this place. But the clatter of tools and the bustle of other workers resonated in Drake's bones alongside hematite's siren song. No more innocent lives should be lost to hematite. They had to find another way to incapacitate the hematite mine.

He swiped at his forehead and glanced to his either side, where Leal and Atanar worked as well. Each of his friends was wholly absorbed in their tasks: Leal's brow was creased, her swings deliberate and even. She'd not said more than a handful of words since the three of them had arrived at the hematite mine a few days ago. Atanar's hammer fell with a resounding clamor that sent tremors through the rock beneath Drake's boots, and the Canderi's bare, broad shoulders gleamed with sweat.

When Nat caught Drake's eye, he paused to regard the rust-red rock before him. "I thought this work would be harder."

"It's pretty sodding hard to me."

Atanar studied him, a faint smile tugging his mouth. "No, but ancestors willing it will be so one day."

Startled by what he took as a flirtatious joke, Drake eyed the blond man, but Nat only hefted his hammer and got back to work. Drake bit back a grin—he wasn't on this mission to flirt!—and glanced at Leal. Out of necessity, she'd shed her Sufani garb in favor of the bland clothing most of the workers favored, but even the muted colors and shapeless tunic didn't conceal her prowess. Thank the One, Adrie had been able to craft a faded tier-mark for her, though Drake often caught Leal rubbing her wrist when she thought no one was watching.

Drake motioned toward the path that led to the lower levels of the open-pit mine. "I'm going to get some water. Want some?"

Leal set her hammer down and kept her voice low. "They don't let us newcomers down there. You've tried. Atanar has tried. I've tried." She exhaled. "This mission is folly."

"It's barely been three days," Drake murmured. "Have a little faith, will you? That tunnel at the base is the only spot we've not been able to access, but I'll rectify that. The guards down there aren't going to be sharing ales with me any time soon, but I've been trying to make friends among them. And we've *all* been working to show that we're trustworthy."

"*Working* is right," Leal grumbled. "My arms are about to fall off. What happens when there's nothing down there but townies and more rocks?"

"Then we find another way to our goal," Atanar said. "I cannot speak for you, but I have caused enough pain in my life. I refuse to take part in more death."

Leal hefted her hammer again, but did not swing. "Fine. Drake, hurry up and make friends with the guards, will you? Otherwise, I'm tempted to let Eris do whatever she wants to this shithole."

Drake considered trying to calm his friend, but decided against it. He needed to save his magical strength. So he only winked at her. "Three coppers says I find something interesting down there."

"You don't have three coppers," Leal said, rolling her eyes. But she slid off her flask and shoved it in Drake's hands. "Very well. But be quick about it," she added, louder.

"Certainly, serla," Drake drawled, and held out his hand to Atanar.

The Canderi passed over his flask as well, and Drake slipped toward the nearest steps. This part of the open mine bustled with workers from Carver's Creek, many of whom shot mistrustful looks at Drake as he passed. He took pains to keep his expression friendly without inviting any questions and descended to the bottom of the mine.

Although winter had not yet fled Stonehaven, the place was as dry as old boots, but as Drake made his way down the steps the air took on a cool, faintly damp tinge. By the time he reached the lower levels, he was in blessedly full shade. The path here was wide, with room enough for several wagons to travel side-by-side. There was also a hand pump that would bring up water, before which a line had already formed. Drake slipped in behind the last person and glanced over at the black tunnel that disappeared into the rock face. Goldie, one of the guards, leaned against the wall beside the tunnel, cleaning her nails with the tip of her dagger.

What in Ea's realm is in there? Drake wondered. *What are they hiding?*

Suddenly, Goldie glanced up. "Get back to work, hemie!"

Drake's heart stuttered but he kept his calm, lifted the flasks, and opened his mouth to reply... And then snapped it shut, for he bore no sentinel mark. He glanced over his shoulder, scanning the ranks of the waiting workers.

Commander Talon stood an arm's length away. Their eyes locked, her lips parted in shock, and Drake's idiot mouth said, "Ea's balls, not *you* again!"

Talon stared at him, and then Goldie rumbled up, glaring at the Forsworn sentinel. When the guard grabbed Talon's wrist, Drake saw that an ugly pink scar marred her sentinel mark. "If I've told you once," the guard sneered, "I've told you a hundred times. No. Hemies. Allowed." She shoved Talon out of the line, sending the former commander stumbling. "Get back to work, sorry sod."

Talon was leaner than Drake remembered, but she still managed to catch herself before she fell, then looked back at the guard. "Jasper is very sick," she said calmly. "I thought he could use some fresh water. We only have–"

"No hemies allowed." Goldie, tall and sturdy in her own right, shoved Talon again, harder, this time knocking her to the gravel. Talon lay still for a few seconds before pulling herself upright, using a pile of rubble as leverage. Drake watched her face transform into an expression of pure rage, a look he recognized all-too-well from when she'd tortured him, before her features smoothed into blank impassivity. Her eyes darted Drake's way before she turned to head back for the steps.

Satisfied, Goldie glanced over at Drake. "What're you looking at, newbie?"

Now was his chance. "Good work, keeping out that hemie bitch," he replied, giving her his most winning smile and extending his hand. "Whatever they're paying you, they ought to double it."

To his delight, she accepted, and they clasped their palms in a gesture of solidarity. The contact was brief, but it was enough for him to soothe some of the particles in her mind, the ones that sparked with distrust over new faces.

When they parted, her regard held less hostility and more curiosity. "You and those friends of yours aren't from Carver's, eh?"

"No, ser," he replied. "We've come from the south, hoping to make a decent living up here."

"Well, you lot work hard," she replied. "Especially that blue-eye with you. I know folks up north are scared of 'em, but I don't have no quarrels with a man who pulls his weight like that fellow."

"You and me both, ser. He's handy to have at my back."

"Aye, I'll bet." The guard nodded to the water pump. "Your turn."

Drake worked the wooden handle and cool water began to flow into his flask. "Thanks. It's hot as Amaranthea's crotch today, I swear."

Goldie grunted. "If you don't like heat, you should look for work elsewhere. You sure you're a southerner?"

"It's not the heat, exactly, but the wild swings in temperature, *and* the dry air." Drake glanced over at the black mouth of the tunnel. "You ever get to cool off in there?"

"The dam's not for me—or you—to visit," she replied. "But sometimes the wind pushes cool air out."

"There's water down there?" Drake asked, working to keep the excitement out of his voice.

Goldie nodded. "Aye, a huge underground river. They had to dam it up to mine the hematite."

"Come on!" someone in line behind him called.

The guard replied with an acerbic remark that Drake missed in his eagerness to thank Goldie and fill his flasks. When he returned to Leal and Atanar, he couldn't help his grin of satisfaction as he tossed them their flasks.

"What's gotten into you?" Leal said as she drank.

Drake winked at her. "You owe me three coppers."

*

Talon trudged back up the path. What in Tor's name was Drake doing here? Was he after hematite? Perhaps he'd come to find some for Stonewall and the others, who must surely be missing the burn at this point. Should she report Drake to Loach? But the thought was fleeting; she was Forsworn, and her word was useless. The burst of energy she'd felt when the guard had shoved her faded, leaving a familiar heaviness in her bones. What did it matter if Drake stole all the hematite in the mine?

He could help free you. The thought sounded oddly like her father, and Talon thrust it aside. No one could help her now. Even if she fled this place, she was as much a prisoner of her body as of her misdeeds.

"Tal!"

She jerked her head up to see Kam barreling toward her down the path, her dark hair loose from its braid. What in Tor's name was Kam doing back? She'd had to meet with Loach, and had said she'd be gone for at least an hour. Heart leaping to her throat, Talon raced toward the other woman. "What's going on?"

"Why did you leave him?"

Talon shook her head. "Jasper just wanted some fresh water... Kam,

234

what's–"

Kam grabbed her wrist with a strength that no longer surprised her, and they rushed up the rest of the path. "Jasper found your hematite," Kam huffed.

"I don't have any…" Talon trailed off, dread coursing through her veins. The raw hematite Loach had given her that she should have discarded. She swore and quickened her pace, even though she knew it would be useless. If Jasper had indeed eaten the piece of unprocessed ore in his current, weakened state, he was as good as dead.

Ignoring the jeers of the workers, the two women dashed to the overburden pit. The two other Forsworn sentinels were tucked in the shadow of the mine's side, Ruddy kneeling beside Jasper, clutching Jas' brown hand in his own. He looked up as the women approached, the whites of his eyes shining. "He's not answering."

"Is he breathing?" Talon asked, kneeling next to Jasper, whose mouth hung slack. His eyes were open and glassy, staring at the ground. Another hacking cough built in her throat, but she fought it back.

"Aye, but it's weak," Ruddy replied.

Kam felt Jasper's pulse and shot Talon a grim look. "His heart's racing."

"But he won't look at me, or speak!" Ruddy bit back a sob. "Why'd you have to eat that thing, Jas? You knew what it would do."

That was probably the point. Talon kept her voice calm. "He's still alive, so all hope isn't lost. We must make him vomit. Stick something down his throat. It won't be pretty, but it should work, though I wish we had some bitterwort."

Kam hesitated. "He wants to go to his next life. Shouldn't we let him?"

Talon stared at her. "He'll suffer a great deal in the meantime."

"But if he ate the entire piece," Kam replied. "He won't suffer long."

"Then why did you rush after me to help him?" Talon asked, narrowing her eyes.

"I didn't think. I just knew he needed help, and reacted. But now…"

She trailed off. Talon shook her head and turned her attention back to Jasper. "He *does* need help, and we're here. We're his brother and sisters in service."

"But we're not sentinels any longer," Ruddy murmured.

The force of Talon's anger startled her, and she had to moderate her grip on Jasper's cheeks so she wouldn't bruise him. "Speak for yourself. Now, help support your brother."

Ruddy did as she instructed, grasping Jasper's shoulders to gently lay him on his side so that he wouldn't choke. She cleaned her hand as best she could, and then pried Jas' mouth open. Thank the One, she didn't have to do this long. Jasper gagged, Talon quickly pulled her hand back and helped Ruddy keep his head positioned. Something wet sopped Talon's boots and the stink of bile filled the air, but within moments, Jasper groaned and leaned into Talon and Ruddy's grips, eyes closed.

"Shoulda...let me... go..." he managed.

Talon rubbed his back. "That's not for you to decide. That's up to the gods."

"'S my life," Jasper croaked, but he shot her a wry look. "Thanks for looking out, though. You're a good sort, Tal."

Something fractured in her heart, but for once the feeling brought no pain. Here was one person she'd not failed. She managed a small smile back. "Well, you can't leave us with all the work."

His laugh dissolved into more coughs. "I guess not."

Talon and Ruddy helped him sit up. Kam brought some water, warm and tasting of dust, and the four of them rested in the shadow of the rock face while the sun went down. For a mercy, no one had come to check on them yet, so the Forsworn sentinels had a few moments of peace. Talon's thoughts turned back to Drake. What was he doing here? She couldn't shake the question, nor her curiosity. But, other than seek him out and ask him herself, she didn't know how she could learn the answers.

Kam sat beside Talon, redoing the braid in her dark hair. Gods above, Kalinda Halcyon was the spitting image of her mother. Talon hadn't found the courage to share her part in Halcyon's story, though she knew—better than most—the truth would come out eventually. Soon, perhaps, for if Drake was here, then Stonewall might be as well, though Talon couldn't think why either of them would come to this place of their own free will.

Footsteps on the path made all four of them tense. Talon rose quickly, helping Jasper to his feet, and went to meet whoever approached. The newcomer turned the corner, and Talon found herself staring at Drake once more, this time accompanied by a slender woman and—of all people—a Canderi man.

"I should quip about us meeting again," Drake said as he came forward. "But I'm afraid we're short on time."

"You know him?" Kam whispered to Talon.

"In a manner of speaking." Talon searched for a sign of Drake's intention, but saw only curiosity. "What are you doing here?"

"My friends and I are looking for information," Drake replied. "Something tells me you might have it."

"Information on what?" Kam asked.

Drake's green eyes swept over her, and widened. "Gods above and beyond... Kali?"

Kam sucked in a breath. "What do you know of that name?"

"We shouldn't talk here," the woman with Drake hissed. "Too exposed."

Talon nodded down the path that would lead to their makeshift barracks. "Follow us."

No one spoke until the unlikely group was gathered around the little table where the Forsworn sentinels shared their supper. Drake and the Canderi man both had to hunch to enter, and the space was crowded, perhaps for the first time in years.

"Who in Nox's void are you lot?" Jasper said, voice still raspy. "Not humble townies, I take it?"

"Long story," Drake said wryly. "But suffice it to say we're no fans of the mines, and I reckon you aren't, either."

Kam kept her voice calm – and determined. "You know my daughter?"

Drake's dark green eyes studied Talon as if daring her to speak, or assessing how much she had already spoken.

Talon decided to save him the trouble of revealing her history with Halcyon. She allowed herself a hacking cough, then said, "She was a mage in my bastion. Drake's brother's lover, if I recall."

Kam gaped between them, and Drake winced. "Nothing gets past you, eh, Commander?" He looked back at Kam. "Your daughter is alive and well, last I saw her, several weeks ago. She's traveling with friends."

Despite herself, Talon exhaled in relief. If her plan to execute Halcyon had succeeded, Kam never would have forgiven her. The thought stung more than it should have.

At Drake's news, a soft sob escaped Kam and she sank against the wall, eyes closed, lips moving in silent prayer. Jasper hugged her shoulders briefly, but studied Drake with a sharp gaze. "Still waiting for an answer on who *you* are."

Drake's story gave an answer – more than Talon had bargained for. There were holes in the renegade mage's tale, no doubt to protect himself or his allies, but overall, Talon judged him to be truthful. But such a truth! It set her blood racing with its old vigor.

"Eris Echina means to destroy the hematite mines," Talon said when Drake had fallen silent, as much to confirm his words as to wrap her mind around them. "And everyone within them?"

Drake nodded, but his expression was grim. "She'll do it, too. There's a fire in her heart."

"Aye, and it sounds like she'll have some magical assistance," Jasper added, rubbing his stubbled chin.

The horror of it all made Talon cold inside, and empty as a chasm. "The workers here are...unpleasant, but innocent. Echina seeks to commit mass murder."

The renegade mage grimaced. "Aye. That's why I'm looking for a *less* deadly way to achieve her aim."

"Whatever she has planned, she must at least let the workers go free," Talon went on, glancing at each of the others in turn. "She *must*."

"I've said as much to her," Drake replied softly. "But..."

Eris, who had known little mercy in her own life, would not show it to her enemies now. Foley would have known what to do, or would have at least had the right words. Talon glanced at Ruddy, Jasper, and Kam, and a fierce swell of protectiveness moved through her. So her own life was probably forfeit; she'd accepted that long ago. But these people deserved *more* than the hand the One had dealt them. Ruddy was little more than a lad, Jasper was a good man caught at the wrong time, and Kam had someone to live for.

Talon's throat stung as she looked back at Drake. "Do you think Eris will meet with me?"

"Highly doubtful."

"I know this place better than you. I can help her cause."

The others stirred. Leal frowned at her. "Eris will not trust you."

"Let Eris decide for herself," Talon replied, though she had little hope.

"It's worth a shot," Drake said. "And Eris has been known to surprise us all."

"I want to meet her as well," Kam said, drawing the others' startled looks.

Drake's brow furrowed. "*Two* former sentinels may be pushing our luck–"

Kam's dark eyes seemed to burn into Drake. "I would like to meet my daughter's friend. And *you* are a former sentinel, one Eris seems to tolerate well enough. A few more won't hurt."

"I suppose." Drake looked at Talon and she read the challenge in his face. "You may not like what Eris has to say."

They continued to make plans, but Talon's worries refused to retreat to the back of her mind. Would Drake tell Kam about Talon imprisoning and trying to execute her daughter? Or would Eris? Regardless, Talon's true villainy would be revealed, and Kam would never look at her in the same way. Nor would the others. Their rejection was inevitable, of course, but still, her heart sank.

TWENTY-FOUR

The metallic stink of hematite permeated the air. To Eris'
annoyance, the smell only heightened her ingrained fear of the ore
– and hatred for those who worshipped the sodding stuff. As she
crept through the dark and silent mine with Drake, Leal, and Atanar, her
hand stole to her bare neck. She could still feel the bastion collar constrict
her airway despite how she hadn't worn the wretched thing in months.

"Where are you taking me?" she whispered to Drake, who led the way
down the stepped path along the mine's side.

"The former sentinels have a barracks, of a sort," he replied in kind. "It's
private, and not much farther."

"If you don't like it," Leal sniped from behind, "just fly away."

Eris glared into the dark sky and did not reply. The whole situation
made her skin crawl, but she had placed her trust in Drake and Leal, and
despite their differing opinions, they had not steered her wrong. Yet. She
shot a look back at the Sufani, who kept her eyes ahead. A pang of sorrow
touched Eris' heart, but she shoved the feeling aside. Leal had *no* idea of
how Eris had suffered—how all mages had suffered—and thus had no idea
why Eris had to burn this stinking, evil shithole off the face of the world.

At last they came upon a hole in the rock face, with a threadbare curtain
drawn over the front. Drake held up a hand in a silent signal to wait and
then peered inside, speaking softly. Someone replied, and Drake waved
Eris, Leal, and Atanar forward.

Eris planted her feet at the cave's entrance. "Bring the hemies out."

Drake exhaled, his breath puffing in the chill air. "Aye, about that... Look, there's something I need to tell you. I wasn't sure *how* to tell you, but you should know the truth."

Seren's light, sometimes she wanted to throttle him. "What?"

"One of the Forsworn sentinels we're going to meet... It's Talon."

Eris stared at the other mage, torn between horror and fury. The latter won. "As in Commander Talon? As in, the sodding bitch who held my friends prisoner – and tortured *you*?"

He winced. "Kind of hoped you'd forgotten."

Eris waved his foolishness away, and turned, preparing to fly into the night. But a hand on her shoulder made her pause. "Talon has knowledge that could help us," Leal murmured. "And there is another sentinel present, one you will want to meet."

It was the most that Leal had spoken to Eris since their argument the previous day, and she could not help her curiosity. "Who is this mysterious sentinel?" Eris asked Drake.

He tensed, no doubt bracing for a verbal attack. "Kali's mother."

"Kali's mother is dead. She was a servant in her old bastion, and died giving birth."

The Sufani shook her head slowly. "Then this woman is a relation of your friend."

"Kam is Kali's blessed image," Drake added quickly. "It's remarkable, really."

"I don't care who this hemie looks like," Eris replied, stepping away from the entrance. "I'm not going in there."

"Eris–"

But she cut off Drake with a shake of her head. "This entire 'mission' of yours is folly. This entire place deserves a bloody death. Nothing here is worth saving."

With that, she made to shift, but Atanar's voice stopped her. "I have no wish to stuff myself into that hole in the ground, either. The night is thick and the guards are few. Can we not ask the others to step outside?"

He spoke to Drake, not Eris, but she appreciated the semblance of an ally. Drake and Leal exchanged glances before Drake ducked behind the curtain.

241

He emerged moments later with two women, and Eris' guts turned to ice when the former sentinel commander straightened. Bathed in Seren's light, Talon was a smudged shadow of a woman. Where hematite armor had once gleamed, only tatters and rags hung from her thin frame, and her once immaculate hair lay limp and dirty about her sallow face. Yet even so, her dark eyes rested on Eris the way a raptor watched a wren.

Eris fought back an involuntary shiver and turned her attention to Talon's companion, and gasped aloud. "Kali?"

The woman had a good two decades on Eris' friend—at least—but the shape of her face was the same: the pointed chin, the dark, curious eyes, and the full lips that so often smiled. But this woman was not smiling now, nor, Eris thought, had she much reason to if the course of her life had brought her to this wretched place. No, the woman Drake had called "Kam" only stared at Eris with naked hope, blinking back tears.

"I'm Kamala," she whispered, pressing a hand to her chest. "You know my daughter?"

Kamala. Eris cast her memory back, but Kali had never mentioned the name. Perhaps she didn't know. "Aye," she managed. "Kali and I grew up together in Starwatch Bastion."

"Starwatch?" Kam took a shaking breath. "Was she–"

"I'm so sorry," Drake broke in gently. "But we *are* out in the open. There aren't any guards about right now, but I don't think any of us have much luck left to push." He nodded to Talon.

Eris tore her gaze away from Kam and looked at the former commander. Bile rose in her throat, so she lifted her chin and crossed her arms. "Speak if you must, hemie."

Talon regarded her calmly. "Drake says you wish to destroy this place. We can help – on one condition."

"You're hardly in a position to make demands," Eris replied.

"How many mages do you have at your back?" Talon asked. "Ten? Twenty? A hundred?" She didn't give Eris time to respond. "All the mages in Aredia won't be enough to fulfill your mission. You need information. You need a plan. You need me."

Eris waved a hand at Drake, Leal, and Atanar. "I'm getting help."

"How long will it take them to gather what you need?" Talon asked. "How long are you willing to wait? They'll be discovered, soon, if they haven't been already." She looked at Drake. "Nothing that happens here does so without Loach's knowledge. He's one of Argent's informants."

Kam nodded, her lips pursed in thought. "It's true. He's got eyes and ears all over." Talon glanced at the other sentinel as if something had just occurred to her, but Kam shook her head. "I've never met the High Commander, only heard stories. But they all end in blood."

Kali's mother had the same way of story-weaving that Kali possessed. Perhaps Kam was also prone to bouts of woolgathering.

"Argent's all the way in Silverwood Province," Eris said. "Even if his spies send word, it'd take days for him to get it, and a week—at least—for his forces to arrive. Your High Commander is of little concern." She looked at Drake. "I've humored you enough. This place will burn."

"How?" Drake asked. "The mine's open to the sky. There's no wood bracing up any tunnels. And I know your new friends are strong, but have they the power to melt rock and stone?"

Sod it all, he was right. But Eris refused to acknowledge his words.

"Tal's right about you needing information," Kam added. She stepped toward Eris. Leal moved as if to intercept and Kam paused, lifting her hands. "You're not alone in hating the sentinels."

The tone of her voice sent a chill down Eris' spine. "Oh?"

The entire world was silent. Kam's hands clenched and her words emerged in fits and starts. "I fell pregnant – a gift from the gods. It must have been, for so few sentinels bear children. And Kali's father was a sentinel, too. But none of us are permitted loyalty other than to the Circle, and I knew my child would be taken away and I would be punished. So I fled the garrison. But Kali's father—Jonas—remained, stuck to his wretched duty like a fly in amber. After Kali was born, when I realized she had magic, I feared she would be thrown into a bastion." She swiped at her wet cheeks. "My sweet little girl. It wasn't fair. We hid with some kind Sufani for as long as we could, until our luck ran out. On that day, my former commander

243

sent squads after me, sent Jonas after me, and that sorry sod came. He stood before our daughter with his sword drawn and told me to surrender." A bitter laugh escaped her. "I made him fight to take her from me. And he imprisoned our baby in a bastion."

Despite herself, tears stung Eris' eyes. She could not let the same fate befall her son. "He died in the bastion. But before that, he stayed with Kali and watched over her." Or so Kali had seemed to believe. "I knew him, a little," Eris added. "Although I never knew he was Kali's father until recently, but he was always…kind to her. As kind as a sentinel can be to a captive mage."

Kam hugged herself. "Then you can see why I have no love for sentinels. I will help you."

It wasn't a request, but for once, Eris didn't mind being told. Desperation was a powerful ally. She only wished she didn't know from experience. "I would be glad of your help, Kam."

"Provided, of course," Kam went on, her voice lighter, "that you destroy this place and everyone in it."

"Hold a moment," Drake said, shaking his head. "That's the opposite of what I'm trying to do."

Talon looked alarmed. "Ruddy and Jas, too?"

Kam glanced back at their barracks, where two men peered from behind the curtain. Other Forsworn sentinels, no doubt. Kam's features softened. "No, not them. They're good lads. They don't deserve to die here."

The lives of two more Forsworn sentinels hardly mattered in the larger scheme, so Eris nodded. "If you say."

"None of those workers deserve to die for your cause, either," Talon said, stepping forward. "You must either strike at night, or evacuate the place first."

Drake grimaced. "Can't believe I'm about to say this, but Talon is right. Tor help me."

"More death is never the answer," Atanar added, and Leal echoed his words.

"Destroy the mines," Talon said to Eris. "I'll help you. But enough blood has been shed on account of hematite. Don't be reckless."

Fury bloomed in Eris' veins again. "Your own mage father died because of your reckless, *selfish* actions. Aye," she said to Kam, whose eyes widened. "Her da was a mage. Did she tell you that? Did she tell you how her father walked free while she imprisoned Kali, collared her like a beast and shoved her into a hematite cell?"

Kam's dark eyes narrowed at Talon. "Why would you do such a thing?"

Even in the darkness, Eris could see Talon's cheeks flush, and her words were more clipped than normal. "Extenuating circumstances. But I never wanted to kill her, even though she'd been possessed by a thrall."

Kam rounded on Eris and Drake. "A *thrall*? You said she was well!"

Atanar spoke next, his deep baritone voice holding a trace of authority Eris had never heard. "Your daughter *is* well. She is no thrall, but a gifted mage." He pressed a hand to his broad chest. "She saved my life. I was a thrall; Kali healed me."

"Kali *was* possessed, it's true," Drake added. "But she cured herself. Now she seeks to help others who've been...turned."

Kam looked at Talon again, her jaw working. "'Extenuating circum-stances?'"

"I did the best I could with what truths I had," Talon said softly. "Please, believe that. I was angry and desperate, and your daughter was a great threat – at the time. I didn't realize thralls could be cured." She looked back at Eris. "Mass murder is Argent's way; you know that as well as I do. Don't become like him. Show mercy."

Mercy. An unwitting echo of Kali's words to Eris, before they'd parted ways. Eris clenched her jaw against the tears that threatened to form and instead stared down the former sentinel with all the hatred she could muster. "I will show mercy where mercy is deserved."

*

Later, after as much discussion as Eris was willing to risk, she and her allies made ready to leave the mines. While Drake, Leal, and Atanar began to sneak out, Eris prepared to shift, as the urge to be flying was a palpable thing. Thank the stars, Talon and the other Forsworn sentinels went back to their barracks, but Kam stayed outside.

"Will it bother you if I watch?" Kali's mother asked.

"I don't mind an audience." Eris took a deep breath, assessing her strength. It was risky to shift now, but she thought she could at least fly to the mine's edge before changing back to human form. The worst pain seemed to occur when she held the crow-shape for longer than a few minutes, but her son was still well.

Kam watched her with Kali's thoughtful, dark eyes. "Does the hematite here affect your abilities?"

This gave Eris pause. She glanced around as if expecting to see the ore littering the ground, but there was only dark red dirt. And her strength, her focus, were as strong as they ever had been. "No," she said. "Should it?"

Kam shrugged. "I have no understanding of magic. I was just curious."

Eris could not help but chuckle. "You really are Kali's mother, aren't you?"

A look of utter heartbreak crossed Kam's face and she stared at the sky, rubbing her right wrist. "I miss her more than words can say. I'll die here. But the One god willing, Kali will never see this place."

Kali had abilities that would be *most* welcome on Eris' mission, but she kept that thought to herself. "No one knows what the future holds."

"Except the One," Kam replied, and Eris fought back a grimace. Kam, heedless of this, studied her right wrist in the wan light. "A thousand times, I thought of leaving, even if it would be in vain. But even if I could leave, I would still be branded a criminal."

Eris frowned. "What do you mean?"

In response, the former sentinel turned her wrist so that Eris could see the three ugly scars where her sentinel mark should have been. "Forsworn," Kam said quietly. "Now and forever. A prisoner of my past no matter where I go."

Despite common sense, Eris' heart twisted. She'd vowed to destroy this place and everyone in it, but Kali's mother had weakened her resolve;

weakened…or changed it. Kam seemed to share her goal, and she clearly cared for the other Forsworn sentinels, one of whom, Eris had learned, had been imprisoned here for aiding a mage and her child. So as much as Eris hated to admit it, perhaps not all sentinels were human garbage. Drake was certainly a good man, and Kam…

Annoyed with herself, Eris held out her hand. "Let me see."

Kam hesitated, but placed her slender wrist in Eris' palm. Seren's light, the woman carried not an ounce of fat; her arm was an iron feather. Eris gently examined the scar with her eyes, and then with her mind, assessing the particles of tissue. Sluggish, gray, and dull in her mind's eye, the particles of Kam's wrist clumped together, remnants of what must have been an excruciating wound. Eris brushed her fingertips over the raised skin, considering. At last she made her decision and layered her will upon the sluggish particles, urging them to dissipate, smoothing their way throughout the rest of Kam's body.

The process took a few minutes. A soft gasp made Eris look to see Kam clutching her wrist, eyes huge and round, lips parted in shock. The scar was gone, as was any trace of a sentinel mark, and Eris felt not even a little tired. Pleased, she smiled, and met Kam's gaze.

"I hope you and Kali will be reunited, one day," she said to the other woman's astonishment. "This should make it easier for you."

Kam stammered a thanks, but Eris had already turned to hurry after Drake and the others. She wouldn't shift now; she wanted to save her strength for Leal. She had a promise to keep.

TWENTY-FIVE

The wine was sweet, but not overmuch, so it trickled down Kali's throat a little too easily. Coupled with the wedding's lively music and the festal air, she could drink a great deal.

Be careful, Kali, she told herself, staring into the rose-colored liquid. *Don't lose control.* She frowned, swallowed half the glass' contents in one go, and shot a furtive glance at her table companions to see if anyone was paying attention. Milo, Marcen, and Flint all seemed absorbed in the gaiety. The ceremony itself had been private, but now that Renata and Svea were officially wed, the entire city had turned out to celebrate. The main street of Dilt was blocked off from vehicles and filled with tables borrowed from every inn, tavern, and home, twinkling lanterns hung over their heads, and flowers of every color, shape, and size decorated every available surface. The two brides, resplendent in their finery, sat with the rest of the Dilt family before the entrance to their home.

Music careened through the streets: viols, gitars, dulcimers, drums, pipes, all urging the guests to step into the wide space cleared for dancing. Kali tapped her feet in time with the music as she watched the twirling throngs, but she tried to clamp down the urge to join. Her knee rarely let her enjoy such merriment. Besides, she had no one to dance with.

For what must have been the hundredth time that night, she glanced across the table at Stonewall, who sat between Marcen and an empty chair. A half-full glass rested before him and he resolutely had not looked her way even once. The thread that bound their hearts remained, but felt twisted, frayed, as if any moment it would snap.

How did he manage to be so calm, so cold? In the two days since their argument over Idalina, they had not exchanged more than a handful of words, spoken or otherwise. Now she wanted to throw something at him, or wrap her arms around his waist and weep into his chest. But she wasn't in the wrong, because she'd been in complete control with Idalina. He simply did not trust her. How could he not trust her, after all they'd been through together?

Eyes burning, Kali reached for one of the decanters to refill her glass and distract herself. She paused when she realized that Sadira, seated beside her, watched her every movement, like Kali was about to catch fire. As Kali poured herself a measure of wine, Sadira lifted one pale brow and Kali flushed, annoyed that this moment, too, would be subject to judgment. Could she do nothing to please anyone?

The hunger for Sadira's magic was still present, but a head full of wine muddled the feeling. Besides, Kali *was* in control. She could handle the urge now.

She offered the glass decanter to her fellow mage. "It's very good," she added.

Sadira pushed her glass forward. Kali filled it, and then clinked hers against her friend's. They each sipped, though Sadira's regard did not cease. Kali turned fully to her friend. "Is Beacon with his family?"

"I believe so," Sadira replied. "Even though he *should* be resting."

"His sister doesn't get married every day. He *should* enjoy himself now."

Sadira plunked her glass down. "His health is of greater meaning than this..." She waved a hand to encompass the celebration.

"He'll be fine. He said he wasn't planning on dancing."

"He'd better not," Flint spoke up from Kali's other side. "Else I'll have to knock some sense into that coppery head of his."

Kali glanced over at the young sentinel. "Are you going to dance?"

"What? Me?" Flint's brows shot to her hairline. "Set me up in a spar – fine. But *that* nonsense?" She grimaced at the throng of dancers. "What's the point?"

"It's fun," Marcen replied as he sipped his wine.

Flint pulled a face. "Doubt it."

"Have you tried?" Marcen asked her.

"What do you think?"

Kali couldn't help her grin. "He's right. You shouldn't dismiss dancing so easily."

Flint took a deep drink. "And yet, here I am."

Marcen rose abruptly, came around to Flint's chair, and stood beside her. For once, no one wore armor, only the soft clothes the Sufani had provided, though the sentinels probably had a few weapons tucked away beneath their silks and velvets. Idalina had even been kind enough to procure the women some proper dress clothes, which Kali would have appreciated more had she been in a better mood. But Flint looked quite lovely tonight. Her black hair hung loose around her face, her cheeks were flushed from the single glass of wine she nursed, and her blue eyes sparkled in the lamplight. Her borrowed dress, a paler blue than her eyes, revealed her shapely back. Marcen certainly seemed to appreciate her, at least.

"Just one song," he said, offering his hand. "Come on. Give it a try."

Flint went very still. "I don't know how."

"It's easy." Marcen smiled down at her. "Let me show you. Please."

She hesitated again, so Kali nudged her shoulder. "At least *try*. I can't, you know, with my knee, so the least you can do is let me live vicariously through you."

Flint rolled her eyes, but rose and took Marcen's hand. "Fine," she said to him. "But no making fun of me if I miss a step."

Kali missed Marcen's reply, but Flint laughed aloud as they walked toward the dance area. Smiling, Kali glanced at Milo, who watched his twin and the mage slip into the crowd. "You should ask someone," Kali told him. "I'm sure many folks here would love to take a turn with you."

He toyed with his still-full glass. "I dunno. Maybe later." He glanced at Stonewall and Kali thought he was about to say something to the former sergeant, but he only looked back at his drink.

Stonewall downed the rest of his wine and didn't say anything, only poured himself another glass, glancing around at the servants who were busy refilling the decanters. Raucous laughter rose from a nearby table, where the guests had settled in with plates of food. Kali's stomach growled, reminding her that she'd not eaten since breakfast. She poured herself another glass of wine and savored the increasingly warm, fuzzy feeling that crept over her mind and heart. Though she could have manipulated the wine's particles to lessen her intoxication, she chose not to. Perhaps soon she'd stop caring whether Stonewall looked her way. The wine, like *biri* smoke, dulled her hunger for magic; perhaps it could dull her heart's desires, too.

"You lot know this is a party, right?" Beacon asked as he plunked into the empty chair. His cheeks were rosy and his grin was wide, though it faded as he surveyed his squad-mates. "Ea's tits... What'd I miss? Look, if someone died, you ought to tell me right away!"

Sadira gave him a stern look. "You have been drinking."

His flush deepened, but his reply was calm. "A tad."

"How much is that?"

Beacon held up his forefinger and thumb, with barely a hint of space between them. "About so. Give or take a smidgen."

The Zhee mage frowned at him. "You are mocking me."

"Oh, yes," he replied, grinning again. "But you bear it so well. I can't help myself."

Kali's head was starting to spin nicely, so her giggle was a bit louder than the situation warranted. "How are the brides?"

"Svea is charming, as usual," Beacon replied, leaning back in his chair, one long arm thrown over the back of Stonewall's. "Ren's about as charming as a rabid porcupine, but Svea loves her. The One help them both. They do seem happy. Svea said she'd get my sister to dance, but I have my doubts. Sadira, if you think *I'm* drunk, you'd be scandalized by Heitor."

"I do not have...a mistake with drinking," Sadira replied. "Except when the person doing it is not at complete health."

Beacon sighed, and then glanced at Stonewall. "Oh, Ida asked about you. She wanted to know if you danced. I said I wasn't sure..."

Something stabbed Kali's heart and she could not catch her breath.

Beacon seemed to realize he'd made a misstep and cleared his throat, his ears now bright red. "Ah…"

"I'm not interested in dancing," Stonewall said aloud. Silently, he sent, *With her.*

Kali nearly replied to him in kind but took another drink instead.

Stonewall did not look her way, only picked up a decanter and poured himself another glass. He offered the decanter to Beacon, but the mender shook his head. "No, thanks. Wouldn't do me much good right now anyway." He gave Sadira a pointed look. "Hematite burns the alcohol away. *You* should be careful," he added to Stonewall. "Since you don't have as much hematite in your blood as I do."

Stonewall drained his glass.

"If you are not drunk, why are you so…jolly?" Sadira asked.

Beacon smiled at her. "I'm home, safe and alive, surrounded by family and friends, most of whom tolerate me. Does a soul need another reason to be happy?"

Kali missed Sadira's reply, because Stonewall caught her gaze. No silent speech passed between them. Instead, she caught flashes of his feelings: grief, anger, and…

Fear. So much fear, centered around her.

What is there to fear about me? She kept the thought to herself and scowled into her empty glass. Stonewall looked away and took another drink.

"Where's your sister?" Beacon asked Milo. The younger man nodded towards the dancers, where Flint and Marcen ducked and spun with the others. Beacon gave a low whistle. "Hard to believe she's the same girl. And Mar cleans up well, doesn't he?"

"Marcen's great," Milo said. "Flint really likes him. I like him too. Well, not in the same way as she does, but he's a good fellow."

"I agree," Kali said. "And they make a fine pair. Flint looks like she was made to dance."

"All that training has its uses," Beacon replied, nodding.

Kali giggled. "Are sentinels trained to dance?"

"Not quite," the mender replied. "But sparring is like a dance, sometimes.

You know... Judging when and how your partner will move and moving yourself in a way that will achieve an end."

"Except in a spar, the goal is to disarm your opponent, or bring them down," Milo said.

Beacon nodded. "Aye, but the principle is the same." He toyed with his glass, then gave Sadira a careful look. "I think a demonstration's in order. Care to help me...?"

She regarded him. "You are not well enough to dance, Abernathy."

Abernathy? Kali could not stop herself from gawking at Sadira. When—and why—had she started calling Beacon by his birthname?

But the Zhee mage ignored Kali and the look she gave Beacon was tinged with regret. The mender sighed and nodded. "Aye, you're right. As usual. Another time, then?"

"Another time." Sadira took another sip of her wine, but not before Kali caught the hint of a smile that crossed her face. Beacon, too, wore a smile, though his was in full view.

Despite her earlier assertions, Kali's gaze crept to Stonewall yet again. Their eyes met. A tendril of...emotion crept from him to her; barely a whisper of love. Her heart sang in response and she allowed herself a smile, a real one. He smiled too, though his was smaller, more guarded...

Then he gasped aloud and dropped his glass. It hit the table and rolled, but did not shatter. Drops of wine spattered the cream linen cloth like blood. That same *fear* spiked from him, but it was so much stronger than before, like a streak of lightning illuminating the entire sky. Beacon and Milo went to his side, but Kali sat stock-still, frozen in place by the force of his emotion. So much fear... Centered on *her.*

"It's nothing," he said to his squad-mates, waving them away. "The wine went to my head for a second. I'm fine."

Beacon studied him, frowning. "Like I said: be careful. You don't have hematite to protect you from the alcohol. Don't overdo it."

Stonewall nodded, though it was clear his attention was elsewhere. He righted his glass and filled it again, and only because Kali was watching him so closely did she see how his hands trembled. She tried to send him a measure of her concern.

Are you...?

I'm fine, he sent back, stark and cold as his namesake. *Don't worry about me.* With that, he stood, wobbling, and nodded in the direction of the banquet tables. "I need something on my stomach. Anyone want anything?"

The others shook their heads, except for Milo, who jumped to his feet. "I could eat. I'll come with you."

Stonewall grinned. "Good. We'll attack together."

Kali did not watch them go. She burned: her cheeks, with embarrassment; her heart, with anger. Finding her glass empty, she refilled it, drained it down again, and rose. "I'm going for a *biri,*" she said to Sadira. "I'll be back soon."

*

"You must relax," Marcen said, a smile in his voice.

Flint gritted her teeth. Bad enough she had to focus on moving her body to the rhythm of the drums while also keeping pace with her dance partner, all while *not* tripping over the hem of the swishing dress. "It's more complicated than it looks. There are a lot of elements to keep in mind." She took the risk and pulled her gaze from her boots to his face. "Like not stomping on your feet, for one."

His grip at her waist tightened a fraction. "I've got good boots. Stomp away."

Heat flooded her, sort of like the warmth from the wine, but far more pleasurable. For one moment, Flint forgot all the complications of dancing at this fancy frips' wedding and just *moved.* Marcen's steps never flagged nor faltered; he led her along the floor with the same easy grace he used to slip through shadowed woods. Skirling pipes and the resonant twang of a gitar underscored the breakneck drumbeat, and the other dancers traded laughs, smiles, and words of welcome.

Mar and I aren't sentinel or mage here, Flint realized. *We're just...people.*

"Tricky step coming up," Marcen said, drawing her attention. Flint tensed

254

in preparation while watching the nearest couple: a pair of laughing young men, cheeks flushed, eyes locked on each other. They did something…an extended arm, a spin, before continuing their dance. The next thing she knew, Mar's arm was outstretched and it was her turn. It was all so fast. One moment she was spinning like a top, the blue dress swirling around her legs like nothing else she'd ever worn; the next, she was pressed to Marcen's solid chest. Their hands had never broken contact.

He grinned at her. "You're a natural."

She flushed again but ignored the compliment. "Where'd a bastion mage learn to dance like a frip?"

"Wasn't always a bastion mage." There was no bitterness in his tone, just a matter-of-factness that sparked more questions and made her feel ashamed, though she could not have said just why.

"What happened?" she asked.

His grip tightened, but it was because his whole body had tensed, and some of his happiness fled his gaze. "Sentinels raided, my…ah…place of employment. Turns out, I unknowingly rattled one of my clients, who decided to tip off the hemies." He winced. "Sorry. The *sentinels*."

They moved past the pair of men and sidled beside an elderly man and woman while Flint turned his words over in her mind. "What sort of work were you doing?"

"I was a whore. In Lasath, if you can believe it." He gave a weak chuckle. "Practically right under Argent's nose."

He watched her like any moment she'd stab him with the knife she'd tucked in her bodice, or at least break the contact of their bodies and turn away.

"Sounds like your client was a horse's ass," she said.

Relief shone in his smile and echoed in his laugh. "Aye, he was. Too bad I didn't realize it until too late." He sobered. "But I was still stupid. I shouldn't have let him—or *anyone*—know what I could do. I knew what could happen. I knew the risks."

"Lot of risks in that line of work," Flint replied as they moved through the dancing throng. "My mother caught the back of more than one client's hand. At least, I think she was a whore," she added, frowning in thought. "Mi and I escaped her pretty young, thank the One, so all I know of her is what little bits and pieces I can recall. We were poor as rat piss and there were always strangers coming through our home. Milo might remember… "

The rest of her words died in her throat and she clenched her jaw against the tears that threatened to fall. *Milo. You're going to leave me behind, aren't you?*

Marcen's touch made her blink up at him. "Have you never been parted from your brother?"

"Never. There was a time when I'd have happily left him on the other side of the world, but now…" She searched the crowd and found Mi and Stonewall sitting at their table, digging into plates piled with Redfern delicacies. Milo was chattering to Stonewall, and the sight of his smiling, happy face made her want to cry in earnest. As far as she knew, he hadn't yet told anyone else about his plans to leave.

Marcen gently guided her over the street with the other dancers. The music slowed its frantic pace; the drums faded to the background while the viols took up the bulk of the tune. On some reckless whim, Flint pressed her cheek against Mar's warm shoulder and spoke into his neck. "What if he gets hurt? Or killed? How would I even know? How can we find each other again?"

"I don't have any answers for you, Flint, though I wish I did."

"He's happy again," she replied. "And I want him to be happy, always. But so much can go wrong." She pulled away to look into Marcen's pale blue eyes, the color of mage-fire at its hottest. "I don't know what to do."

Slender, strong fingers tightened over hers. "What would he do if you told him not to go?"

She frowned. "He'd stay. I think."

"And how would that make him feel?"

Resentful. Angry, probably, though she'd only seen Milo truly angry a handful of times. But resentment would be worse, because it would poison Milo's pure, sweet nature. "He would grow to hate me," she managed as

256

they swayed.

Marcen gave her a sad smile. "Sounds like you know what you must do."

"Aye. But I don't have to sodding *like* it." Her heart felt oddly lighter, though still weighed down by sorrow.

They moved with the music a bit longer before she turned her thoughts from one man to another. In a physical sense, Marcen reminded her of Dev, her dead lover and the squad's former commanding officer before Stonewall had come around. Both Mar and Dev were pale and fair-haired. Both men were slender, though Dev had been more muscular than Marcen, and his being about ten years her senior made him seem more distinguished. But there, the comparisons stopped.

Another gentle squeeze at her waist. "You look like you're a thousand miles away," Marcen said.

Flint managed a smile back. "Only a couple hundred."

He had a beautiful smile and his laugh sent a shiver across her skin. There was a strength in him that went deeper than his lean frame. She might have told him that, or simply lain her head against his shoulder again just to savor the movement of his body so close to hers. She might have done many things, but instead, she asked, "Do you still love Kali?"

He froze, causing the elderly couple nearby to break their rhythm to avoid crashing into them. Flint muttered an apology and urged him onward before they got more than a few dark looks.

"Well?" she asked once they were moving again.

His ears and neck were bright red. "Love is a strong sentiment."

Flint rolled her eyes. "Fine. Do you still want to fu–"

"Seren's light," he muttered, interrupting her as he directed them toward a relatively isolated spot. "You don't mince words, do you?"

"That's not an answer."

Marcen's mouth opened to respond, but his gaze crept toward their friends' table, where Stonewall and Milo sat with Beacon and Sadira. Kali was nowhere to be seen, but it hardly mattered. Flint's heart sank into her guts; her punishment for prying.

"I don't blame you," she heard herself say. "She's kind, and smarter than the rest of us put together."

Somehow, he flushed even deeper, though he was frowning. "It's not like that. I don't...love her, Flint. I never *loved* her. I never knew her well enough to love her. It's just... I never had a chance."

This was enough to make Flint pull away. Dancing was just as pointless as she'd expected. "Sorry to hear that. I'm sure it's been very hard for you – in more ways than one."

She turned from him, no clear idea where she was going other than *away*, then...

"Flint." Her sentinel name, not her birthname. Why did she want to hear him say *Mira*? She gritted her teeth as he caught up to her in a few steps. "Flint, I'm sorry. I was just being honest. I didn't mean to–"

"I'm not angry," she said, and meant it. She took a deep breath to shore up her calm. "But I won't come second. To anyone. That's me being honest with you."

With that, she slipped away from him once more.

TWENTY-SIX

K ali leaned against the tree and exhaled a stream of *biri* smoke into the night. Chilly air clung to the upper level, away from the lights, people, and music, and she'd neglected to bring her cloak, but she didn't care. Even the short trip up the curving wooden stairs made her knee throb. She didn't care about that, either, because right now it was better to be cold, alone, and in pain than warm and close to *him*.

As she was peering through the canopy at the stars, the sound of footsteps on the walkway's wooden planks made her turn. A figure approached, shadowed by the tree and the lights below, but she could make out enough to know it was a man. Tall, slender... At first, she thought it was Beacon, then he came closer and she recognized Heitor Dilt.

She tried to ignore the sudden leap of her pulse. Idalina had sworn she would not breathe a word of Kali's true nature to anyone. In fact, the youngest Dilt had been eager to speak to Kali of mage-related matters, particles and such, and the two of them had spent much of yesterday in conversation. No, Idalina would not have betrayed Kali to her eldest brother.

But that thought did not set Kali at ease right now.

Heitor paused about ten paces away. "Ser Green?"

She fought back a grimace at her hasty pseudonym. "Serla Dilt. Nice to see you."

"You, too. I needed some fresh air." He came closer, inhaling the *biri* smoke. "Although... You don't have another one of those, by any chance?"

"Not on me."

"Ah, shame." He inhaled again and leaned against the tree. "My wife, Iona, hates them, but I like to indulge occasionally."

Kali took a long draw and released the smoke into the night. "Your family certainly knows how to throw a party."

He chuckled. "All Ren and Iona's doing. I've no head for party planning."

"No doubt you've other matters on your mind."

He was quiet, his gaze on the forest around them as his hand stole to a pendant around his neck – a hematite pendant, judging from the dull silver sheen. Music and laughter filtered up from below, but not loud enough to drown out the chirping crickets and the wind shuffling through leaves. "Ida has spoken highly of you and your companions," he said at last. "You, especially. She is *quite* taken with you."

The wind rippled his silk tunic to reveal he wore more than just a hematite pendant. Heitor dripped with hematite: flat bands around several of his fingers, at least two bracelets resting on his slender wrists, and three necklaces – that she could see.

A knot began to form in Kali's belly but she tried to keep her reply calm. "I like Ida a great deal, as well."

He looked down at her, pale eyes catching the dim light. "Of course, I know what she is."

The knot tightened and Kali shored up her energy reserves in preparation for self-defense. She considered reaching out to Stonewall through their bond but decided against it. She could handle this on her own.

Heitor's voice was steady. "She's got a way with our crops and livestock. Besides, she's blood and I love her, so I won't endanger her. But I cannot condone magic–"

"Magic is not a choice," Kali broke in, more sharply than she meant to.

Now he turned to face her, keeping one shoulder against the tree. Stars and moons, he was so tall. Though he did not have Stonewall's strength, or even Beacon's, he could still break her over his knee if he wanted. Instinct screamed at her to flee, but he blocked the only way down.

But she was not helpless.

A part of her leaped at this chance to *take* what she wanted, unfettered, unhindered by caution or virtue. Hunger tugged at her mind, urged her closer to the Dilt man, whispered in her ear as the Fata had done. *Sweet blood. Give it to us.*

She took a final draw of the *biri*. No. She was stronger than this desire. *Better.* She was in control.

"Magic has ripped this country asunder," Heitor said, his voice dropping to a low growl. "And magic could not even save my mother."

"I'm sorry you've lost loved ones, but magic can still do a lot of good."

A strong, slender hand grabbed her right wrist, pulling her close enough to smell the wine on his breath. She tried to jerk out of his grip, but he held her fast. "Mages are a curse," he murmured into her ear. "If I had my way, I'd see them purged from the country."

"But Idalina—"

"Ida is a good girl who offers no threat," Heitor interrupted. His grip tightened. "But you... You are the reason the word 'danger' exists. She never said as much, but I could tell what you are from the way she spoke about you."

He trailed off, gaze locked on hers. Kali's vision pooled to his pale eyes as she gathered her strength. Nothing for it now. She had to defend herself.

"You don't know anything about me," she managed, hoping to keep him talking.

"You are a mage. A pretty one, but that makes you more dangerous. Pretty faces like yours think they can sway men's minds with a mere smile."

Anger swelled within her, making her entire body tremble. But she savored her new-found strength and reveled in her righteousness; for once, no fear bled through her voice. "How fragile you must be, to let a smile vex you so."

Heitor made a noise of disgust and pulled her closer, as if demonstrating how easily he could move her where and how he wanted. He twisted her wrist up, tugging down the sleeve of her borrowed dress, but there was no mage-mark to reveal. "Ah. More of magic's treachery, I see. Well, it hardly matters." His voice was cold. "Do you know what sentinels do to errant moon-bloods?"

"Better than you do."

Focusing on his particles, she grabbed his arm with her left hand, shoved her fingers under his sleeve to touch bare skin, and *pulled.* Heitor Dilt had not a drop of magical blood in his veins, but he had strength enough for her to take. Kali drew his energy into herself, sighing at the pleasant tingling that filled her from within. Strength blossomed within her, sparkling through her veins sweeter and brighter than any wine. *Cold* and *pain* became distant memories; all she knew, all she cared to know, was *power.*

Eyes wide, Heitor tried to shove her away.

Tried.

"Do *you* know," she whispered, flushed with raw power. "What errant moon-bloods do to dregs like you?"

"Please," he groaned. "Have mercy... Please..."

Her blood sang in her veins. Her heart soared, too full of joy and strength to care about his words. *Yes,* her hunger crooned, eager, desperate for all she could take. The sentiment echoed in her memories of the Fata's voices. *Sweet blood. Give it to us. Now.*

"*No,*" she cried, releasing him. But he was already weak as a fawn, so he stumbled backward, glanced off the tree and slid down. The faint scent of a burning *biri* rose from the wooden planks where she'd dropped the smoking end.

Dizzy, drunk with power as much as wine, Kali swayed in place before leaning against the solid oak tree, staring down at the slow rise and fall of his chest. He deserved much worse than this, but she hadn't killed him; she had kept control. The hunger for more power built to a roar, thrumming through her whole self. She had to get away, had to do something *good* with this energy while it lasted.

Only one thing came to mind, and she all but flew back to the party, back to *him.*

*

"Nox's frozen tits," Beacon said, laughing. "You're drunk."

Stonewall glowered at the other man, who'd gone annoyingly blurry. "I'm not."

Before he knew he'd made the decision to rise, he was on his feet, though he swayed and had to brace one hand against the table. Which tilted beneath him. *Stupid, wonky thing.* "I'm *not* drunk," he said again. "I can prove it."

Flint guffawed from her seat. "How?"

No sodding idea *how* he was going to prove his decidedly sober state, but that hardly mattered considering her blatant insubordination. Stonewall leveled her with his most stern look and she laughed harder.

"Burnies," he scoffed, drawing himself fully upright before pointing at Flint. "You may think you know everything, but you're as green as... As..." He looked around—too fast, for the world began to spin—and caught sight of the bouquet of wildflowers resting at the next table. "As green as spring leaves," he said at last, pleased at the poetry pulled from his imagination.

Beacon snickered. "Nice one, Sarge."

Stonewall chose to ignore the mender's sarcasm. He glanced around again, slower this time. When his gaze fell upon an unused walking stick propped against a nearby table, a plan coalesced. But his legs refused to cooperate and instead sent his chair skittering over the street, sliding to a stop a few paces away. Frowning, Stonewall marshalled his body to order, ignored his squad's raucous laughter, and tried again, intent on his mission.

He grabbed the walking stick and returned to his audience. Milo was off talking to Beacon's brother, Vestain, but that was all right. Mi had been so troubled lately. He obviously needed counsel from someone more suitable than Stonewall, who was only capable of making situations worse.

As he'd done over the last two days, he searched for Kali, both with his eyes and through the bond they shared. She was not in sight and he could get no clear sense of her. To his consternation, the image clearest in his mind was of Kali's slashed throat, covered in blood, her eyes blazing like stars. A thrall, or dead, or both. The image had come to him before as suddenly and sharply as a knife in the heart. It had ambushed him when they were all seated together, making him spill his wine, thinking, just for a moment, she really was *gone*.

263

It wasn't a vision, he told himself again, shuddering. *It was just my own worries talking.* But his conviction, like his sight, was blurry and unfocused, and he was tired of being afraid. So he hefted the stick, testing its weight and balance.

"What in the blazing void are you doing?" Flint asked, taking a deep drink from her glass.

Stonewall grinned at her. "Fire-dancing. Sadira, would you be so kind…?"

"No," came the Zhee mage's reply, though he could tell she was hiding a smile.

"Mar?"

"Tempting. But a hard pass."

"Fine," Stonewall replied. "You'll just have to use your imagination."

"Oh, I'm on tenterhooks," Beacon said, leaning back in his chair and clasping his hands behind his head.

Stonewall honed his focus to the stick in his grasp. It didn't take much to pretend the ends were burning, and while the effect would have been more impressive, perhaps Sadira was right not to light them right now. Not because of *him*, of course, but because a lot of people were nearby, in various states of sobriety, and he didn't want any of them to stumble into his path.

The nearest table was empty so he shoved it aside, only faltering a tiny bit. The chairs toppled over the street, for he'd forgotten about them, but the result was the same: he now had an open space to perform. The walking stick was lighter and shorter than he would have preferred, but desperate times and all. One hand grasping the middle, he held it horizontally in front of him and faced his companions.

Beacon, still grinning, propped his boots on the table. "Tor help me, this is going to be good."

"How long before he hits himself in the face?" Flint asked.

"Have a little faith," Stonewall said, though the words came out more slurry than he'd meant.

The mages exchanged glances, but settled into their seats as well, and for the first time in many years Stonewall had an audience. A deep breath, a moment of concentration. Through memory, he transported himself through time and distance, back to Pillau, back to his childhood. Salt air mingled with baking bread wafting from a nearby shop; lapis-blue buildings stood solid beneath an impossibly blue sky; merchants entreated potential customers to stop by their stalls while those customers jabbered to one another. And beneath it all, the susurrus of the ocean whispered, ever-present in his mind no matter where he was in the One's world.

If only Drake were here.

But for once, the thought of his brother did not cause pain, nor bitterness. Drake was alive and well, and if he were here, he'd be at Stonewall's back, just like old times.

Calm settled over Stonewall; not the warm-blanket feeling wrought by his patron god, but a weightier sort that came from within.

Again, Stonewall's body moved on its own accord, but this movement was a wave caressing sand. The walking stick whirled and spun with only a flick of his fingers, a few turns of his wrists. Displaced air whistled softly and only because he listened so close did he hear the faint sound beneath the music. A small part of his mind noted the rounded "O" shapes of his friends' mouths, but he kept most of his focus on the spinning walking stick. On a whim, he tossed, then caught it neatly amid a few flower petals its passage shook loose from their garlands.

Someone clapped. Someone else whistled in appreciation. A few copper and silver coins landed at his feet. Stonewall grinned, beads of sweat rolling down his back, and tossed the stick again.

Desire kicked him in the chest. Not his, but Kali's, and stronger than a roaring fire. Startled, Stonewall glanced over to see her standing a few paces away. Even had her emotions not been so clear, he knew the look on her face, and his body responded in kind. Her desire incited his own and suddenly he wanted nothing more than to hold her close and kiss her senseless. Everything else fell away, leaving just him and her. They would figure out the mess of her magic, of the thralls and the Fata and all the other nonsense. Only love mattered.

His revelations only took an instant. She glanced up, reached out, and the walking stick landed in her grip. Smiling tentatively, she came to him on smooth steps, the stick extended. *A peace offering,* she said through their silent speech.

Stonewall gripped the smooth wood and used it to pull her closer, then dropped the thing and cupped her cheek, pressing their foreheads together. His head spun, though his focus centered on the woman in his arms. *Accepted.*

He kissed her hard. Her mouth opened; she took him in with eagerness and wrapped her arms around him.

But of course, they were not alone.

Whistles and jeers came from the audience Stonewall had captivated with his imaginary fire dancing. A bread roll bounced off his shoulder as Flint shouted, "Ea's balls, get a room! Bad enough we have to hear you grunting and moaning whenever we're camped together."

Stonewall reluctantly broke the kiss and glared at his fellow sentinel. "Insubordination won't be tolerated."

Flint stuck her tongue out at him. "Save the rough talk for the bedchamber."

Kali dissolved with laughter, slumping in his arms and pressing herself even closer. Her euphoria echoed through their bond and a smile crept to his own face despite his best efforts.

"I have to agree with Flint," Beacon piped up. "That's not the kind of display I was hoping for."

"You just wanted me to bust my face open," Stonewall replied.

"It *would* be entertaining," Marcen said.

"Only for a minute," Beacon replied. "Then I'd have to stitch him up. *That* gets old, believe me. He's squirmy."

Kali leaned against Stonewall's side, one hand wrapped around his waist, the other pressed to his chest before it drifted down his stomach to spark another thrill of desire. "I'd rather have him in one piece anyway," she said to the mender.

Distracted as Stonewall was, he almost missed her next words. "But if you're in the mood for mending, it looked like Heitor needed some help."

Beacon sat up. "What's wrong? Where is he?"

A flare of apprehension rose from her, but when Stonewall glanced down, she looked calm. "On the walkway leading to the beacon moth stables," she said. "I think he had too much to drink. He...had some trouble standing, so I told him I'd send some help."

The mender was on his feet in an instant, though he immediately grimaced, clutched his side, and then sank back into his chair. "Ah... right. I think you should find Vestain. Or Ida."

"I'll go," Flint said, rising.

"Thanks." Kali smiled at her. When Flint slipped off, Marcen asked Beacon a question Stonewall didn't catch, and soon the others were engrossed in their own conversations.

Kali looked up at Stonewall again, a question in her eyes.

Is everything all right? he asked through their bond.

"I want to dance," she told him.

His heart sank. "I would like nothing more than to dance with you, but your knee...?"

Her eyes flashed with anger, though it was brief. Only because he was so attuned to her did he catch the emotion before it faded into her usual wry humor. "My knee will be fine tonight."

Gods above, she was so beautiful, softly lit by lamplight, stray flower petals caught in her dark, unbound hair. Idalina had found her a dress the color of ripe plums that clung to her hips and the curve of her breasts; only some of the places he loved to kiss, to suck, to savor. Desire swam through his veins, stronger than wine and hematite together. Nothing would be better than to sink into her, to lose himself with her, and within her.

We could go upstairs, he ventured. *Our rooms will be empty for a little while...*

She laced their fingers together. "Later. I just want to dance with you now." *Please, Elan,* she added silently.

Tor help him, he was not strong enough to resist her under the best of circumstances, let alone when she called him by his birthname. So he squeezed her fingers and drew her closer to whisper in her ear. "Let's dance."

TWENTY-SEVEN

Two days after meeting the Forsworn sentinels, Drake squinted through the final rays of sunlight that crept up the mine's sides. "Where in the blazing void is Talon?"

"Most of the workers have left for the night," Atanar said. "Leal was right to remain at camp. We'll be missed. We must be out of sight – now."

"Hold a few more minutes, Nat. We need Talon's help to get past the guard."

Atanar shifted. "I don't like waiting."

Drake placed a hand on his companion's shoulder. "I know, but please be patient a while longer, all right?"

Atanar's gaze flickered to Drake's palm. "Do I seem as if I will break again?"

Cheeks hot, Drake lowered his hand. "No. I'm sorry… I'm not trying to…*influence* you too much, only buck up your spirits. I won't do it again."

The Canderi rubbed his hands together. "I fear there can be no calm within me without your *influence.*"

"Well, I don't believe that," Drake replied. But was Atanar right? He cursed silently. He'd have to be *extremely* careful not to use his abilities overmuch, lest he rob another of their free will.

"We can't poke around without a guide," Drake continued, hoping to change the subject. "The guard won't let us. We must wait for Talon – or *Tal*, I should say." He snorted. "Elan will never believe I'm about to trust her. Ea's balls, *I* can hardly believe it."

Atanar stared at the black void of the nearby tunnel, where a single guard

269

stood on duty, picking her teeth with her fingernail. When Atanar did speak, his voice was quiet. "Must we enter?"

"I'm afraid so. But we'll be quick."

Atanar did not slide his gaze from the mouth of the tunnel. "*Tang Yaarok*," he whispered.

Before Drake could respond, Talon and Kam came into view, stepping over the scattered rocks with practiced grace. Talon held an unlit lantern.

"Sorry we're late," Kam said as they approached the two men. "Loach summoned me."

"Everything well?" Drake asked.

"As well as it ever is," Kam replied.

Talon nodded to the tunnel. "We shouldn't linger."

Kam made to walk toward the guard, but Drake stopped her with a light touch at her forearm. "We can't just...stroll in, right?"

"Kam has...a plan," Talon murmured, though she was frowning.

"I do, indeed." Kam grinned at Drake and went to the guard, who straightened as the four of them approached. "Well met, Goldie," Kam said to the guard. "It's been too long since we had a good chinwag. My fault, entirely, but I'd hoped to make it up to you tonight. How are your little ones? And has your husband recovered from his illness?"

"Rose and Violet are fine girls, and hale as ever," Goldie replied. "But Ronny's cough is still pretty bad. Stubborn sod refuses to rest. Not that we can afford to. The crop was next to nothing this past harvest season." Her gaze fell upon Talon, Drake, and Atanar. "What's this shifty-eyed lot doing with you?"

Kam did not miss a step. "Watermill's stuck again. We need some muscle to unstick it, and these little lambs were too slow to leave with the evening bell. As I'm still getting Tal acquainted with her duties, I figured I'd escort them here and let them work while you and I catch up."

A coy smile came to Goldie's face. "Unstick it. Right."

"It's a *very* important task," Kam replied, dark eyes sparkling with merriment. "Right, Tal?"

She elbowed Talon's ribs. The former commander gave the most forced smile Drake had ever seen. "Aye. We're quite...desperate."

Goldie rolled her eyes and stepped aside. "Kam, you're such a generous soul. Fine, I'll play your game. Go on," she added to Talon. "Go 'unstick' your mill. Just don't take too long."

Talon grimaced, but Kam laughed and waved them along into the dark tunnel while she and Goldie began to chat. Talon entered cautiously, Drake and Atanar on her heels. Blackness closed around Drake and for a few moments he lost all sense of direction, until light flared before him as Talon lit the lantern with a tinderbox. The passage they were within pressed too close around them. Drake could place both flats of his hands on the walls on either side, and his head almost brushed the ceiling. Atanar wasn't faring much better.

"I mislike this," Atanar murmured, sidling close to Drake. His breath was hot on Drake's cheek. "I would rather wait outside."

"Please, stay," Drake whispered back. "It'll be too suspicious if you go back now." But Atanar began to tremble, so Drake took his hand and squeezed once. "I'm right here, Nat. We'll go together and be quicker than greased otters."

"Step lively," Talon called from a few paces ahead. "No time to waste."

Drake gritted his teeth, but they didn't have time to bicker. So he swallowed his protests and continued onward. Atanar followed, still clutching his hand.

Away from the sun-warmed rocks, the air was cool, almost pleasant, with a faint metallic scent that reminded Drake of hematite. The path twisted down in a series of sharp angles, at times turning into steps that would have sent Drake stumbling to his knees without the bobbing lantern. He did almost fall, once, but Nat caught him, adding a soft smile as he steadied Drake on his feet. Drake smiled back, his stomach fluttering despite himself. He tried to ignore the feeling. Mind on the mission, after all.

About five minutes into their journey, a faint rumbling sound trickled up to them, like the distant roar of the White River. Drake and Atanar exchanged looks. "What's that?" Drake asked Talon, who still marched ahead.

"Nox," came Talon's reply.

Dread, old and deep, flooded Drake's veins and he froze, one hand braced upon the tunnel wall for support. He stared after the flickering light without seeing it until a warm hand squeezed his shoulder and Atanar said his name.

Drake shook himself out of his state and shot the other man a wry look. "Sorry. Just…" But words failed him. Even he couldn't make light of this moment.

Atanar's brows knit. "This place troubles you, too?"

How to explain? Drake began to walk again, hurrying to keep up with Talon, who had not slowed nor paused to look back. "Nox is the name of an Aredian goddess," he said quietly, as if speaking her name too loudly would summon Nox herself.

To his surprise, Atanar nodded. "Yes, the goddess of death." The way he said the words made Drake think he was trying not to roll his eyes. "I am no sapling in your country."

"Aye, Nox is the goddess of death – sort of. It is Nox who brings our souls to the great river, Nox who weighs and measures our actions in this life, and Nox who determines how and when we can cross the river to our next lives." A chill crept up his spine, making him shiver.

"Your gods and such are real? I thought they were all…" Atanar waved a hand. "Fantasies."

"The people of Carver's Creek call the river Nox," Talon called back. "They're morbid, that way, but…" She bent over into a coughing fit. When it ended, she continued. "There is no goddess here. Just the dam."

"Glad to hear it," Drake replied. He glanced at his Canderi companion. "Some folks believe the gods and their stories are metaphors – or fantasies. Some don't."

In the shadows of the tunnel, Atanar's eyes were still somehow so blue, bluer than anything Drake had seen in all his years. "What do you believe?" Atanar asked.

What, indeed? Drake shook his head. "I believe in the One. Beyond that…" He shrugged. "Who knows the truth? But speaking of Nox still makes me uneasy."

272

The lantern disappeared. Drake's heart seized until he realized the former commander had simply turned a corner. When he and Atanar followed, he couldn't help but let out a gasp at the sight that met them. They'd come upon a vast cave. The ceiling stretched so high, it faded into shadows and Drake could not find where it ended. While he stood gaping, Talon was busy lighting a few staked lanterns by the edge of a lake. The glow did not penetrate the water, but painted an inky blackness marred by faint ripples of current that cast a dancing light upon the lower portions of the walls. There was no scent of hematite down here, only cool water and stone, and smoke from the lanterns. Beside the rocky shore where they had emerged, rested a stone dam that spanned the lake's edge, built against the cavern wall.

"Impressive, isn't it?" Talon said, pulling Drake from his awe. She'd come to stand beside him by the dam.

He scrubbed his face. "Aye."

"See those pipes coming out of the water? The windmills above pump the water up to the refinery once the raw ore is ready to be processed."

Drake knelt by the dam, built flush against the cavern wall. A massive wooden lever sat along the side nearest to them, pointing toward the shore where he and Talon stood. "What's this for?" Drake asked.

Talon pointed to several openings in the cavern, across the lake from where they stood, where Atanar lingered alone. "Those lead to the base of the mine, where the overburden is stored. Kam says that every few years, they release the dam a little bit so that it washes away the overburden."

"There's enough water to flood the entire mine?"

They both looked at the retaining wall again, where the reflected lantern light danced over the stones. Talon's voice was weighted. "More than."

Drake considered the layout of the mine. As just another grunt with a pickaxe, he had not been privy to the facility's inner workings. "Where does the overburden go?"

"This area's full of caves. Most are connected by an underground river." She nodded toward the tunnel they'd entered. "There's another cave at the opposite end of the mine's base. But don't ask me how anyone engineered this place to work as it does. It's beyond my understanding."

"Mine as well."

Talon toyed with the lever. "Drake, I... I know nothing I say will change anything, but I...I'm sorry for what I did to you and your brother. I have no explanation for my actions, only regret, though I know it's too little and too late."

He wanted nothing more than to throw her into the dark waters, never to be seen again. But he recalled Hazel's tale of the slaughter at Whitewater Bastion, and could find no room in his heart for anger. "I'm sorry, too." When she looked at him, stunned, he only sighed. "I heard about your father. I'd call Argent a piece of shit, but that'd be unfair to shit."

The woman who stared at him, brown eyes gleaming with tears, was not *Commander Talon*. She was Tal: worn and frayed. "Aye," she whispered, and looked at the water. "Thank you."

A soft splashing sound made Drake turn to see Atanar standing waist-deep in the water, staring up into the shadows of the ceiling. The Canderi man stepped forward, the water sloshing. His eyes were wide and his mouth hung open, and the water around his waist rippled with the force of his trembles.

What in Tor's name was wrong? Drake rushed along the shore to Atanar. He reached for the other man's arm, to tug him back onto solid ground. "Nat, what in the void's gotten into–"

When his hand closed around Atanar's wrist, the Canderi whirled, gripped Drake's arm, and slung him into the basin. The shock of the icy water stole Drake's breath but he was a strong swimmer, thank Tor, for he could not touch the river's bottom and the current was swift.

"Nat," Drake tried again, trying *really* hard not to be ticked off. "Nat, what're you..."

Tal had come up to Atanar as well, though had wisely kept away from the water. "*Kutanya?*" she asked.

Drake knew little of the Canderi language, but knew enough to understand she was asking after Atanar's well-being. At the sound, Atanar seemed to come out of a dream. He blinked hard, turned, and looked at the woman standing on the shore – then he lunged. Three strides brought him to Tal, who took several steps backward. But she was not fast enough, nor strong enough, and Atanar's hands closed around her throat as he knocked her to the ground. She cried out once, struggling beneath him, but even she could not hope to match his strength.

"Get back," Atanar snarled at Tal in Aredian. "You will not take him. You will not harm him. Get *back!*"

Shit! Drake plunged back through the water, swimming to the other man with powerful strokes. Icy water cascaded down his back and arms as he scrambled upon the shore. He leaped upon Atanar and wrapped his arm around the Canderi's neck to pull him off Tal, who even now struggled and fought, swiping at Nat's eyes with her fingernails.

With effort, Drake broke the Canderi's hold, but when Atanar released the Forsworn sentinel he whirled on Drake, blue eyes wide and unseeing as he swung his fist toward Drake's jaw. Drake had no time to duck completely out of the way, but managed to avoid the worst of Nat's considerable force. Still, his jaw stung from the impact; a swell of heat followed, then pain. That would probably bruise later. Nat swung again. This time, Drake avoided the blow, adding a tug at the Canderi's arm to further goad him away from Tal. As he did, he searched for signs of thrall possession, but saw no agitation in the other man's particles, nor a trace of starlight in his eyes.

Atanar was lost to his own mind. He struck at Drake again, this time shoving all his weight into the punch, but Drake was ready. Rather than duck out of the way, he caught the Canderi man's fist and used the momentum to draw them both backward. He toppled over onto his back, Atanar atop him, still caught in whatever madness had taken hold of him. Atanar reared up to swing at Drake again, but Drake stopped him, grasping Atanar's wet, bearded cheeks, pressing his palms against the other man's face and neck. Atanar's pulse raced. Magic coiled within Drake; faint as a far-off whistle, but still clear and bright in its own way. Drake exhaled and drew Atanar closer, willing, *Calm.*

Atanar froze, still straddling Drake, leaning over him. *Calm,* Drake

275

pressed again. Atanar's chest heaved, but the wild look in his eyes faded. He blinked several times before leaning over heavily, bracing his weight on his arms on either side of Drake's head. Water dripped from his hair and beard, pattering onto Drake and the cavern floor. Neither one spoke before Drake smoothed back the tangled, dark blond strands of the other man's beard. "Atanar."

The Canderi struggled to his feet and went to stand by the lake once more, shoulders hunched.

Drake rose as well, slowly, and glanced over at Tal, who was bent over, hacking and coughing. "Are you all right?"

"No worse," she managed between coughs, and nodded at Atanar. "Is he?"

Good question. Drake brushed mud and gravel from his back, rubbed his already aching jaw, and made his way to the Canderi man. His boots squelched upon the rock. "Nat?"

Atanar looked at the water, arms braced around his middle. "Do it."

"Do what?"

"What you promised." Atanar inhaled deeply before dropping his arms and raising his chin to expose his neck. "I will offer no resistance. You have that knife in your boot?"

"Nat, what in the blazing void are you—"

"You promised," Atanar broke in, shooting Drake a look that fell somewhere between anger and desperation. "If I harmed anyone, you promised to kill me. Don't you remember?" He faced the lake once more and pulled back the soaking, matted tangle of his hair. "Be quick."

Drake swiped water from his face, hoping to buy some time. "What happened, Nat?"

"You promised—"

"I know what I promised," Drake broke in, placing a hand upon Atanar's shoulder. "But before any bloodshed, please tell me what happened."

Atanar had tensed beneath his touch, but now he sagged against Drake, who, after a hesitation, rested his palm against Atanar's upper back. The Canderi was warm, even now.

"Tang Yaarok," Atanar whispered. "It was a cave like this one, where I slaughtered my brother and my hunting party. I was looking at the water, just now, thinking of that night, and..." He trailed off with a shaking inhale. "Ancestors help me. I am still possessed."

"It's all right," Drake said quietly. "You're not a thrall any longer, Nat. You're just...remembering. I've seen it before," he added at Atanar's confused look. "With sentinels who've gone through a particularly harrowing mission. Such things change a person; the memories linger and can resurface when you least expect it. But you're no thrall." He offered a faint smile. "Trust me. I'm a mage. I can tell."

"I saw them: my brother, my friends. All dead by my hand. I could smell the blood. I could *feel* the anger within me, the foreign presence."

"It wasn't you who killed your brother and your friends," Drake replied. "It was the thrall. You're innocent."

Atanar shook his head. "I am responsible. I should have been stronger." He exhaled again. "I am a monster."

"I promise you, Nat. You're no monster. Just a man."

Atanar looked at Drake, his brilliant blue eyes wet. "You saved me. You and Kali. You brought me back to myself – twice now." His regard shifted; his gaze seemed to soften and heat all at once, like steel in a blacksmith's forge.

Drake's vision clung to those two beautiful eyes, the rugged blond beard, the muscled shoulders. Desire flushed through him, and he very nearly forgot himself and closed the last of the space between them.

But.

Although Atanar bore no physical wounds, his mental scars were still healing. Perhaps one day, they could explore whatever lay between them, but for now, Atanar needed a friend more than a lover – especially a lover who could quite literally *change* his mind. So Drake gave the other man the most reassuring smile he could muster under the circumstances. "You're no monster, but neither are you...whole. You must be patient with yourself."

"I will try." Atanar's brows knit. "But something is amiss. Have I apprehended you?"

"Offended," Drake corrected, though Atanar wasn't far off, in a way. "And no, you've done nothing wrong. Well…" He rubbed his stubbled jaw, welcoming the brief distraction of pain, then nodded to Tal. "I think you owe our guide an apology."

Atanar grimaced, but drew himself upright, swiping at his face and clothes to rid himself of what water he could. His bearing changed as he walked toward Tal; he held himself like any first tier.

Tal tensed but did not run. Atanar knelt before her, palms open, and murmured something in his native tongue. She regarded him, and then replied in kind, and Atanar ducked his head. Tal glanced at Drake. "He's asked for forgiveness."

"I gathered." *But did you give it?* Drake wanted to add.

She looked back at Atanar. "He said Kalinda saved his life. Is that true?"

"Kali's the only mage who can cure thralls," Drake replied. "She was trying to teach others to do so when we parted ways."

"So he was a thrall?"

Drake nodded.

Tal knelt in front of Atanar, touched his bearded chin, drawing his gaze up, and said in Aredian, "Forgiven."

*

Eris sucked in a breath as mist bloomed around them. Jensine's eyes were closed and her face was tight with concentration as the mist settled over the rust-red rocks that surrounded their camp. Seren's Children, who had gathered to witness their leader's act of power, faded from Eris' view, and only when she placed a hand on Brenna's shoulder did she confirm that her fellow mage was still beside her.

The rocks were little more than faint shadows in the mist; the fire, only a soft glow beside Eris' feet. She squinted at the sky but saw only that pearly gray sheen, rippling with white. "It's incredible," she whispered. "But how can she manage it? The air is so dry here… Where's she getting the moisture?"

Brenna did not answer immediately. "I don't understand much about my mother, but I know she likes showing off."

The mist began to dissipate, allowing Eris to make out Caith and Jensine taking a seat on an obliging bit of rock. The older mage met Eris' gaze and lifted a brow in silent inquiry.

Eris stepped around the smoldering campfire to Jensine's side. "Impressive. That will be a fine distraction."

"It makes better cover," Caith replied.

He was right, but the idea of hiding from the hemies—again—made Eris' lip curl in distaste.

Jensine swiped her brow and accepted a cup of water that one of the others offered. She drank deeply before regarding Eris. "My magic will do its job, provided your friends' information about the dam is correct."

Eris fought the urge to glance in the direction of Carver's Creek, where Drake and Atanar were—hopefully—gathering more details on the underground dam. "It is."

"Working with disgraced hemies to destroy the mines." Jensine scoffed. "I suppose there's a sort of poetic irony to it all, though I hope you aren't planning on bringing any of *them* into our number once our business here is finished."

Eris brushed aside a strand of hair—still shorter than she expected—and met Jensine's gaze. "The hemies will never be my allies."

Which wasn't *entirely* true. Kali's mother presented a dilemma. Eris' only certainty was that she couldn't let Kamala perish before Kali saw her. Beyond that... Well, she could only make so many plans. Life had a way of changing even the best-laid ones.

She glanced between Jensine, Caith, and the other mages. "So it's agreed, then? We'll attack in two days' time?"

Caith crossed his arms. "Why not now? According to Drake, their latest hematite shipment is nearly ready. We ought to stop it before it leaves the mines."

"We will," Eris assured him. "But we must also send another message, one that shows the hemies and the Circle that we have as few scruples as they do. Apparently, the sentinel High Commander sends several squads to escort each shipment where it needs to go. Everything is carefully timed; we must act when they are here, so that we may inflict as much damage upon the hemies as possible."

Jensine held out her cup and one of the other mages took it away. "I like the thread of your thoughts, Echina, but last I checked, hemies know how to swim. Flooding the place won't be enough."

"Which is where the rest of you will come into play." Eris stepped over to one of the nearby boulders where she'd used their gathered intelligence to sketch a rough picture of the mine's layout. "Hematite lives here, but so does wood and earth – and particles. The flood is our first step. Magic is at our command: it's time to use it for the greater good."

Brenna frowned. "You still mean to kill everyone there?"

"Let it go, Bren," Caith snapped.

"Apologies for not condoning mass murder," Brenna replied. "I think drowning the place sends a clear message – without turning *us* into the villains."

"The plan is set," Jensine replied. "If you don't like it, leave. Otherwise, keep your thoughts behind your teeth." She nodded to Eris. "Let Drake and his hemie friends do as they will. Our magic will prevail."

The rest of Seren's Children exchanged approving looks, with a few even grinning with the same sort of feral excitement Eris had often seen upon Gid's face. What would Gideon say about her plans? *Good work, love.* She could see his smile in her mind's eye, feel the warmth of his gaze upon her. *You're a true leader.*

Movement in the corner of her eye caught her attention. Leal strode by, spear clutched in one gloved hand, traveling pack and water skin slung over her shoulder. Eris excused herself from the others and picked her way through the rocks toward her Sufani ally.

She caught up with Leal a few paces from the spindly creek the mages had made their camp beside. "What are you doing?" Eris asked.

Leal had set her spear and pack aside to kneel by the creek's edge, water skin in hand. She did not turn. "You have eyes, don't you?"

Eris bit her tongue against her own swell of anger. "Why *now?*"

"I should have left already." The Sufani grabbed her spear and pack. She made to brush past Eris, but Eris stood in her way. Leal exhaled. "Move."

"Weren't you going to help Drake?"

"Drake doesn't need my help. Nor do you. No, I cannot stay here a minute longer." Leal's voice dropped to whisper something in her native Sufa; Eris caught the word *kotahi,* but nothing more, but the regret on Leal's face was clear.

"Fine." Eris lifted her chin and stepped aside.

Leal stared at her, tightening her grip upon the spear. She had only taken one step when Eris said, "You weren't wrong, you know. At least, not in the end."

"What?"

Eris held out a hand, palm up. "I keep my promises. I'm ready if you are."

Leal had stopped at Eris' words, but now seemed to go utterly still, not even breathing. "You said using magic was dangerous for you now. Dangerous for your babe."

"If I've learned anything since leaving Whitewater City, it's that I'm stronger than I realized," Eris said, thinking of Kam's magic-smoothed skin. "I can at least *start* to help you now. Besides, we made a deal, one you've upheld far better than I have."

"You're with child," Leal replied, although she did not look Eris' way. "Some would say that means you're not in your right mind." Eris bristled, but Leal shrugged, adding, "Children change everything. At least, that's my understanding."

"Do you want any?"

"One day, maybe." Leal gave a low laugh. "Though I have no wish to bear them."

"Fair enough." Eris risked a touch against Leal's solid shoulder. "For what it's worth, you will make a fine father."

Now the Sufani looked at Eris fully, green eyes wide. "You think so?"

Eris could not help her smile. "Let's find out."

They found a secluded spot beyond the creek, well out of sight from the camp, although they weren't out of shouting range. As Leal set down her belongings, Eris took a seat upon the ground, gathering her concentration and focus, testing her own strength. She'd not shifted in a few days, so she was fairly brimming with magic. Her little one—her son!—was peaceful and quiet within her womb; part of her attention was always on his presence, and would remain so while she worked her magic on her friend.

Leal settled in front of her, rubbing her arms and glancing around them before gazing at Eris. "You're certain this won't hurt your babe?"

"When we went to the mines, I healed a very old, deep scar upon one of the Forsworn sentinels and felt no ill-effects."

"Which one?"

"Does it matter?"

The Sufani frowned. "It was the woman—Kam—wasn't it? The one who looks like Kalinda."

Eris studied her friend. "Why don't you look impressed?"

"I don't trust her. She's too..." Leal considered. "She is not a godly woman, though she pretends to be."

"She seemed quite pious."

"Aye. *Seemed.* But anyone so eager to kill is not acting by the One's edicts." Eris braced for another censure of her own plans, but it did not come. Leal only regarded her and added, "I have no magic to speak of, but I know *people.* I was right about that other sentinel—Rook—and I'm right about Kam. Don't trust her."

Eris cleared her throat, anxious to steer the conversation back to the business at hand. "In any case, if I feel any pain from using magic on you, I'll stop at once." She hesitated. "Before we begin, you should know that I've never attempted anything like this before, so I don't quite know what I'm doing. But...well, there are differences between men and women's particles, so my plan is to simply coax yours into those of a man, and let nature take its course. It may take a long time—months or more—for you to fully feel the effects. It may take hours. We may have to do this more than once, and even then, it might not work as you hope. I truly don't know."

Leal, who by now had some inkling of how magic worked, nodded. "I understand."

"Do you?" Eris asked. "I've been another shape. Not permanently, of course, and not because the one I was born with wasn't right, but still. A new body is...well, it's strange and often frightening. Are you completely certain you want to go through with this? I'm not sure I can reverse what I do."

Pale green eyes, almost gray with anxiety, met Eris', but when Leal extended her bare hands, neither one trembled. "I've wanted this my whole life, Eris. I want this with everything I am. Even if it's folly, I must try."

Eris smiled at her friend. "Well, then I suppose only one question remains: Will you choose a new name?"

"Ah." Leal scrubbed a hand through her short hair, displacing her hood. "I've hardly dared to consider such a thing. That is a question for later, I think." She took a deep breath. "It's time."

Leal's hands were slender and strong, cold from the wind and calloused from years of labor and training. Eris delved her concentration deep into Leal's particles, searching for those she identified as feminine. Both masculine and feminine particles looked the same, at first glance, but each held a different energy; each *felt* different in a way Eris could not quantify. The best comparison she could draw was that of a song with two distinct but complementary harmonies. But as much as Eris wanted to understand the differences, she didn't need to in order to perform her magic. As she did with her body's own particles when she urged them into a crow-shape, she laid her will upon Leal's feminine particles and coaxed them to change.

They resisted at first, but Eris was prepared. Her initial attempts to shift herself had brought about much the same result, so patience and perseverance were key. *Don't force it,* she thought, settling further into her focus. *Be gentle.*

Eris focused on a handful of feminine particles first. Their energy hummed in a familiar tune, so Eris coaxed them to a different melody. At first, they kept resisting, but then the hum of energy shifted, transformed, and the masculine particles' song grew – and maintained their new melody.

Heartened by this small success, Eris moved to another handful of particles, and another, and another still. Her head began to feel light, but not overmuch, so she pushed on. Leal's hands were shaking and the Sufani made soft, hiccupping sounds that Eris associated with tears, but she didn't dare to look. Surely Leal would say if she was in pain, so the magic must be working. For the first time in Eris' life, she was performing true, powerful magic on someone she cared for, with the intent of making her friend's life *better*.

Dizziness threatened to steal Eris' concentration, but she ignored it and worked faster, harder, shape-changing her way through as many of Leal's particles as she could reasonably focus upon at a time. Magic hummed through her own veins, responding to her urging in a way it never had before. Seren's light, she was strong! So much stronger than she ever knew. *This won't take more than one session,* she realized with awe. *I can help Leal now. Forever. As long as—*

Pain shot through her abdomen and the thread of her concentration snapped. Eris came back to herself gasping, doubled over as the force of the pain seemed to rip out her insides. Dimly, she heard someone calling her name—a man she did not know—but she couldn't open her eyes, couldn't do anything more than clutch her stomach. Her body felt leaden and weak, and her sight became shadowed. Was she dying? Would her and Gid's son die, too?

"Stay here," the man said. "I'll bring help."

"Save him," she managed, though she did not know who she spoke to, for the stranger had risen and run away. "Please… Save my son."

TWENTY-EIGHT

onsciousness trickled in slowly. Something warm and solid rested at Kali's side, curled close without touching. She inhaled and found *Stonewall*: leather, sweat, and wine, and that scent that was purely him. Without opening her eyes, she eased closer to the bulwark of his body, resting her head on his bent elbow and pressing against his chest. Still asleep, he grunted, and then gave a soft hum of pleasure and nuzzled her hair, his stubble and breath both tickling her cheek. In her mind's eye, the thread that bound their hearts sparkled, bright and gold.

Her body was leaden and her mind weary, so she tried to drift back to sleep, but the longer she was awake, the more she noticed other pressing needs: a full bladder, a mouth stuffed with cotton, a roiling stomach, and an aching head. And her knee… Sweet fucking stars, she wished she were asleep again, because the moment she realized how her knee burned, she thought someone had pierced her skin with a knife pulled straight out of a blacksmith's forge.

Sleep was a lost cause. Groaning, she rolled away from Stonewall's warmth and shoved back the blanket to get a look at her knee, just in case someone really *had* stuck her with a knife. But the moment she opened her eyes, she regretted it, for too-bright daylight cleaved through the round window of the room they'd stumbled into last night. A chorus of birds and cicadas serenaded her, but the shrill sounds only made her headache worse. She gritted her teeth lest she yell at the birds to shut up, and examined her knee. Other than some faint swelling, the joint was fine.

And honestly, aside from her less-than perfect physical state—nothing

285

new there—she soared with the admittedly wine-drenched recollections of the night before. Her memories of their dancing were blurred; mostly she recalled the feel of his body moving with hers, the press of his hands to her hips, and the molten gold of his eyes as he gazed at her like she was something sacred. He'd been drunk, of course, probably more so than her, otherwise he might never have danced with her for fear of hurting her knee.

For the first time in her memory, she'd danced to her heart's content. Not only that, she had controlled her magic. Yes, she had acted out of anger, but Heitor should never have threatened her so – especially if he knew she was a mage. No doubt he was still fast asleep along with the rest of the city, although she and her friends would have to leave very soon. But what mattered most was that she'd proven her mastery over herself and her desire for power, and used the energy to carouse with Stonewall.

He would probably not be as pleased with her news, but she could convince him. She hoped. One more peek reassured her that he was still sleeping, so she struggled to her feet, threw on her clothes, and stumbled for the door. It was still early enough that no one else was awake, so she made it to the latrine without meeting anyone. The small wood-paneled room held only a chamber pot, and ewer of water, a basin, and a round window the size of her head that looked over the canopy. After the welcoming shock of icy water on her face and neck, Kali tipped the basin's contents back into the ewer, purifying the particles so that the next occupant would find only clean water. She'd already done the same for the chamber pot. If she'd had more time, she would have taken a proper bath downstairs, in the guest bathing room, but she was unwilling to risk running into one of the Dilts.

Slightly refreshed, she slipped out of the latrine and into a bright spring morning. A wooden walkway wound around the outside of the branch, leading back down to the rest of the Dilt home. Kali's headache and throbbing knee made the journey slow going, but she didn't have the energy to be annoyed at such inconvenience. Even though the fallen oak that housed the Dilt family was lying on its side, it was still massive enough to allow a view of the upper levels of the few nearby normal trees who managed to grow in this forest of giants. The massive oak trees loomed overhead, dwarfing Kali. This place really was marvelous.

Only one guard stood on duty within sight of the hatch on the level where she and her friends had been staying. The woman ignored Kali as she made to slide open the wooden panel to step within. But the moment Kali's fingers touched the hatch, it slid open to reveal Sadira.

"Oh, good morning," Kali said, hoping she sounded less hungover than she felt. "I was just going to–"

Sadira's power rolled off the Zhee mage like heat swelling from a fire. The force of it cut off Kali's words and knocked her back a pace. Hunger overtook her, strong enough to blur her vision, and she took a step forward, heedless of her knee's protests, one hand extended as if to grab–

No! Kali snatched her hand back as if she'd been burned. With effort, she backed up further, hoping to put more distance between herself and her friend. Her heart raced and sweat trickled down the small of her back with the effort of keeping her hunger at bay.

Sadira was not fooled. She regarded Kali with that same calm calculation she used when examining an injured patient, before she spoke. "I was going to find you, too. Come with me."

She continued down the walkway from which Kali had just come. Kali hesitated. Should she follow? Or would the urge for Sadira's magic prove to be too strong? Well, she couldn't stand here, debating, so she hurried after her friend as best she could. After all, she was in control.

Once they were out of earshot of the guard, Sadira's stride slowed, finally stopping once they'd reached a shaded spot on the walkway.

"Beacon and I saw Heitor last night," Sadira said without preamble. "Vestain thought he was only drunk, but I felt there was something else." Her eyes narrowed. "I was right."

Kali looked away, scratching her nail along the tree bark. Everything was fine. Probably. "Was Heitor...?"

"He was very near his next life," Sadira replied, and Kali's stomach flipped. She hadn't taken *that* much of his energy!

"A few more moments, and you would have killed him," Sadira went on. "He sleeps now and I believe he will recover. But Kali…" Sadira took a deep breath, as if *she* were fighting for control. It was so unlike the Zhee mage that Kali looked up, alarmed. She met Sadira's gaze and saw, for the first time, true anger burning behind those pale eyes.

Heat swam through Kali's veins, although this time she did not look away. She was blameless. "But what?"

Sadira's voice was low. "What if you had killed him?"

"He knows I'm a mage." Kali rubbed her wrist, for she could still feel his iron grip. "He sought me out, threatened me while he wore enough hematite to outfit a sentinel garrison. I had to protect myself."

"Yes, you did," Sadira agreed, though Kali took no pleasure in her tone. "But you could have done so without abusing your magic. Your actions bring danger to us all."

"I had no other choice," Kali shot back, close to tears. She clenched her jaw against the feeling, focusing instead on her throbbing knee.

Sadira's intricate white braids swayed as she shook her head. "Rarely have I seen you so happy as last night, when you returned to dance with Stonewall. You enjoyed stealing Heitor's energy, did you not?"

Kali swiped back her unbound hair and tried for a distraction from the sudden, heavy weight upon her chest. "Look, if it makes you feel any better, he doesn't know about you or Marcen. We'll leave right away, and…" Kali trailed off at the stricken look on her friend's face. "What?"

But Sadira ran her palms down her already smooth dress. When she did speak, she did not look at Kali. "Beacon is not fit to travel. He must remain here for some time. But you should go. At once."

Realization dawned and Kali could not help her surprise – or her shame. "You don't want to come with me."

Sadira hesitated before she met Kali's gaze. "It is best if you and I part ways as well. At least until you have your…addiction under control."

Kali's jaw dropped. *"Addiction?* I think you've got the wrong word."

Pale-blue eyes bored through her skull to her very soul. "I know what I say. Do you not feel it now? The urge to take my power for yourself?"

Sweet blood. Sweet magic. Give it to us...

The hunger had never left; she'd only ignored it, like she so often did with her sodding knee. And it was so much worse around other mages. But every time she'd taken power, even from a non-mage, the hunger grew too pressing to shut away. What would happen if she could no longer ignore it? Kali could not find the words to answer the other mage. She dropped her gaze to her scuffed boots, her eyes stinging, her face hot, and every part of her in pain.

"I have no wish to be away from you," Sadira said softly, though Kali could not bring herself to look up. "But there is much you don't tell me. But I know I make your...situation difficult to bear. And I cannot..." Sadira exhaled. "I cannot cause pain to those I care for. I have done that, enough."

"You would abandon our mission?"

"For now."

Neither spoke until Kali managed to lift her gaze. "I was right to fight back."

"Yes," Sadira said. "But you also used magic with anger. That will only lead to despair."

"So I should have just let him attack me?"

Sadira lifted one hand as if to touch Kali's arm before drawing it back, clasping it with her other. That, more than anything else, told Kali the depth of Sadira's fear. "All I know," Sadira whispered, "is I would wish a path for you other than the one you keep choosing."

For only the second time since knowing her, Kali saw true tears brighten her friend's eyes. "You must leave," Sadira added. "The sooner, the better."

Tears stung Kali's eyes too, but she tried to speak normally. "Will you go as well?"

Sadira's dark cheeks flushed but her voice was steady. "I will remain with Beacon for now." A faint smile touched her lips. "Heitor seems to think I am some sort of Zhee courtesan, so I believe my abilities are still secret. The moment Beacon is fit to travel, we will leave this place."

"Heitor doesn't seem all that fond of Beacon," Kali replied, frowning. "I'm worried the two of you won't find sanctuary here much longer."

"Do not concern yourself with us. We will be fine." Sadira gave her a soft, sad smile. "Take care, Kali. I believe in my heart that we will see each other again."

With that, she bowed and slipped past Kali, back the way they had come. Once she was out of earshot, Kali whispered to the trees. "I hope so."

*

Kali returned to Stonewall's room to find her sentinel still curled in the bed, head sandwiched between two pillows. She eased herself down to sit beside him.

"Sweet Mara's mercy," he groaned. "I can't decide if I want to puke or cut off my own head."

His misery was a welcome distraction from her own. She turned fully to him, careful not to bump her knee, gently urged his arm and the pillow down, and pressed her fingertips to his temple. "Let's try something less messy first."

Stonewall hissed in pain and tried to squirm away, but Kali held firm. "Be still," she murmured, concentrating on the particles in and around his head, while she slid her other hand down to his stomach. His particles pressed together too tightly, pulsating with unreleased tension; little wonder he was suffering. There was only a trace amount of hematite in his blood, so it was simple to ease his discomfort. A few minutes of focus, then the pillow fell back and he heaved a great sigh, and cracked one eye open to regard her.

"I have never loved you more than I do at this moment," he murmured.

Remember that in a few minutes, Kali thought, trying to smile. "Feeling better?"

"Leagues." He rubbed his head and sat upright, slowly. "But what was in that wine?"

"Nothing unusual, as far as I could tell. You're just not used to drinking without hematite in your system. Beacon tried to warn you. Do you remember?"

"Most of last night's a blur. Most." He gave her that boyish grin that made her heart stutter. "I remember *you* very well."

"So glad to hear it." She tried to summon the same levity, but her throat was tight and tears threatened to fall. *No*, she scolded herself. *Sadira's wrong. Everything will be fine.*

He skimmed a hand down her bare arm. "What is it?" He frowned. "You're feeling rough as well, aren't you? Do you need Sadira?"

"I'll be fine," she said, too quickly. She looked away from him, at the clothes scattered across the room the men had been allotted. Her cheeks grew warm. "Where did Mi and Mar have to sleep last night? Since we took their room."

"I don't know. In Beak's room, maybe. We'll apologize to them, I promise." He tipped her chin up so that their eyes met. "We never really talked about... anything, did we?"

Would he be angry or only disappointed? Of the two, she would rather have the former. But either way, she had to be truthful. She had to tell him. She took a deep breath to gather her courage.

"What happened to you last night?" she asked instead. "When you dropped your glass? It felt like you were suddenly...afraid."

Light brown eyes, tinted gold by the morning sunlight, studied her. She had not fooled him. But his hesitation to answer came from another place. "I...had a vision," he said at last, slowly. "It was..."

"Bad?" she asked when he trailed off.

"Terrifying." His gaze grew distant even as he looked at her, and he reached up to trace the raised scar on her neck. "You were at Parsa again, only you were a thrall this time, too. Your eyes..." He shuddered. "They burned. And the blood..."

He wrapped his arms around her, pulling her close, burying his face in her hair so that his words were muffled. "It was like you were dead. I couldn't *feel* you, and the only thing I could see was..."

Say it, she told herself when he trailed off. *Tell him what you did!*

But she was a coward. "You didn't have a vision, Stonewall. Just a drunken dream."

"I was awake." His annoyance flared like a struck tinderbox. "And yes, I was drunk, but I wasn't delusional. No…it was a vision, sent from the gods." His voice softened. "Well, from Tor. It's not the first time, but I hope it's the last."

Her disbelief was real, not only borne of a desire to distract him. Still, she chose her words carefully. "Have any of these 'visions' come to pass?"

"Not yet." He studied her. "You don't want to talk about using your magic on Ida, do you?"

Kali's knee still throbbed and her body was still angry about her shenanigans the night before, but she could bear the pain for a little while longer. She went to the window, hoping the necessary words would come easier if she didn't have to look in his eyes. She stared at the glass without seeing the forest beyond. "Well, there's good news, and bad news."

Stonewall swore. "What happened?"

Kali tried to swallow the lump in her throat. "The bad news is…Heitor knows what I am."

He swore again. "How?"

"Last night, during the party… I ran into Heitor outside. He…" Her words died as her eyes burned, and she hated herself for even the inchoate tears.

It was not yet true anger that pricked at him, but the beginnings of it, as if he were shoring up his battlements in preparation of an attack. "What did he do?"

Kali shook her head. "He knows Ida's a mage. He figured out I'm one too, and he grabbed me, threatened me. I'm fine," she added at his spike of alarm, "I just don't like being manhandled, especially not by close-minded bullies. So I used my magic on him. I took some of his energy for myself, to teach him a lesson. Then I went to find you."

Stonewall's transformation was instantaneous. One moment he was lying on the bed, as relaxed as he ever got. The next, he leaped to his feet, his shoulders squaring and his gaze darting to his weapons and gear, as if assessing how quickly he could suit up before danger struck. The change was not only physical; his sudden tension reverberated through their bond like a drumbeat.

All of that, Kali could have borne without chagrin. Stonewall was a soldier at his core and a part of him would always be prepared for a fight. What cut her to the quick was the lack of surprise, both in his face and in the invisible ties that bound them. On some level, he had believed she would cause trouble.

She rushed to add, "But the good news is I *never* lost control, not even a little. He's still alive. I didn't go too far, with him or with Ida. I'm not–"

"Don't," he broke in. "I can't. Not right now."

He grabbed his gear and stalked toward the door. Kali's heart fell into her stomach, suddenly tangled in knots. She jumped up, winced from the pain in her knee, and started after him, reaching for him through their bond as she did. "Elan–"

The current of emotion between her and Stonewall trickled almost to nothing, as if he had pinched a vein. He stopped at the threshold, his back to her. "Don't," he said again, and slipped out of sight.

TWENTY-NINE

D rake's boots crunched against the rocks of Stonehaven Province. The sound echoed in the silence between him and Atanar, a silence that had not completely fled in the few hours since the incident in the cave. The *incident*. Drake resisted the urge to rub his throbbing jaw.

Gods above, they'd spent longer in the dam than he'd intended; now it was almost dawn. *Another day, another disaster*, he thought wryly.

When Carver's Creek was out of view, Atanar cleared his throat. "I think you may be correct about how I am still...troubled. But I don't know what to do about it."

"Nor do I," Drake replied. "But as they say, 'time heals most wounds, unless the Laughing God finds you first.'"

Atanar scowled. "The Laughing God. I will never understand your Aredian customs."

"That's probably for the best," Drake said. "A lot of them are quite silly."

Atanar said something else, but Drake missed it, for a somewhat familiar figure came sprinting toward them from the direction of the mages' camp. *Somewhat*, because the figure was decidedly male in form, yet when the person drew closer, Leal's face came into view. Her usual Sufani hood and veil were gone, and her face was...well, it was Leal's face, but different.

"She did it," Drake breathed.

"Is that Leal?" Atanar asked.

Before either of them could say more, Leal bounded up to them, breathing hard. "Come, quickly," she—*he*—said, pointing toward the camp. "Eris is

294

in trouble."

Drake's heart stuttered but he and Atanar followed Leal, who gave a summary of what had happened. At least Eris had used her magic for good, but Drake would not forgive himself if she died on his watch. Gid certainly wouldn't have.

"Jensine and the others are with her now," Leal said. "But I don't trust any of that lot as far as I could toss them."

"Nor do I," Drake admitted.

Leal paused, blinking hard. "She was only trying to help me. I should never have–"

"Stop that kind of talk right now," Drake broke in. "Eris always does as she pleases. You know that. You're not to blame for her actions."

They reached the mages' camp to find the fire blazing and the mages clustered around Eris, who lay upon a padding of blankets, curled on her side. Her eyes were closed and her brow was furrowed in pain, but she was breathing, thank Mara.

Brenna hurried to meet them. "She's fine. The babe is fine. Everyone will be all right."

Drake made to step past the renegade mage. "I want to see for myself."

Brenna grimaced. "That may not be as easy as you like. Mother's in a mood."

"Bully for her. Let me see my friend."

But Caith met him, blocking the way to Eris. "What do you hope to do for her, metal-licker?"

Drake glared at the other man. "This again? Sass doesn't suit you, Damaris. Let us by. Let us help our friend."

"She doesn't need your help," Caith shot back. His gaze fell upon Leal and his eyes narrowed. "You, least of all. What were you thinking, allowing her to put herself in such danger, all for the sake of your vanity? Sodding dregs. Is there no end to how you use us? Don't you have any regard for her child? Or are you a murderer as well as a Sufani heretic?"

Leal's mouth opened but no sound came out. It took every ounce of Drake's self-control not to flatten the other mage. "There is no *vanity* here,

Damaris, nor is Leal a murderer. Though you can't say the same, given what you've been planning. And that's a fine way to thank us, by the way, for risking our asses for *you* every day, while you hide, sniveling about how the world treats you unfairly. Well, I've seen unfairness. Hell, I've sodding *lived* it, more than any of you. So shut your idiot mouth and stand aside before this gets ugly."

Caith's hands tightened into fists. "Make me."

"That's enough." Brenna placed a hand on her brother's arm and looked back at Drake, her blue eyes wide. "Both of you."

"This is not the moment for bloodshed," Atanar added.

"When is it ever?" Drake muttered, but managed to shake away the worst of his fury and looked over at Eris again. "She's really all right?"

"She will be," Brenna said, visibly relaxing at the change in Drake's mood. "Mother and Adrie have seen to her – and the babe. They're both fine. Eris just," her gaze flickered to Leal, "pushed herself too hard. But she knew better."

"She told me she'd stop if—when—she reached that point." Leal's voice was hoarse, and deeper than Drake had ever heard.

Brenna offered a pained smile. "She probably meant to, but sometimes magic runs away with us."

Drake opened his mouth to argue, but a glance at Leal's slumped shoulders made him pause. Maybe Brenna was right. He couldn't do anything for Eris; none of them could. "Adrie's with her?" he asked.

"Aye, and she agrees with us that Eris needs to rest. If you like, I can ask her to come speak with you."

"That would be good. Thanks. We'll be around." Drake waved a hand toward the separate site where he, Nat, and Leal had been bedding down. The three of them slipped past the Damaris siblings and headed for their bedrolls and the pile of embers that was their fire. Without a word, Leal knelt to rekindle the flames, while Atanar went to gather some of the meager fuel that the group had collected.

"Let me," Drake said as Leal blew over the embers. A little bit of concentration was all it took to coax a few flames back to life, but for once, Drake took no pleasure in the magical act.

Leal waved him away. "Get our dinner ready. I'll tend this."

Drake considered arguing, but didn't have the energy. As he dug through their rations, he rubbed his temples to hopefully stave off the impending headache. Gods above, what a sodding mess this all was. Seren's Children—he inwardly rolled his eyes at the pretentious name—were too fond of Eris, and now her babe. Were they drawn only to Eris' powerful magic, or was there some other nefarious reason? And now he wasn't even *allowed* to speak to her?

Later, as sunrise painted fiery reds and golds over the lonely, rocky province, Drake, Nat, and Leal shared a meal before the fire.

"Your transformation is *very* impressive," Drake said.

Leal shot him a wary look. "Truly? I haven't yet seen for myself."

"You won't be disappointed. Do you feel...different?" By the One, he hardly knew what to ask.

"I feel...more at home."

"Did it hurt?" Atanar asked.

Leal picked at the boiled juca root in his bowl. "Not as much as I feared. It felt..." He lifted a hand to skim along his jaw. "Strange. Like when you sleep on your arm wrong, and wake to it being numb. When the blood rushes back to the limb, how the whole thing tingles? It felt like that, but... everywhere."

"Your voice is...wider," Atanar replied.

"Deeper," Drake corrected, digging into his own bowl of juca and lentils. The food wasn't particularly flavorful, but it was hot and filling, and after last night's events, that was enough. It wasn't too chewy, either, which his jaw appreciated. "You look good," he said to Leal. "And I've got high standards."

A flush crept to the Sufani man's cheeks. "I did not expect so much, so soon. It will take some getting used to."

"Are you happy?" Drake asked.

Leal shifted his shoulders. "I don't know. It's not real yet."

"How...ah..." Drake coughed into his hand. "How widespread are the changes, if I may ask?"

"I haven't made a complete…examination," Leal replied, flushing again. "But I don't feel entirely…masculine. Eris said the magic may take time to work fully."

They all glanced in the direction of the mages' camp. They couldn't see Seren's Children from here, and there was no sign of Adrie yet. Drake looked back at his meal, but his appetite had fled. He was no sentinel, but clearly he didn't belong with other mages. Where did that leave him? But he had little wish to dwell in self-pity. He had new friends, and his brother didn't hate him. Surely, that was all anyone needed.

"Aredians and their magic," Atanar muttered, stabbing his fork into his bowl. "I'll never grow used to it."

Something in Drake's heart tightened at these words, and he was reminded of Ben all over again. "You don't like magic? Or is it mages that make you uneasy?"

The Canderi man met his gaze. "Both. Neither." He exhaled. "My people have no magic, so all of this," he waved a hand around them, "is new and strange, still. And I feel it's the same for you and your people. But it is not a bad thing. Magic is like a weapon. In the wrong hands, it can be used for evil. But in the right hands…" His gaze crept to Leal, who seemed to be only half-listening as he studied his forearms. "Magic can be good, too," Atanar finished. His gaze upon Drake softened but lost none of its intent. "Very good."

"Agreed." Drake's heart had crept up to his throat, and he could not find another reply.

And then, as if coming from inside his own head, Drake heard his birthname – and his brother's voice. *Bahar?*

*

Stonewall's hands shook as he tried to buckle on his gear, but even the familiar weight of his weapons brought him no comfort and his head ached again. His thoughts spun in useless circles. *How could she have done this?*

Barely morning, and the day had gone to shit. He had to find the others so they could leave this place as soon as possible. Guts churning, Stonewall hurried through the Dilt home's corridors, taking care to keep his steps as noiseless as possible.

Beacon's room was empty. Stonewall stood at the threshold and fought back a twist of despair and panic, because neither would serve him in this moment. His squad was counting on him. He slipped out of Beacon's room and made his way to the bottom level, which would grant access to the street. Flint, Mi, and Marcen had been spending a great deal of time at the local temple. Perhaps he could find them there. As for Beacon and Sadira... Stonewall had no idea where they might be, but he had a hunch it was together. Another time, he might have allowed himself to be happy at how his brother-in-arms had found close companionship with the Zhee mage, but in his current state, he scowled. Mages only brought trouble.

But that's not true, he told himself. For every measure of trouble Kali had caused him, he'd experienced far greater portions of joy. He was angry and disappointed *now*, but surely that would not last forever. So while he probably shouldn't have stormed out like a petulant child, it was for the best he not be with her until he had cooled off, lest he say something he could never take back.

The party had lasted long after Stonewall and Kali had left last night, so thank the gods he met no one as he traveled through the Dilt family home. Not until he reached the lowest level did he encounter another living soul, but when Idalina said his name, he froze, wishing it were anyone else.

"There you are," she said as she hurried down the stairs after him.

He turned to face her, ensuring that each movement was crisp and professional. "I'm sorry, serla, but I'm in a hurry."

"So you know, then."

Stonewall tensed, glancing over his shoulder for the nearest guards, but they were stationed outside of the door, not within the atrium. Still, he kept his voice low. "Aye, so I have no time to waste."

She nodded. "I've ordered the guards to delay them, but I don't know how much longer they'll be willing to wait."

"Thank..." Stonewall frowned at her. "What are you talking about? Who's 'they?'"

Her eyes widened and she stepped closer, her voice hushed. "Last night, a group of sentinels arrived at the city gates, as the party was in full swing. Thank the One, I was the most sober Dilt around, so the guards notified me first. I sent the sentinels some food and wine as a courtesy, along with my regrets that no one could speak with them until today. The Dilt guard captain is with them now."

A hundred swears rolled through Stonewall's mind, but he only said, "Shit."

"Indeed. I trust Captain Jemos with my life, but you and your friends shouldn't linger here."

"Is there a way out of the city besides those gates?"

She nodded. "Let me make some preparations. I'll meet you at your rooms in an hour. Will that give you enough time to gather your people?"

"Yes, thank you." He made to step out the door, but something Kali had said made him pause and look back at her. She looked so much younger than he remembered, even from a few days ago, and her face mirrored the despair in his own heart.

Mages only bring trouble. True, perhaps, but he could not stop himself from adding, "You're not safe here. Come with us."

Whatever she had expected him to say, it was not this. Her lips parted but she shook her head. "This is my home."

"But your brother–"

"Will protect me no matter what," she broke in. "Blood is blood."

Her faith in her family made his throat too tight to speak, so he only offered her a warrior's salute and slipped out the door.

Spring had arrived in Dilt but the warm air could not banish the chill that seeped through his bones. Evidence of last night's festivities still littered the streets: flower petals, empty cups, and a few scraps of food not yet consumed by any local fauna. But the town seemed to be back to normal, with folks bustling to and from their homes and the shops. A few servants wearing Dilt livery swept the walkways and gathered the

300

detritus. Stonewall strode down the street, senses alert for danger. Perhaps he should have made Kali come with him. But as she'd proved, she could take care of herself. The thought made his steps quicken.

The temple was not far from the Dilt home, but Stonewall's attention meandered as he watched the street sweepers collect a heap of flower petals the same plum color as Kali's dress. Memories of the night before trickled back: Kali's smiling face, softly lit by lamplight; her body in his arms as they danced, for once unhindered by her knee or fear of discovery; his own voice raised in laughter. The love that bound them, shining brighter than the sun.

He could not remember a similar night they had shared. Perhaps the closest was on their first journey together, when they had spent the night at the Jessamin Inn on the way to Whitewater City. There and then, they had been in their own world.

A sense of longing pinned him in place. Would he and Kali ever share that kind of peace again? The longing sharpened, deepening into despair. Stonewall stood at the edge of the street but did not see the Dilt servants or the flower petals scattered by a mischievous breeze. He and his squad had to leave this place, but what then? Where would they go? Should they keep trying to cure thralls? How long would *that* take? How long before their luck ran out and someone else got hurt – or worse? And even if every attempt ended in success, how long would it take to cure all the thralls in Aredia? How could a handful of people stop such evil?

Stonewall was out of ideas, but he could not give up, not yet. He needed to move, yes, but he also needed guidance, and his mind went to his elder brother. His earliest memories were of Drake watching over him, guiding him, protecting him. Even though Drake was probably leagues away, Stonewall could not help but try to find him along the thread of love that bound them.

Bahar, he thought, imagining his brother's face. *Can you hear me,* relah?

Nothing at first and Stonewall felt foolish for the attempt. Then...

Elan? Shock radiated from Drake. The emotion was faint, as if stretched thin by distance.

Stonewall's heart leaped and he grinned despite everything. *It's me. You're not mad. Well, not about this.*

Amusement replaced some of Drake's shock, and he gave what Stonewall could only think of as a mental chuckle. *Well, that's a relief. What's wrong? Are you all right?*

How to explain? Their connection was tenuous; a slender filament. How to quickly and clearly get across what he needed to? *I'm fine. I'm in Dilt – for now. But we'll have to leave in a hurry, and I just...* He trailed off, throat tight. *I don't know what to do next.*

Come here, Drake replied immediately. *To the hematite mine in Stonehaven.* Traces of worry bled through their bond and Stonewall felt his brother's concern for Eris and whatever she had planned, though he could not sense the specifics.

Leaving Redfern was their only option, but they could not use conventional means. Stonewall would have to use his magic again, sooner than he would have liked, but perhaps this was Tor's way of telling him it was time to fully embrace his new abilities. Perhaps he'd been given this power for a reason. Besides, Tor favored Stonewall enough to send him visions, though they still made his blood run cold.

But perhaps the terrifying visions were their own kind of test; a chance to prove his dedication to his patron god, to his chosen path outside of the sentinels – and to Kali.

For Kali had the best, kindest heart of anyone he knew. Although her choices lately left him unhappy, she had never let him down before – she had never broken his heart, the way he had done to her, back in Whitewater Bastion. If he loved her, he ought to stand by her side, no matter what.

Together.

So he reached for his brother again. *We'll leave here today. It won't take long to reach Stonehaven. I'll contact you again soon.*

Warm affection flickered from Drake, and more worry, though it was the sort Stonewall thought his brother always held in reserve for his younger sibling. *I'll be here,* Drake said. *Take care of yourself, little brother.*

You, too, Stonewall replied, and the link faded.

"Are you trying to get killed?"

Flint's voice shook him out of the haze wrought by his mental communication with his brother. Everything was vivid, almost glaring, and the sound of her voice seemed louder than he recalled.

"Flint?" he said, stupidly.

She stood before him, fully kitted up, a scowl on her face. At his words, she grabbed his forearm and dragged him out of the street, toward an awning in front of a closed shop. "You nearly got flattened by one of those giant sodding beetles. Why are you just standing there?"

"I…got distracted," he admitted, rubbing his aching temples. His body had not yet forgiven him for his forays to the bottom of his wineglass, and despite Kali's efforts, he had a headache to end all headaches.

Flint blew out a breath. "Shouldn't you be with Kali?"

Stonewall's hands crept to his daggers. "Our luck has run out. We've got to leave."

He'd expected her to snap into action, but instead, her face fell and her shoulders slumped. "When?" she asked.

"Within the hour. Where are the others?"

"Mi's practically living at the temple. I think Beacon and Sadira are at the Dilt's."

"And Marcen?"

"How should I know?"

This was the Flint he knew, though there was an edge to her voice that made him think she was more upset than she was letting on – which was saying something. So he nodded in the direction of the temple. "Get Mi. I'll find Mar, Beacon, and Sadira, and we'll meet back at our temporary barracks."

"Fine." She gnawed at her lip. "Do you think I'm a good person?"

Tor help him, this had to be a trap of some kind. "What would make you ask such a thing?"

"Milo's leaving. He's going back to sodding Whitewater Province – after we fought and bled to get away from that place! He's going to join the Circle and help people who've been attacked by thralls or Canderi or whatever.

The only person who's ever loved me is leaving – and the only reason he stuck around so long is because we're family. Everyone leaves, and it must be because I'm so awful that no one can stand to be near me for more than a little while, and I know we need to hurry, but I can't..."

The last words broke as she choked back a sob. A few passers-by shot the pair odd looks, with some added glares in Stonewall's direction.

They had so little time, but he couldn't just bark at her to shut up so they could leave, so he put a hand on Flint's shoulder, drawing her attention. Bright blue eyes, wet with tears, looked up at him reluctantly. She'd said a lot, but one bit stuck out. *Milo's leaving?*

Another member of his team – gone. The knowledge was at once a kick in the chest and a new weight upon it.

Flint swiped her eyes. "Rook left, too. And Marcen..." She scowled and shook her head. "Anyway. They all leave." She hesitated, then gave him a look that was almost pleading. "Am I really so terrible?"

Stonewall's heart tightened. Best leave the subject of Marcen alone for the time being, as he was not qualified to give advice about mages and romance.

"You're not the easiest person to get along with," he said slowly, and her face fell. "But you're brave and loyal, and though I've seen you stumble, I think you make the best choices you can. I think you are a good person." Although his blood raced to be moving, he took care in forming the rest of his reply. "Milo's state has nothing to do with you, Flint. As for Rook... Her actions weren't your fault, either. You know that. Right?"

"I thought we were on the same side, but she betrayed me. She betrayed all of us."

Kali is lost, my son.

With effort, Stonewall shook away the memory of his divine vision. "Only the gods know what lives in a person's heart. Rook unseated all of us when she left, which makes me think she'd been hiding many secrets for a long time. But still... That's not your fault. She didn't leave because of you. It's the same with Milo. He loves you, but I think he's on his own journey."

Why was it easier to say these things to Flint than to himself?

Because she wasn't a leader. She had trusted him with her life – not the other way around. And as far as he knew, no god had ever spoken to her directly. The weight on his chest pressed heavier, harder, trying to steal his breath.

Flint looked away from him, her lip quivering again. Her voice was uncharacteristically soft. "Maybe." After a few breaths, she squared her shoulders and looked back at Stonewall and bowed a salute. "Consider your orders followed."

Stonewall gave her what he hoped was a reassuring look. "Thanks."

He watched her hurry down the street before making his way back. As he went, he sought his patron god again, hoping for guidance about Kali. Surely Tor would advise compassion and trust, both qualities Stonewall could not seem to grasp for more than a few moments at a time.

But he found only that same plea resonating through his entire spirit: *Come home, Elan.*

Stonewall bit his tongue against the bitter swell of despair that he could not seem to fully banish. *Mind on the mission*, he ordered himself.

But his fingers sought the leather pouch at his belt, slipping inside to free a single vial of precious, purified hematite. The little glass bauble nestled in his palm like it belonged there, reflecting the trees above his head, whispering sweet promises of warmth, strength, and fortitude. *Need* clawed at his chest with icy talons. Surely just a half-dose would suffice. After all, he needed help to solve the problem at hand, and he was not at his best after last night's activities. A *biri* would dull the edge of his hunger, but it would also dull his mind. He needed to be sharp. His squad—his family—needed him at his best.

Just a half-dose, nothing more.

Before he could change his mind, he ripped out the wax stopper and poured the dark-gray powder into his cupped palm, careful to shield it from the breeze. But his hand still trembled and instead of only half, most of the dose spilled out. Rather than risk losing any hematite, Stonewall swallowed the entire dose in one go, being sure to lap up every bit of the crushed ore. The bitter, metallic taste on his tongue made him grimace even as the delicious bloom of power flowed through his veins, soothing his body, heart, and mind even as it spurred all to action.

Several shaking breaths brought him through the nausea, and it wasn't as bad as he remembered.

THIRTY

Flint found her brother deep within the Dilt temple, engrossed in conversation with a pair of Circle priests. His back was to her, so he did not see her step into the simple wood-walled room that smelled of lavender and herbs, meant to inspire peaceful contemplation.

Gods above, she was starting to hate this fucking place. "Milo," she said. "Come on, we've got to..."

He turned and she trailed off, for he had a dove-gray initiate's cloak tucked beneath his arm and he wore the most delighted expression she had ever seen. "Look what I got," he said with a smile. "Think it'll fit?"

Too well, she thought, her throat tight. But she forced a smile and said only, "It'll be a pain in the ass to keep clean."

The Circle folks scowled, but Milo only laughed. "I'll manage."

"Stonewall wants us back at the Dilt's," Flint said, jabbing her thumb toward the door.

Milo furrowed his brow. "I was hoping to stay a while longer. Can it wait?"

Flint clenched her jaw. "No. And he's still in charge."

"Funny to hear *you* talk like that," Milo said, but there was no malice behind the tease. There never was malice in anything he said or did.

Her heart sank even further. "Are you coming with me or not?"

Milo hesitated. One of the Circle priests, a fellow about Milo's age, cleared his throat. "We really could use the help..."

"I know," Milo said at last. "But duty calls. I'll be back as soon as I can." He bid goodbye to the priests and followed Flint out of the temple, carefully folding the robe as he walked. Once they were on the street, he shot her a curious look. "What's going on?"

Flint quickened her steps. "Not sure, exactly, but keep a sharp eye. Stonewall said we have to leave in a hurry."

He glanced around. "Folks here seem all right to me."

"That's because you've spent the whole time doddering around the temple. You're so blind, I'd be shocked if you could find your own arse."

It was a testament to his good mood that he didn't respond to the insult. No, the lout only chuckled and smoothed out the robe he'd slung over his injured arm. "I like it here."

Flint's throat went tight again. "You know those Circle idiots are just using you, right?"

"They're good people doing good work," Milo shot back, and Flint hated her own swell of satisfaction at his sharp tone. "And I'd be proud to call myself one of them. Why do you hate them so much?"

Great work, moron, she told herself. *You brought him back down to reality.* She tried to remember the counsel from Stonewall and Marcen, but their words, so sensible at the time, burned out of her mind like river mist beneath the sun. She may as well have been a child again, cowering beneath the bed while a storm raged outside.

"They don't care about *you*, Mi. They only care about what you can do for them."

"At least the Circle *wants* me around. At least they *need* my help. I'd rather be where I'm needed than be a burden."

Flint's face flamed. "You're not a–"

"No one wants to say the truth, but you've all thought it: I'm useless. I'm a waste of space. I'm nothing." He looked away from her, down the street, back toward the temple. "Just let me go, Mira. Let me be useful again."

Her foolish heart fell to her guts and she clenched her fists lest she strike him. "If you want to go," her voice was hoarse, "then sodding *go*. I don't care any longer."

With that, she turned away from him and hurried toward the Dilt house. With each step, she told herself, *Don't you dare look back.*

Kali willed her trembling fingers to steady as she lifted her viol from its padded case. Even within the confines of Beacon's room, the woodgrain still shone as if newly polished. Thank the stars, she'd not broken any of her new strings – yet. She withdrew the bow and slipped it over the strings a few times, checking the tuning and savoring the familiar weight in her grip. The music from the reception last night still buzzed in her mind; she tried to recreate some of the melodies she'd heard, but couldn't recall more than a few notes. It'd been too long since she'd gotten to properly play and there was no telling when she'd get a chance.

The weight of her beloved instrument turned leaden. With a sigh, Kali returned the viol and bow to their padded home, latched the case, and set it with the rest of her friends' belongings that she'd collected in the corner of Beacon's room.

The door opened and a sudden heat strengthened the floral scents wafting in through the window, before Sadira stepped in. Any other time, and Kali would have relished the added sweetness, but Dilt's beauty had lost its luster. She couldn't leave this place fast enough.

Sadira regarded her as one might an unfamiliar dog. The bloom of power that clung to the Zhee mage caught in Kali's senses like the scents of spring, but she ignored her own hunger and made a show of stepping away from her friend, hands raised in surrender. "Don't worry. You're safe from me."

Sadira did not rise to the bait, only met Kali's gaze. "This decision is *not* for always. We will see one another again."

Her earnest tone brought heat to Kali's eyes and her sarcastic reply died on her tongue. "Dealing with my magic has been difficult *with* you, but I fear it will be worse when you're gone."

Sadira hesitated, and then came over and took Kali's hands in both of hers. Kali tensed at the renewed swell of her own hunger, but the Zhee mage's voice was calm. "You have everything you need within you to face this challenge."

If only that were true. Kali's voice fell to a whisper. "I'll miss you."

"And I, you. You are the first true friend I have known in many years."

"I'd hug you, but..."

The Zhee mage squeezed Kali's hands before releasing them. "The One has a plan for you, Kali, whether you believe it or not. Everything will turn out as it should."

Just then, Marcen swept into the room, a pack slung over his shoulder. "By the One, what crawled up Stonewall's ass? He shouted at me to get over here like I was one of his sodding burnies..." He trailed off as he noted the women's stricken expressions. "Damn. What'd I miss?"

"You shouldn't come with me, either," Kali blurted out.

Marcen lifted a pale brow. "All right...but...what's going on?"

"We have to leave Dilt," Stonewall said from the doorway, where he was helping Beacon. "Good. You're all here. Flint and Milo are right behind us." He surveyed their supplies and glanced at Kali, but she turned away from him to stand out of the way. Their silent connection still held, but as before, she felt nothing from him. Perhaps that was for the best right now.

Once the entire group had assembled in Beacon's room, Stonewall relayed the increasingly dismal news. Despite this, though, he stood at the center of the group, fully armored and shoulders square, determination radiating off him, eyes blazing with purpose. "Idalina should be here soon. She said she has a way for us to leave aside from the front gates."

"Yes, but why go to *Stonehaven*?" Beacon asked. "And how do you know your brother's there?"

Stonewall stalked across the woven rug, clutching his dagger grips with trembling hands. "I'm getting to the latter. As to the former... I don't know the particulars, but Eris is planning something at the mine. Something *big*."

Kali's heart stuttered. She met Stonewall's eyes, and she did not need their connection to sense his fear, beating in time with her own.

Marcen rubbed the bridge of his nose. "Eris' plans tend to turn bloody, but I thought we were curing thralls? Isn't that the priority?" He looked at Kali. "Not all mages want chaos, right?"

Before Kali could reply, Flint interjected from her place by the window. "I'm sure there's plenty of thralls in Stonehaven. But I'll bet my daggers it's Gray at the gates, since we saw her before, when Kali used her magic to bring us here."

"We will be using magic to leave this place," Stonewall said, a little too quickly. "But it won't be *Kali's* magic." He tensed. "It'll be mine."

The others were silent, although Sadira and Marcen both shot Kali startled looks, but Kali lifted her gaze to meet Stonewall's. His expression was still guarded, but softer. *It's about time, isn't it?* he asked.

Aye, she managed, though she couldn't resist adding, *That wasn't so hard, was it?*

A faint smile flickered over his mouth in reply, and her heart lifted. Maybe they could get through this trial, too.

"What he says is true," Kali said to the others.

Beacon stared at Stonewall with eyes as huge as those of his namesake moth's. "*You're* a mage?"

"Not exactly. I can't heal anyone, and hematite has no effect on my... abilities."

Sadira inclined her head. "Which are?"

Here, Stonewall faltered and glanced at Kali, who took pity on him. "Stonewall used his magic during our escape from Whitewater City."

Flint sucked in her breath. "You held us together on the waterfall?"

"No, that bit was Kali's doing. My part came after, when we were on the river proper."

Beacon, Flint, and Milo exchanged wide-eyed glances, while Marcen merely looked thoughtful. Sadira shot Kali another astonished look, to which Kali merely gave a weak smile and a shrug. The Zhee mage sighed heavily, clearly piecing the story together. "*You* carried us to Redfern after the thralls attacked."

Stonewall nodded. "I can also...speak to my brother, despite the distance between us. Don't ask me how that works, though."

"I wasn't going to," Beacon muttered. "But if you're no mage, how can you do magic?"

"That's...a little trickier to explain," Stonewall said. "As I'm still figuring it all out, myself. But I think—Kali and I think—that it has something to do with the Fata."

"He's got Fata blood," Kali added. "When I was possessed by a thrall, I could *feel* what they felt; sense what they sensed. And the Fata recognized Stonewall as 'kin.' I know it sounds mad," she said when the others exchanged further, dumbfounded looks, "but it's the truth – as far as we can tell."

Flint gave a dark chuckle. "So you could *both* be mad, rather than just him."

"I wish I were mad," Stonewall said. "Truly. It would be much simpler. But truth is stranger than any fantasy." He began to pace, the movements jerky and halting. His words came a little too quick and his eyes gleamed with a familiar fever.

Did you take hematite? Kali asked.

He gave no answer other than a flare of guilt which he immediately suppressed. Kali closed her eyes against the sudden ache in her chest. *He took it because of me.*

But she was *not* responsible for his actions. He knew better; he'd told her as much. Besides, how dare he be angry with her when he'd acted even worse? At least her magic wouldn't kill her. At least she wasn't a slave to crushed ore within tiny glass bottles.

"This...ability of yours," Beacon said. "I suppose it's difficult to manage or control?"

"Aye," Stonewall replied. "Otherwise, I'd have used it more. But it's not exactly reliable, as you've seen."

"Too bad," the mender said with a sigh. "It would save you a lot of walking."

Milo rubbed his temples, clearly struggling to understand – as they all were. "So...if Stonewall has Fata blood, does that mean he can turn people into thralls?"

Stonewall shuddered. "I hope not."

The others peppered him with more questions, but Kali only studied her own hands, flexing them a few times. They felt weak now, while a hunger for power, stirred by Sadira's presence, stirred deep in her bones. *Sweet magic.*

It was uncharitable and unkind of her to demean Stonewall's struggles. But that didn't mean she was going to follow him blindly.

"I agree that we must leave," Kali said suddenly, breaking into their chatter. "But I don't think we should go to Stonehaven."

Stonewall paused to regard her, though his leg twitched as if he couldn't bear to hold still. "I've told you *why*. Drake said that Eris–"

"Eris has made her choices," Kali interjected. "As have we all." She gave him a knowing look and he had the decency to wince. "But our mission hasn't changed."

Stonewall resumed his pacing and the floor shivered as his steps fell harder. "We have allies and an achievable objective in Stonehaven: prevent further loss of life. After that, we can resume curing thralls."

"We can cure thralls on this side of the world," Kali protested. "Or go north. I just don't–"

"*You* are the reason we must leave so quickly," Stonewall broke in.

A wave of bitterness crashed over her, stunning her into silence. Kali stared back at the man she loved and allowed her own anger to churn through their bond in response. He looked away first, and she hated her satisfaction.

Marcen lifted his gaze to the ceiling. "What in Seren's light *happened?*"

"Heitor grabbed and threatened me," Kali said. "So I used my magic to defend myself. I took some of his energy, as I've done with other people. As far as I know, no permanent harm was done."

Marcen studied her, but Flint nodded. "Good. Sorry sod had it coming. And we'd probably have gotten kicked out of here eventually, anyway."

Kali braced for additional censure from Stonewall, but he only said, "Aye. Heitor brought the trouble on himself."

Please don't use your magic like that again, he added to Kali through their bond. *I couldn't bear it if something went wrong. I'm...sorry.* For the first time since their argument, she felt the thread that bound their hearts brighten with love; it had not died, he'd only dammed the flow.

An answering promise bubbled up in her mind, but she could not make it. She was not like him; she could not sling oaths like arrows, and expect them all to hit their marks. But nor could she refuse this peace offering.

"I'm sorry," she said, ostensibly to Beacon. "I didn't want to hurt him."

I know, Stonewall replied, and the thread brightened.

Beacon gave her a warm, if somewhat exasperated look. "I love my brother, but he has a way of making enemies. I'm sorry he pushed you to that point, but I'm glad you're all right." He looked down at his folded hands, his voice quiet. "Well, wherever you all go, I wish you a safe journey."

Stonewall froze, eyes wide, gaze fixed on the mender. Shock crackled through his and Kali's bond like white-hot lightning.

"You're not coming with us, either?" Flint asked, jaw agape.

"At the moment, I'm not fit to do much more than lie here," Beacon replied. "Sadira and I—and Vestain—think it's best if I take it easy for another week or so. Too long for you lot to linger. And what do you mean 'either?' Who else is staying behind?"

Spots of color appeared in Flint's cheeks but she was silent.

Stonewall was not. "You'd abandon your squad?"

Beacon blanched but, to everyone's surprise, it was Milo who shot back, "Beak's not 'abandoning' anyone. He just said he's not fit to travel."

"Right, and this isn't forever," Beacon rushed to add. "We can make plans to meet again. Maybe in Pillau, say in about three months?"

"Very well," Stonewall said after a beat. "You know of the seawall?"

"Aye. We'll meet there. Give or take a week or so," Beacon said wryly. "You'll have to step up," he added to his fellow sentinels, though Milo only looked at his boots. "That's two less sets of blades in your party. At least you'll have all three mages, though. That should come in handy."

"Two mages," Sadira said. "I remain here."

Beacon gaped at her. "What are you on about, woman?"

So Sadira had *not* informed Beacon of her plans. Somehow, Kali was not surprised, though Marcen and the twins certainly seemed to be. Sadira, however, remained as cool and unruffled as ever as she regarded the mender. "Can I not?"

"For all its charms, Dilt's not exactly a mage-friendly place," Beacon replied.

314

Kali winced. Thank the stars Idalina had asked that Kali not speak of her abilities to Beacon. *That* was a conversation she had no wish to be a part of.

"If Kali got found out as a mage," Marcen added. "You might be, too."

"I will not remain here overlong," Sadira replied.

Flint snorted. "Why should she be afraid? She's like a living flame in a forest of kindling. They should be worried about *her*."

Sadira grimaced but did not respond. Kali ached to take her friend's hand, to offer reassurance, but that probably wouldn't help, given her situation. She tried to catch Sadira's eye, but the Zhee mage faced resolutely ahead.

"You have anything to add?" Stonewall asked Milo.

Milo hesitated, then met his former sergeant's gaze. "There's a bunch of folks from the Circle going up north, to help those who've been hurt by the thralls. I'm going with them. Vestain said he'd vouch for me."

"The Circle!" Beacon pinched the bridge of his nose. "Mi, you never cease to surprise me, you know that?"

Milo gave the other man a careful smile. "Um…is that good or bad?"

"I don't sodding know." Beacon made a noise of agitation and looked at Flint. "*You* can't possibly think this is a good idea."

"And why not?" Flint growled. "You don't think he can take care of himself?"

Milo drew back his cuff to show his wrist, which bore no sentinel mark. "No one can tell I'm Forsworn. I'll be fine, Beak. I promise."

Beacon's shoulders slumped and he looked at Stonewall. "You can't let him run off like this."

"I don't have much of a choice, do I?" Stonewall shot back, hands fisting.

"Milo's life is his own," Flint said. "We can at least agree about that."

Stonewall glared at her. "Milo swore an oath. He's part of a team. He doesn't have the luxury of leaving us to chase some fantasy life."

Flint met his glare with one of her own. "I don't want him to leave, either, but he deserves to be happy. So if running around in a sodding robe like some lunatic will make you happy, Mi, then you'd damn well better be the best lunatic out there."

Milo had followed the exchange with wide eyes, but now he stared at his sister, a mixture of astonishment and joy on his face. "Mira..."

She reached for his left hand, moving his fingers so that they laced with hers. "Don't be stupid. Be careful. I love you."

Milo embraced her with his good arm. "I love you, too, *relah*. Take your own advice, all right?"

"I'll try." They parted and she looked between Beacon and Stonewall, and outstretched her hand. "All right. Give it here."

Beacon frowned at her, but Stonewall's hand stole to his belt-pouch, and he gave Flint a dark look, his anger belied by the lance of despair Kali felt as keenly as if it were her own. "Mind on the mission, burnie," he said, his voice too low.

"You're one to talk, *Sarge*," Flint replied. "Give me the hematite. You obviously can't be trusted."

"Besides," Kali added, trying to sound reasonable despite the thrum of her own irritation at his hypocrisy. "You'll need to split it with Beacon before we part ways."

Stonewall stepped backward, his heel hitting the door. "It's fine. I'm fine. Here." He dug around the pouch and tossed a small sack to Beacon, who caught it neatly. "That's half."

He met Kali's eyes, and she felt rather than heard his resolute, *Already divvied up. I'm no cinder.*

No one said you were, Kali replied, biting the inside of her cheek to keep from shouting the words aloud.

Silence hung in the room like a hammer poised to fall, until a knock sounded at the door. "Abe?" Ida called. "I hear voices... Are you with your mercenary friends?"

Her voice was a little too loud. The sentinels tensed and Stonewall, being the closest, opened the door to reveal the young Dilt woman. She rushed into the room without preamble. "You have to go, now," she said. "I tried to stop them, but that Captain Gray wouldn't hear me. She and her sentinels are in the city. Ves and our guards are trying to stall them, but I don't know how much longer-"

"Vestain is in on this?" Beacon broke in.

Ida drew up her shoulders. "He thinks they're after *you*. But they won't have you." She glanced around the room, her eyes landing on Kali. "Any of you. Not while Ves and I draw breath. They have no authority here, and I have given our guard captain leave to expel them by any means necessary. But it would help," she faltered, "if you did not give us more than one secret to hide."

"Then Beak needs to come with us," Stonewall began.

But Ida was already shaking her head. "He's not fit to travel. Don't worry; he'll be safe here. Even if Heitor was awake, he would not allow an outsider to drag our brother away, sentinel or not."

"Sadira and Milo aren't leaving with the others," Beacon said.

Ida's eyes widened, but she nodded. "They can all hide here until the sentinels leave. But the rest of you must flee at once."

THIRTY-ONE

T his parting is not forever, Stonewall told himself. Sadira and Marcen spoke a few quick words before Beacon urged her and Milo out of the room, to lie low while the others made their escape. Stonewall tried not to watch them leave. He had to focus on the task at hand, not on the lump in his throat. His blood hammered with the promise of a fight and he almost—*almost*—wished they were not fleeing so he could face down Gray. A foolish desire, to be sure, but some primal part of him wanted to meet at least one problem with his blade.

Idalina led him, Kali, Flint, and Marcen down the stairs. But when they reached the base, a familiar voice outside the door sent Stonewall's stomach tumbling to his knees.

"We tracked the deserters to this city, serla," Gray said, her voice muffled through the door. "Along with our mages. We *will* find them."

"You *will* respect the authority of the Dilt family in our own home," Vestain replied.

Stonewall grimaced. They'd lingered too long over planning and goodbyes. He glanced at Idalina, who gestured back up the way they'd come. "We'll have to take another route," she whispered. "It's not as direct, but..."

Vestain's voice rose again. "As you have been told, repeatedly, there are no mages here."

"Then prove it," Gray shot back. "Let us see for ourselves."

She called to the other sentinels; a thud against the door made Stonewall snatch his daggers free of their sheathes. How solid they felt in his hands;

how *right.* "Gray wants a fight," he said, angling himself toward the door. "We'll give her one."

A hand at each shoulder pulled him back. He turned to face Kali and Flint, both glaring at him while Mar and Idalina stood back, clearly confused.

Kali's eyes, darkened by shadows and her own fury, seemed black. "*Nobody* wants a fight, Stonewall."

Flint said nothing, but he read her disappointment with him in her face before she looked back at Marcen and Ida. "We're going now. Lead the way, Serla Dilt."

Idalina turned to bound back up the stairs. The others followed as silently as they could until Kali stumbled and slapped her hand over her mouth lest she yelp in pain. Unthinking, Stonewall scooped her and her belongings up, trying to ignore the shame coursing through his veins alongside the hematite-granted energy. His spirit was weak, but at least he could carry her to safety. The group scrambled through the hatch on the second level, where a network of wooden bridges and curving stairs hung like spider webs. Thank Tor, Idalina knew her way around. The youngest Dilt bounded across hanging bridges and over stairs with the speed and agility of familiarity, and did not falter at the continued shouting between Gray, Vestain, and the Dilt guards who must have arrived.

Idalina did not stop until they reached the beacon moth stable in the canopy. By then, sweat ran down Stonewall's back and face, and every muscle was starting to burn. He set Kali down so he could make sure no one followed, but for the first few seconds, he could only hear blood pounding in his ears.

"You want us to fly away?" Kali was saying as Idalina brought out a beacon moth from its stall.

"The moths know what to do," Ida said. "You just have to hang on."

The moths were already saddled, so she began to fiddle with the girths, but Stonewall eyed the multitude of straps with skepticism. Was all that really going to keep a rider from falling to their death?

He wasn't the only one with misgivings. Kali shot him an aghast look, and Flint and Marcen, too, exchanged glances.

We don't need this, Stonewall realized. *I could just...* But he glanced down and the world seemed to spiral away. Too many unknowns to use his new abilities now – and no doubt he'd have to use them soon enough, anyway. It was wiser to save his strength for later and accept the help freely offered. Even so, he bit his tongue to keep from shouting in exasperation. Why would Tor have granted him this power if not to sodding *use* it?

"Ida," Kali said, stepping forward. "We don't have time to learn to fly these creatures. How can we possibly–"

"They'll respond to a rider's commands the same way as horses will," the Dilt woman broke in.

"Well, then we have nothing to worry about, I suppose," Kali replied dryly.

Flint glanced at Marcen. "Hope you're not afraid of heights."

"It's the falling part that worries me," he replied.

Sooner than Stonewall would have liked, he and Kali were astride one of the moths while Flint and Marcen clambered upon the other. Everyone's packs were strapped down tight. Ida talked the entire time, giving them last-minute instructions on how to take off and land, although none of her words truly stuck in Stonewall's mind.

At last, Ida stepped back to fling open the stable door, revealing filtered sunlight and the canopy. "One last thing: they won't fly past one of the waystations at the provincial borders. It's a stupid old tradition," she added when Flint opened her mouth to ask. "Don't get me started."

"What do we tell the folks at the waystations?" Kali asked.

But the Dilt woman shook her head. "They're not occupied. We only send scouts to replenish the supplies. Go now!"

Stonewall positioned both arms around Kali, who sat before him, and gripped the reins before nudging the beacon moth's sides with his heels. The creature crept forward, feelers waving. When it slipped out of the stable and onto the branch proper, it moved quicker, rocking its passengers from side to side. Stonewall caught a glimpse of the forest floor—so far below!—and his stomach lurched. This was not at *all* like riding a horse!

"Keep calm," Ida shouted after them as Flint and Marcen's moth followed.

"They can sense when you're afraid."

Before Stonewall could ask her what would happen in that case, the moth shoved away from the branch, and they were airborne. The entire world dropped away, spinning, before his vision righted and he got his bearings. Stonehaven was to the west. Stonewall ignored the rapidly shrinking treetops and used his bodyweight and the reins to steer the moth away from the rising sun. The creature's wings swept up and down on either side in strong, steady swoops, unlike those of their smaller relations. After several minutes, Stonewall mustered the courage to look down. A blanket of green met his gaze, the leaves shining in the sunlight. Despite his fears, he could not help but smile. What a marvelous world the One had created.

The whistling wind tore Kali's hair from her braid, sending the dark strands whipping in his face as she peered behind him. "Flint and Mar are still with us," she called.

Stonewall's eyes watered as he squinted ahead, searching for a familiar landmark. But his training had never prepared him to view his country from so high above and he could not make sense of the scenery. Instead, he faced forward as best he could, given the wind and the moth's bobbing feelers, and ensured his grip on his mount—and on Kali—was secure.

Kali kept her thoughts to herself. A hundred times, Stonewall almost reached for her through their bond. A hundred times, he didn't. Now that they were relatively safe, the fire in his veins had abated, leaving him colder than the wind that buffeted them. He would have attacked Gray and her retinue out of sheer, hematite-induced stupidity, and his weakness would have gotten his squad killed. No, he couldn't speak to Kali, at least not now, so he focused on keeping his seat.

They flew for hours. The sun crept up into the sky, casting the world below in brilliance. The gentle rhythm of the moth's beating wings was a comfort and soon Stonewall relaxed enough to look back. Flint sat behind Marcen on their mount, gripping the reins. Stonewall couldn't make out either of their expressions, but Flint lifted her hand in a sentinel sign for "we're all right."

Eventually, a patchwork of browns and reds began to mottle the green blanket below, and the smudge of the Argus Mountains to Stonewall's right sharpened into jagged peaks. They crossed over a shining thread of silver—the White River, if Stonewall's estimation was correct—and the moths began a spiraling descent. The trees drew closer; no longer the looming, old-growth giants around Dilt, but their humble cousins.

"There's a tower over there," Kali said, pointing ahead.

It resembled little more than a wooden box on stilts, with a broad platform outside, large enough to accommodate the moths. As they swooped closer, Stonewall could make out vines and creepers that had clambered up the tower, camouflaging the structure's base within the rest of the canopy. The beacon moths alighted upon the platform, settling with only a few small shifts, their pale green wings folding up to cocoon their riders. Stonewall extricated himself first and slid behind the massive wings down to the platform. The moment his boots touched the wood, he felt heavier, and briefly lamented that the flight was over. But there was no time to do more, for Kali needed to follow, so he held out his hand to help her dismount.

Still astride the moth, she stared at his hand before accepting. When she was on her feet, she regarded him, dark eyes searching his. *You are enough, Elan,* she sent. *Never doubt that.*

Too late, was the only reply he could make.

Once all four riders were safely on the platform, Stonewall came around to the moth's head and reached out one hand to brush against the bobbing, feathery feelers. They tickled his palm as the moth's glittering, multifaceted eyes studied him, and he couldn't help his smile.

Kali joined him and stroked the front of the creature's furred head. "Thank you for carrying us to safety. I hope you find your way back home safely, too."

The moth nudged Kali's palm, wings fluttering, before shifting to pass beside the humans, making for the tower's entrance. Stonewall peered past the massive wings to see that the room had no windows, and was covered in dried moss and leaves, clearly meant for the moths to rest. Flint and Marcen's mount followed, and the humans were again on their own.

322

"It's warmer than I expected," Flint said as she checked over her gear.

"Well, it's still too cold for me," Stonewall replied.

Marcen shouldered his dulcimer case and squinted over the mottled brown canopy. "We're on the edge of Redfern now?"

"Aye." Stonewall withdrew his map of Aredia, decidedly more stained and torn than it'd been a year ago, and they all gathered around. Kali helped him hold up the map while he pointed. "I think we're about here."

Kali gave a low whistle. "We still have to go all the way through Silverwood and *then* into Stonehaven. Where's the mine?"

Flint tapped a section of triangular symbols near the left side of the map. "We've a long way to go." She looked at Stonewall. "Can you manage, *Sarge?*"

The honorific held no admiration. That would have been bad enough had Stonewall's stomach not flopped at the notion of using *his* magic.

Well, he'd wanted a chance to use his abilities – perhaps this was Tor's way of granting his wish. But it took more effort than he'd have liked to keep his nerves in check as he folded up his map. "We ought to get down first."

They all peered over the edge to see how the creeping vines and mist obscured the tower's base. After some reconnaissance, Marcen spotted a hatch in the platform. When opened, it revealed a sturdy, ironwood ladder that descended into the canopy. Other than some creepers clinging to the rungs, the ladder seemed secure, but Stonewall insisted upon going first to make sure. Flint came next, and then Kali, while Marcen brought up the rear. The ladder creaked beneath their weight, but held fast. The late winter wind whipped through Stonewall's gear as if trying to tear his grip away from the rungs. While this part of the world was not as cold as Whitewater Province, it wasn't exactly balmy, and he found himself sorely missing home yet again.

When the group was all truly earthbound once more, they gathered around the tower's base. Stonewall's body was leaden and he glanced back up at the tower with longing. The Redfern moths had saved them days and days of travel; he should be grateful and nothing more. But apprehension tumbled in his veins as he looked at what remained of his squad. So much was riding on his magic. Could he do this?

"What happens now?" Flint asked.

Dark eyes met Stonewall's and Kali smiled at him as she held out her hand. "Away?" she asked softly, eyes closing.

Together. Stonewall slid off his glove and clasped her fingers in his own as he gathered his own strength, shored up his own resolve. "Away," he echoed, and concentrated.

THIRTY-TWO

Flint gripped Mar's arm as the world shifted and the air rippled, like waves of heat above a roaring fire. The brown, slumbering forest around them faded, blurred, and wind ripped through her hair like she was back on the stupidly giant moth. The ground rushed beneath her boots but she held still. Her stomach twisted in rebellion and her fingers tightened around Mar's forearm. The blond mage had shut his eyes, sweat beading on his forehead while his face had turned a sickly green. Stonewall and Kali held each other close, both deep in concentration, so Flint resolved to try and keep *her* wits about her, at least, but then the world lurched again, her knees began to buckle, and dizziness overtook her.

Just when she thought she was going to faint, the world righted. Kali fell toward Flint, who caught the unconscious mage out of reflex, though she wasn't far from collapse herself. Stonewall stumbled backward to catch himself on a nearby rock formation. There were rocks *everywhere*, and hardly any trees in sight. Dry air caught in Flint's throat and each inhale brought the scent of dust.

Mar groaned. "Did we make it?"

Stonewall pushed himself off the rock and rubbed his forehead. "I think so. Let me get my bearings."

"I've got her," Flint replied, easing the mage to a seated position against another nearby boulder. "You figure out where in Ea's realm we *are*."

While her former sergeant tugged out his map, Flint examined the mage. Kali was out of it, all right, and looked like she'd been on an all-night bender, judging from the sunken shadows beneath her eyes and her gaunt cheeks.

If not for her soft breath, Flint might have thought her dead.

Marcen knelt beside them. "Is she...?"

Ea's balls, Flint had almost forgotten she was cross with him. "She's alive. You look like shit."

He gave a weak chuckle. "Last couple times we did that, I wasn't conscious enough to feel it."

Flint glanced over at her former sarge. "Stonewall?"

He was looking between the map and the arid, rock-strewn landscape around them. "We're in Stonehaven, but I don't know exactly where."

"Well, figure it out," Flint snapped.

"I'm trying," he shot back. "Is Kali–"

"Yes, Kali's fine," Flint broke in, rolling her eyes. "Why don't you worry about where we are? Unless you need more hematite first," she added beneath her breath.

Stonewall frowned at her but kept his reply infuriatingly neutral. "Then help me out, will you?"

Flint huffed but went to stand with him, and the two sentinels examined the map. "If we managed to travel in something of a straight line, as I've managed in the past," Stonewall said. "I think we're somewhere here." His finger circled a wide patch of Stonehaven Province.

"But did we? Is that how your," she grimaced, "magic works?"

"I'm not sure," he admitted.

"You've been stationed here before. Don't you know this province?"

"Not every nook and cranny." He squinted up at the overcast sky. "We could have only another day of travel to reach the mine – or several days, if not more. Either way, Kali needs to rest."

Flint grunted assent but glanced back at the mages. Marcen had carefully placed his and Kali's belongings on the ground so he could lean against the rock next to her, running a hand through his hair. He still looked pretty green. His pale eyes met Flint's and he offered her a shaky smile.

She looked back at the landscape. The magical travel had deposited the group between some large, rust-colored boulders, sheltering them from the worst of the wind and—hopefully—shielding them from the view of any would-be attackers. But there was no wood in sight, only distant mountains and lots and lots of rocks.

"There's no fuel for a fire," she said.

"I can manage a little one," Marcen replied, sitting up.

Flint scowled. "We can't have one. We'd risk being seen."

"But you just said—"

"Don't argue," Flint interrupted.

Marcen rolled his eyes. "I told you, I don't love her. I never did. What's your damage?"

Face hot, Flint swept her arms around them, indicating the landscape. "In case you haven't noticed, we've a few more concerns than your stupid feelings."

"Do you hear yourself?" he replied. "Or is it just a river of nasty commentary running through your brain? I. Don't. Love. Her. Grow up, Flint." He looked at Stonewall. "I can create a fire without smoke. I'd really like a hot meal right now. How about you?"

Stonewall had been studying his map a bit too intently. "Sounds good, Mar. Thanks."

He had good reason to be annoyed with Marcen, but he'd never shown one trace of irritation with the mage who'd harbored an attraction to his lover. Nor had Kali. She and Mar had only ever acted as friends would. Heat flooded Flint's face and neck. Forsworn or not, she had taken an oath, so she was still a sentinel. She ought to act like one.

"I'll scout around," she offered, and slipped off before anyone could say more.

The past few weeks—hell, the past few *months*—had been a parade of insanity. It was a relief to get away from the others for a few minutes and give herself something practical to focus on. Carefully, she crept through a patch of large, rust-red boulders, until she gauged her surroundings safe enough to climb to the top of a promising bit of rock. Exposed here, a chilly wind whipped her hair and slipped beneath her gear, but she ignored the discomfort and searched the desolate landscape for any sign of danger.

Nothing.

Her attempt at a distraction failed. Milo's face appeared in her mind's eye. Would he escape Redfern in one piece? Would they ever see each other again?

The only person who ever loved me is gone. Dev had liked her, but nothing more. She knew that now. He'd never looked at her the way Stonewall looked at Kali, or even the way Mar looked at *her.* He'd been kind and considerate, but there had always been a distance between them, one she'd accepted without question due to their different ranks. Now she'd driven Marcen away and Stonewall was losing himself to the burn and she was alone.

Something wet slid down her nose and she swiped the tear away with a dirty glove, scowling. Self-pity was stupid and useless when she had a job to do. She pulled off her glove and rubbed her eyes again, and then looked back up and ahead, where a cloud of dust bloomed up from the rocky horizon. Heart in her throat, Flint squinted through the afternoon light, trying to glean some sense of who these folks were. If they were merchants, or other civilian travelers, there was no cause for concern. But the group moved too quickly to be civilians, and when they drew closer she realized they were mounted – and heading her way. When she spotted hematite winking in the sun, her stomach churned as she scrambled down the boulder's side and raced back to their camp.

Stonewall and Marcen sat before the mage's smokeless brush fire, which burned despite a lack of proper fuel. Mar was rummaging through one of their packs, while Stonewall still stared at his map, brows furrowed. Kali was still asleep, curled next to the former sergeant.

"Sentinels," Flint said without preamble when she reached the others.

"Where?" Stonewall rose, careful not to disturb his sleeping lover.

Flint pointed. "Not a mile off, heading this way."

"We should assume they're looking for us," Stonewall said grimly.

"How could they be?" Flint asked. "We just got here. Unless I'm the only sentinel who *can't* flit all over Ea's realm."

Stonewall's reply was too sharp. "We've been on the run for over a month. I expect Argent has alerted every garrison in the country. We need to move out."

"And even if they're not looking for us now," Marcen added. "I'm sure they'll be *curious* about our little party." He closed his pack and placed his hand on the ground beside the yellow flames, which began to sputter and die.

Flint began gathering up their packs, including the mages' instrument cases. "Can you wake her up?"

Stonewall hesitated. "She must rest."

"We *must* get out of here," Flint replied. "Can you use," she winced, "your magic, then? On your own?"

Her former sergeant shifted, his boots scuffing up little flurries of red dirt. "I don't know."

"Well, now's the time to learn." Flint secured her and Kali's packs.

He grabbed his own pack and looked down at Kali. "I don't know where we are, so I don't know how to get where we're going, and I'm not..." He swallowed hard. "I'm not sure how strong I am on my own. I don't know if it will work."

"Then wake her up," Flint said.

Stonewall straightened. "I'll try it on my own. Could you both help her stand? I'm not sure I can manage carrying her and *us*."

Without hesitation, Flint knelt and wrapped Kali's arm around her shoulder, all but slinging the mage to her feet. Marcen did the same with Kali's other arm. Kali murmured something, but Flint ignored her and nodded to their former sergeant. "We're ready."

Stonewall looked positively ill but closed his eyes. Marcen cleared his throat. "If it helps, try picturing somewhere near the mines, somewhere you're familiar with. Maybe that's all you need to do. First creating a clear picture in my mind helps me when I'm testing my abilities."

Stonewall motioned them closer, so that they all stood where Mar's fire had burned moments ago. Other than a faint smudge of charred ground, there was no evidence a fire had been there at all. Flint shifted Kali's weight more comfortably and glanced around them, waiting for the air to shimmer and change as it had before. Stonewall gripped their wrists and murmured beneath his breath, "Away."

Nothing happened.

Hoofbeats sounded, too close for Flint's liking, and the ground trembled. "Sometime this sodding *year*, Stonewall," she hissed.

Stonewall's grip tightened. The hoofbeats grew louder, blending with the drumming of Flint's heart. Just when Flint was about to shake out of her former sergeant's grasp and meet the oncoming threat with drawn daggers, the world shifted and blurred again. Her stomach flopped as it had before but she forced her eyes to remain open, lest their potential attackers come upon them at the last moment – or Stonewall magicked them all into the middle of the Stonehaven garrison. But her body protested; she grew dizzy and lightheaded again, and had to shut her eyes before her last meal came back up.

The next thing she knew, she was stumbling in the dirt. Kali was gone. Flint looked up wildly only to see her in Mar's arms, but barely, as he staggered backward against an unfamiliar rocky outcropping. She went to help him, but tripped over something large and solid. It was Stonewall, who lay unconscious, face pressed against the gravel, mouth slack and breathing steadily.

"I've got her," Marcen said. "Help him."

"He's fine," Flint replied, drawing her daggers and breathing deeply to banish the nausea. "I must make sure we're alone."

They were in another barren stretch of land where only a few boulders provided any sort of shelter. The only plants were scrubby brushwork and some spindly trees, and other than a few beetles that scuttled away beneath Flint's boots, no creatures stirred. After the obscenely lush forests of Redfern, Stonehaven was indeed a desolate patch of the world. But the one advantage to so much *nothing* around them was that Flint could get a good look at their surroundings, enough to realize they were truly alone. She still had no sodding clue *where* in Stonehaven they were, but at least no one in their immediate vicinity wanted their blood. Good enough for now.

Flint returned to find Marcen struggling to prop Stonewall into a more comfortable position. She considered letting Mar sweat it out on his own, but decided to help him, if only so that Stonewall wouldn't chastise her later about being left in the dirt. Her fellow sentinel was a heavy sod, so it took her and Mar together to move him, eventually deciding to lay him and Kali beside one another on a blanket.

Once the lovers were situated, Marcen swiped his forehead, leaving a streak of pale skin amid the dust. "You said we're safe?"

"For now."

"Good. They need to rest."

"How long, d'you think?"

Marcen rubbed the back of his neck, considering. "Not sure. Kali probably needs an entire day, at least. But I have no idea what sort of magic Stonewall's calling upon, let alone the toll it took on him."

"We'll camp here tonight, and reassess in the morning." Flint began rummaging through their packs, searching for rations. She tossed some bread and dried fruit to Mar, but the mage didn't eat.

Instead he looked at Kali, sleeping peacefully next to Stonewall. "I meant what I said," Marcen said softly. "I never loved her. I wanted to, at one point, but that was before I knew about *him*. And now...well, I still think of her as a friend, but nothing more. I've turned my attention elsewhere." Pale blue eyes fell upon her. "You're not 'second' to anyone, Flint."

"Mira." Her birthname escaped, breathless.

"Mira." There was a smile in his voice. "No one else even comes close."

Ea's balls, her face was on fire. Flint toyed with a piece of jerky and tried not to look at him. "I guess you're all right, too."

"No." Suddenly he was before her, not touching, gaze deliberate and open. "Don't play tough or brassy – not about this. Not right now, at least."

She glared. "That's how I am."

"Aye, but you're more than that attitude of yours." His features softened. "You're fierce and loyal, and the bravest person I've ever met. And I think—maybe—I could love you one day. What about you?"

"I hate myself, most of the time." She tried to smile, to show him she was joking, but he only looked at her in that earnest way of his. At last she sighed. "I could love you, too. One day. Probably a long time from now."

Because she couldn't make anything easy for anyone, she glared at him again and added, "But don't rush me."

Marcen's answering smile shone. "Wouldn't dream of it." He hesitated, and then held out his hand. Flint's heart picked up and she accepted, her glove settling easily within his fingers, which closed around hers with a strength that no longer surprised her. "Can I kiss you?" he murmured.

Rather than answer, Flint tightened her grip, pulled the mage to her, and kissed him first. She'd meant for it to be a sweet, soft kiss, like in all the stories, but when they parted, his lips and cheeks were pink, and her own were hot and bothered – like the rest of her. They grinned at each other like fools.

THIRTY-THREE

The scratch of quill upon parchment grated in Drake's ears and filled Loach's office. The small space was too neat for Drake's liking; the desk and bookshelves each held carefully stacked towers of paper and books, while maps of the mines sprawled over the otherwise bare walls. The sun was rising, but the air was stuffy, and Drake's skin prickled with sweat. Leal and Atanar stood on either side. None of them spoke. Loach had not given them leave to do so when they'd entered after his summons.

The quill scrawled.

Just when Drake was about to risk speaking out of turn, Loach shifted his hand, allowing Drake a peak at what he was writing. Well, not the exact words, but Drake knew sentinel script when he saw it. Why in the void was this fellow writing in the sentinel code? Who was he writing to? Drake tried to tilt his head to get a better look without *looking* like he was snooping. Easier said than done.

The scratching stopped as the mine's administrator set down the quill and glanced up between the three men who waited before his desk. He'd not looked at any of them too closely upon their hiring, so he didn't bat an eyelash at Leal's somewhat changed features.

"I summoned you here," Loach began, "to discuss your employment in this facility. Specifically, its termination."

Atanar stared at the administrator, brows furrowed as if scanning a map for a known location, but the tension in Nat's posture made Drake think his attentiveness wasn't due to a lack of understanding.

Leal cocked an eyebrow at Loach, but it was Drake who replied. "You're letting us go? Why?"

Not that he minded the thought of leaving this sodding place for good, but he had wanted to poke around the dam again. And given Loach's use of a code only taught to sentinels, this place evidently held more secrets he could learn.

Loach exhaled through his nose in a sharp, mocking laugh, and began to tick off points on his fingers. "You're late all the time – when you bother to show up. Your efforts are pathetic. And Goldie told me you've been sneaking down to the dam to...well, only the gods know what, but I'll not tolerate any foolery under my watch. You're all dismissed."

With that, he set the first parchment aside and picked up another, this time writing in the common Aredian script that Drake recognized, but had never learned to read. Atanar still stood frozen until Leal tapped his arm, and the two of them turned to leave.

But Drake had to know what was on that parchment.

"What about our earnings?" he heard himself ask. "We don't work for free."

"Room and board," Loach replied without looking up. "And meals. You're lucky I don't care to see your faces here any longer, else I'd be making *you* compensate me for the amenities provided to your sorry selves."

"Amenities?" Drake snorted. "That slop you call porridge?" He risked a step closer to Loach's desk, eyes darting to the first letter. "This is..."

Relah? Bahar?

As it had back at the Sufani camp, his brother's voice appeared in his mind, as surely as if Elan had been standing beside him. Drake trailed off, mouth agape, as Elan added, *Brother?*

"Elan?" Drake whispered.

Loach sighed. "What's that?"

"Drake," Atanar's voice was soft but urgent.

Drake squeezed his eyes shut to concentrate better. *Relah*, he managed. *Are you in danger?*

I'm in Stonehaven, Stonewall replied, relief coloring the words. *Where can we meet you?*

To have traveled so quickly! Drake had hardly dared to hope for such a miracle. He tried to picture his and the wild mage's campsite, adding, *Brother, you and I need to have a nice long chat about this new ability of yours.*

We will, Stonewall assured him. *Thanks, relah. See you soon.*

And he was gone.

"What in the void's wrong with him?"

"I don't know, serla," Atanar said, squeezing Drake's shoulder. "Drake? Drake, are you–"

"Sorry," Drake said, blinking hard and resisting the urge to shake his head. In Tor's name, speaking like that—if it could even be called *speaking*—was sodding *strange*! "I'm fine. Just...tired. Sorry, serla," he added to Loach. "What were you saying?"

The administrator did not look impressed with his explanation. "This is a business, not a charity. Besides, you're clearly unfit for duty."

With that, Loach snatched up a small bell at the edge of his desk. Three rings later, Ottis strode into the room. The bear-like man filled the doorway, impressively muscular arms tense as he swept his gaze over the three former miners.

"Serla?" Ottis asked.

Loach pointed to Drake. "Remove these dregs."

"Yes, ser." Ottis stepped toward Drake, who raised his palms.

"We're going, we're going," Drake said, casting one last look at the parchment before making for the door. "No need to get riled up."

Loach did not reply. Ottis followed the three men out of the office and into the cool morning, the sky still tinted indigo. They passed the mess hall, where a group of Carver's Creek townies smoked outside, and watched them with varying degrees of suspicion. Atanar stared back, that same searching expression on his face.

"What're you looking at?" Leal asked.

Atanar shook his head. "I cannot yet say."

Well, that boded ill. But despite the knot of anxiety in Drake's belly, his heart was light. His brother was here!

"Can't say I'm upset at leaving for good," Leal said, though his tone was suspicious. "Drake, we earned enough coin, right?"

"We earned as much as we could," Drake replied, thankful they'd worked out a simple code for their mission here. "Met some good people, at least." He thought of Talon and added, "Well, some are better than others."

Ottis followed them until they passed the refinery, then the guard hung back, watching them leave. Was it Drake's imagination, or was it easier to breathe now that they were away from the mine? The red dirt road was hard-packed, but they kicked up dust as they went. Drake scanned the horizon for a glimpse of his brother, but saw no sign.

"What happened back there?" Drake said to Atanar as soon as they were out of Ottis' earshot.

"I should ask that of you."

"I'll explain in a moment," Drake said. "First, are you well?"

Atanar's brows knitted. "That man... I knew him. No," he frowned, "I recognized him. He's...bound to *them*."

"Them?" Leal asked.

Atanar shuddered. "The...what do Aredians call them? The glimmers."

Drake froze in his tracks. "You know this for certain?"

"No," Atanar admitted. "It was a feeling of...kinship, but not a true knowing. More of a memory." He sighed. "Perhaps my mind deceives me."

Leal shot Drake a wary look. Drake had no answer, either, so he only squeezed Nat's shoulder. "We'll ask Kali when we see her, which should be soon." His companions gave him startled looks but he picked up his pace. "I'll explain on the way. I must speak with Eris."

*

Kali leaned against a chunk of Stonehaven rock and exhaled a stream of *biri* smoke into the dawn light. The sun had just broken free of the horizon, scattering saffron and pink through the clouds, and streaming gold across the red rocks and towering boulders. But the province held a harsh beauty, for no foliage dotted the landscape, only the occasional scrubby bush whose thorns warned against getting too close. Kali could not sense even a hint of water in the air. Although she'd been away from Whitewater City for well over a month, now was the first time she truly missed the White River's rumble. Even back at Starwatch Bastion there had been lakes and streams in abundance. But here, there was only dust.

She felt Stonewall's presence before she caught the crunch of his boots over the ground. He came to stand beside her, arms crossed as he surveyed the landscape, a sense of accomplishment emanating from him like ripples in a pond. Kali blew out another stream of smoke and passed him the *biri*. "Success?" she asked.

He accepted, exhaling his own smoke before he offered the *biri* back to her. "Yes, I managed to contact Drake. From what I could tell, we're not far from his location. I truly didn't believe my magic would work." He whispered the word *magic*. "Let alone bring us so close to my brother."

There was much unspoken between them—too much, really—but the *biri*'s gift, a languid, easy warmth, softened the edges of Kali's agitation and granted her the fortitude to ignore the persistent pulse of her frustration. "Bringing us here on your own must have taken everything you had."

He slanted her a sideways look that was not quite a smile. "Close to it." She offered the *biri* again but he refused, and his gaze drifted to the horizon. "I just wish I knew why."

"Why, what?"

He gestured to the landscape. "Why Tor saw fit to grant me these abilities, and what my magic *means*."

Kali finished the *biri* and resisted the urge to light another. "You have Fata blood, Stonewall, so this magic is your birthright. I think the more pressing question is what else can you do?"

He frowned. "The more I learn about myself and the world, the less I understand."

A hollow laugh fell off her tongue. "Truer words. I suppose we should get underway?"

He nodded, but didn't turn back to the camp that Marcen and Flint had set up while Kali and Stonewall were indisposed. They had been in this place for a full day but only now did Kali feel somewhat rested. But even as the *biri*'s calm slipped through her veins, her stomach churned at the thought of what they would find when they reached Eris and her new allies – and what they had abandoned to come here.

"What do you think of Stonehaven?" Stonewall said suddenly.

In response, Kali used the boulder for balance and knelt to grab a small hunk of rock. She delved her focus deep. Its particles were sluggish, with none of the echoes of life and movement that she'd sensed from other stones. It had been the same for every bit of Stonehaven rock she'd touched. "This place is barren," she managed, looking around again. "Nothing grows here; nothing is new. Everything just…dies." She closed her hand and brushed her intention over the stone's particles again, and the rock crumbled to dust. "Is the whole province like this?"

Stonewall squinted through the dawn light again, bringing his hand up to shield his eyes as the sun crept higher. "It's worse in areas around all of the different mines."

A seedling notion turned some of her anxiety to excitement, and she studied the landscape with new eyes. "What would it take," she murmured, "to bring life to this dead land?"

Now he turned, but it was only to face her, and she caught the shiver of his apprehension along the thread that bound their hearts. "No, Kali."

"You don't know what I'm–"

"No," he said again, sharper, though the next word was a whisper. "Please."

She scoffed. He was so sodding stubborn! "I don't need your permission to have an idea."

Almost-gold eyes fell on her and his fear was like the wind-kicked dust swirling at their feet. "I know your heart."

Sweat pricked at the small of her back but she kept her voice—and her heart, thank you—steady. "Aye, so you should trust me."

He looked back at the horizon. "This is where my last vision took place."

Kali made a show of looking around their feet. "Quite a coincidence."

She'd hoped to draw out a chuckle, but his face went blank, like it did in the heat of battle. "You died here."

So much for her meager attempt at humor; she really should know better by now. "It was just a dream," she told him, though she didn't quite believe the words. "Everything will be fine. Besides," she could not help but add, "*you* were the one so keen on coming here, remember?"

"I know," he whispered, the words almost stolen by the wind.

"We could still leave," she ventured. "Grab Drake and Atanar, and just... go." She gestured to the horizon.

"Do you believe that?"

She opened her mouth to say, *of course.* But now that she was here, she could not turn away from Eris, especially if Eris truly intended to create whatever destruction loomed in her heart. Nor could Kali turn away from her own foolish hope of doing *some* good with her magic.

Stonewall embraced her then, too close for mere comfort; he held her like she would crumble to dust otherwise. She could not, did not *want* to break the contact, so she pressed her cheek against his cuirass, savoring the scent of leather and *him*, and straining to hear his heartbeat. The drum was faint, but steady, and she savored it, too.

They returned to the camp to find Marcen kicking dirt over the remains of their fire and Flint running a whetstone over her sword, occasionally squinting down the blade. She didn't look up as Stonewall and Kali came into view. "Back already?" she asked as she swiped the whetstone a final time. "That didn't take you very long. Kali, he's not being selfish, is he?"

Stonewall rolled his eyes but Kali chuckled. "Stone's the least selfish person I've ever had the pleasure of spending time with," she said lightly as she reached for her viol case. "And easily the *best* with his–"

Don't encourage her, Stonewall broke in through their silent speech.

The only way to fight fire is by smothering it with too much information, Kali replied in kind.

Indeed, Flint made a show of wrinkling her nose as she hefted her sword before sliding it into the sheath at her waist. "Ugh, never mind. Sorry I said anything." She grabbed her own traveling pack. "You know where we're going right?"

Kali shot Stonewall a raised brow.

He rolled his eyes again. "All too well."

The journey to Drake and Eris' location took the better part of the morning. By midday, Kali's knee screamed in agony, refusing to be ignored any longer. But she said nothing, unwilling to slow their journey any more than necessary or be the focal point of anyone's sympathy. Besides, the pain was, as ever, a distraction from her own churning thoughts.

Even had she and Stonewall not shared their strange connection, he would have known she was distressed. But he tried, in his way, to keep his feelings to himself. He tried. When they stopped for a midday meal, she sucked down half a *biri* like it was nothing, but saved the rest, as she was reluctant to burn through their meager supply. So she ate and chatted and smiled at Flint and Mar, and tried not to let twice the worry overwhelm her heart.

As the balance of the day tipped toward evening, Stonewall's head jerked up and a grin came to his face. He'd been walking in the lead, but now he rushed ahead, where a trio of familiar figures had appeared on the trail: Drake, Atanar, and a man who looked an awful lot like Leal.

Drake swept his brother into a massive hug that lifted Stonewall off his feet. "Thank Tor and the rest of them," Drake said as Stonewall struggled in his grip. "I really thought I was just hallucinating all of that silent speech stuff."

"Ea's tits, put me down," Stonewall grumbled, but when his brother released him he was grinning harder. "I wondered that, too."

Atanar had filled out, and the shadows beneath his eyes had receded. "You look well," Kali said to him. "Any trouble from... anything?"

A broad statement, but he seemed to catch her meaning. He glanced at Drake, and then shook his head. "Not from thralls." He studied Kali, brows knitting. "You look...unwell."

Drake cleared his throat. "We'll swap war stories on the way back. Oh, but before we head out, I should make introductions."

The man who looked like Leal rolled his eyes.

"I'm too much of a gentleman to pester a lady," Drake continued. "But seeing as you're one of us fellows, consider this your manly due." He swept into a fair approximation of a courtly bow. "Leal, this is everyone. Everyone, this is a different, albeit still thorny, Leal. The difference is courtesy of Eris."

So Eris had made a non-mage's life better with her magic. Perhaps all hope wasn't lost. A glow of pride suffused Kali's veins and she beamed at Leal.

"Leal?" Stonewall said, eyes wide. "By the One... You look..."

"Happy," Kali said, regarding the Sufani man, who was trying and failing to hide his amusement at Drake's teasing. "Are you?"

Leal still wore a hood, but no veil covered his face, revealing traces of stubble on his jawline. "It was a little strange at first, but now I feel..." He exhaled deeply, squaring his broader shoulders. "For the first time in my life, my outside matches how I feel inside."

Flint's eyes went rounder than a moon. "I don't understand."

"You don't have to," Drake told her. "Just accept."

Flint regarded the Sufani again. "Well, I wouldn't kick you out of bed."

Marcen snorted a laugh and Leal's cheeks flamed, though he lifted his chin. "How comforting. But if you've quite finished making asses of yourselves, we have a massacre to stop."

THIRTY-FOUR

By the time the group reached the wild mages' camp, Kali's head was spinning. She had thought her group's adventures were the stuff stories were made of, but their trip to Redfern was *nothing* compared to what Drake had related. Eris was in league with wild mages. The name Seren's Children had a poetic ring that Kali appreciated, but Drake's account of their hatred of non-mages was troubling, to say the least. Destroying an entire mine, workers and all... It was an unthinkable act of violence. Far worse, though, was that she *could* imagine Eris taking part in such a plan.

"Tor willing," Drake was saying, "you'll be able to talk her out of bloodshed." His next words were quiet. "The One knows I haven't."

Kali tried to give him a reassuring smile. "I'll do my best."

"And I'll try not to murder Talon," Flint added, for she'd cursed Drake after he'd related news of the former commander's presence.

"At least, not right away," Kali said. "Believe me, I'm not fond of her, either, but we can't be too choosy about the help we can get right now, beggars that we are."

"I know, I know," Flint said, sighing. "It's just... Milo."

"Milo isn't here," Stonewall replied curtly. "Keep your mind on the mission, Flint."

Drake paused just out of earshot of the wild mages' campsite and gave Kali a serious look that reminded her of Stonewall. "Eris has told Jensine and the others about your magic. They were *most* interested in your abilities. If I were you, I'd be careful about getting recruited."

Kali was no slouch at serious looks of her own. "That's the least of my concerns right now, but thanks for the warning."

"Understood," Drake replied, and gestured toward the boulders that sheltered Seren's Children. He led the way, Atanar on his heels while Leal followed last, watching the weary travelers' backs. Seren's Children looked...normal, though Kali didn't know why she had anticipated anything else. All were dressed simply and practically, and all wore wary gazes as the newcomers approached.

Eris was not among them.

Before Kali could worry, a familiar figure shouldered through the wild mages and darted down the sloping ground. Marcen surged toward her. "Adrie!"

"Mar!" The two former Whitewater Bastion mages met in a few strides, embracing amidst the scattered boulders. Adrie pulled back first and rested her palms on Marcen's cheeks. "Seren's light, it's good to see you again! You look too thin; have you been eating? Where's Sadira?"

Chuckling, Marcen placed his palms over Adrie's. "I've been eating plenty, I've just been running a whole lot, too. Sadira..." He hesitated and shot Kali a glance.

Adrie looked over as well, and lowered her hands. She made no move to embrace Kali, and her voice was civil. "Kalinda. I'm glad you're well, and that you made it here safely. Where's Sadira?"

"Safe in Redfern," Kali said, smiling tightly. "I'm sure she sends her regards." *Even though you never cared for her.*

Nodding, Adrie glanced at the sentinels, and her eyes narrowed. "You're here, too. Eris won't be pleased."

"That's nothing new," Stonewall muttered.

"What happened to the others in your squad?" Adrie asked, brow furrowing as she surveyed Stonewall and Flint.

"We'll get to that soon," Kali said. "First, I'd really like to see Eris. How is she?"

Adrie scrubbed a hand through her hair. "Resting, but she's...well, she's waiting for you. I must admit, we hardly believed Drake when he said you

343

were coming here." She studied Kali and Stonewall. "Where were you? How did you get a message to him?"

Drake had said that he'd been vague about his knowledge of Kali and the others' imminent arrival. Stonewall answered. "We weren't far, and my brother and I have ways of reaching one another." He nodded to the path ahead. "We shouldn't linger."

Adrie frowned at him, but evidently decided not to question him further as she turned and picked her way back to the wild mages, who had not moved.

Kali identified the Damaris family from Drake's description. But even if she'd not been able to, the first of Seren's Children who came to greet her was clearly their leader. Jensine Damaris radiated magic; the sweet essence of it drenched the dry air around her, soaking into Kali's senses like jessamin blossoms in full bloom. The rest of Seren's Children were strong in their own rights, but their leader was the most powerful.

Jensine Damaris stood with arms crossed, surveying the newcomers with open suspicion. "Which one of you is Kalinda Halcyon?"

Here we go. Kali fought to ignore her longing for the other mage's power. If she couldn't conduct herself normally around these folks, she had no hope of a peaceful resolution to the situation. She needed a moment to collect herself.

That in mind, Kali gave her prettiest smile as she pointed to Stonewall. "Right here. The name throws people off."

Stonewall did not move, though Flint snickered. Kali stifled a chuckle. At least Flint could appreciate her sense of humor. But the moment of levity helped her steel herself against what would surely be a test of her self-control.

"*Kali* is joking," Adrie said, sighing. "The man is Stonewall. There's Marcen, my friend from Whitewater. And that's Flint."

"Drake told us about you," Jensine replied, glancing at the sentinels. "Such courageous souls, to defy the sentinel order to rescue your mage allies." Her snide tone belied the civil words before she added, "I would welcome you among us, but you still stink of hematite."

344

"They must still ingest it for a little while," Drake said. "Otherwise the loss will kill them."

Jensine harrumphed but offered no further comment, which set off a warning in Kali's mind. "We've had a very long journey," Kali said. "May I please see Eris?"

The wild mage studied her before nodding once. "Fine. This way."

She slipped through the nearest boulders without looking back. Kali limped after, Stonewall and the rest of her allies on her heels. The other wild mages brought up the rear, though some remained outside of their camp, presumably to stand guard – or to prevent anyone from leaving. Kali tried not to let that thought stick.

"There," Jensine said, pausing before a couple of boulders, where the trail wound ahead and through. The path between them was narrow, probably too narrow for Drake and Atanar, and the sentinels with their gear.

Kali glanced behind her at her allies. "I should go alone." At Stonewall's spike of concern, she added, "I'll be fine."

He set his pack down to guard one side of the opening, despite Jensine's stony gaze. "We'll be here."

Kali picked the rest of her way down the narrow path. She sensed Eris' power before she saw her old friend. Eris had always been strong, but the magic within her had been leashed, held fast to her being. Now, though, magic seethed around Eris, brimming in the air. The force of it hit Kali like a slap, making her stumble. Her knee, already burning from the day's journey, screamed in protest, and only the rocky path, so close on either side, prevented her from tumbling to the rough dirt. Stonewall's mind brushed hers and she caught his concern.

I'm all right, she sent through their bond.

Are you?

Of course, there was no fooling the man so attuned to her every mood. Kali took a deep breath. *I will be.* She smoothed out her hair—sod it all, her braid had come undone again!—and slipped past the boulders to find her friend. Eris sat cross-legged on a bundle of mats and blankets, a semicircle of candles before her, along with what looked like a map of the surrounding countryside. She did not glance up as Kali stepped into the clearing.

"Drake told me you were coming here to 'talk some sense into me,'" Eris said. "I'm afraid you've wasted your time."

Kali could not help but laugh. "Oh, now that's too easy."

Eris looked up, green eyes narrowed. "We must destroy the mines, Kali. We must cleanse the world of hematite. It's the only way our people can truly be free."

Kali awkwardly slid down the nearest boulder. Once seated, she rubbed her throbbing knee and tried to ignore the pull of hunger for her friend's power. "I agree."

"But?"

"You know 'but.'"

"You and Drake," Eris scoffed. "And Leal, too. No stomach for what must be done." She turned back to her map, but her gaze seemed far away. "Seren's Children understand."

Rather than reply right away—for all the good arguing would do—Kali scooted over so she was nearer to her friend. The hunger for magic did not increase too much, which was a relief, and Kali thought she could bear the feeling a while longer. So she only studied Eris from head to polished boots. "You don't *look* like you're an inch away from dying."

Eris scoffed again. "Drake's being dramatic. I'm fine. Really." She held up a hand as if staving off protest. "I pushed myself a little too hard—with good reason, I should say—but I'm better now. All of you are worried for nothing."

"We care about you," Kali said. "We all want you to be well. And Drake was truly frightened, by the sound of it."

Eris made a noncommittal noise and then eyed Kali. "You look dreadful."

Something hot stung Kali's eyes. "Life has been...difficult since our parting, which was bad enough on its own."

Eris was silent.

"You were right," Kali added. "People hate mages, even when we try to do right by them. Perhaps *especially* then, because our power is nothing compared to the Laughing God's."

"Since when do you believe in–"

"I don't. But all the magic in the world can't bring a soul back to its body." Kali rubbed her temple. "Even with everything we can do, it's not enough. I don't know if it will ever be enough."

"Enough for what? To stop the dregs from fearing us?" Eris' voice was dark. "That's a losing game, Kali. They'll never come around. They'll always see us as *other*."

Kali stared up at the darkening sky, where stars had started to prick through the inky veil. "There must be a way we can all live together in harmony. Isn't that the One god's greatest edict?"

"I wouldn't know. And I'm a little concerned at your sudden piety."

"It's not piety." Kali scrubbed her eyes. "Just hope."

"Well, you can hope in one hand…"

Despite herself, Kali chuckled. "I suppose." She leaned against the rock, still warm from the sun. "Leal looks…incredible."

A pleased half-smile crept to Eris' face, but her voice was neutral as she studied her map again. "Aye, he does, doesn't he?"

"Is he truly changed? All the way?"

"Nearly. He grows more masculine every day, but his particles are still shifting. It's as if my magic set something in motion, but the full transformation is still underway."

Kali smiled at her friend. "You did a good thing, Eris. For a non-mage, no less."

"Leal's a friend." Eris exhaled. "And I made a promise."

"I only wish you'd taken more care with your own well-being."

Eris rested one hand on her rounding stomach. "I'll do anything to let my son have a brighter future."

Kali's breath caught. "Son?"

"Aye. Can you believe it?"

Tears pricked Kali's eyes, but she welcomed them; brought, like Eris' smile, by happiness. "Stars above, if he's even a little bit like you and Gid, you're going to have your hands full."

Eris wore the first true look of joy Kali had seen since Gideon's death. "I

347

know."

Kali swiped her cheeks and looked back at the map. "That's the hematite mine?"

Nodding, Eris skimmed her fingertips along the outline, which reminded Kali of a giant thumbprint. "I have never seen a greater stain upon the world. Don't try to change my mind," she added, firmer than before. "It's quite made up."

In response, Kali reached for a nearby stone, turning it over in her palm as she considered how best to proceed. Eris' conviction was firm, but Eris herself wasn't evil. She wasn't a monster. She just had to see the bigger picture. Kali stared at the sketch of the mine, remembering what Drake had told them of Eris' plans of blood, bone, and fire. There had also been talk of flooding the place. The result would be catastrophic.

Unless... Kali delved her focus into the stone once more. Yes, it was cold and empty, but if she concentrated, if she looked deeper, she sensed something she had not caught before: a memory of life. Perhaps this lonely province needed a reminder. Kali inhaled softly at the notion, and the stone crumbled into dust as she squeezed.

"I agree that the mine should be destroyed," Kali said slowly, brushing off her hands on her tunic. "But what then? What happens after the waters settle and the fires die? What will you do? Move on, and leave the survivors behind to clean up your mess?"

Eris stiffened. "The hemies–"

"Drake said there are only a few sentinels there. The rest of the folks have homes and families and lives. They're trying to survive, Eris. Just like you."

"They bring evil into the world."

"If you destroy the mines *and* the folks who work there, you will be no better than those you hate so much. *You* will have spread evil, with grief and fear and loss. Everyone who hates us will have their worst fears confirmed. Everyone who might be your ally will turn their backs, and we'll be worse off than ever."

"What else can we do?"

Kali found another chunk of Stonehaven rock and pressed it into her friend's palm. "This place is sick. Can't you feel it?"

Eris's eyes closed and her slender fingers gripped the rock. Heartened, Kali steeled herself, and pressed both of Eris' hands around the stone. "This place is barren and dying...but it's not dead yet. We have great power at our disposal. We can heal this land, Eris, change it enough so that those who live here have other options than digging up the ground. We can shape this place, and the world, into something better.

"I know you're angry. You have every right to be angry. But you must be stronger than your anger, or it will hold you prisoner."

Seconds passed, and Kali hoped she'd struck the right note. Then Eris wrenched her hands free, sending the stone to the blankets around her. "Your heart is too soft. 'Healing the land.'" She snorted. "Silly fantasies, even for you. Your eyes are clouded. It's not your fault, I suppose, given your...history with hemies. Don't look at me like that. The mines *will* be destroyed," she added firmly. "But...I understand your concerns about the loss of life. As such, we'll strike tomorrow night, after everyone has gone, rather than the daylight hours when all the workers are around. Will that suit you?"

This was...unexpected, but not unwelcome. Eris could see reason after all. A massive boulder seemed to lift from Kali's chest. "It will suit me just fine," she said, beaming. "Thank you."

Eris looked back at her map. "What exactly did Drake say about the Forsworn sentinels?"

"Nothing much," Kali said. "Actually, he seemed rather uncomfortable about the subject. Why?"

Eris' gaze slid toward the direction of the mines. "Someone's there you ought to meet."

Kali's stomach fluttered. "Who?" Her mind went to Gannister, the sentinel back at Starwatch Bastion who had been her late father's close friend. Gan had loved Kali too, in her own way, and Kali had always thought of her as a dear aunt. But Gan had never been a troublemaker. Why would she have been sent here? "Who is it, Eris?"

349

Eris took a deep breath and met Kali's eyes. "Your mother."

＊

The following morning, just after the sun had crested the horizon, Eris and Seren's Children gathered to go to war. They had made no secret of their leave-taking, so Eris was not surprised when Kali, Leal, Mar, and their sentinel allies came charging up from their camp several yards away.

"What are you doing?" Kali huffed as she limped over. "You said you wouldn't set out until tonight!"

Dark circles ringed her eyes and her hair was messier than usual; had she slept at all? Eris shoved aside her concern. "I did say that."

Kali's eyes widened. "You lied to me."

Eris looked over her shoulder, where Adrie, Jensine, Caith, and Brenna waited. "Go on. I'll be along in a moment."

Brenna shot Eris a dubious look but the Damaris siblings turned to go. Adrie and Jensine, however, stood with Eris.

"We could use your help," Jensine said to Kali.

Eris shook her head. "She won't. Right?"

Kali only glared at her, hands balling into fists until her hemie lover murmured her name. She relaxed a little but the angry look upon her face did not abate. "If you do this, Eris, you'll be no better than Argent."

Eris welcomed the surge of her own fury. She *should* be angry; she *should* be willing to do whatever it took to free mages everywhere. "Aye, and Argent accomplishes what he intends to. So will I. And he will find that Seren's Children are a force to be reckoned with."

"You'd kill my mother?" Kali shot back. "After I only just learned she still lives? Even you can't be so heartless."

"Kam can take care of herself." Eris glared at the hemies that stood with Kali. "As can all sentinels. And Sufani, apparently."

Leal frowned, but said nothing. What could he say? Their bargain was finished; he was free to do as he wished.

"Eris," Drake began, stepping forward.

350

But she cut him off with a lift of her hand. "You've done your duty to your fellow mages, Drake. The information you gathered about the mine will serve us well. Although we won't bother with the dam, I thank you for your assistance. Your intentions are good. I don't expect you to remain with me, although I wish you would. Stay with your hemie brother if you like. Your life is your own." She looked back at Kali again, turning over the words she'd been considering since their conversation the night before. "I see now there's no use in convincing you to abandon the sentinels, but consider this." She pointed to Stonewall. "Hematite has ruined him, body and mind, and will steal his life far sooner than you would like, as it did your father's. Your own mother's life, too, has been destroyed by hematite."

Eris stepped closer to Kali, boring her eyes into Kali's wide, dark ones. "You have suffered and you *will* suffer so much pain and loss because of hematite, and yet you *still* claim those who keep the mine alive are worth saving. Your compassion is noble, but misplaced." To her surprise, heat pricked her eyes and she had to fight to keep her voice as steady as it needed to be. "The world is changing, Kali. You must, too."

Tears streaked down Kali's face, but she swiped them away. "Compassion is *never* misplaced, Eris. But if you won't show mercy to strangers, think of your friends." She nodded to Jensine. "How do you think today will play out if you stroll up to the mine in broad daylight? Aren't you afraid your own people will suffer?"

Jensine snorted. "We have *nothing* to fear."

"Aye," Eris added, nodding. "We are stronger than our enemies."

"Your objective," Stonewall said slowly, "is a mine filled with hematite."

Eris should have ignored him, but she opted to give the hemie her best withering look. "We aren't there to destroy the hematite, just the place where it lives and those who bring it into the world. Besides, most of Seren's Children have never been hematite's prisoner. Their strength has never been diminished."

"Enough talk," Jensine said. "We've got work to do." She turned to leave, but something held Eris in place. She met Kali's eyes again and spoke so that only her friend could hear. "Come with me."

But Kali shook her head. "I won't be part of this destruction, Eris. There is another way. Please, take it."

Something caught in Eris' throat. Kali didn't understand. She never would. Was this how nearly fifteen years of friendship would end? This loss did not cut the same as Gid's death had, for Eris had never looked upon her husband and thought *enemy*. So her voice shook more than she would have liked when she said, "If you're not with us, you're against me."

Kali's cheeks were still wet but she wasn't crying any longer. "Be safe, Silver Girl."

Eris' heart sank. She turned her back to Kali and hurried after the other mages, Jensine and Adrie at her heels. Leal did not follow, and that was the final straw. Eris' heart clenched but she forced herself not to react to that betrayal. Only when she was certain she was out of Kali's sight did she duck her head and weep.

THIRTY-FIVE

Stonewall did not spare the shape-changing mage or her allies another glance. They weren't worth the effort. Instead, he touched Kali's arm. *You did all you could,* he sent through their bond.

She swiped her wet cheeks with her sleeve. *Maybe.* "How far away are the mines from here?" she asked Drake.

"A couple hours on foot." Drake clasped Leal's shoulder while the Sufani watched Eris and the others walk away. "We could probably outrun them… "

He trailed off as Kali shook her head. "No running for me." She looked at Stonewall. "How fast can *we* get to the mines?"

He caught her meaning at once. "A few minutes, probably," he said, squinting through the massive, rust-red boulders in the direction Seren's Children had gone. "Maybe less. I'm not sure."

"Could you manage it alone?" she asked.

"Why?" He searched her eyes and heart; the quiet certainty he found sent a chill through his blood. *You want to conserve your strength? What are you planning?*

She lifted her chin. "Can you manage it or not?"

His allies' collective gaze settled upon him and Stonewall fought the urge to reach for the vials of hematite stowed in his belt. He'd used this magic before; he could again. Perhaps his abilities were Tor's way of showing him that his worth was more than swinging a sword. This thought eased some of the weight on his chest. "I think so," he said. "I could at least get us closer in far less time than it'll take Eris and the others."

Drake beamed at him. "Atta boy, *relah*."

"What of the guards?" Atanar asked. "Or will you fight them all as Eris intends to?"

"There aren't a lot of guards at the mines," Drake added. "But even a few could slow us down, for certain. And...well..." He spread his hands. "Killing anyone goes against what we're trying to do."

"But even if we got back into the mines, unharmed," Leal said. "The miners won't listen to us. They'll never leave."

"They will," Drake replied. "But if not, we'll drag them out."

A strong wind blew, kicking up dust and sending Kali's dark hair whipping around her face as she watched the path Eris had taken. "Stonewall..."

Gods above, he knew what she was going to ask him before she'd finished saying his name. But he didn't know if he could manage moving them across the province *and* using his shadow-self. "As we discussed last night, there's more to my," he grimaced, "magic than just traveling quickly. I can... disappear into the shadows. I'm still figuring it out," he added as the others exchanged startled looks. "So we shouldn't rely on it overmuch."

Flint sighed. "Will this magic spin my insides like a top like the other kind?"

"No idea," Stonewall told her. "But it beats slogging across this wasteland and needless killing."

"Leal, Nat, and I will handle the workers after we arrive," Drake replied. "But Leal's right; they likely won't be eager to leave." His gaze slid to Kali. "Your mother has a way with the guards. Could you persuade her to help us?"

Kali studied him. "Why didn't you tell me about her? You said that Loach fellow was writing in sentinel code, and you told us about Talon. How hard was it to say, 'by the way, your mother's a sentinel, Forsworn, and is in the mines, too?'"

"I wanted to," Drake replied. "But Eris...said she wanted to tell you herself. Sorry about that."

Kali swept a hand through her hair. "I'll talk to her, but I can't promise anything more."

Flint shifted into a battle-ready stance. "I'll help clear folks out, or keep watch, or whatever's needed."

"I'll help, too," Marcen added.

Atanar took a deep breath. "Will this truly work?"

"Of course it will," Drake replied. "Have a little faith, eh?" For all that he tried to keep the trepidation out of his voice, Stonewall sensed it anyway: the distant ring of a hammer striking stone.

Kali looked at him. "Stonewall?"

No actual words crept through their bond, but unspoken questions – and a hope.

He nodded slowly. "Let's move out."

The group collected their weapons and other necessary gear, stowed the rest, and gathered around Stonewall. His heart raced and doubt clouded his thoughts, but just when he knew he couldn't manage this feat, Kali touched his mind again. *Yes, you can. You will.*

The thread between their hearts was still strained and frayed, but love looked back at him through her gaze. Doubt receded. He squeezed his eyes shut to better concentrate and the others linked their hands. Stonewall pictured the underground dam that Drake had described in detail last night; the brothers had poured over Stonewall's weathered map as they recalled their time in this province. At first, all he could see in his mind's eye were scribbled lines of ink, which were not clear enough to guide him. Panic set in, pounding through his throat.

No. He would not surrender to doubt. *I can do this.* He marshalled his courage and concentrated.

Images swam into Stonewall's thoughts: rust-red earth, a stained fingerprint that delved deep into the ground; reflected waterlight flickering on a cavern ceiling; a stone wall, a bulwark against the underground river. Stonewall leaped upon the images, urging his will to follow. *Away.* Only when the scents of water and iron and clay filled Stonewall's nose did he open his eyes. Darkness met him head-on, until his eyes adjusted and he exhaled in wonder at the sight of the dam and the water.

The air was heavy, as the world felt minutes before a storm descended. The water before him was mirror-smooth, but when he knelt beside it, he swore it lapped at his hand. A chill swept over him; warning and a welcome, intertwined. *I should not have come here.*

"Gods above..." Drake whispered, rubbing his eyes as he looked around the cavern where Stonewall had brought them.

Flint stood close to Marcen. "Well, at least I don't feel as much like puking this time."

"Me too, thank the stars," the mage replied.

"Speak for yourselves," Drake muttered, for he, Atanar, and Leal were hunched over and groaning.

"Buck up, boys," Flint said airily, then she nodded to Marcen. "Let's see what we're up against."

The two darted toward the single spear of light thrust down into the cavern: the only way in or out. Stonewall knelt by the water and watched the play of light and shadow on the walls. The water beckoned; the utter blackness of it seemed to resonate in his mind, a promise of pain as much as pleasure.

Come home, my son.

Kali knelt beside him and dipped her fingertips in the water. "Oh," she whispered. "It's colder than I imagined. It's dead, too."

Stonewall frowned but did not take his eyes off the water. "What do you mean 'dead?'"

"The water's particles feel...empty, just like the ground." Kali wrapped her arms around herself. "Seren's light, if curses exist, this place is cursed."

The reflected light coalesced until a vision of Tor, the golden-eyed god, swam before Stonewall's waking eyes. *Soon, my son.*

"Not cursed," Stonewall murmured. "Waiting."

Kali shot him a curious look, but before she could speak, Flint and Marcen returned, faces tense.

"Guards and miners all over the place," Flint said as she trotted back to the group.

"Ready to show us what else you can do, brother?" Drake asked.

But Stonewall heard him only dimly, for he could not tear his eyes away from the water. Everything else seemed distant and hazy, like figures on a far horizon. A sense of lightness filled him; a feeling that he was not entirely in this place and time.

Come home, Elan.

Leave now, Stonewall's better sense screamed. *Leave now and never look back.*

"Stonewall?"

He did not know who said his name, but the familiar sound brought the world back into focus. "I'm ready," he said to his allies. "Get close to me again."

As they clustered around him, as he fought to focus on that one desire—*hide*—Kali touched his arm. *Are you well?*

Stonewall tried and failed not to look at the black water one last time. *I don't know.*

Shadows closed around them, darkening the world. Flint sucked in a breath and Atanar muttered something in Canderi, but otherwise, no one made a sound. The group crept toward the surface and the shadows followed.

*

When Drake led the group from the tunnel, Kali squinted in the sunlight, craning her head back to take in the full scope of the hematite mine. From her vantage point at the base, the stepped sides loomed high enough to touch the blue-gray sky, making her dizzy. As they began to climb the path to their destination, Kali's stomach twisted and her knee screamed, but she held back all protest for fear of giving her friends away. She and the others moved through the mines as if in a dream. They clung to the shadows cast by the looming sides, and no one—not the miners hefting pickaxes and shovels, not the glaring guards—paid them any mind.

She could not help but look beside her at Stonewall. Though his eyes were open, his attention was wholly inward, reminiscent of a mage in deep focus. His concentration writhed like a living thing, and the sweat beading his brow gave away his efforts. Hoping to ease his burden, Kali sent him a soothing pulse of her own energy, but his attention shied away. Kali drew her focus back and faced forward, her heart stinging along with the antics in her stomach and knee. If he wanted to go at this alone, she would let him. She had too much else to worry about right now.

No one spoke as they climbed, until Drake paused before a fissure in the rock face: little more than a hole in the ground with a tattered blanket fixed over the opening. Atanar frowned at Drake, who shrugged and made a show of hunching over so he could step in. The others followed. When Kali stepped inside, the shadows stole her vision and a sense of closeness overtook her, contrasted by how she'd been under open sky moments ago. The sour tang of body odor made her nose wrinkle. A few steps behind Drake revealed how the path sloped gently downward. Once her eyes adjusted, she made out the wide, low tunnel that led to a larger space which held a table with several people seated around. But all other thoughts fled at the sight of her mother.

Kam—for surely the wiry, dark-haired woman was Kam—sat with Commander Talon and the two men Kali supposed were the other Forsworn sentinels. But Kali barely noticed anyone else, even Stonewall, even the former sentinel commander, and stood frozen while the others milled around her as Drake muttered hasty introductions.

Jasper rose, but did not drop his gaze from Kali. "Ea's tits, Kam, she really does look like you. Well met, Kalinda," he added, bowing.

Kali blinked up at him before giving a brief smile. "You too." Her gaze slid back to her mother. They had the same dark eyes; surely Kali wore the same, stunned expression. Kam held out her hands: weathered, slender, and no doubt strong. Like the rest of her. What sort of life had she led in this wretched place?

She had this life because of me. Kali stepped forward, her throat tightening. Was this really happening? Another hesitation, and then she allowed Kam to take her hands and pull her close.

"You're alive," Kali whispered, her voice breaking. "I thought…"

"I know," Kam murmured. She hugged Kali close with arms as solid as the rock on all sides. "But the One spared me."

Kali could not fight her skepticism any longer, and buried her face in her mother's neck. Kam smelled of earth, water, and hematite, as if the ore in this place had seeped into her bones. This sparked tears anew, and Kali sobbed without caring how everyone was probably staring. *Let them.*

"Kali," Stonewall murmured at last.

He added a reluctant brush against her mind, reminding her of all they had yet to do. Kali pulled free of her mother and nodded, swiping her eyes. "Right."

Drake saluted the Forsworn sentinels. "Good to see you again." He turned to Leal. "Told you they'd stick around to help. That's five coppers you owe me. I'll add them to your tab."

Leal rolled his eyes and muttered something in his native tongue.

"So as you lot might have guessed," Drake continued. "We've had a change of plans. Right now, Eris and her friends are marching to the mines, set on burning the place to ashes."

Kam had not torn her gaze from Kali's, but now her eyes flickered to Drake. "You want to *stop* them? I thought you were set on destroying the mines, too?"

"There's no stopping Eris," Leal replied, his mouth a thin line. "Our aim now is to evacuate the mines to prevent a massacre."

"Aye," Drake said. "And once the mine's empty, we'll flood the place. Everyone wins. Kam, I'll need your help to convince the guards to abandon their posts. You've got a way with them, and–"

"My place is with my daughter," Kam interrupted, hugging Kali close. How solid she felt, though the situation was still too surreal for Kali to wrap her mind around. All she could do was lean her head against her mother, savoring that solid strength.

Drake frowned but Stonewall spoke. "Ser Kam, Kali will be helping us talk to the miners."

Kali's calm shattered. Stonewall must have sensed her feelings, for he glanced her way, a question on his face. Her own cheeks warmed, but she

359

couldn't delay any longer.

"Actually..." Kali squared her shoulders, trying to inject some of Kam's strength into her own bearing. "I have another plan. It's a good one," she added at Stonewall's leap of alarm. "But I may need some help. I want to treat with Eris again. I *know* I can stop her. I just need a little more time."

"You know she won't listen." Stonewall stared at Kali, understanding prickling through their bond like seedlings through black earth. *What are you really planning?* he asked.

There was no emotion in the words. Kali did not return the favor. *Show the world what* good *deeds mages can do.*

"How?" he asked aloud, causing everyone to start. Kam shot him a glare, but he ignored her.

Kali held up her empty hands. "You know how." *I can heal this land, with help,* she added silently. *But I'll only take just enough from Seren's Children to manage it. No one will be hurt. I can do this. I can control myself.* Aloud, she added, "Trust me."

Fear crackled through their bond and Stonewall shook his head, eyes wide and beseeching. "Kali..."

The others cast helpless glances at the lovers until Talon gave a deep, racking cough that echoed in the small space. "There's no time for discussion," the former commander managed. "Drake, if Kam won't help you, I will. We'll find Ottis, first, then try some of the guards. Then we'll go to the dam."

Stonewall did not drop his gaze from Kali's. "Go," he said to his brother. "We'll join you soon."

Kali bristled at the implication, but held back her argument – for the moment.

"Fine." Drake glanced at Talon. "Can't believe I'm about to say this, but... lead the way, Commander."

"I'm no one's Commander any longer," Talon said.

"No shit," Flint hissed. She'd shown remarkable restraint so far, but couldn't contain the hatred in her voice. "You're a monster. A filthy, lying, sack of useless trash. Death is too good for you."

"I know." Talon had the grace to look down, but her repentant stance only made Flint's hands clench.

As the group filed out, Flint stayed at Stonewall's side, casting a wary look at Kali. "What are you–"

"Help Drake," Kali broke in. "Please."

Flint looked at Stonewall who nodded. She made to dart off, but froze when Marcen spoke. "I don't know what you're really planning," he said to Kali. "But I know that look in your eyes; I've seen it in Eris. As your friend, I'm asking you—begging you—not to do anything that will make us mages look even *worse* to the world."

Kali gaped at him but recovered her mental footing at once. So he thought she acted like Eris? Very well. She gave him her coldest glare. "Noted."

His pale brows knitted but before he could respond, Flint touched his arm. Something unspoken passed between them before they, too, hurried out of the tunnel.

Kam did not watch them go, only took both of Kali's shaking hands in her own steady ones. "We must leave, dearest heart. Now. Trouble is coming."

"That's nothing new for us," Kali said.

Stonewall studied Kam with eyes that missed nothing. "You know more than you're letting on."

The way Kam would not meet Kali's gaze was its own answer. Kali worked to keep her voice calm. "Tell me what you know. Please," she tested the word in her mind before adding aloud, "Mother."

Kam rubbed her eyes with the heels of her palms. "I told Loach."

Drake had shared his experiences with the mine's administrator, so Kali knew the name. She wished she didn't. Her stomach knotted. "Told Loach...what?"

"Everything. Eris' plans, our involvement." Kam's eyes were wide. "I didn't know you were coming. When I learned you were still alive, I had to think of some way to get to you. The only thing I had of any value was information. I used it; Loach assured me that my loyalty would gain my freedom. It was risky," she added at Stonewall's noise of disbelief, "but what choice did I have?"

"What are you saying, exactly?" Stonewall ground out.

"Loach—and sentinels from the Stonehaven garrison, I believe—intend to ambush the renegade mages."

"And us, too," Kali said, clenching her fists. That settled it. She had to warn Eris. "How could you? Eris trusted you."

"Eris is out for blood," Kam replied sharply. "Let her have it. Let Argent have her. I don't care. I didn't know you were coming. But we have time. The Stonehaven sentinels will no doubt be here soon. We can still run away, Kali. We can still be free. Together."

She squeezed Kali's hand, but Kali felt only the press of hematite cuffs at her wrists; memory overtook the moment. "I have a duty," she said softly. "I have to help this place. *Someone* has to help–"

"This place is cursed," Kam broke in, tears brightening her eyes. "Let it die."

"I can't do that. Not if I can help."

Anger darkened Kam's features. "You have your father's foolish, stubborn heart."

"And glad I am for it," Kali said, swiping at her cheeks. "Leave if you want. No one will stop you. But I have a plan."

"Aye," Stonewall said, causing both women to look his way. "About that."

"Not this again," Kali said before she could stop herself.

Their bond crackled again but his voice was flat. "Your *plan*–"

"Is solid," Kali interrupted. A familiar tingle of hunger skated up her spine and into her brain. "This place is near death, but with some...coaxing, I think it could be brought back to life. And then the world will understand that mages are capable of much more than healing cuts and illness."

"The strength of the magic needed to perform such an act is..." Kam blew out a breath. "It's beyond any mage's ability."

Sweet blood. Sweet magic. Give it to us. Now.

Kali had long since been rid of the Fata possession, but remnants of their hunger merged with her own eagerness at the promise of more magic, more power. Her mouth watered at the thought. But no. She shoved the desire aside—with effort—and took pains to keep her voice steady. "It's beyond any *one* mage's ability, that's true. But–"

"You can't," Stonewall broke in. "You *can't.*"

"What did you think I was planning?" Kali asked him.

"Something like you did with the jessamin vines back at Whitewater. But Kali, you can't do *this.*"

"It will be fine," she replied. "I know my limits."

His mouth twisted with anger before he controlled himself. "You can't lie to me, Kali. I *know* your heart. This act will kill you, or someone else. It's not worth the risk. You can't."

Kam's head whipped between them as she tried to follow the argument. "Kali, what's he talking about?"

"She can *take* power from others," Stonewall said. "Mages and non-mages. But the cost is too great. It's..." He trailed off, shaking his head. "It will kill you, one day. Maybe today. It could kill others. Please, there must be another way."

"No one's going to kill anyone," Kali replied. "Besides, we've come this far. There's no turning back now."

"Like hell there isn't," he muttered, rubbing the bridge of his nose. "How will you do this, anyway? Walk up to Eris and her friends, and ask to use their magic?"

Kali toyed with her unraveling braid. "Actually...I was hoping to have your aid – again."

Stonewall stared at her, and then swore under his breath. She caught no silent speech from him, only a deep, pervasive frustration that must have taken all his concentration to keep at bay.

"You have incredible abilities at your command," Kali added. "And when we work together, we can do anything. Why are you so afraid of what you can do? Why don't you want to test your own strength?"

"The same reason I don't slice bread with a sword. It's too much, Kali. There are too many variables. We don't know what will happen."

"That's life," Kali replied. "Yet we move forward, anyway, because the alternative is the void."

Stonewall said nothing.

363

Kam cleared her throat. "If you have abilities that will keep Kali safe," she said to Stonewall. "Then you must use them. She means well. Why not aid her however you can?"

"With respect, ser," Stonewall bit out. "You don't know what you're talking about."

Kam lifted her chin. "If you love her, you'll do as she says."

"If I do as she says, you'll outlive your daughter."

Kam's mouth fell open, but Kali's frustration replied. "It was a vision, Stonewall! Akin to a dream, and no more real. I can do this. You have to trust me."

Sweet blood. Sweet magic.

Her voice softened. "I can't go forward without you by my side." *I love you,* she added through their bond. *Please, help me.*

He ran his broad, scarred hands through his hair before exhaling. To Kali's consternation, cold grief poured through their bond, followed by a reluctance that made her heart ache.

"I'm sorry," she added, softer. "Once this is over, we can start our lives together. You can show me the ocean. We can..." Her face flamed. "Get married. If you want."

He let out a laugh that wasn't much of a laugh at all, more like a sharp exhale. "Don't tempt me."

"I mean it," she said, taking his hand and ignoring her mother's scandalized expression. "We've both been through...well, a lot. After this, we should move on. Try to make the most of the time we have together. But we can do something good here." She watched the indecision upon his face and regret coursed through her, almost as strong as the call of power. "I shouldn't coerce you," she murmured. "I shouldn't dangle a future in front of you. It's unfair and cruel. I'm sorry."

Silence.

"Wishing you'd just left me in that carriage?" she added, only half in jest.

He stared at her. His emotions were a wall to her again, and his expression was just as blank. "If you do this," he said slowly. "I can't support you and I can't go with you. But I can't watch you kill yourself – or anyone else. I can't…" He took a shaking breath and freed his hands, and his honey-brown eyes bored into hers. "This is your last chance to do the right thing."

She should have been sick with despair, and a part of her was, deep down. But her heart pounded and heat stung her eyes, and her anger erupted. "The 'right thing?' As in chug hematite every chance you get? Is that the 'right thing?'"

He drew back as if she'd slapped him. "Hematite only hurts *me*."

"That's not true." Kali pressed a hand to her chest. "How long do we have, Stonewall? How many years until you're gone, too? Each dose steals more of our time together, more of your *life*, yet you keep taking it."

"I'll die otherwise."

"You were supposed to cut back," Kali replied, fighting back her tears. "But you're not, are you?"

His hand stole to his belt-pouch before he checked himself. "I've tried. Gods, I've tried."

"Well, so have I," Kali managed.

Kam had kept silent so far, but now she looked at Kali with hard eyes. "He'll never be able to give you a normal life. He's already dead."

Shock and anger burst through the bond Kali shared with Stonewall, and it was not all his. Eris' earlier words came back in full force and for one terrible second, Kali was utterly hollow; she would have shattered with a feather-touch. Every word was true.

"But you've managed without it," Kali said. "You must tell him–"

"I've not managed without," Kam broke in, gaze dropping briefly. "Loach…helps me, sometimes. Hematite will never let go."

Stonewall's shoulders sank.

"I love him," Kali whispered, more to Stonewall than to her mother.

Kam squeezed her hand. "Love only brings despair."

Panic buzzed over their bond, like a viol string struck too hard. "Kali, please," Stonewall whispered. "Don't do this. We'll find another way to prove mages are good. I swear it."

"Eris is coming. I have to meet her." Her voice broke. "Go to your brother. Be safe. We'll find each other again." *I love you,* she added through their bond.

I love you, too, was his ready reply as he closed his eyes and disappeared into the shadows.

Kam stared at the empty space where he'd been, then turned to Kali. "I know it hurts, dearest one, but you're better off without him."

Perhaps heartbreak should have felt like *more*, but Kali was numb inside. She gestured to the tunnel's exit. "I doubt that very much."

THIRTY-SIX

Careful to keep out of sight of any miners or guards, Flint crept out of the tunnel and surveyed her potential fate: a Forsworn laborer in the wretched mine. It would be Mi's fate, too, if the Circle ever found him out. A vivid blue sky made the landscape seem even more barren by contrast, and the gaping fissure in the earth, ringed with graded steps, made Flint's skin crawl. The sight was organic but somehow *wrong*.

"I can't believe Kali's doing this." Marcen muttered as the wind kicked up his hair. "She's barking mad. She's as bad as Eris."

Flint squinted across the chasm until she spotted a group that was surely Drake and the others, making slow but steady progress toward a group of workers at the base. "I don't like this, either, but our enemies are coming. Stonewall will talk some sense into her, so as soon as they come out, we should–"

"That's the problem. Eris and Adrie *aren't* my enemies. They're my friends. This whole situation is shit." He rubbed his arms as if he were cold. "They both hardly spoke to me last night. And I wonder if they're wrong to hate me. I left, after all."

She thought of Milo and her voice softened. "You came with us to help all kinds of folks, not just mages. Eris is selfish; you're not."

Now he met her gaze, his eyes harder than she'd ever seen. "Maybe so, but you've never worn a collar or had your hands shackled because of the blood in your veins. You won't ever understand."

Her mouth opened, a sharp retort on her tongue, ready to strike back.

But he still wrapped his arms around himself, like he was shielding his insides from an attack. From her.

Tell him to go fuck himself. Aye, then she could snarl at him to leave, and end any dilemma. No doubt she'd be better off if he left *now*, rather than one day in the future when she cared a whole lot more.

But those thoughts felt more barren than the province around them.

Flint stared at Marcen and saw a juncture in the landscape of their... whatever they were. "You're right," she said softly. "I don't understand what it's like to be a mage. Hell, I barely understand what it means to be a sentinel, let alone if I still am one." She judged his stance and determined it was safe to step closer. "All I know right now is that I want to make the world a better place. I think you do, too. No matter what, you should have the freedom to live the life that makes you happy."

Marcen's pale blue eyes rounded as he stared at her, his mouth falling open like a fish. Before she could say anything else—and probably ruin whatever she'd tried to do—he reached for her gloved hands, pulled her close, and captured her lips with his own. More heat flooded her, albeit a far more pleasant kind than anger or embarrassment, and Flint wrapped her arms around him, deepening the kiss.

When they parted, he was still smiling. "Always keeping me on my toes."

"You don't seem to mind."

"I do wish things were different," he said. "But I'm glad I'm here. Well, not *here*," he amended, his ears going red. "But..."

The mission had probably already gone to shit, but she laughed anyway. "I know."

Just then, Stonewall appeared beside them, having apparently just slipped out of the tunnel to the makeshift barracks. He was alone.

"Where's..." Marcen trailed off at the pained look on Stonewall's face. "Shit. *Shit.*"

"I'll get us to Drake and the others," Stonewall ground out through a clenched jaw. "I just need a second to concentrate." He grabbed Flint and Marcen's hands and shut his eyes, but he couldn't disguise how his own hand trembled. And no amount of stoicism would hide the tears slipping down his cheeks.

What in Atal's name had happened to turn the world upside-down? More importantly, what should she say? What would Milo do?

She squeezed Stonewall's hand and when he looked her way, she bumped his shoulder with hers. "We're with you, *relah*," she murmured. "It'll be all right."

A smile ghosted across his mouth before he took another deep breath, and the world around them blurred once more.

*

"It's clear," Kam said as she peered around the curtain covering the barrack's tunnel. She glanced back at Kali and held out her hand. Kali stared at her mother's tanned, weathered skin. Was she dreaming? She could still feel her bond with Stonewall, but it was muted, while her mother—whom she'd thought long dead—stood within arm's reach.

"Kali?"

Kali tried to smile as she reached back. "Sorry. Just woolgathering. Do I get that from you?"

Kam squeezed her palm. "I'm afraid so."

She led Kali outside the tunnel and paused to examine the area again. The sunlight blinded and Kali squinted as her eyes adjusted. "I don't exactly know where Eris is," she admitted. "Or how long she'll take to arrive."

"Drake described the area where her friends were camped. It's not that far, so I imagine she'll be here soon." Kam set off on the path that wound up to the mine's rim. "If nothing else, we can meet her on the road."

Kali followed as best she could, glancing around warily as her mother strode along. "Are the guards here so terrible at their jobs that they'll let us just…leave?"

Her mother paused to wait for her. "No. But with Drake and the others causing a distraction," she waved in the direction of the base, "I imagine we'll slip by." Kali reached her but Kam did not move, and her eyes darted to Kali's left knee. "Does it hurt?"

"Only when I use it."

Kam's lips trembled and she pulled Kali close again, clutching her tightly. "My sweet girl. I'm so sorry."

They had to hurry. They had a mission, and there was no telling if Kam's theories on the guards were right. But still, Kali could not resist sinking into her mother's embrace, desperate for some small comfort. Kam held her for what could have been seconds or hours, then pulled away enough to cup Kali's cheeks. "I've missed you, dearest one. I've thought of you every day."

"There's so much I want to know."

"Me as well," Kam replied. "But we mustn't dally too long."

Reluctantly, both women began to walk again. The path curved around a large boulder that obscured the way, and Kam paused, then lifted her hand in a gesture that clearly meant, *stay here*. She then picked her way forward around the boulder. "Goldie! Thank the One I've found you!"

The woman who emerged towered over Kali and Kam. Like Kam, her skin told the story of a life spent in the elements, but her solid, muscular form made Kali think she was no mere worker. Indeed, Goldie hefted her spear, but she relaxed when she caught sight of Kam. "You all right?" she asked the shorter woman. "Heard there was some kerfuffle near the mess hall, so I'm on my way." Her gaze slid to Kali. "Who's...? Ea's balls, she looks..."

Kam hugged Kali's shoulders again. "This is my daughter."

Goldie's eyes rounded. "This is little Kali?"

"Aye. She learned where I was, and came all the way here to find me."

Kali's pulse leapt and sweat prickled her back, but she kept silent. Kam was clearly on good terms with this guard. Perhaps that would be enough to let them pass.

"How can this be?" Goldie asked, no small amount of wariness in the words.

Kam pressed a hand to her heart. "The One willed it. I'm truly blessed."

Kali held her breath as the two women studied each other. At last, Goldie jerked her chin to the path behind her, which continued to the top of the mine. "Best get on your way, then. Be safe."

"We will."

Kam turned to go, but Kali spoke. "Drake's at the base, trying to warn the others. You must listen to him."

Goldie frowned. "Warn them of what?"

Kam spoke quickly. "He said he noticed a problem with the dam, and fears it may break soon. Loach sent him away before he could say anything, but he returned to warn us. You should get everyone out as soon as possible. I wish I could stay to help, but my place is with my daughter. I know you'd do the same if Rose or Violet were here."

"I would at that," Goldie replied, bowing slightly before she tossed Kam the spear. "The One keep you, Kam. Good luck."

The former sentinel caught the weapon neatly and bowed in reply.

After they parted ways, Kali let out a long, shaking breath. "Friend of yours?"

Kam glanced back at Goldie's retreating form, then faced ahead. "The One has a plan for us all. Come on." She took Kali's hand and began to walk. "We must keep going."

As they went, Kam glanced Kali's way again. "Eris told me you grew up in Starwatch Bastion. That your father brought you."

"Aye, Jonas was captain there."

"I'm surprised he told you of your connection," Kam said, the words tinged with coolness.

"He didn't," Kali replied. "I discovered it quite by accident, when I caught a glimpse of his particles. He denied anything at first, but I wore him down eventually."

If Kam knew of particles, she said nothing. "I didn't want you to live in a bastion. That's why I tried to run away with you. To keep you safe. But..." She exhaled. "Well, it doesn't matter now. You're alive."

"What happened to my knee?" Kali asked. "I thought I was unlucky from birth, but a healer friend told me I was injured very young. Do you know anything about that?"

At first the only sounds were their boots on the rocky ground. "Aye,"

371

Kam said at last. "But…it was so long ago. Surely it would be healed by now…"

She trailed off. They had so much to discuss and so little time, but Kali had to know. "What happened?"

"Before you were born, Jonas and I were part of Shadow Squad – High Commander Cimera's personal squad."

"They're called Silver Squad now, I believe," Kali said. "Under Argent."

Kam's nose wrinkled. "Different tastes, I suppose. Cimera always had a flair for the dramatic. In any case, she tasked us with carrying out missions she couldn't entrust to anyone else – including hunting renegade mages and any sentinel defectors. We were a close-knit bunch, as you can probably imagine. Jonas and I had joined around the same time and the others thought of us as 'burnies,' though we weren't much younger than they. He and I became…closer than the rest. When I realized I was pregnant…" She swiped a tear from her cheeks. "I knew it was the One's will at work. Pregnancy among sentinels is so rare."

Kali nodded. "Most sentinel women don't even have cycles."

"Aye, so I was surprised, to say the least. But you were a gift from the gods. I knew this in my heart." She jabbed the spear's end into the ground as they walked. "Your father did not agree. He wanted to… He wanted me to get rid of you."

It was as if Kali had plunged into the White River falls again. She stood, unable to take a proper breath, until her mother urged her forward.

"I refused," Kam continued. "We argued – for weeks. Like a fool, I held onto hope that he would come around. I had fantasies that we would run away and raise you together, as a family. I even started tapering off of hematite in preparation, and out of concern for how it would affect you. But when Jonas threatened to report me to our commander, I finally understood that he wasn't just frightened, as I was. He was truly set in his duty. It was the only thing that mattered to him. I fled, and took refuge with a group of Sufani I had befriended during my time as a sentinel. I gave birth, and life was pleasant for a time."

When she said nothing for a few moments, Kali found her voice. "What happened, then?"

"You had magic. You began to show signs of it quite early, and the Sufani were…afraid of what would happen should the Circle find us among them. I can't blame them for their fear. So I left, again. During my time in Shadow Squad, I had found signs of some small groups of renegade mages, but never the mages themselves. I found them, this time. I convinced them to allow us to stay with them for a while, although they weren't pleased at the arrangement."

"Can't imagine why," Kali said weakly.

Kam's smile was broken. "One of them told me, 'we would not separate a mother from her child.' I still feel ashamed, for I did such a thing during my time as a sentinel. But I am grateful for their compassion, too. Without it, you might not be alive." Another frown touched her face as she continued. "But not all of the wild mages were so…accepting. I don't know exactly what happened, but I think one of them sent word to the garrison in Lasath."

They were approaching the rim; the rest of the mine splayed below. If Kali listened, she could make out an echo of voices near the base. Was Stonewall there?

He'd left her.

Again.

Mind on the mission, Kali told herself. She did not want to hear how this story would play out—she could guess—but she needed the knowledge she had so long been denied. Even so, bitterness flooded her heart.

"I woke up one morning to the wild mages gone, and Jonas and Shadow Squad bearing down upon us," Kam said after a few seconds. "I think I must have been drugged. You were wide awake, though, screaming your head off. Shadow Squad didn't quite know what to do with you, but Jonas…" She seemed to force the words out. "Jonas recognized you as a mage and demanded that I release you to his custody. Mages are so dangerous, as you know."

Tears stung Kali's eyes. "He never acted as if he felt that way."

"A renegade mage killed his parents when he was a lad," Kam replied, not unkindly. "Perhaps your arrival made him rethink his position. In any case, he wanted to bring you to a bastion. I refused, and gathered you up to make a run for it. Foolish, I know, but there is nothing fiercer than a mother when her child's life is at stake. I ran. Jonas pursued." She took a shaking breath and met Kali's eyes. "We fought. He struggled to pull you out of my arms, and in doing so...his dagger slipped and struck your little knee.

"You stopped crying. That was the worst part: the sudden silence. You'd wailed the entire time, but at the first touch of pain, you fell silent. For one terrible second, I thought you were dead. I think Jonas did, too. We worked together to wrap up your leg, and by then the battle-haze had faded. I begged him again to run away with us, to leave the sentinels behind, to put our family first. And as he held you, as he stared into your face for the first time, I truly thought he would." Kam's eyes closed and her voice softened. "I could see our future, as if the One had painted it in my mind. Then Shadow Squad found us."

Her eyes opened again and Kali realized she was not the only one weeping. "They wanted to kill the mage child, but Jonas claimed you were innocent of wrongdoing and would be taken to a bastion. They wanted to kill me for treason, but Jonas insisted I be brought to the Pillars for trial. The Pillars sent me here."

They crested the lip of the mine, revealing the road and the rocky landscape. A single crow marred the otherwise blue sky; surely it was Eris, scouting. No doubt Seren's Children would find them soon. Kali didn't know how to feel about that.

Tears streamed down her cheeks, blurring her vision and stealing her breath, but she forced herself to think clearly. There was so much she needed to know! "What happened to Da after all that? Did no one suspect he was my father, even after you were lovers? How did he get sent to Starwatch with me?"

"I don't know," Kam admitted. "Before my trial, we had a moment alone. He swore to me that no harm would come to you while he lived. The other sentinels assumed I'd bedded a mage, and Jonas did not say otherwise, for doing so would have drawn suspicion on you and him, and he could not protect you if he was sent to the mines, too. I don't know how he came with you to Starwatch." Another faint smile touched her mouth. "He hated the cold. I imagine he felt that station was penance of some kind."

"It's fairly isolated as well," Kali added, still trying to wrap her mind around what she'd just learned. "He kept his word. He never spoke of you. He spun some tale about my mother being a worker in the bastion who'd died in childbirth."

The mine was just behind them now. Guilt and bitterness warred within Kali's heart, and every second of forced calm was a battle of clenched jaw and fisting hands. Seren's light, she needed a *biri*, but she'd smoked her last one this morning. *Calm down*, she schooled herself. Surely, they would come across Eris soon, and Kali would never manage the complex magic she was planning if she was so distraught.

Kam clasped her hand. "Thank the One, we've found each other now. Only the Laughing God will part us again."

Don't say that, Kali wanted to reply, but the words stuck in her throat. Each step along the dusty road sent searing pain through her knee; each step carried her farther from Stonewall. Leaning into her mother's side, Kali tried to reach him, but he had closed his heart.

He's wrong about me, she told herself. *He loves me, but he's wrong.*

As if reading her mind, Kam squeezed her hand again. "Don't fret over that sentinel of yours, dear heart. Focus on your task. The One will guide us both." She tensed and pointed ahead, where a group of people strode toward them. "Is that Eris?"

Kali's stomach flipped when she recognized her friend's form. "Aye," she managed. "It's Eris and the rest of Seren's Children."

She concentrated, testing her strength and resolve for the magic to come. Yes, she could do this. Yes, she was in control.

*

Drake gritted his teeth and forced himself not to shout at the miners. "I don't know what the mages are planning, exactly, but it's going to be bad.

You all should clear out."

The miners exchanged wary looks. Drake couldn't blame them. The whole story sounded suspicious, and despite how he, Nat, and Leal were all somewhat familiar to these folks—though not as familiar as Jasper, Ruddy, and Talon—they were still, to the miners' way of thinking, outsiders.

"There are no mages here," one of the miners replied. "And even if there were, we're in a *hematite* mine. Or did you forget?"

Drake fought back a glower. Damn Eris for making him incriminate his own people just to save these–

He cut off the unkind thought.

Atanar lifted a brow. "Do you understand so much about mages to ignore a warning such as this?"

A few workers turned away, scoffing, but others remained. A burly fellow called, "What's your angle, dregs? Why d'you want us out of here so sodding badly?"

Some of the other miners echoed his words. Drake tried to look into each miner's eyes as he replied. "Because you'll die if you stay."

"You like living, don't you?" Leal added.

A few miners grumbled and shot the Sufani dark looks; a few more rolled their eyes and turned away. Drake's shoulders sank. But what else did he expect? This plan was folly; these people were about to get caught in the mages' war. He should give up this foolish idea and take Nat and Leal south, where they could ride out the approaching storm in peace.

Then Talon called, "Is this place worth your lives?"

Some of the miners glared at her. The man who'd spoken before said, "Not this place, no, but without my wages, my children's bellies will be empty."

"Ottis, you know you can find work anywhere," Talon said. "But this place is a stain upon the world, and there are those who would see it washed away. None of you deserve to die for hematite."

"Aye," added Jasper. "And we'd know, better than anyone."

The remaining miners exchanged glances: some wary, some considering. At last, Ottis threw up his hands. "Well, I'll not be caught in whatever foolishness is coming. The hemie's right; we can find work in the silver mines, or elsewhere. If there's trouble on the way, I'll not stay to see it."

"But Loach will–" began one of the other miners.

"Loach can suck my left pinkie toe," came a new voice. Drake glanced over to see Goldie approaching the group. "Listen to Ottis, and Tal. Let's clear out. If nothing else, we can just blame the Forsworn hemies. Or the mages."

"Everyone else does," Drake could not help but mutter. Thank Tor, no one heard him, although a strange feeling crept up his spine, like he was being watched. He glanced back at the side of the mine's rocky base, but saw only shadows.

Talon shot Goldie a grateful look, but Goldie ignored the former sentinel and went to her fellow workers. "We all ought to clear out. Loach can't dismiss everyone, can he?"

"Are you sure, Goldie?" another miner asked, biting her lip. "I need this job."

"You need your life more," Goldie replied.

There was some discussion among the miners, but many appeared to have made up their minds. Goldie and Ottis both spoke to Talon. "We'll try to clear out as many folks as we can," Ottis said. "But it's likely some won't be willing to budge. I'll send a runner to Carver's Creek as well, to get word to the sentinel garrison."

Talon exchanged looks with Drake. "Thank you," she said, bowing. "Whatever you can do will be most welcome."

Drake echoed her words to the miners, but inside he was reeling. Bringing sentinels here would no doubt end badly, but he couldn't argue the plan without giving himself away. Besides, with any luck, the mines would be flooded well before the messenger even reached the garrison.

Drake snorted. Because they'd had *so* much luck before now. Llyr, the god of luck, was either drunk or asleep. Either notion was preferable to the thought that the god of luck had it out for him.

As the miners began to dissipate, that strange feeling came upon Drake again, but stronger this time, like a ghostly tap on his shoulder. He whirled to face the shadows, bracing for a blow, but there was only Stonewall, Marcen, and Flint, emerging from the darkness. Drake's grin threatened to crack his face as he went to meet his little brother. How talented Stonewall had become! But the bitter sorrow in Stonewall's bearing pushed back Drake's brief joy, and then he saw heartbreak in Elan's eyes.

And there was no sign of Kali.

A hundred scenarios ran through Drake's mind, but he kept his tone light. "Nice work," he said to Stonewall once they met. "I didn't even see you all arrive." He hesitated. "Is Kali...?"

"She's with her mother," Stonewall replied quickly. "You seem to have things under control here."

"That's the hope." Drake led them back to Leal, Atanar, the Forsworn sentinels, Ottis, and Goldie. "We have reinforcements," he said to the miners, gesturing to Stonewall, Flint, and Marcen.

"Good," Goldie said, nodding. "Leal and I think it's best if we split into two groups. The others won't listen to you lot on your own, but me and Ottis have sway with them."

"When d'you think the mages will get here?" Ottis asked.

"I wouldn't bet on more than half an hour," Leal replied.

Goldie spat upon the ground. "Figures that mages would be trouble, even here."

"Not all mages are trouble," Marcen said.

"If that was true, lad, we wouldn't need hematite," Goldie replied. She skimmed her gaze over Marcen, Flint, and lastly Stonewall, then shrugged. "Well, there's no use dawdling. We'd best get to work."

They divided into two groups, with Stonewall, Drake, Atanar, Flint, and Marcen following Ottis, and the others going around the mine's base with Goldie. Soon enough, Drake found himself climbing back up the mine's sides, heading for the refinery and nearby workshops. The blue dome of the sky made him dizzy, so he kept his gaze on the path – and on his little brother, trudging at his side. Flint walked on Stonewall's other side, eyes scanning all around, but always coming to rest on her former sergeant.

Other than Flint, no one was ostensibly listening to them, so Drake took a chance. "Want to talk about it?"

Stonewall faced ahead. "There's nothing to say."

"Your eyes say otherwise."

A pause, then, "I can't do it, *relah*. I can't watch her destroy herself – or anyone else." Stonewall glanced up, as if trying to peer over the mine's lip.

Drake looked too, but could only make out a couple specks on the path that wound into the rocky landscape. But if he guessed right, that was the direction Eris and her allies would come from.

"It's too much," Stonewall added in a whisper.

What could Drake say to this? He resorted to basic comforts, and covered his little brother's shoulder. When Stonewall glanced his way, Drake nodded once, like how he used to when they were both sentinels, about to head into a dangerous mission. *I'm with you.* It was a small gesture, but some of the heartbreak fled his little brother's face. Flint strode at his other side, clearly ready for whatever lay ahead.

"You're not alone, Elan," Drake murmured.

Stonewall ducked his head.

"There," Ottis said, pointing to a long, low building. "There's the mess hall. A lot of folks'll be at midday meal."

"This isn't an ambush, is it?" Drake asked, not quite joking.

Ottis' brow creased. "No one here cares enough about you to attack you."

Drake gave a hollow laugh. "Well...that's something."

As Ottis made to lead them into the building, Atanar paused just outside, brow furrowed as he searched around.

"What's wrong?" Drake asked.

The Canderi shivered despite the warm air, and did not answer.

THIRTY-SEVEN

Eris folded her wings and alighted upon Adrie's outstretched arm. The rocky ground did not offer many convenient places to land and shift, and since Eris was trying to exercise restraint with her abilities, she needed to take care with every aspect of her magic. Adrie set her down, and moments later, Eris was a woman again. A brief assessment of her unborn son assured her that he was well, though the dull, aching cramps in her abdomen made her uneasy. She had not been in crow-shape that long, but clearly, she had to be even *more* careful.

She glanced between her allies, who had gathered around her in the shadow of one of the massive stones near the gaping maw of the hematite mine. "The miners appear to be either in their common building, or near the base, and I saw no additional fortifications, guards, or any indication that anyone is aware of our presence." She paused. "Kali and Kam are on their way to us."

The others exchanged glances, and Jensine's eyes narrowed. "A trap of some kind?"

"Doubtful," Eris replied. "That's not Kali's way. Besides, if there's to be a trap for anyone at this accursed place, it's a trap we'll spring. I imagine Kali intends to try and 'reason' with me again, but no matter what she thinks to do or say to stop us, we're going to make this place hurt."

Jensine lifted her hands and a thin veil of fog began to swirl around her legs, snaking up to her torso and shoulders, and faintly obscuring her features. "About time, I say."

"There's no excuse to be reckless," Brenna said, glancing in the direction of Carver's Creek. "Eris, did you see any soldiers or sentinels?"

"No," Eris replied. "But that township is within easy step of the mines, and the sentinel garrison isn't too far off, either. We must prepare for the worst."

"Good thing we've got a lot of practice," Caith said grimly. "Shall we meet your friend?"

Eris and the Damaris family took to the main road, which ran parallel to the rim of the mine and then down into the base. Each step brought Kali clearer into view, and Eris worked to shutter her heart against the naked hope she saw in her friend's face.

Eris met her friend perhaps five meters from the mine's edge. "What in the blazing void are you doing here?"

Kali seemed to steel herself and her voice rang out clearly. "We came to warn you. This is a trap. I don't know the numbers, but word has been sent to the Stonehaven garrison. Sentinels will likely be here soon."

Silence hung in the air before Jensine gave a booming laugh. Caith and the others followed suit, and Eris smiled. "Let them come. We are not afraid of hemies or dregs." She narrowed her eyes at her former friend. "But how do you know this?"

Kali grimaced, but Kam answered. "I told Loach."

Eris glanced at Kali. "Disloyalty bides in your bloodline, I see."

When Kali said nothing, Eris made a noise of disgust and turned to Jensine. "We should start up here; an avalanche should do nicely."

Jensine barked an order and two other mages knelt in preparation of churning up the ground.

Kali's voice was high with desperation. "This is your last chance. Please, don't turn to violence."

"Listen to her," said Kam. "Leave this place. Find another battle to fight."

Last chance? What in the stars was Kali talking about? Eris did not care enough to tease out her meaning. "We've both made our choices."

Kali's voice was resigned. "Aye, so we have."

Despite her better sense, Eris glanced back over her shoulder. So she saw what happened, although at first she did not understand.

Kali darted for the two kneeling mages, then grabbed their exposed wrists and yanked them toward her. The mages shouted, trying to struggle out of Kali's grip, but she held them fast. The rest of Seren's Children erupted with fury and a few lunged toward Kali, but Kam shoved them back. A tongue of flame burst from Caith's fingers, but it did no more than dance across Kam's chest.

"Your magic won't touch me," Kam warned, as Caith stumbled back. "Stay away from my daughter, or I'll toss you over the mine's edge and into your next life."

Meanwhile, Kali's eyes closed and concentration strained her face. The two members of Seren's Children shuddered in her grip, but soon grew limp, sagging to the dirt until they fell, their chests rising in a slow but steady rhythm. Eyes still closed, Kali released them and pressed her palms against the dirt path that led to the mines. For the space of a heartbeat, everyone was too stunned to do more than stare, until...

"Sweet fucking stars," someone gasped.

Spindles of grass inched through the rusted ground beneath Kali's palms...and all around her. Something tickled Eris' boot and she started at the sight of more grass creeping up at her feet, where her allies stood, where the two mages whose power Kali had stolen lay sleeping. Eris gasped as the grasses grew higher, thicker, nearly obscuring Kali and her mother from view.

"Eris!"

She whirled to where Brenna was pointing and sucked in a breath. Green blanketed the world around them, covering the rocks in bright lichen and the ground in shades of emerald fading to honey-gold-green. Spots of pink and white and yellow flowers speckled the grass, soaking the air with their sweet scent that still couldn't drown out the stink of hematite.

But more flowers bloomed every moment – because of Kali.

"Healing the land," Eris whispered.

A rustle in the grass made her look back at Kali, to see Kam kneeling beside her, hand on her shoulder. "That's enough," she heard the former sentinel say.

Kali looked up and met Eris' gaze. The sun beat down, and cast her eyes in shadow, but she leaned forward, as if reaching for another mage. This snapped Eris out of her trance and she turned to her allies. "Stop her!"

*

Drake did not follow Ottis into the mess hall, but pulled Nat to the side. "What's wrong?"

Atanar's gaze flickered to Stonewall, Flint, and Marcen, who stood nearby. Talon, too, hung outside the low building. When Nat looked at Drake again, his eyes were wide. "I can hear them," he whispered. "The...glimmers. They're close." He trembled again, harder, eyes still huge and round. "Don't let them have me. Please."

"Fata?" Drake asked. "Here?" He glanced around out of habit. "No one's going to take you again," Drake said, grasping the Canderi's shoulder as his mind whirled. "You're safe with me." He looked back at his brother. "Can you–"

Stonewall gasped and jerked his chin up. "Kali!"

He turned as if to leave, but Drake snatched his arm. "Calm down," he said, praying the miners would not hear. "*Relah*, what's–"

But Stonewall slid out of his grip. "She's in danger. Ea's tits! I'm a fool; I shouldn't have left her side." He stepped away from the group and the air around him shimmered.

"Don't go alone," Flint said before Drake could.

Take me with you. The words came to Drake's throat and died, and he glanced at Nat. He'd *just* promised the other man safety; now he wanted to run off?

Thank Tor and all the gods, Stonewall paused and glanced back, shifting his feet. "I can't take everyone."

A soft touch at Drake's arm heralded Nat's voice. "Your place now is with your brother."

Drake met those bright blue eyes and saw only certainty. He clasped Nat's forearm briefly before darting away to Stonewall's side, then followed his brother toward the road that led around the mine's rim.

Once they were out of earshot, Stonewall paused. Drake braced himself for the upcoming surge of nausea—he hadn't forgotten the last time he'd traveled like this—but his brother only dug into one of his belt pouches. Only when Stonewall brought the vial to his throat did Drake realize what he was doing.

"What's gotten into you?" he hissed, reaching for Stonewall, but the younger man swerved out of the way and downed the entire dose. "I thought you were giving it up!"

Stonewall cast the vial into the mine and grabbed Drake's arm. Facing the full sun, his eyes blazed with gold fire. "I can't," he said, ducking his head. "Not yet. I need..."

"You need to never touch that shit again," Drake said when his brother trailed off. "It's killing you."

"It helps," Stonewall shot back.

"Aye, until it doesn't."

Stonewall swore. "I don't need this now." He released Drake's arm, closed his eyes, and disappeared, leaving only a ghostly shimmer in the air where he'd been.

*

Eris held her breath as Caith darted for Kali. Kam jabbed her spear at him again, but Caith ducked out of her way and surged for Kali, palms blazing with mage-fire. He snatched her shoulders and lifted her up from the ground, flames licking them both as it caught on the newly-made grass. Fire and smoke distorted Eris' vision as Kam barreled through the flames and tried to wrench Caith away. But Kali held his face in her hands, their foreheads pressed together. Her eyes sparkled and her breath came hard and fast, and Caith didn't move as the fire around him shrank to embers, then charred ground.

"Caith!" Jensine rushed forward, but the sinking feeling in Eris' gut told her it would be too late.

Kam cried Kali's name, but she did not react. Caith's eyes rolled back

384

in his head before Kali released him. He crumpled to the ground, sending flecks of ash spiraling into the air. Kali knelt, still breathing hard, and pressed her hands against the earth again. More grasses bloomed, with delicate trees this time, and brilliant green vines snaked up from the rust-red dirt to creep across nearby boulders. The air grew heavy with the scent of growing things.

All this happened in the space of a breath, then Jensine's shriek of rage rallied the rest of Seren's Children and they descended upon Kali. Horror flooded Eris as she realized their folly, but they ignored her cries of warning and surged toward the dark-haired mage.

Seren's Children fell upon Kali. She spread her palms—in welcome, or challenge, Eris could not tell—and let them grab her. They were too many; surely she would be torn to pieces! But one-by-one, the wild mages collapsed, dead. A few stumbled out of Kali's grip, reeling as if drunk or injured. But Jensine did not retreat. She struggled the longest, but even the ornery woman was helpless against Kali's power. Only when someone grabbed Eris' shoulder did she realize she'd backed well out of Kali's reach. She whirled to see Stonewall, eyes wide and wet.

"What's she doing?" Eris gasped, too stunned to wonder where the hemie had come from.

He shook his head. "She won't listen to me. I can't..." The ground shuddered as a copse of slender trees burst through the barren earth, further blocking Kali from view. Even so, Stonewall urged Eris farther away, to where Adrie and Brenna stood frozen with shock.

"You must leave," Stonewall cried.

Something hot ran down Eris' cheeks as more green sprang to life around them; life borne at the cost of so many deaths. Kali's doing. "What's happened to her?" Eris whispered.

"She's...lost." His head jerked up and his eyes widened, and he shoved Eris backward. She stumbled, nearly falling, but Adrie's strong grip caught her before she hit the grass.

Brenna and a few other mages who had not attacked huddled nearby. "We must get out of here, Eris," Adrie said, pulling her upright. "Now!"

Eris looked back at Stonewall, who had drawn his sword and gone to Kali's side, though Kali did not react to his presence. So her friend was truly gone.

"Aye, let's go," Eris managed. She and the others turned to run, but the grass surrounding them rippled, revealing flashes of burning starlight – thralls' eyes. An otherworldly chorus of shrieks pierced the air.

*

Thrall screams echoed through the mine and within Talon's chest. Her skin prickled, her blood sang a warning, and her hands itched for their absent weapons. Two solid presences at her back sent her pulse leaping, but it was only Jasper and Ruddy, thank the One. They stood with her, poised between the miners and the path that led into the mine's base; they were ready to fulfill their oaths and protect these folks, despite everything. Heartened, Talon pushed aside the wave of instinctive fear and scanned the rocky base, but saw no sign of thralls.

Goldie and the other miners, who had been debating the truth of Drake's claims, shouted and swore, hefting their pickaxes and other tools, and clustering together.

"You said mages were coming, not sodding *thralls*," one of the miners cried.

"Well, I was wrong," Goldie replied. "Why'd I have to give Kam my spear?"

Ruddy's head swiveled. "I hear them, but does anyone see them?"

Jasper pointed up. "Sounds like they're near the rim, but I don't see anyone heading down." He looked at Talon. "You've fought thralls before. Why would they come to this shithole?"

"I can hardly say." Talon glanced at Goldie and the other miners. "You should find cover. The dam–"

"I'm not going in that cursed hole," Goldie spat, with a few others chorusing in agreement. Someone handed her a spare pickaxe which she hefted. "They might be after the mages. If that's the case, we can get away."

"We can't stay down here," another miner said. "We're trapped!"

Goldie gestured to the path. "I'll take my chances getting out. I'm *not* dying in this place. Come on!"

As the miners barreled up the path, Ruddy made to follow, but Jasper held his ground. "What about the plan? Are we still going to flood the place?"

They all looked toward the black maw of the tunnel that led to the underground dam. Talon's stomach turned at the sight, but she ignored her instinctive fear of the darkness. "Aye. I'll go. You both take the chance to get away."

Jasper and Ruddy exchanged nervous glances. "Releasing all that water's going to be dangerous," Ruddy said, eyes wide. "If you can't get out in time..."

Talon considered her own death with the same detachment she'd cultivated as a sentinel commander. But this time, she was not acting. "I'll be fine. But there's no reason for you two to stay when freedom awaits."

"Now might be our only chance to leave," Jasper added, glancing between Talon and the path out.

Ruddy looked at Talon, silently pleading for instruction. But she could not give it to him. She'd failed as a leader once. She could not do so again. More innocents could not die because of her foolish actions. "Do as your heart tells you," she said to the lad. "Your spirit won't steer you wrong."

She raced for the tunnel. Even the brief sprint set her throat to burning, and by the time she'd reached the entrance, she doubled over with the force of her racking coughs. Out of habit, she covered her mouth, and when she pulled her hand back, spots of blood dotted her palm. Talon stared at the crimson speckles before wiping her hand on her trousers and hurrying on.

The lanterns had burned out. Several steps into the tunnel, utter blackness swallowed her whole. After cursing her lack of foresight in not bringing a lantern, Talon had to find her way by touch, shuffling her boots in the dust lest she stumble. She continued for what felt like an eternity before she caught the scent of water. When her hands felt the wall no more, the scope of her small world changed; the clean scent strengthened and the air held a chill that the tunnel had lacked. She was in the cavern.

Talon stepped forward, slowly, feeling for the water's edge, until her boot touched something colder than the air; the water's chill permeated even the tough leather. Still taking the utmost care, she followed the shore, bending every so often to brush her fingertips into the icy water, reassuring herself she was heading in the correct direction. Gods above, it was so *still* here. Her careful steps grated against the silence, and when another of her coughing fits struck, the rasping sounds echoed.

At last her extended hand brushed solid stone: the cavern wall. More groping led Talon to the dam itself, and the sturdy wooden lever that would release the seal. She wrapped both hands around the smooth wood and took a deep breath. Once the cavern started to flood, she would probably not have time to find her way out through the darkness.

But the knowledge of the Laughing God peering over her shoulder did not set her heart racing with dread. Perhaps she had not brought a light source because she was meant to die here. The One had steered her to this place; the One had preserved her life until now. What for, if not for this?

Honor. Service. Sacrifice. She'd destroyed the first to perform the second. Now she could only fulfill the third and final part of the sentinel oath. Perhaps she and her parents would be reunited in another life.

Talon's hands tightened around the lever. She braced her body, glad of her height and what strength she had not lost, and pulled. The stubborn thing didn't move. Gritting her teeth, Talon dug her heels into the stone floor and put all her weight into the effort until something metallic groaned and creaked beneath the wall, and the lever lurched toward her. A bubbling, rippling sound came from nearby and something cold crept up to her ankles. She gasped at the icy sensation, which sent her into another coughing fit. She leaned against the wall, sucking in air while her eyes burned with tears, and so did not see the glimmer of lantern light until it was almost upon her. When she marked the light—and the two figures with it—her heart both sank and swelled. "Ruddy, Jasper, what are you doing here?"

The men rushed to her side, sloshing through the rapidly rising water, panting with their efforts. "What's it look like?" Jasper muttered, grabbing her arm. "Come on. We don't have much–"

Talon tried to pull free, but Jas was stronger than he looked. Ruddy grabbed her other arm and they began to haul her away, plunging through water now waist-high. It would fill the cavern within moments. They had no time!

"Leave me," Talon said, still trying to free herself.

"Not on your life," Ruddy said, gripping harder. "With respect," he added quickly.

"Drowning's a shit death, anyway," Jasper added. He'd taken Talon's hand by now, lacing their fingers together. "Besides, it's time for payback."

They reached the tunnel's entrance within minutes, but the water slapped at their heels. Jasper shoved Ruddy forward first, then Talon, who scrambled after the young man, fighting back the urge to cough at the effort. "Payback?" she managed as all three clambered up the tunnel, the sound of the black water rushing in their ears. Water splashed up around them, sucking at their feet and making the walls slick. "For what?"

"You know what," Jasper said. He was only a step behind her, the lantern swinging in his hand and casting wild, dancing shadows on the tunnel walls. "Feel free to rough me up later, once this sodding battle's over."

Talon wanted to curse him or cry, or laugh, but all her energy went toward getting herself and her companions out of this tunnel. Yes, the One had brought her here for a reason. Perhaps she just had not yet discovered why.

"Thank you," she managed.

Jasper chuckled behind her. "That's more like it, Tal."

*

Stonewall did not remember drawing his sword, but savored its weight. Thank the One he did not stumble over the bodies of Kali's fellow mages, although the sight sickened him.

Kali did not look up at his presence; he reached for her through their bond but found her attention solely on the earth beneath her feet and the power flooding her body. Kam spared him a glance but no more. Water rumbled in the distance, adding a sinister undercurrent to the thralls' cries. Stonewall gripped his sword and maneuvered around Kali, braced for the thralls' attacks. Shots of starlight gleamed in the corner of his eye. He whirled and struck, and a man in sentinel armor fell back shrieking through the grass, eyes burning. Another leaped forward. Stonewall aimed for her gut. Later, he would allow himself to mourn taking her life, but the only one who could help them was lost to magic.

More starlight rushed forward on all sides. The grass shuddered. Two more thralls shouldered into view, gripping the hilts of their swords with gloved hands. They struck at him in unison, each movement smooth, as if they'd been born in these bodies. Strange. No other thrall he had fought moved its human host so well. Stonewall felled one and Kam knocked the other back, but more were coming, their attention wholly on Kali.

At some point, he caught Kam's eyes and saw their shared realization: this was no fight for victory, but a desperate bid for survival. Thank the gods for his hematite-granted strength. But he and Kam could not face this threat alone. He had been lucky so far, but his luck would not last. It never did.

Two more thralls appeared; in the moment before they struck, Stonewall called to his brother through their bond. *Relah!*

Drake's reply came at once. *Almost there.*

Relief surged through Stonewall even as sweat rolled down his back, his face, his arms. Something caught his side, but he could not spare a moment to assess the damage. It didn't matter, anyway, for he would fight until he fell. Were these scouts running ahead of a larger force? Or were they toying with him, biding their time until they could surge over Kali with greater numbers?

Someone charged over the trampled grass, then Drake leaped to Stonewall's side, a pickaxe swinging in each hand. Without a word, he and Stonewall drew up back-to-back, and Stonewall was never so relieved to be in his brother's shelter. Atanar thundered up as well, spear in hand, then the Forsworn sentinels—including Talon—each armed with mining tools. A familiar battle cry cut the air as Flint swept in front of

Stonewall, sword already painted crimson. Marcen was at her heels, fire flickering in bloody fingers.

None of the thralls' attention had shifted from Kali. Kali, still lost to her magic; Kali, who brought life to this barren world amid death and destruction.

She is lost, as I warned you she would be. Come home, my son.

Stonewall ignored the familiar call of his patron god. His allies fought around him. He caught a glimpse of Marcen kneeling beside one of the injured thralls. The mage's eyes were closed, his face was tight with concentration as Flint stood over him, poised defensively. But the thralls wanted nothing to do with the pale-haired mage.

"I can't cure him," Marcen shouted over the din, the shrieking, the clatter of steel and bone. "I don't know what's wrong!"

"They're not moving like normal thralls," Stonewall called, back still pressed to Drake.

During a few seconds of reprieve, movement near Kali caught Stonewall's gaze. He whirled to see Eris scrambling over the matted grass and between the bodies of Seren's Children, reaching for her friend. Tears streamed down the black-haired mage's cheeks and her mouth moved in speech Stonewall could not hear, but could guess. Kali's name; a plea for her attention.

But her efforts were in vain. She looked over at Stonewall, her lips parted. He read the shape of her words. *Help her!*

I can't, he wanted to say, but their enemies were upon them again.

Another burst of flame, this time accompanied by the scent of water, and splatters of rain upon the slick, trampled grass. Stonewall spared a glance to see Adrie and a few other mages who had come with Eris. Leal fought with them, his spear gleaming in shafts of sunlight that cleaved a low, magic-made storm cloud.

A veritable army at Stonewall's back, yet he had no room in his heart for hope.

THIRTY-EIGHT

Fly! Fly! Fly!

Eris' arms ached to beat against the air, but she could not risk a shape-change so soon after the last, which still pained her. It was foolish to remain in the middle of a battle she could not join, but she still struggled to reach Kali's side. Foolish, as well, for her friend was lost. The sight of Jensine's lifeless eyes and Caith's slack jaw made her guts churn, but she forced herself to look away from her dead allies – were they ever truly her *friends*?

So she focused on Kali. She had to shake Kali from whatever trance had taken hold of her, lest more mages perish. But Kali was not *Kali* any longer. She was a goddess of death and life; both intertwined and at her command. Flowers sprang up all around, only to be crushed beneath the boots of the sentinel-thralls.

Another thrall shriek cut through Eris' skull. Tears burned her eyes. The scent of iron hung in the air; iron and rain and other sickening smells Eris did not want to identify. She had never seen a thrall before. Was this what Kali had tried to warn her of? These…monsters? No trace of humanity burned behind their starlight eyes. Only death.

"Eris!" It was Leal, braced for another attack even though he'd felled the thrall before him. "Fly, Eris! Get away!"

She wrapped her arms around her still-aching abdomen. "I can't."

"Your son will die with you if you stay," Leal broke in, sparing a glance down at Eris. His hood had fallen aside; blood and dirt streaked his face. "Please, Eris. Save yourself. I cannot defend you forever."

Eris looked around, where Brenna and Adrie stood back-to-back with Marcen and—of all people—Flint. The earth churned beneath Adrie's hands, sucking down thralls, while Brenna called rain from a single cloud that drifted overhead. And Marcen... Fire bloomed at his fingertips, although once it left his hands, it roared over the grass. If not for Brenna's rain, they would have all been in a firestorm. Despair filled Eris at the sight of her friends. She had power, yes, but nothing like theirs. She was no warrior.

"Eris!" Leal cried again, but Eris ignored him and continued to Kali and the sentinels who stood before her. But while Stonewall and Kam had failed her friend, Eris would not.

"Kali," she cried as she drew closer. But she dared not touch Kali, who still pressed her hands to the ground. The distant scent of water and green, growing things came to Eris as if in a dream. She called Kali's name again.

No response.

Eris' throat burned. "Kali, please! Kali, stop! You've killed them!"

Kali turned. Dark eyes fell upon Eris, but there was nothing in Kali's face that Eris recognized: no anger, no fear, no wry humor. No sorrow. Only a gaze as black as the void. A slender hand closed around Eris' wrist, then a sense of exhaustion swept over her, as if she'd run across the whole world. She tried to jerk free, but she was powerless in Kali's grip. She tried to catch Stonewall's attention, and Kam's, but they were preoccupied with the battle. Leal had been right. She was going to die. Her son was going to die.

Then someone snatched her up. She met Atanar's vivid blue eyes as the Canderi lifted her from the wreckage of Kali's magic and dragged her away. "Fly," he cried, shoving Eris out of Kali's reach. "Fly!"

There was no other way to survive. Eris summoned her remaining strength and shifted. She threw her crow-body upon the wind, catching an updraft that sent her spiraling above the battle. Airborne, she surveyed the world below, and cried a crow-call in shock at the sight of so much *green*. Seren's sweet light... It was as if spring had ambushed the mine and everything around it, blanketing the once rusted ground in verdant life.

Water gleamed within the vast chasm, spilling over the sides, racing toward Eris' friends and now-allies. She cried out again in desperate warning. Did anyone understand? Did anyone even hear?

Yes! Leal looked up, then shouted at the mages. Drake caught the Sufani's words and called out as well, pointing away from the waters. Eris' heart swelled as Adrie, Brenna, and Marcen scrambled out of the surging water's reach.

But Drake, Stonewall, Kam and the other non-mages had not fled. They stood together, fighting at Kali's side as more thralls descended.

*

Burning starlight pinpricked Stonewall's vision even after his foes fell, but he would die before he let them take his soul-bonded. He knew this as surely as he knew the coppery scent of blood and the weight of his sword.

He sank into that weight and cinched his existence to the heft of his weapon and the necessary motions to survive and protect. Such focus always kept him sane in battles when others would lose their minds to fear. So he ignored the growing ache in his muscles and the acrid stink of smoke, the thralls' shrieks and the cries of his friends, and lost himself. Drake's solid presence at his back helped. It had been too long since they had fought together.

But the brothers were not alone. Every few seconds, he spared a glance at Kam and the other Forsworn sentinels, who moved with far more grace than expected, given the lack of hematite in their veins. Perhaps the ore left its memory upon their muscles. Kam was a cyclone by her daughter's side, unrelenting in her fervor. Between her, Stonewall, and Drake, no thrall had a chance to get close to Kali. Talon fought bravely as well. She had always been a gifted warrior, but there was a ferocity to her strikes that he did not recall from his time under her command.

When he could, he reached for Kali through the bond they shared, trying to shake her out of whatever trance she'd surrendered to. *Kali! Stop this! Kali...please. I'm sorry.*

394

But the scent of spring grew in the air, overpowering the scents of blood and smoke. Little white flowers bloomed among the dead. If Kali heard him, she did not answer. He could feel their bond, see the golden thread shining in his mind's eye, but he could not reach her. Magic had devoured her heart and mind.

Come home, Elan, Tor pleaded. *She is lost. You will be, too. Come home.*

I'm not done yet, Stonewall wanted to shout in reply.

Pain jolted him back into the moment. A dull pain, but it was a warning. He struck without thinking and a tall, male sentinel screamed at him, starlight eyes dimming before he dropped like a stone in a river. Someone else cried out: a human woman. Stonewall ignored the burning in his side, the warm wetness sliding down his hip, and darted for Kam. Two thralls were about to overwhelm her while she held a third at bay. Stonewall kept within two steps of Kali, but he'd be damned if he let Kam die now, after Kali had just found her again. His sword met one of the thralls in time to stop a blow, but he miscalculated the other's strike. Sloppy. The thrall's dagger gleamed as it tore through his armored cuirass – such strength behind that blow! Stonewall didn't feel the blade's bite, only a coolness on his belly, made cooler by the warm river of blood—his blood—that fell to mingle with the green, green grass.

Shit, he thought. *That one was bad.*

All strength fled his limbs and he knelt in the grass, gasping for breath that would not come. Something wet and cold slid up and around his knees, and he could smell water beneath the blood. His vision swam with shadows; the thralls' cries mingled with Kam's and Drake's, and they all faded to the background of his mind, like the shrieks of seagulls. The grass was cool and soft against his cheek.

He tried to push himself upright, but his arms had turned to sand and he could not take a proper breath. Someone called his name. The starlight cut into his brain. The glaring sunlight and too-vivid green everywhere stung his eyes. He wanted to sink into the quiet shadows, but something held his eyes open. Instinct, maybe, or stubbornness. He tried to swallow, but his throat refused to work, and he gagged on wet copper. Cold crept over his limbs, reaching for his heart. Only then did true fear take over; the latent terror that dwelled deep in his bones, that knowledge each living being possessed. All things die.

Kali. He reached for the shining thread that bound their hearts but found nothing at the other end. She could not hear him, or would not. He had closed himself to her, so she had done the same to him. The cold feeling wrapped around his chest, encasing him like water on all sides. He tried to say her name aloud, but his tongue was leaden and his throat was full of iron.

Then someone laid a warm blanket over him. The shrieks and scent of blood receded like the tide and a sense of peace filled his heart. Once more, he heard his patron god. *Elan. Come home, my son.*

Gods above, he was so tired. His entire life had been a struggle, but he could not do it any longer. He had fought – and failed. Perhaps he would be better in his next life. Perhaps he would deserve happiness.

He pictured Kali's face. Not the ravaged, power-filled specter of death that she had turned herself into, but the wry sweetness that had captivated his heart. *I'm so sorry,* he sent her. *I've failed you.*

No response. The thread between their hearts wavered as if caught in a riptide and pulled out to sea.

With one final breath, Stonewall surrendered.

THIRTY-NINE

D rake's heart stopped when his little brother fell. Only Nat, close at his side, prevented him from getting struck down too, but as it was, it took everything Drake had to shove aside the thrall he faced and scramble toward Elan. Not Stonewall now, no, but skinny little Elan with eyes too old for his face, who clung to Drake every night after their mother and siblings died, sobbing himself to sleep in Drake's arms. Somehow, Drake knew he was shouting, but he felt only a faint burn in his throat. He reached his brother as the floodwaters did, bubbling up from the sodding dam down below. How quickly water changed the shape of the world. Heedless of everything else, Drake clung to his brother, searching for breath or heartbeat.

But Nox would claim her due. The waters kept coming; newly-made currents sucked at Stonewall's body and ripped him out of Drake's arms. Even all of Drake's strength was not enough. The river stole his little brother and carried him out of sight.

A strong grip at his shoulder made him look up, into Nat's eyes. "We must go."

The rushing water pummeled Drake's chest, threatening to steal him too. Stupidly, he shook his head. "He's gone, Nat."

Atanar laid a broad, calloused palm against Drake's cheek. "Yes. But you must get up, Bahar. *Now.*"

With effort, Nat tugged him to his feet. Drake did not think, only followed, concentrating on not getting swept away. When he realized he could only hear the slosh of water, he looked around, blinking. The thralls were gone. Kali was gone. The mine was gone. Tall grasses stuck up from the water; a strangely vivid marshland amidst the barren landscape.

"Where is..." he began, but the words died on his tongue.

Atanar gripped his hand. "Our friends left before the worst of the water came. The thralls are..." He squeezed Drake's hand, harder. "Gone. They have Kali."

Drake dug in his heels. "He died trying to save her. We can't–"

But Atanar would not relent. He grabbed Drake's shoulders and pointed him toward the refinery, which sat untouched above the water. Several sentinel squads had rallied there, a petite, unarmored woman kneeling in their midst, hands bound, dark hair falling like a curtain across her face. Kali. Drake tried to jerk out of Atanar's grip, but the sodding Canderi was strong, and grief and battle had sapped Drake's vigor.

"Look at their eyes," Atanar hissed in his ear. "No starlight burns there, Bahar. They are human again."

So they were. Drake ran a sopping hand over his face, as if he could clean off the stench of death that clung to him. "How?"

"I do not know," Atanar replied grimly as he began to lead them to safety. "I can sense them, but only little. Perhaps their aim was *her*."

Elan was dead.

Drake clung to Nat's arm and wept.

*

Sweet blood. Sweet magic.

Kali knew no pain, nor anger, nor fear, only the raw rush of power she had fought against for what felt like a lifetime. But here, now, she surrendered to that desire, that strength – hers for the taking. Each inhale brought the scent of rain and flowers. All other sensations had retreated to mingle in the back of her mind; her friends' cries and the metallic taste of blood were no more than mountains on the horizon, veiled in mist.

Save one sensation: a meager brush against her awareness, like a hand outstretched as she passed by. Her name, not spoken aloud, but whispered

398

in her mind in helpless entreaty. *Kali, please.*

Somewhere in her heart, she knew that voice, but in this moment, there was only magic.

A woman cried out and Kali's eyes cracked open in time to see a dark-haired, familiar form collapse, sending up a spray of icy water. But magic beckoned and her borrowed strength would not last forever, so Kali squeezed her eyes shut once more, determined to bring this desolated province back to life. She'd done so much already, but there was still endless work ahead. Although she had not looked, she could sense the new life all around in the form of grasses and flowers, of twisting saplings and stocky shrubs.

Kali... I'm sorry.

That same silent speech. Perhaps it was familiar, but her awareness belonged to her magic. Even so, the desperation in the word gave her pause. Who called her? Why? Something cold and wet climbed up her legs and arms, but she dared not open her eyes, not when she was so close to the end of her strength. The rush of power slipped away like sand between her fingertips. There was no mage around her strong enough to borrow from, so Kali poured herself into her task. What did it matter if she died? Her magic would remake the world.

At what cost?

She shook the thought away. *Focus.* She was still in control. She had pulled just enough energy from Seren's Children to let them live. She would put it all to good use, and add her own, besides. She would make people see the good in magic and those who wielded it. She just needed a little more time, just needed to try a little harder...

Something within her snapped. She could not explain the feeling, other than visualize it as a thread wound around her heart, severed. A sense of loss flooded her, stronger than any magic. It stole her breath and forced her eyes open, but she saw only rippling water. The world reeled. Kali lost all sense of direction, for something anchored deep within her heart had vanished. But her focus returned and her attention veered back to herself, and she realized the truth.

Stonewall was gone.

She looked for him, but her vision blurred and her eyes were hot, and she could not make sense of the sunlight dancing upon the water and the vibrant green all around. She reached for him through their bond, but found only a thread waving in the void, like a cut fishing line. "Elan?"

Water sloshed. Someone pulled her upright. Kali looked into the sentinel's helmet as he clapped a set of hematite cuffs around her wrists. No starlight looked back; just a set of watery eyes bracketed by crow's feet. The world dimmed. The sentinel nudged her forward. "Come on, Mage. Serla Loach wants all the survivors brought to him."

Kali wrapped one hand around his arm, but no magic answered her summons, for she had spent herself almost to nothing. When she tried to take a step back, her knee burned and she could not help her scream. Her body collapsed, dropping her to the icy water, and she had no strength to rise.

The sentinel let out a long-suffering sigh and scooped her up. "Thank Tor you're little," he muttered as he sloshed through the waters. "Otherwise, I'd be cross."

Kali struggled in his grip, not to escape, but to look behind him, where she'd last seen Stonewall, Kam, or any of her friends. She saw only a marshy wetland, kissed by sun and water, shining, new. Although the hematite cuffs dulled her vision, the new growth was still obscenely bright against the arid landscape. Where the waters had not reached, the grasses and trees had taken complete hold. Lichen bloomed along the sides of the great, rusty boulders near the road. Even when viewed through the veil of hematite around her wrists, the scope of the magic stole Kali's breath, but she could find no room in her heart for wonder. Stonewall was gone.

The thought was not real. It was like she'd read it in a story or heard it in a song. *Stonewall is dead.* The truth of it threatened to shatter her. As much for distraction as to seek information, she peered up at the sentinel carrying her. "Where are the thralls?"

His neat beard was almost white, but she guessed him to be no older than forty summers. "What thralls?"

She tried to twist in his grip again, to see the battlefield, but he held her fast. "You were thralls," she said, looking back up at his eyes. "Don't you remember?"

When he looked down at her, there was no malice in his eyes. "There are no thralls here, little mage. Only your kindred, set on destruction. Thank the One, Serla Loach received word of the attack, and sent word to our garrison. Even so, a lot of good sentinels died today. Who knows what damage those renegades would have done otherwise? Though, why *you* would kill your own kind is a head-scratcher, for sure. Ah, well. Suppose you're Loach's problem now, and Argent's."

Kali stared at him, uncomprehending. "Mages...were killed?"

He huffed, though she thought it was in part due to the incline as he carried her toward the hematite refinery, well out of the water's path. "Never seen the like. You're your own star, that's for sure. Always thought mages stood with their own, but perhaps I was wrong. You saw wrongdoing, and righted it. Right?"

Surely, she'd not lost herself to magic. This fellow must be mistaken. She fought to remember and slowly, as the sentinel trudged up the grassy hill, the memories returned. She wished they had not. Her head grew light even as her stomach twisted. The cuffs hung like massive bangles on her wrists, and her knee still burned. Her heart still ached. She could feel the raw power surging through her; only a memory now, but clearer than anything else.

Her mother was surely dead. She couldn't see Eris, Drake, Flint, or Marcen. And Stonewall...

She closed her eyes. "I killed them."

"Yes, indeed," the sentinel said. "Perhaps you should take the Burn, eh? If the High Commander would allow it. You'd be a force unto yourself."

Elan, she thought, clutching at the strange sentinel's cuirass. *You were right. I'm sorry. Please forgive me. I love you.* Tears spilled down her cheeks. She was a murderer. A monster. And she'd destroyed everyone she loved. "I *killed* them," she whispered again.

The sentinel chuckled. "Ah, moon-bloods. Addled in the brains. Well, no matter. We'll get you to Argent, let him sort you out, and anyone else left standing in this gods-forsaken place."

*

Kam was heavier than she looked. Talon hefted the other woman's weight until they were both clear of the rising waters. She found a patch of grass in the shadow of one of the massive rocks, and laid Kam gently down. Crimson spilled from several wounds in the Forsworn sentinel's chest and side, but her face was unbloodied and her gaze was clear.

"Kali?" Kam whispered.

Talon wrapped one of Kam's hands in both of hers, squeezing as if she could force life back into the other woman. But that was a false hope. She'd seen Kam's wounds. All the hematite in the world would not save her.

"The Stonehaven sentinels have Kali," Talon said.

Kam's brows knit but the expression smoothed into one of determination. "Help me up. I must..."

She trailed off, coughing. Talon wiped away the blood on Kam's lips and shook her head. "I'm so sorry."

"It's my time at last, isn't it?" Kam frowned. "Sod it all, I knew I'd die here. I hate being right."

Despite everything, Talon chuckled and smoothed away a strand of dark hair, threaded with silver, that had stuck to Kam's cheek. "Me too. But you're not alone."

Not like Foley had been. Although Talon had been within arm's reach, her father had died alone, in pain, and afraid. Her eyes stung but she hardly noticed any more water on her face. A wind blew, making her shiver and reminding her that she was soaking wet.

Kam squeezed her hands, the weak pressure forcing Talon back to the moment. Kam's dark eyes were hard as iron. "Stonewall fell," Kam whispered. "She'll be alone. Don't let her stay that way. Watch over her. Please."

Talon stared at the other woman. "I can't..."

402

Tears streamed down the sides of Kam's face. "Why else would the One have sent you to me? Keep my daughter safe where I have failed. Please, Tal."

What else could Talon say to a dying friend? She nodded once. "I will. You have my word."

How she would keep such a promise was anyone's guess.

As if reading her thoughts, Kam's face relaxed into a faint smile. "You're resourceful. You'll manage." Her eyes widened, her gaze fixed upon something Talon could not see. "The river came to meet *me*."

"I know," Talon murmured, gripping Kam's hand. "You'll be in your next life, soon."

Kam closed her eyes. "I'm so tired."

"I know."

Kam's breathing ceased, and her body went still. Talon held her a moment more before she ducked her head. "Nox bring your spirit safely over the river. Tor guide your steps into the next life."

"The One keep you in all your days." Jasper crouched beside her, brushing his fingertips over Kam's cheek. Ruddy knelt with him, head bowed, murmuring his own prayer.

As gently as she could, Talon released Kam's hand, and then looked between her fellow Forsworn. "I told you to leave."

"You're not my commander," Jasper said, swiping his eyes.

They went to stand in the shadow of the towering rock face. Ruddy skimmed his fingers over the soft green moss that blanketed the rock. "That little mage did all of this?"

"Looks that way," Jasper replied.

Green covered the world, in places almost to the horizon. But Talon had seen the cost. Many mages were dead because of Kalinda. Had Kam realized? She'd seen Stonewall fall, at least. That loss panged at Talon's heart, surprising her. He'd died defending the one he loved most. There were worse ways to leave this life.

Talon rubbed the raised scar on her wrist. How could she fulfill her promise? She glanced between Ruddy and Jas again. "Did you see any more thralls?"

Jasper frowned. "As best we can tell, they're all gone. But so are your new friends."

"I saw Loach, Goldie, and Ottis by the refinery," Ruddy said. "With a bunch of sentinels from Stonehaven – and Kam's kid. She was cuffed."

"Probably on her way to Argent," Jasper added.

A plan coalesced in Talon's mind – a foolish plan, but she had little else but effort and chance now. She looked back at Kam's body, resting among the flowers. "Will you...see to her?"

"Of course, but..." Jasper stared at her. "You're going after Kam's daughter."

"I made a promise."

Ruddy opened his mouth, but Jasper shook his head, silencing the younger man with a look. He nodded to Talon. "Do as your heart tells you. We'll take care of her."

Talon's throat burned, but she managed to swallow another coughing fit. She gripped Ruddy's forearm, then Jasper's, and met their gazes in turn. "Thank you both. You have your freedom now."

Ruddy nodded, and Jasper's gaze upon her was firm. "Aye, our lives are our own." They parted and he gave her a warrior's salute. "Tor protect you, Tal."

Tal. A new name; a new life. Another chance to make amends.

"And you," she said, returning the bow.

Tal slipped away from them and waded through the water toward the refinery, careful to avoid the open area where the mine was. Used to be. The air smelled fresh, but she could still taste blood on the wind. Her path led her out of the water and she came upon the refinery, where a bevy of sentinels milled about, no doubt taking stock of themselves after a harrowing battle. She searched the gray armor until she spotted a familiar dark head, seated upon the ground, hands bound before her.

Tal stumbled forward as if her minor injuries were much worse. When the sentinels caught sight of her, a handful of them darted over to grab her arms and shove her to her knees. She offered no resistance. "Please, help me," she said as pitifully as she could between hacking coughs. "The moon-bloods..."

She said no more, hoping they'd interpret the rest to her advantage. One of them, a lieutenant, grabbed Tal's wrist to examine her scar, then shoved her back, snorting. "Forsworn," the sentinel officer muttered. "One of the workers here, no doubt."

"Serla Loach said to collect all the survivors," another sentinel replied.

The lieutenant sighed. "So he did. At least there's no civilians." She jabbed her gloved hand in Kalinda's direction. "Put them together, for now. We'll let Argent sort it out."

More sentinels shoved Tal forward, but she went willingly, silently thanking Llyr for her luck. As she went, she shot a glance at one of the sentinels who led her. "Did you see any more thralls?"

The sentinel, an older fellow, rolled his eyes. "Again with the thralls. You and that moon-blood are of the same mind, aren't you? Well, I'll tell you what I told her: there are no thralls here. Never were. That little mage did her part, but those wild moon-bloods killed our brothers and sisters in sacrifice. And mark my words, they'll pay for the lives they stole."

FORTY

Salt and water mingled in the air. Gull cries and the susurrus of crashing waves filled Stonewall's head, and something soft—like warm sugar—cradled his back. Slowly, he opened his eyes to a blue, blue sky laced with wispy clouds. He struggled to sit upright, sugar sand falling from his arms and tunic, and his gaze fell upon the ocean for the first time in many years. The Sea of Asherat, judging from the shape of the cove around him and the broken chain of islands reaching for the horizon. Which meant...

He turned and his mouth fell open at the mighty sea wall. Sun, surf, and wind had bleached the stones white long ago, but beyond them, the Blue City waited. Every building in Pillau contained the same blue stone: lapis.

Home. He was home. Stonewall leaned forward, head in his hands as his vision spun. Memory escaped him, but if he concentrated, he caught flashes of the past: a battle, thralls' cries, rushing water, and Kali...

A shadow blocked the sun. He looked up, into the face of a man who might've been blood, had Stonewall's heart not told him otherwise. Tor smiled down at him. The god's eyes did not glow, but Stonewall knew his patron god anyway. Heart racing, he knelt forward, touching his forehead to the sand. Was it wrong to look a god in the eye, even if that god had claimed a mortal form?

A low, gentle laugh met him. "None of that, now, son. Look at me."

Swallowing hard, Stonewall straightened but did not rise from his kneel. Tor's eyes were like his: that same light brown, albeit with flecks of gold glinting in the sunlight. How could that be?

406

Tor smiled at him. "You have many questions."

"Aye, serla," Stonewall managed.

Tor settled down beside him in the sand with ease, though his face was that of a man at least twenty years Stonewall's senior. "Well?"

Stonewall glanced again at the ocean and at the city of his birth. "Am I dead?"

The god chuckled. "No, my son. You're home. As I promised."

Home. Stonewall shook his head and struggled to his feet. If he wasn't dead, he had to get back to Kali and Drake, and the rest of his friends. Only when he was standing did he realize he felt no pain. He pulled aside his clean cotton tunic—one he had never owned—and skimmed his fingertips over his abdomen. His old scars remained, but there was no trace of a fresh wound.

He looked at Tor again. "I should be dead."

Tor was on his feet in a flash, though Stonewall did not mark his movements; one moment he sat in the sand, the next he stood. "That's not a 'thank you.'"

"Forgive me." Stonewall nearly dropped to a kneel again, but Tor stopped him with a hand upon his shoulder. It was a strong hand of flesh and blood and bone. "What happened?" Stonewall asked. "A thrall cut me down, I couldn't reach Kali, and then..."

The god smiled at him once more, but this time the expression held a trace of sorrow. "It was all a dream, my son. You will understand soon."

"No. It was real. I must return to Kali and Drake, and–"

Tor pressed a palm to his cheek and drew him close, so that their foreheads brushed. Stonewall reeled from the god's touch, but before he could speak, Tor said, "You cannot return to your old life. You are here now, Elan. You are home."

Stonewall frowned. "No, serla. I must go back. Kali..." He swallowed. "Kali is my home. We're soul-bonded. I must–"

"No, Elan." Tor's voice took on a deeper resonance, silencing any further protest. "Look at me," Tor said, soft once more, holding Stonewall's gaze. "You don't belong there any longer. You are safe here, far from the darkest hearts of our people."

"'Our people?'" Stonewall's voice was a whisper. "But I'm no god."

"No, you are not." The corners of Tor's eyes crinkled with his smile, more real than the sand beneath their bare feet. "Humans call us 'glimmers.' I've never decided if I like the name."

Stonewall's breath caught; he tried to pull back, but Tor held him fast. "The Fata," Stonewall managed. "You're a Fata."

"Yes." Tor pressed his other hand to Stonewall's chest. "And my blood flows in your veins. But you know this, don't you?" His breath was warm and smelled of the sea. "It's time I showed you the truth of what you are."

Everything grew dim and distant, as if a veil had been placed over the entire world. Memory faded. The gull cries and crash of ocean waves receded to the back of Stonewall's mind; everything shrank to Tor's golden eyes, to the deep, resonant voice that had followed Stonewall through the last few months of his life. But he'd always known that voice, somehow. This was his patron god, after all.

Right?

Tor smiled at him again. "Yes, you know me, Elan."

Elan swallowed hard, struggling to recall why his heart raced, why panic had coiled through his guts. He was on the beach of Pillau, his favorite place in the world. Out of the corner of his eye, he spotted the bleached sea wall, the high stones that had protected the city for as long as anyone could remember. Something about the wall tugged at his memory.

"Elan..."

He looked back into the man's golden eyes, struggling to recall why the two of them stood so close. Perhaps sensing his confusion, the older man released him, and rested a hand upon his shoulder. "You have been lost for so long," he said to Elan. "Your return fills my heart with joy."

And he knew the truth, then. "Father," he said, blinking hard as the salt air stung his eyes. "I've missed you."

His father smiled again. "Welcome home, Elan."

Hi there! I hope you enjoyed the fourth installment of the *Catalyst Moon* series! Please share your thoughts by leaving a review.

The saga concludes in Sacrifice (Catalyst Moon - Book 5)! Interested in Atanar's story? Read his book, Exile, for free at this link: https://bf.laloga. com/surrenderfreebie

If you or someone you know is suffering from substance abuse, know you're not alone: https://www.samhsa.gov/find-help/national-helpline

Did you spot typos or errors? Awesome! Please let me know so I can correct them: lauren@laloga.com

Thanks for reading, and stay awesome,

Lauren

The world of Catalyst Moon

Author's note: I realize there's a lot to keep track of in this 'verse, so here's a rundown of the relevant info for this book. Please let me know if you find this helpful, or if there is anything else you'd like to see: lauren@laloga.com

* * *

Mages

Magic first manifested in Aredia about three centuries ago. Mages are often identified at a young age, taken from their families and placed in secure bastions, where sentinels guard them at all times. Mages use magic by manipulating particles: tiny pieces of matter that make up everything in the world.

- Kalinda Halcyon: Nicknamed "Kali." Originally from Starwatch Bastion, transferred to Whitewater Bastion following the death of her father, the sentinel Captain Jonas.
- Eris Echina: Birthname – Eris Nassor. Leader of the mage rebellion. Escaped Whitewater Bastion with Drake and Leal's aid. Shape-changer, able to transform into a crow.
- Gideon Echina: Founder of the mage rebellion. Married to Eris. Deceased.
- Adrie Talar: Member of the mage rebellion who fled Whitewater Bastion with Eris, Marcen, and others.
- Marcen Selle: Member of the mage rebellion who fled Whitewater Bastion with Eris, Adrie, and others.

- <u>Sadira</u>: Mage from Zheem, (country to the south of Aredia). Capable of powerful fire magic.
- <u>Foley Clementa</u>: Former First Mage of Whitewater Bastion. Father to Talon. Deceased.
- <u>Drake</u>: Birthname – Bahar. A former sentinel who faked his own death to escape the order. A mage and member of the Assembly, an alliance of folks seeking to abolish the tier system. Older brother to Stonewall.
- <u>Hazel</u>: Young mage from Whitewater Bastion.

* * *

Sentinels

These elite warriors are known as much for their bonds of kinship as their unnatural resistance to magic. This resistance is granted by ingesting hematite, an ore mined in the province of Stonehaven. Magical resistance is necessary when tasked with guarding mages, which is the sentinels' primary function. While hematite will not completely obliterate a mage's abilities, it does dispel the effects and allow the bearer to safely handle the mage. Most mages cannot work magic on hematite, which accounts for the ore's presence in sentinel armor, weapons, and other implements used on or near mages, such as cuffs and collars.

A sentinel's first full dose of purified hematite is called *The Burn*; subsequent doses are also "burns." Young sentinels who have only taken their first Burn are called *burnies*. Older sentinels who have been taking hematite for a long time are called *cinders*. Given hematite's highly addictive properties, most sentinels are unable to live without ingesting it on a regular basis. Hematite grants enhanced reflexes, strength, and stamina, but also dramatically shortens a sentinel's lifespan.

Sentinels are generally brought into the order as young children, often orphans. The Circle controls the sentinels, and provides food, shelter, training – and hematite.

- <u>Stonewall</u>: Birthname – Elan. A sentinel who has been stationed all over Aredia, most recently at Whitewater Bastion. Younger brother of Drake.
- <u>Milo</u>: Sentinel formerly stationed at Whitewater Bastion, twin brother to Flint. Unlike many other sentinels, he goes by his birthname.
- <u>Flint</u>: Birthname – Mira. Sentinel formerly stationed at Whitewater Bastion, twin sister to Milo.
- <u>Beacon</u>: Nickname Beak, birthname Abernathy Dilt. A sentinel mender (healer) recently stationed at Whitewater Bastion.
- <u>Talon</u>: Birthname Talaséa Hammon. Formerly Commander Talon, leader of sentinel garrison in Whitewater City.
- <u>Rook</u>: Former squad-mate of Stonewall, Flint, Milo, and Beacon. Reports to High Commander Argent.
- <u>High Commander Argent</u>: Leader of all sentinels in Aredia. Stationed in Lasath, the capitol city, located in Silverwood Province.

Others

- <u>Atanar</u>: Canderi man, formerly a thrall.
- <u>Aderey</u>: Leader of his group of Sufani nomads, married to Ytel and father of Leal & Dianthe.
- <u>Leal</u>: Sufani nomad and ally of Drake's. Child of Aderey & Ytel, and sibling to Dianthe.
- <u>Ytel</u>: Sufani nomad, husband of Aderey and mother of Leal & Dianthe. Healed by Kali in Book One: Incursion.
- <u>Dianthe</u>: Sufani nomads, youngest daughter of Aderey and Ytel, sister to Leal.

* * *

The Provinces

Starwatch

Located in the northernmost reaches of Aredia, Starwatch shares a border with the country of Cander. Given its mountainous, wild terrain, Starwatch is generally considered the most hostile and isolated of all the provinces.

Silverwood

Home to the capital city of Lasath, Silverwood Province contains sweeping grasslands in the heart of Aredia. Legend has it that the province once held forests of towering silverwood trees, but they grew sick and died out. Naturalists and historians alike cannot say why.

Whitewater

Known for its famed Whitewater City, built on a massive waterfall on the White River, this northern province is integral to the Aredian trade system. The province is also home to rich farming and merchant communities.

Stonehaven

This province is located in the western region of Aredia and is the home of many mining ventures, including hematite. The terrain is predominately rocky desert.

Greenhill

A sparsely-populated province in the southern central region of Aredia, famed for its fertile soil, lonely moors, and treacherous marshes.

Redfern

This province is located on the eastern side of the continent, and is known for its dense, lush forests with towering trees.

Indigo-By-the-Sea

The southernmost province lies along a varied coastline of sandy beaches and thick, uninhabitable jungle. The province's capital, Pillau, is famed for its mighty seawall and bustling harbors.

* * *

The Circle

This is the predominant religion in the country of Aredia. The leaders are three powerful folks called Pillars. Ciphers are prominent priests/priestesses who provide tier marks, thus bestowing upon each Aredian citizen their proper place in the One god's world.

The One is the most powerful deity in the Aredian pantheon. All other gods are children of the One. There are a multitude of deities, but these are the most common:

Ea is genderfluid and is often portrayed as a steward of plants and animals. *Atal* is a warrior god, and he is tasked with keeping order among humanity. *Llyr* is the god of luck and commerce, and his temples usually feature moving water. *Mara* is known for her healing and compassion, and is often called upon in times of crisis. *Amaranthea*, the sun goddess, is often called upon by artists and poets, for the touch of her fire in the mind is akin to inspiration in its purest form.

Seren is a goddess of some contention. She is named for the second moon, which appeared several hundred years ago – along with the first recorded instances of magic. As such, some consider Seren to be the goddess of the mages, although others simply use the name to refer to the second moon.

Acknowledgements

Infinite gratitude to my editors, Imke and Isabella, who have been with me since the beginning of this journey. Special thanks to Kate, M.E., and the rest of my ARC trooper team, who helped smooth out the last few wrinkles in this tale.

Thanks also to my long-suffering bearded half, who not only encourages my endless woolgathering, but supplies me with coffee.

And as always, my thanks to you, Dear Reader, for the gift of your time and attention.

About the Author

Lauren finds Real Life overrated, and has always preferred to inhabit alternate realities, both self-created and created by others. However, after being burned by certain fandoms one too many times, Lauren decided to focus her reality escape attempts on her own creations. She's much happier now, although she still enjoys fandoms - in small doses.

A believer in love, hope, compassion, and similar squishy ideals, Lauren endeavors to create stories that both gut-punch and elevate her readers. Emotional rollercoasters are what make fiction fun, after all.

When she's not avoiding Real Life responsibilities, Lauren enjoys dancing at music festivals, spending time in nature, and tending to her cat's every whim. She lives in North Florida with her partner and assorted furred critters, but can be found online at laloga.com

You can connect with me on:
- https://laloga.com
- https://twitter.com/lalogawrites?lang=en
- https://www.facebook.com/laloga
- https://www.goodreads.com/author/show/15266429.Lauren_L_Garcia

Subscribe to my newsletter:
- https://laloga.com/newsletter

Made in the USA
Las Vegas, NV
20 July 2022

51916940R10249